FIRST LOVE, SECOND CHANCE

FIRST LOVE, SECOND CHANCE

Colin Shindler

headline

First published in Great Britain in 2002 by
HEADLINE BOOK PUBLISHING

10 9 8 7 6 5 4 3 2 1

British Library Cataloguing in Publication Data

Shindler, Colin
First love, second chance
I.Title
823.9'14 [F]

ISBN 0 7472 7456 8

Typeset by Palimpsest Book Production Limited,
Polmont, Stirlingshire
Printed and bound in Great Britain by
Mackays of Chatham plc, Chatham, Kent

HEADLINE BOOK PUBLISHING
A division of Hodder Headline
338 Euston Road
London NW1 3BH

www.headline.co.uk
www.hodderheadline.com

To Lynn

Who has shown me what spring is like
on Jupiter and Mars

ACKNOWLEDGEMENTS

As ever, my greatest debts are to Luigi Bonomi, my valued and trusted literary agent, and to my perceptive editor at Headline Books, Jane Morpeth.

For help in the areas of music and golf I am grateful to Denis King, a man greatly gifted in both fields. In California my researches were made much easier by the help afforded me by Michael and Shelley Chadwick, Steve and Freda White and by Jacques Pierre Schlumberger of Michel-Schlumberger Wines Ltd.

Since this is a novel about the deepest of human emotions, I wish also to acknowledge my debt to Joe Royle and David Bernstein, who have allowed me to find love again.

PROLOGUE

Dear Tom,

Today I am getting married — but not to you. A part of my heart will always be yours even though you are a complete bastard.

The way you left me convinced me that we never had a chance. I would always have come second in your life.

Anyway, I thank God now because I am so happy to be marrying Mike. He is everything you're not — caring, thoughtful and unselfish. It took some courage on his part to stick with me throughout that wretched final year at Oxford. I was a worthless cheque, a total wreck, a flop, but Mike was . . . well, I guess you can fill in the rest.

The Casualty Department of the John Radcliffe Hospital in Oxford is an unexpected place to meet your future husband. Oh no, don't go giving yourself a swollen head. I didn't slash my wrists the moment you abandoned me (though I think you owe my tutor a letter of apology because my essays were awful the whole year and I only just managed a miserable third-class degree).

My friend Helen — you remember, the girl who introduced us — suggested I see a psychiatrist because then they'd give me bottles of Valium to keep me quiet and she fancied taking some herself but couldn't get a prescription. I was feeling miserable because they were making me re-read Beowulf. It was just too depressing and it was a dull, bleak, grey November day. Unfortunately, the Mozart clarinet concerto was on the radio, that haunting and beautiful slow movement, and I remembered how we had made love for the first time in your rooms in Balliol with that music oozing from your stereo.

I reached for the happy pills and struggled with the child-proof lock. Is it my imagination or is it only children who can open them? Eventually I tore it off and tipped it towards my open palm and about seven of those small white things rolled out.

They were so small, Tom, tiny, white, inoffensive little things. What harm could they possibly do? And you know me, Little Miss Julia Sensible you called me once. I'm not exactly given to acts of great melodrama, am I? Valium's just like sleeping pills, isn't it? Shows you what a deep fund of pharmaceutical information I am. I thought they'd just send me to sleep for a while, there wasn't much to get up for and it would postpone the dreadful prospect of opening Beowulf again.

Which is what they did. Only when I woke up the room was plunged into almost complete darkness. I was very cold and I had a splitting headache and then I remembered what I'd done and thought that perhaps I shouldn't have.

Helen was living in the room across the staircase so I dragged myself off the bed and knocked on her door. I don't remember much else but there was an ambulance and a very loud siren and I rather liked the attention for a while. Helen came with me and she told me later we raced through the streets of Oxford and I groaned so much about Beowulf that the paramedics momentarily thought I'd been attacked by a wolf.

Anyway, when they found out I had just taken too many Valium I was instantly downgraded from 'urgent priority' to 'stupid cow, make her wait, that'll teach her'. I did try to make them understand that this was neither a desperate suicide attempt nor a frantic plea for help. The truth of the matter was far more mundane but of course nobody was interested enough to listen to my side of the story. As far as the hospital staff were concerned I was just another silly student.

A sadistic nurse at Reception told me I was going to have my stomach pumped and that it would be deeply unpleasant and that it served me right. It makes you wonder where these nurses do their training.

Finally, after two hours, Helen's sympathy disappeared. She got a bus back into town and there were only two of us left in Casualty. Me and a nice-looking boy in a very muddy football shirt and shorts with very cute legs. He smiled at me and it was the nicest smile I ever saw. It was sort of sheepish and apologetic but he was obviously laughing at himself, which was more than I was able to do.

Mike was there because he'd climbed down a bank into a ditch to recover the football, tripped and fallen head first into a nest of wild hornets. Apparently it was the third time he'd been in Casualty that term and he claimed he was better known to the hospital admissions staff than he was in his own college. He told me the previous week he had put his back out while bending to recover the coin after tossing up to decide which team started the match. Can you believe that? It made me laugh, even in Casualty. I hadn't laughed for a thousand years before then.

When I got out of the stomach-pumping room for distressed ex-girl friends, Mike was waiting for me. I liked him even more then. You know at the end of a long flight, when you just want to get home and into bed, it's always wonderful if you come through Customs and see a friendly face. Especially if the face has a car to drive you home.

That's how I felt when I saw Mike waiting for me. He had even ordered a taxi, a bit extravagant considering our student poverty but neither of us fancied the prospect of waiting at a bus stop in the cold of a November night. I offered to pay half but he wouldn't hear of it. He's much more of an old-fashioned gentleman than you are, Tom, which sometimes has its advantages for a girl.

I didn't think he could possibly have fancied me in the condition I was in so what he did came from the kindness of his heart and he has got a kind heart, Tom. He is the kindest, sweetest, gentlest man I have ever met and he adores me.

He has a very huggable quality. Does that make sense to you? He's broader across the chest than you are but shorter too so he stands four square and solid. And I love his smile and the way his whole face seems to crack open when he laughs, just like a baby's. He's a good sport, Tom. He doesn't have your sharpness of wit but I'm not worried about being the butt of his humour either. Well, I couldn't be – not if you saw his dress sense.

I love him. And he wants to have children. I know I'm only 22 and you and I spent most of our time when we were together making sure we avoided having children but the moment I met Mike I knew he would make a great father. I never felt like that about you, Tom, although God knows I felt plenty of passion.

Mike's not here, in case you think he's reading this over my shoulder. He's gone to a hotel for the night. I wanted our wedding day to be special and I didn't think it would be if we got out of the same bed together in the morning. I want him to see me for the first time on this special day in white coming down the aisle rather than in an old T-shirt getting out of bed.

Tonight we shall be somewhere in Greece in a hotel and I shall be Mrs Julia Ramsey. Does that sound strange? Mike's booked a hotel on a little island called Mykonos. It sounds romantic, doesn't it? It's a small hotel, probably without a wishing well, but we shall be there together – me and Mike and our unborn child.

I'm pregnant. And we're going to call her Emily. If it's a girl. If it's a boy, we haven't yet decided. Probably not Tom.

Wish me luck,

Love always,

Julia

CHAPTER ONE

'Do you think Mummy will like this, Daddy?'

Emily proudly pointed to the tray with Julia's breakfast on it. Two soggy Weetabix sat in a dish soaking up the milk. Two pieces of cold burned toast lay on a plate next to a saucer of marmalade and the tub of butter which Emily had taken straight out of the freezer because she couldn't find any in the fridge. She was currently mashing a tea bag against the side of a mug as she attempted to squeeze its essence into the lukewarm water.

Mike broke off his yawn and his casual glance at the Sunday newspaper to appraise his daughter's efforts at the start of Mother's Day. The fact that the breakfast was inedible was as nothing compared to the enormous effort that had clearly gone into the planning and execution. His heart swelled with pride as he picked up his daughter and hugged her.

'I think she will love it.'

'I did it all myself. Jamie didn't help me at all.'

'Where is Jamie?'

'Watching television.'

Mike wandered into the living room and saw his five-year-old son watching the antics of Mr Happy with rapt attention.

'Is that Mr Smiley?'

Jamie shook his head.

'Do you want to come and have a family cuddle with Mummy?' Even as the words were still forming in his mind he knew that they didn't represent much of an attraction. 'Or would you prefer to stay here and let Emily give Mummy her breakfast?'

Jamie didn't even bother to nod. It was clearly a rhetorical question. If a five-year-old could see that, why couldn't a 29-year-old?

Mike and Emily went upstairs and stopped outside the bedroom door.

'Let's knock,' Mike suggested.

'Why?'

'Because it's like a hotel. We can be the Room Service. Go on, you knock. I'll hold the tray.'

Emily tapped on the door very lightly.

'I think you'd better knock a bit harder. She's probably still asleep.'

Emily battered on the door with the force of the Drugs Squad breaking down the front door of a suspected dealer.

From inside the room came a sleepy but worried 'Whaaat?'

Mike opened the door and handed the tray to Emily.

'Happy Mother's Day to you,' they both sang as Julia struggled to sit up in bed, her head still ringing from the abrupt manner in which she'd been woken. The song gave her time to arrange her mouth in the right shape to indicate pleasure.

'I did it all myself,' said Emily, firmly dumping the tray down on Julia's lap and then hurling herself onto the bed to lie next to her mother, causing the tea to slop over the side of the mug. 'Jamie didn't help at all.'

'Well, Emily, how did you know that this was just what I wanted?'

'I thought so,' said Emily, now distracted by the sight of a blank television screen, an abomination in the eyes of a small child. Particularly as she knew that her brother was enjoying the Mister Men downstairs.

'Can we watch television?'

Mike turned on the set and tossed the remote control onto the bed, grabbed his dressing gown and departed for the bathroom.

'Eat up and I'll give you a massage,' he said as he left.

'Well,' said Julia, still trying to blink the sleep out of her eyes, 'how can this day get any better?'

Emily tried to snuggle up to her mother in order to accomplish just that and in so doing she upset the saucer of marmalade which, unseen by either mother or daughter, leaked its way slowly into the remote control.

When Mike returned from the bathroom it was to find the Morning Service addressing two sleeping figures. Emily, who had been working on the breakfast since seven thirty, was exhausted by her efforts and slept contentedly on the reclining body of her mother who had gratefully returned to her slumbers.

Mike smiled and picked up the remote control to snap off the television. The off button didn't work, nor did the mute button. He swore softly as he discovered the reason on his fingers. The marmalade had crawled remorselessly into the inner vitals of the remote and gummed up the works. Mike turned off the television in the conventional manner, got dressed quickly and went downstairs to see what mischief his son had been up to.

Julia wasn't sure that she wanted to spend this 'special' day driving out into the country but Mike seemed so determined to ensure that she had a good time that she decided to grit her teeth and pretend to an enjoyment she didn't entirely feel. The grey clouds, ominously heavy with rain, scudded across the Hertfordshire sky. The occasional flurry of rain splattered onto the windscreen and was smeared across it by the wipers.

They left the car outside a busy village pub and began to walk across the fields as the wind whipped up and drove the rain clouds towards the Midlands. It was supposed to be just a small outing but, as with most such trips with young children, it soon became an expedition fraught with complexity and danger. Both children had insisted on bringing their bikes, and Emily was now wobbling unsteadily on her two-wheeler with stabilisers at the back and Jamie was somewhat recklessly driving his tricycle straight into the nettles. Each child required constant monitoring.

Julia slipped her arm through Mike's.

'Thanks.'

'For what?'

'For marrying me.'

'I had to marry you. Your father was loading his shotgun.'

'My father wouldn't know where to find his glasses let alone a shotgun. You know what I mean.'

'Yes, I know what you mean but I take no credit for loving you. Who in the whole world could possibly lay eyes on you and not love you?'

'The newsagent for a start.'

'Oh well, that was just a misunderstanding.'

'What was there to misunderstand? I went in there a week before we went away and cancelled all the papers. I saw him write it down.'

'Apart from the newsagent then, who else could possibly not love you?'

'British Rail.'

'British Rail don't love anyone. They don't count.'

'Eric at work.'

'He's a berk.'

'But he doesn't love me. Even you would have to admit that.'

'All right, apart from Eric at work, the newsagent, British Rail—'

'The parent at Jamie's school who said I tried to run her over.'

'And the parent at Jamie's school who said you tried to run her over, who else could possibly fail to love you?'

'Nobody. I guess I'm just about perfect.'

'I guess you are.'

They kissed tenderly. Barely had their lips touched, however, than the sound of a high-pitched scream caused them to spring apart.

Emily's bike had collided with a tree root, depositing her into a ditch filled with rain water. Jamie cycled blithely on. Mike ran to recover him as Julia rescued her daughter from the indignity caused by the mud.

They returned to the pub where they had left the car and Julia made an attempt to clean up her daughter in the loos while Mike negotiated with the landlord for four bowls of vegetable soup. The landlord's initial reluctance to serve them appeared to be born less of a fear of losing his licence by admitting children into a corner of the saloon than by the aggravation of having to open two tins of vegetable soup, pour them into a pan and heat them up. His bad temper was not improved when Jamie accidentally knocked over his soup bowl. Mike pressed a five pound note into the landlord's hand and hurried his family back to the car.

'Is this what we've got to look forward to for the rest of our lives?' said Julia, turning down the football commentary on the radio.

'What?' asked Mike, adjusting the level so he could still hear it.

'Going out, falling off bikes, getting cold and dirty, driving home.'

'Not at all. I should think that when we're in our eighties our children will be perfectly able to ride their bikes without falling off.'

Julia smiled. Mike's hand left the steering wheel and dropped onto her knee. Instinctively Julia turned to see what the children were doing in the back seat. They were both fast asleep, their heads lolling against the door handles. Julia put her hand on top of his and squeezed it gently.

'I think we should wait till we get home, don't you?'

'Absolutely not. A nice lay-by on the A1 can be very romantic.'

'Only to an AA patrolman.'

'All the books recommend a change of location.'

'I would imagine that means the dining room rather than the bedroom. I doubt it means doing it in the front seat of a Vauxhall Cavalier.'

Mike swung the car off the main road.

'Mike!'

'Plan B.'

He drew up in front of a garden nursery that was just closing for the day.

'Come on!' He grabbed her hand and dragged her out of the car, closing the door quietly and hoping that the children would continue to sleep after the engine was turned off, which they usually took as their cue to wake and cry. He was lucky. They snorted but failed to wake.

Inside the greenhouse Mike was clearly looking for something in particular. One of the assistants appeared by her attitude to be related to the pub landlord.

'Sir, we're just closing.'

Mike ignored her.

'Mike? What are you looking for?'

'There!' He seized a small potted plant, held it up and showed it to her triumphantly. 'I've been meaning to get one all week. Couldn't find it anywhere.'

'It's an orchid!'

'It matches your eyes.'

'It's pink! I don't have pink eyes.'

'I was referring to the cost.'

'It's very expensive.'

'Exactly.'

'Do I have very expensive eyes?'

'Of course you do. Think how much it would cost to replace them.'

'But that applies to everyone's eyes.'

'Do you like it?'

'I love it.'

Mike handed the plant to Julia. 'Happy Mother's Day. Even though, strictly speaking, you're not my mother.'

'But I'm the mother of your children.'

'That's good enough for me.'

Julia cradled the plant all the way home. She always preferred a pot plant, that could be nurtured and loved, to cut flowers whose life span was considerably more limited. But it wasn't just the orchid that so warmed her, despite its beauty, expense and potential longevity. It was the fact that Mike had been thinking about it all week that made her feel so loved.

After the children had been fed and bathed and read to and tucked up in bed, and after they had cleared away the dinner plates and stuck them in the dishwasher and set the table for breakfast, and after they had prepared everything they needed for their respective jobs in the morning, Julia and Mike finally had some time for themselves.

Mike turned up the heating, took the cushions off the couch and laid them on the floor in front of the radiator. He draped a bath towel over them.

'The doctor will see you now, ma'am.'

'Do I really have to take all my clothes off?'

'Is there any point in a fully clothed massage?'

'I'm really quite shy.'

'Very well, you may keep on your shoes.'

'Oh, but I wanted you to massage my feet.'

'I'm afraid that means complete nudity.'

'All right, but you won't look, will you?'

'If you insist. You may not know this but I have recently completed a correspondence course with a guru in the mountains of India.'

'No, I didn't know that.'

'The Maharishi of Giggleswick has taught me the ability to sleep with my eyes wide open so even though you will think that I am devouring you with my eyes as you slowly take off all your clothes, in fact I shall be fast asleep.'

'Oh goody, that's all right then,' said Julia as she unhooked her bra and slipped it provocatively off her shoulders, waved it under Mike's allegedly unseeing eyes and draped it round his neck before lying full length on the cushions.

'Mike! What kind of a massage do you call this?'

'I call it the "It's About Time Massage". It has elements of Swedish, Finnish and Australian massage.'

'What's an Australian massage?'

'This.'

'Oh!' she squealed. 'What a good name for it.'

Afterwards they curled up on the couch together and watched an old black and white film with Cary Grant and Katherine Hepburn who really loved each other but spent eighty-five minutes in denial until the last five minutes when they realised what the audience had known all along. It was utterly predictable and totally charming, and long before the fadeout kiss, Julia and Mike had fallen asleep in each other's arms, oblivious to the emotional and comic misadventures being paraded in front of them.

Dear Tom,

We've just been away for Easter to St Ives but that's not what I want to write about. There are two pieces of really big news. I've finally landed a decent job. I begin on September 6th, the day Jamie starts his new secondary school, working in the copyright department of Lee, Bell and Book, the famous London music publishers. I shall be clearing the copyright on all those songs you spent so long teaching me.

The other news, which we heard about just before we left for our holiday, was that Emily had passed her Grade Eight violin with distinction. As far as I'm concerned, this puts her pretty much in the Vanessa Mae class, not that I'll be encouraging her to pose standing in the ocean in a see-through skirt or whatever it was that little minx did.

She is an absolute delight — so far. But she is only 13 and I am very conscious that puberty has already started and relations between teenage girls and their mothers can become a little stressful. I remember avoiding speaking to my mother for years. Do boys go through the same kind of hormonal sea of change? For some reason I don't feel nearly as protective towards Jamie as I do towards Emily. But that could be because he's only interested in his computer games and golf. We don't have to worry about his wanting to go to parties at the weekend or anything like that, but then he is only 11. Emily of course is always practising her scales and her pieces and she's so talented (and knows it). I hope it might help to protect her against those awful teenage pangs of angst and self-doubt.

I wish you could meet Emily and hear the sound she makes with her violin. I know you'd adore her — maybe she'd remind you of me when you first met me — so naive and full of enthusiasm.

You remember what I was like — always the second violin, always Sigmund Nissel, never good enough to play first violin like Norbert Brainin. Well, Emily is not going to be just the first violin in an orchestra or a string quartet, this little lady is going to be good enough to have a solo career. As God is my witness I state for the record that before she is thirty I will see my daughter playing the Mendelssohn E minor concerto with one of the major orchestras. Next year I am going to enter her for the Young Musician of the Year competition which the BBC televises. She won't win the first time but she will before she's 16.

Am I boasting? Yes, I probably am. Mike, too, is proud of Emily, but he isn't proud of her like I am. Mike knows she's good because other people tell him so, but he doesn't know how good because he has no real understanding of music — not the way you have, Tom.

What Mike does understand is golf, and he reckons Jamie has the makings of a first-class golfer. As you know, my knowledge of sports is nonexistent but I'm sure not many kids of his age can even play golf. Jamie apparently has natural talent. But I worry about the way Mike puts thoughts into Jamie's head about becoming a professional golfer. I mean, he's only 11 years old with a lot of exams and schooling to come. Mike shouldn't be filling his head with a bunch of false hopes, should he? Mike thinks that playing golf well and playing music well are related, but as far as I can tell, you just stand there and bash a little ball with a big club and then walk after it and bash it again. Mike says I have no understanding of the finer points of the game and he's right!

I sometimes wonder what sort of children you and I would have had. Would our combined genes have produced the sort of musical talent Emily has? Music brought us together in the first place. I felt I could tell you anything. You understood me so immediately, so instictively, even though you come from northern California and I come from Kenilworth. And what you didn't understand you wouldn't judge. Sometimes Mike can be very disapproving.

Tom, I do love writing to you like this. I mean I'm a happily married woman and all that but sometimes I need something that marriage can't provide, that even my best friend Sarah can't give me. You always had that magical ability to understand what I was feeling rather than what I was saying. I tell Mike that something is bothering me and he tries to fix it. He doesn't understand that I just need to talk. It's almost as though he'd rather try and fix the unfixable than discuss the situation with me. That's what you were so good at. Just listening.

And that's what I feel you're doing now. Listening. That's why I never need to post these letters. My pleasure comes just from writing them – I don't even have to buy stamps, which makes this a wonderfully cheap form of therapy. Not that I need therapy of course. I am English, as are my well-adjusted husband and children, and we're all incredibly normal, rational and balanced in this country – despite your caustic observations to the contrary.

If I were to post these letters you would no doubt feel the need to reply, and that would never do. It's much better for me just to hold in my mind that strong image of you, arms folded across your chest, laughing at me or the pompous university dons or Mrs Thatcher or the Duke of Edinburgh and wonder and wonder ... Did you marry one of those young, thin, blonde, tanned Californian girls who grace the covers of magazines? That would depress me no end!

In fact I won't think about that. I'll keep our love just the way it was when we first met. If we start a grown-up correspondence we'll inevitably end up talking about schools and house prices and you won't be Tom any more, you'll just be another husband and father. So it's not that I don't wonder what happened to you – whether you married or how many children you have – it's that I'm going to remember what it was like in your college room in Oxford in 1982.

Besides, I'd then have to tell my best friend Sarah. We have a pact: we tell each other everything, or at least almost everything!

She does know about you, Tom. I had to tell her. I mean, she told me about her first boyfriend and it was only fair that I spilled the beans about you. I suppose I could have made up a fictitious lover but it was just after our children were born and we were lying, exhausted, in neighbouring beds in the same maternity ward. It was the time for total honesty about the past and our anxieties and hopes for the future, so it didn't seem right to lie.

But I reckon it's OK not to tell her about these letters I write you because I don't post them, but if I sent them and you wrote back I'd feel obliged to share them with Sarah. And I don't want to. I don't think she'd understand. I love Sarah and I treasure our friendship but I really want to keep our love all to myself. And I don't think Mike would understand either – after all, he knows all about how much you hurt me and how long it took to put me back together again after you'd gone. He especially would be shocked that I still think about you.

Julia put her pen down and looked out of the window.

CHAPTER TWO

IT WAS THE BEST FAMILY holiday of their lives. Julia's own childhood memories of summer holidays had been of cheap hotels and windswept promenades, freezing sea water and omnipresent grey clouds. Mike could scarcely even remember a family holiday as such. Usually, what had passed for such an event involved his mother taking him and his sister to the cinema in Brighton or Ramsgate whilst his father disappeared into the betting shop. Not until he emerged frowning or smiling would they know the nature of their hotel accommodation that night. Neither set of parents was enamoured of holidays abroad, which they deeply mistrusted. The overwhelming combination of strange language and different coinage saw to that.

Julia and Mike were the polar opposites of their parents. The more exotic the location, the happier they were. They had backpacked and interrailed around Europe during their student days, and they both had an easy familiarity with languages, and a thirst for absorbing other cultures. For a brief period they even experimented with food at home, investing heavily in a variety of cookbooks detailing increasingly exotic recipes which reflected the happy memories of their travels, but eventually a combination of the exhaustion of commuting and the convenience of the microwave and the takeaway put an end to their hunger for gastronomic experimentation.

They retained, however, their abiding love of travel, and even when the children were young they dragged them on to charter flights at the first opportunity. Although they had been to Italy many times, they had never ventured south of Rome before and what made this summer holiday even more appealing was that they were going with two other families who also had teenage children. Julia's best friend Sarah had found the villa in Ravello, high up in the hills on the Amalfi coast, in the pages of a travel agent's brochure. It offered five bedrooms, a concrete patio and glorious days of endless sunshine. Mike's squash partner, Tim, was a member of three different airlines' frequent flyer clubs as a result of his business travelling and managed to get all the families into a VIP lounge at Gatwick, which took much of the sting out of the four-hour delay before they could take off.

The villa, astonishingly, was every bit as wonderful as they had all hoped it might be. The cool bathroom tiles and the terracotta walls were decorated with a mosaic of Roman times. The shower worked, the kitchen was large enough to accommodate the demands of three families and there seemed to be enough chairs and sun loungers on the patio for all of them to be comfortable. Besides Emily and Jamie, there were five other children — Tim and Louise had three children, Sarah and John had two.

The first day they woke late — even the children slept until a civilised time in the morning, so exhausted had they all been by the journey. While the women explored the amenities of the villa and compared them with the inventory, the men took the children down the hill into the piazza, off which ran a number of attractive small streets with shops that sold everything a tourist could want, from fashionable shoes and handbags to cheap wine and pasta and a variety of ice creams.

John was particularly taken with the lemoncello, the local aperitif which, to the amusement of the children, was stored in the freezer compartment of the fridge.

'Why doesn't it freeze?' asked Martin, Tim and Louise's eldest.

'Because there's something in it that stops it,' said his father.

'What?'

'Some kind of chemical or something.'

'What chemical?'

'Oxygen.'

'Are you sure?'

'Come on, everyone, food's ready,' called Sarah, saving Tim from further embarrassment.

That first meal was a melange of bread, wine, salad, pasta, Coca-Cola, pizza and, because it was still technically the first meal of the day, Sugar Puffs. It was widely adjudged completely satisfying, although the children were unimpressed by the milk.

'It's horrible,' they chorused.

'Tastes like cats' pee,' said Jamie, delighted with the metaphor.

'How do you know how cats' pee tastes?' asked Martin, back in his Jeremy Paxman role.

'I think he just means it's bit watery,' said Julia quickly.

After brunch they walked down a steep path towards the beach they could see in the distance but which, oddly, never seemed to get any nearer.

'It's getting further away,' observed Mike.

'Optical illusion,' said Emily.

Despite the complaints, it was agreed that aborting the journey and returning home was impossible to contemplate as it was entirely uphill, so the intrepid party trekked on, sustained only by bags of sweets and pop songs which all the children and none of the adults knew. They responded by harmonising incongruous Christmas carols which turned out to be the only songs to which they all knew the words.

'I'm going to get everyone Frank Sinatra CDs for Christmas,' complained Julia. 'Next year we're all going to sing, "Young At Heart".'

When they eventually finished their descent by the beach at Minorai they were too tired to do anything but search out the nearest pizzeria. Food was clearly going to become the leitmotiv of the holiday. Afterwards they looked up the hillside towards Ravello, whence they had descended, and were all deeply impressed with the journey they had made. Armed with double and triple scoops of ice cream, they made their way back to the villa by bus.

That night in bed Julia felt the cares of the world slip from her shoulders. There had been a minor crisis at work just before she left and Mike had been putting in such long hours at the investment bank, where the working hours only increased and never diminished, that he had contributed almost nothing towards the preparation for the holiday.

Now that they were all here, though, and the weather was glorious, the villa was clean, the views spectacular and the families seemed to be getting on with each other she felt she could plunge herself into the hedonistic delights of a real family holiday. Next morning, toasting gently in the warmth of the hot sun, Julia dozed, airport novel face down on her stomach, and surrendered to the pleasure of physical relaxation.

The following day they all took the bus down the mountainside into Amalfi with the intention of carrying on to Positano and even Sorrento further down the coast but after they had walked the length of the jetty in Amalfi and been disappointed at the lack of amenities apparently on offer for teenage children, they decided that they were better off spending most of the holiday staying in Ravello and in the villa.

The women, however, had observed the departure of the daily boat to the Isle of Capri.

'We have to go,' declared Sarah.

'All of us?' asked Tim who saw only the logistical problems of six adults, seven children and unreliable foreign public transport.

'No, just the ones who deserve it,' replied Sarah, teasing him.

'It's expensive,' said John staring at the prices displayed on the board next to the wooden hut where the tickets were sold. 'Children's prices stop at twelve years old.'

'Oh, John, not now. We're on holiday,' said his wife wearily.

'Girls day out,' announced Julia.

'All the girls?' asked Emily, torn between wanting to be entirely free of her mother and being considered sufficiently mature to join them as a proto-adult.

'No. Only those girls over the age of fifteen.'

So it was settled. It was to be the women's day to themselves, on holiday, in the sunshine, free of domestic responsibility for once.

The men took up what they perceived as the women's challenge. Not only would they look after the children and enjoy themselves but they would cook a gigantic meal for when the women returned in the evening.

'That's not a challenge,' observed Louise tartly. 'It's what we do three hundred and sixty-four days in the year.'

'Without complaining,' added Sarah.

'And without expecting to be congratulated for it,' finished Julia, looking at Mike who gave her a 'What did I do wrong?' look in return.

Over breakfast the men decided to do things rationally. Women were emotional creatures, ruled by the moon or the changing tides or their own changing bodies. They made far too much of perfectly mundane tasks. Mike took a piece of paper and drew three lines down it representing the tasks allocated to each of them. Then he drew various horizontal lines to indicate the hours of the day after the women had left until they were expected back. Into the boxes went the details of the children's activities, the household chores and the food arrangements. After half an hour the men had organised the whole day. All that was necessary was to consult the master plan which they pinned to a cork noticeboard in the kitchen.

Mike was in his element. He loved his children and regretted that he could never be with them as often as he wanted. It irritated him that he had to spend so much time at the bank, building his career in conventional areas slowly but surely, earning less than if he'd taken the risk of going into the City as a trader. But he was only too aware that at thirty-eight he was no longer regarded as a high-flyer and he wasn't going to be earning the huge bonuses

that the City handed out to those whom they had marked for spectacular success. He was not going to join the dot.com world either which he had always
regarded as an unsustainable bubble destined to burst sooner rather than later.
The security of his family had always been top of his list of priorities.

This holiday was his chance to spend time with his children and he had
every intention of seizing it. He appreciated how hard Julia worked to reconcile
the different demands of her job and their children and he was delighted that
she seemed to be able to relax from the moment they had arrived in the villa.
There was even a physical closeness between the two of them that had not
existed for some time.

He had always been close to Jamie. There was an easy familiarity between
the two of them which had grown up on the golf course and so far he had
managed to avoid the strained relations which so often followed the onset of
puberty. It had been some time since he had seen Emily in a swimsuit and
he was surprised by how much she had developed. He swelled with pride.
His kids were great, his wife was happy, the sun was shining. It was turning
out to be the best holiday ever. When he kissed Julia goodbye it was the kiss
of a profoundly contented man.

When the women set off on the bus down the winding road from Ravello
to Amalfi at eight thirty-five, the sun was already shining out of a cloudless
blue sky. Despite being up in the mountains the temperature was already in
the seventies and likely to climb far higher in the next few hours.

The journey to Capri took them parallel to the coast dotted with tiny white
houses among the omnipresent orange and lemon blossoms to Sorrento, then
across the spectacular Bay of Naples haunted by the awe-inspiring sight of the
foreboding proximity of the volcano of Vesuvius. The funicular which, like
the boat, was crammed to bursting point with tourists, took them from the
Marina Grande and deposited them onto a Moorish opera set of shiny white
houses, tiny squares and medieval alleyways hung with colourful flowers and

boasting some of the most hideously expensive designer label stores in the world, each displaying tasteful credit card symbols in the window.

Over the centuries the island had been occupied successively by the Phoenicians, the Greeks, the Romans, the Saracens, Moorish pirates and invading armies of the French and British Empires. None had managed such a complete triumph as Visa or American Express.

Fighting desperately against the urge to race into every shop and grab armfuls of summer dresses, evening gowns and business suits, Julia forced herself resolutely to walk along the Via Vittoria Emanuele towards the domes of the Certosa di San Giacomo. In the window of the very last shop was a powder-blue silk scarf with an edging of small white squares. How much could a scarf cost? she wondered.

'*Centocinquantamila lire*,' said the bored shop assistant.

'A hundred and fifty thousand lire,' translated Louise.

'Sixty-five, sixty-six pounds,' said Sarah who had already signed credit card slips to the sum of £430 and wasn't entirely sure how she was going to tell John.

Julia picked it up and ran it through her fingers, luxuriating in the sensuous feel of the silk. The others pinched it between their fingers and squealed in delight.

'Isn't that just heaven?'

'Oh, Julia, you've got to have it.'

Julia draped it across her bare shoulders, conscious that she had rubbed large amounts of Ambre Solaire onto them during the boat journey and hoping that none of the cream would be transferred to the scarf. In the end she didn't have the strength to resist the combination of the wonderful feel of the material, the way it lit up her face in the full-length mirror and the entreaties of her friends. She fished her credit card out of her purse with a palpitating heart.

Emerging from the shade of the store into the bright noonday sunlight,

Julia felt herself opening up like the petals of a flower. She had forgotten what it felt like to be Julia Cowan, single woman, having long ago submerged that identity into Julia Ramsey, wife and Mrs Ramsey, mother of two. For the first time for ages there was no time pressure on her, no commuter train to catch, no office rumour to worry about, no shopping or dry cleaning to collect.

'Oh, isn't this just the best time ever?' she sighed.

'No meals to cook, no house to clean,' agreed Sarah.

'No clothes to wash, no silver to polish,' concluded Louise.

'You polish the silver?' asked a surprised Sarah.

'Well, I don't think it's fair to ask the cleaning woman,' said Louise in self-justification.

'How much silver do you have?'

Julia wandered across the narrow street, anxious to maintain her current serenity. How long had it been since there had been no one to worry about but herself and nothing to think about but enjoying herself to the full? A long time.

Back at the villa in Ravello, everything was going according to plan, the plan that was secured to the noticeboard with a drawing pin. Mike wasn't exactly preening but he was certainly experiencing a warm glow of satisfaction. He believed in planning. He had always made lists, from the time he was a schoolboy — book lists, record lists, football league tables, lists of potential careers, lists of worst Eurovision Song Contest winners, lists of U S Masters champions. Lists allowed him to impose harmony on an unruly world.

His reverie was interrupted by the arrival of a bad-tempered Martin, Tim's sixteen-year-old son.

'Where's my dad?'

'Check the board.'

'Can't you just tell me?'

'Not without checking the board.'

'What the hell does SHP mean?'

'Shopping. He's gone to get the ingredients for dinner. What's the problem?'

'I'm bored. The TV out here is shit, there's no videos, no computer, I can't e-mail my friends, it's too hot and your kids are too little. I've got nothing in common with Jamie. I'm nearly seventeen.'

'I get the message. Any solutions?'

'I want to go swimming.'

'What about the others?'

'That's what they want too.'

Cursory questioning suggested that Martin might be right. There was an indefinable air of tension stemming from the fact that the seven children were already finding the villa too limiting. Mike wished now they had plumped for the more expensive house that had also been on offer. It had only four bedrooms but it boasted a pool. If the weather remained hot they were going to need a pool or the sea.

He discussed the situation with Tim and John when they returned from the shops laden down with pasta, vegetables and bottles of wine. They decided to have lunch at the house and then catch the afternoon bus to Amalfi and find a bus that took them down the coast. Somewhere there would be a beach that would allow the teenagers to let off steam.

The air suddenly filled with the sound of Bach's Air on a G String.

'What's that?' asked John.

'It's that advert for Hamlet cigars on the telly,' said Tim uncorking the day's first bottle of vino rossi.

'No, it's not,' said Mike. 'It's Emily.'

The other two men stopped and listened as the violin continued on its wonderfully assured path.

'Blimey!' John breathed. 'That's fantastic.'

'You've heard her play before.'

'Not for a year or so. I mean that's just amazing.'

'So when does she turn pro?' asked Tim.

'As soon as she graduates from university,' replied Mike.

'You're not going to wait till then! She could do recordings and TV concerts like that Welsh girl, whatsername?' interjected John.

'Charlotte Church?'

'Yeah. That's the one. Why doesn't she do that?' John demanded.

'Because she's got her GCSEs next year and Julia doesn't want to turn her into a freak show.'

'She's fantastic. Stop work now, become her manager and make a fortune,' suggested Tim.

'It's something to look forward to,' agreed Mike tactfully. 'Now where's that large boiling thingy we used for the pasta last night?'

After lunch they telephoned for two taxis as they had missed the noonday bus down the mountain and the next one didn't leave until five thirty. The taxi drivers were asked to take them to a beach where they could all swim. A rapid-fire conversation followed in which one driver clearly disagreed so strongly with the other that he got into his car and slammed the door violently. Emily looked at Mike.

'That guy's a psycho, Dad.'

'We'll go with him. You kids get in the other car.'

The taxis set off at a furious pace, screeching round the narrow hairpin bends as they vied with each other for the right to be the first to kill all their passengers. The three men and their children emerged, blinking into the sunlight, half an hour later, grateful to be alive. Mike thrust a fistful of lire into the drivers' hands and didn't begrudge the enormous tip, so relieved was he that they were all in one piece. 'I think we should get the bus home,' he said.

The party made its way onto the beach and spread out their towels.

'Well, at least it's not too crowded,' said John.

'Is it safe to swim out there?' asked Emily.

'I think so,' said Mike. 'It looks placid enough. Just don't go too far out.'

'I'm not going yet anyway. I'm going to do twenty minutes in the sun on each side then go in the sea.' Emily coated herself very carefully with suntan lotion. 'Can you do my back, Dad?'

Mike looked at the bottle. 'SPF 15. Is that strong enough?'

'Mum bought it. And I've got sunblock on my face.'

'OK. You're a good girl, Emily.' He coated her back and neck with the lotion and rubbed it carefully into her skin then called a preoccupied Jamie for the same operation.

'I don't need it.'

'You do.'

'I've already done it.'

'When?'

The fractional pause was tantamount to an admission of defeat.

'This morning.'

'That's no good. You need it again. Come on, or your mother'll bollock me.'

Jamie reluctantly submitted to the humiliating ordeal.

Mike read two pages of his novel before giving up the unequal struggle against the combination of the warmth of the sun's rays and the effect of the lunchtime red wine. He dozed off and awoke only when he was aware that he had started to snore.

He raised himself into a sitting position and noticed that ten yards away Tim was fast asleep with the previous day's copy of the *Independent* over his face. Two of his children were sunbathing with their personal stereos operating at full volume and Jamie, Martin, John and John's son Jordan were playing football with other holidaymakers and/or the local youths.

Idly, Mike looked around for Emily but couldn't see her. The two periods of twenty minutes' sunbathing on either side had obviously elapsed. She was probably in the sea somewhere. He strained his eyes. The sun was dancing on the water, making it hard to distinguish the jumping, splashing figures on the horizon. He thought he recognised Emily then changed his mind. He decided to walk out to check. Besides, he was feeling the effects of the heat and he could do with immersing himself in the water for a while anyway.

He walked tentatively into the sea, the water washing over his ankles in a deferential but refreshing manner. He saw Emily's little face in the distance and smiled, waving at her. She turned slowly onto her front and swam away from him, at which point he realised he had been waving at a strange girl. He examined the other bodies in the water more carefully and then walked over to the football game.

'Have you seen Emily?' he asked Jamie.

'Yeah, she's over there somewhere,' said Jamie vaguely.

'Where exactly?'

'I don't know. There.'

Mike looked in the direction of the pointed finger but none of the frolicking children was Emily. He turned back to his son.

'When did you see her?'

'I don't know. Twenty minutes ago, maybe.'

Mike swam slowly out to the mass of children in the water, but then decided that Emily was probably back on the beach sunbathing again. He stood up in the water, looking for their bags and towels. He soon spotted Tim flicking a Frisbee with his daughter Megan and waded towards them.

'Have you seen Emily?'

'No.'

'Is she with John?'

'No, John went to the shops with Nicky.'

'He's not hungry again, surely?'

''Fraid so.'

'Megan, did you see Emily?'

'She was swimming way out. I don't like swimming out of my depth so I stopped.'

A cold hand clutched at Mike's stomach. Tim sensed Mike's anxiety and said comfortingly, 'It's OK. She'll be one of those kids out there.'

'I've been out there. I couldn't see her.'

'Come and play some Frisbee with us,' offered Megan.

'I'm going to look for her,' said Mike, and walked back towards the water, the anxiety starting to grow.

By the time Mike had swum the width of the beach both ways, he was starting to feel tired. He stopped by Martin and Jamie, who had abandoned the football game in favour of a relaxing swim.

'I can't find Emily.'

'Oh, stop fussing, Dad. What could have happened?'

'I don't know, that's why I'm asking you to help.'

'Dad!'

'Now, Jamie. You too, Martin, if you don't mind.'

The three of them swam up to every body in the sea but Emily wasn't there. Mike made his way back to the beach. John had left the game and soon caught Mike's mood. By now Tim was concerned as well. He tossed the Frisbee at Megan and tried to keep Mike calm.

'It's OK, Mike, she's fifteen, not five.'

'Maybe she's just swum round the headland to the next beach,' suggested John.

'Christ, John, she doesn't do this sort of thing, you know that. She's always so careful and thoughtful.'

'Who's got the best Italian?' asked Tim.

'Sarah,' replied John immediately.

'Not much help now. Let's be rational about this.' Tim was always rational. 'One of us should go out there and start talking to the kids. Someone else should perhaps go and report this.'

'Who to?' wondered Mike.

'Is there a lifeguard?' asked Tim, scanning the beach.

'This is southern Italy, not California.' Mike had experienced the laissez-faire nature of Italy's bureaucracy on previous excursions.

'The kids probably speak English,' volunteered John. 'They all do and there's probably lots of English tourists to help.'

'OK. You two go out there. Megan and I'll go and find who the authorities are.' Tim was assuming control and Mike was grateful.

'Will our bags be safe here?' asked John.

'Oh, for God's sake, John.'

'OK. Sorry. Let's go.'

They spent the next mind-numbing hour swimming frantically around the bay, checking the beach and wondering when Tim and Megan would reappear with some sort of authority figure. Nobody knew anything. Nobody remembered seeing Emily. She had simply vanished and now a second and even more frightening thought gripped Mike.

'John, what if someone's taken her?'

'Taken her?'

'You know. A paedophile.' Mike could scarcely pronounce the word.

'No. Not a fifteen-year-old. They like kids under ten.' John was trying to be reassuring, but it wasn't working.

'Well, someone else. Someone like that,' said Mike impatiently.

'If she's gone off with anyone, it's some Italian boy, some kid with a full head of hair unlike me who's taken her to a coffee shop and is chatting her up.' John was sensitive about his increasing baldness.

'She wouldn't do it, John. She would always come and ask me first. She'd never want to cause me that kind of worry.'

'Kids do thoughtless things sometimes, Mike.'

'Not Emily. Not ever Emily. What if it's someone who wanted to have sex with her and when they couldn't—'

'Mike! Come on, man! Get a grip. Look, there's Tim and Megan.' John started waving.

They ran towards them.

'Did you find her?' asked Tim, hopefully.

'No!' snapped Mike. 'For Christ's sake. Have you brought anyone?'

'There's one small police station in the next town along the coast,' explained Tim.

'Well?'

'The bloke spoke no English. Best I could get was he was alone and couldn't leave the shop unattended.'

'Shit!' Mike smacked his right fist into his open left palm.

'Mike, don't get hysterical. That won't help,' John warned.

'It's only been two hours or so . . .' Tim was still trying to be rational.

'Two hours. Do you hear yourself?' Mike was almost screaming.

'Mike, calm down.'

'It's all right for you. It's not your daughter!'

They went in and out of the water a dozen times. They spread out across the beach, they talked to everyone. Tim and his children hired a taxi and drove to the next beach but it was round the rocky headland and a long way away from where they had started out. Emily would never have swum that far, couldn't have swum that far, according to Mike.

The crowds began to melt away. The temperature dropped and T-shirts were slipped over sunburned flesh. The sun moved behind the mountains and the light lost its glare and became very still. By now Mike was living in a different world.

'Emily! *Emily!*' He continued to shout at the unhearing waves as they lapped gently onto the shore. Tim and John gathered the children together and discussed in low tones what they might do. Tim went over to Mike and put his arm round him.

'Mike, we have to get some help,' he said slowly, 'and we have to get the kids back to the house. We're going over to that Tabac place on the shore and I'll ring for two taxis. I'll drop the kids off and go down to Amalfi. I'll wait by the jetty and bring Julia back. OK?' He was expecting another wail but Mike simply nodded.

'Where could she be, Tim?'

'I don't know. She's just gone missing. Kids do these things to you. She'll show up. She will.'

'She's dead, Tim. I can feel it.'

'Oh, bollocks, don't be such a prat. Just stay here. We'll be back.'

Jamie came over to his father and took his hand. 'She'll be OK, Dad. I know Emily.'

Mike nodded. ''Course she will.' And he hugged his son so hard, Jamie felt the life was being almost squeezed out of him.

The taxis started on their journey back towards Ravello. Mike heard a horn honking. He waved but couldn't make out whether they were responding. He turned back to the sea that had swallowed his daughter. Oh God, please, please, I'll do anything. I'm sorry. I'm so sorry for everything I've ever done. Please give Emily back to me, please, I'll do anything you want. I'll go to church three times a day. I just want my daughter back. Please, God, please.

The little waves crashed onto the shore twenty yards away and rolled gently towards his feet.

'*Emily!*' he yelled, his voice lost in the infinity of space. '*Emily!*' This must be what it is like to lose your mind, thought Mike. I can feel it now, inside my head, literally becoming unhinged.

When Julia, Sarah and Louise tumbled off the ferry from Capri at the jetty in Amalfi an hour later, their arms full of shopping bags, their faces wreathed in smiles and their tongues loosened by the second bottle of vino rossi they had consumed since lunch, it took a full minute for them to absorb the enormity of what Tim was telling them. Julia felt that from that moment on she lost the ability to laugh or smile ever again.

CHAPTER THREE

THEY FOUND EMILY AT NOON the following day. Her body had been washed ashore at the next beach, two miles from where she had entered the water. Some children who were playing on a rock saw her head trapped under a jutting stone and dived in to explore.

Nobody in the villa in Ravello had slept much that night. The phone had rung at seven o'clock in the morning but it was just to inform them that there had been no sighting of Emily. They knew then that there was little chance she had gone off with anyone willingly or unwillingly. When it rang again shortly before one o'clock Mike knew even as he grabbed the receiver that the news was bad.

'Thank you, *grazie*,' he said blindly and put the phone down.

Sarah had ushered all the children out of the room to wait anxiously in the kitchen as the red-eyed Julia looked desperately at her husband. He felt her eyes on him and moved away with the receiver in his hand, unwilling to let her see the moment when he knew. But she felt it anyway. He turned back to her slowly, reluctantly, tears already welling in his eyes.

'Oh Mike, no!'

'They've found her body. We have to go down and identify it.'

'No! No, I won't! *No!*' Julia started to beat Mike's chest. He held her two fists apart with his hands but found it impossible to hold her close until he felt her body collapse, wracked by sobs and pain.

*   *   *

The paperwork surrounding the formalities in Italy had seemed endless and it was two days before they had been able to return to England with the coffin. Mike and Julia had made a token effort to convince the others to remain at the villa and finish the holiday they had paid for in advance but they wouldn't hear of it. None of them had much felt like a holiday any more.

The funeral was sparsely attended. Most of Emily's friends were away on holiday and news of the tragedy had not yet reached them.

Jamie had no formal suit and was forced to wear his school uniform to the funeral. He felt utterly bereft. His parents had retreated into their own world, maintaining just enough sanity to get through the unreal saga of the preparations that were required of grieving parents. There was nothing left for him. Whatever excess energy his father had was directed at attempting to look after his mother. There were so many questions Jamie wanted to ask his parents. Would they have another baby to make up for Emily's death? What would happen to her room? What would happen to their lives? Would they move house? He knew that some people moved house after a divorce or a death if the memories were too sad. He didn't want to move house. All his friends were round here.

There were other problems. What did he tell his friends? What did he tell anyone who asked him about Emily? He knew he had to be respectful and sad but was he supposed to stay sad for a long time? If so, how long? Could he go out with his own friends and have a laugh or was that somehow hurting the memory of Emily? He wanted the answer to all these questions but he didn't dare approach his parents. His dad was constantly flustered by the slightest inconvenience and his mother didn't seem to be inhabiting her own body any longer. She was in the room with him sometimes, like when she was sitting at the breakfast table, but he could tell that she wasn't really there. Her spirit seemed to leave her body when Emily was lost.

Sarah's constant presence unsettled him too. He understood that she was there to help but she didn't help him. It was always awkward when people came to stay. There was just the one bathroom for a start and whenever he wanted to use it Sarah was always in there. Both his parents seemed to leave the running of the house to her and, devastated as they all were by what had happened, it seemed to Jamie that Sarah's presence was discouraging a speedy return to their family routine and therefore making things worse. When the time came to leave for the funeral service it was Sarah who checked the knot in his tie and the smoothness of his hair, tasks that had traditionally been undertaken by his mother.

Jamie sat in the church in the front pew staring at the vicar as he recited Emily's list of accomplishments. He wondered whether they would mention her neck. It was what he remembered most about his sister. When she wore her hair in a ponytail it revealed her neck which he always thought was the most attractive part of her — it was so white and vulnerable. He hoped she hadn't suffered when she died. He couldn't imagine what it must have been like. They had been told that she had probably had cramp or a sudden seizure of some sort and been unable to manoeuvre her body. He hoped it had been quick. Just thinking about it made him cry. Unlike in other social circumstances, tears now would be expected of him. He knew there were others in the pews behind him who were crying because he could hear their stifled sobs during the service but he knew, too, that he was not supposed to turn round and see who they were. He was on parade, like in the CCF at school.

It was so unfair that he was expected to behave well just at the time when he was more upset than at any other point in his life. And he didn't even have Emily to help him through it. He missed her. He didn't think they had been that close, quite frankly. She had always been that annoying superior older sister. She had her friends and her music and her clothes and her make-up and she spoke for hours on the telephone and he had his golf and his own friends and not much interest in anything else outside television and his computer.

But now that she was gone he realised how much a part of his life she had always been. She had just always been ... well, Emily. She'd been in the house, in the bathroom, on the phone, in the kitchen, usually just when he wanted to be there. She'd been a pain a lot of the time but the house was so weird now. His parents were so weird now for a start and probably would be for ever. The sheer unfairness of it all overwhelmed him. He hadn't done anything to deserve this terrible punishment and nor, he was pretty sure, had Emily. He started to cry audibly. His father laid a hand on his thigh. Was it an instinctive paternal gesture of comfort and support or an equally instinctive parental warning, telling him not to submit to the ease of breaking down in public?

Jamie stood with the others as the coffin containing his sister's body slid towards the roaring flames that would consume it. He didn't like this part of the ceremony, he found it rather frightening and he wondered why his parents had opted for it. Not that the alternatives were a whole lot better but he wanted somewhere to come in future and just stand over her body and pay his respects. If there was no grave he didn't know how he could do that. He didn't know if his parents were going to scatter her ashes somewhere. But where? Outside the Royal Festival Hall where she had said once she wanted to make her debut as a soloist? On the lacrosse field at school?

Christmas cards were always addressed to Mike, Julia, Emily and Jamie, in that order, as if to stress their declining scale of importance in the scheme of things. He always felt diminished by that constant mantra and yet now that Emily was gone and he was promoted to number three he didn't want it, didn't think himself worthy of it, knew that every time he read the three names together like that it would only emphasise the hole in his life that used to be filled by Emily.

Jamie was surprised and quite pleased when they filed into the Garden of Remembrance and he saw the newly engraved plaque with all their names on it. Now he knew he would have somewhere to come and think about

Emily. He wouldn't come with anyone else unless it was to show a friend who might be interested; it would be a private place for him and his sister. He hadn't talked to her much in life. He hadn't needed to. He knew what she was thinking. She regarded him as a nuisance, usually dirty and untidy as well, but now, somehow when it was no longer possible for them to be physically close any longer, he felt extremely close to her spiritually. He looked again at the inscription: 'Beloved sister of Jamie.' That was true. Whenever he had seen the word 'beloved' before, he had thought it was a stupid word, old-fashioned and somehow untrue, false and sentimental. Now he knew what they meant. She was loved. Always and for ever. She'd never grow old. He could talk to her about their parents. He had a feeling he was going to need her advice.

After the last mourner had left the house, Jamie raced up to his bedroom and slammed the door shut with enormous relief. He tore off his school uniform which he felt made him look ten years old and grabbed a T-shirt and a pair of jeans out of his wardrobe. He turned on his computer and played his favourite Soccer Manager game with total concentration for over an hour. It was nearly six o'clock when he became aware of how hungry he was. He turned off the computer and padded downstairs slowly, becoming increasingly more conscious with every step of how unnaturally silent the house was.

'Mum?' he called softly. There was no answer. Nervously he opened the lounge door, anxious at what he might find in the room. Julia lay on the sofa, her eyes staring at the ceiling. Jamie thought she might have fallen asleep with her eyes open. He had heard from other boys at school that it was possible for this to happen.

'Mum?'

Slowly Julia turned to him.

Not again. Jamie thought. He knew she was upset; he was upset, they were all upset, but his mother seemed to have physically collapsed.

'When's tea?'

Julia tried to answer him but the mere act of talking seemed almost too great for her. Haltingly, she told him to go and look in the fridge.

'There isn't anything.'

'What about the food in the dining room?'

'There's only some salted peanuts left.'

'I'm sorry, Jamie.'

'Where's Dad?'

Julia just shrugged.

Eventually Jamie managed to find a tin of baked beans and open it, a difficult task with the old-fashioned can opener they still used. He had just tipped the beans into a pan and turned on the electric ring when the back door opened and his father came in with a large bag which emitted an inviting aroma.

'I thought you'd fancy some fish and chips.'

'You thought right.'

'OK, grab some plates and let's see what we've got here.'

'Shall I get a plate for Mum?'

'I'll go and see.'

Mike left the room as Jamie put out three large dinner plates and started dividing up the chips as evenly as he could.

'She's not hungry. It's just the two of us.'

'Good. I'm starving. I can eat hers.'

After this bright beginning the conversation gave way to silence as they chewed their way through soggy chips and deep-fried batter.

'Dad?'

'What?'

'Is Mum going to be like this for a long time?'

'Like what?'

'You know. Like she is now. Lying on the couch and everything.'

'We all have to do our grieving, Jamie. We just do it in different ways and it will take us different amounts of time.'

'What should I do?'

'Get out on the golf course every day and practise till you go back to school.'

'Won't Mum think I'm dissing Emily?'

'No. I think she'll be grateful you're out of the house.'

'What do you think I should be working on?'

'Same as usual.'

'My short game?'

Mike nodded, collected Jamie's plate from the table and began to scrape the remains down the waste disposal. He felt ashamed for pushing Jamie back on to the course. He realised it was what he wanted rather than what the boy needed.

Mike had seen Julia stretched out on the couch, practically catatonic, and been unable to reach out and help. Whether this was because he felt overwhelmingly guilty for his part in Emily's death or resentful that Julia appeared to be blaming him for the tragedy he could not tell. He always thought he had loved both his children to the same extent even though the past couple of years with Emily had been slightly awkward, as she had become increasingly adolescent. It had all got so complicated with Emily not saying what she actually meant but hinting instead at how she felt. Mike never understood why women found it necessary to play this ridiculous guessing game. Running upstairs, slamming the bedroom door and bursting into tears because you had been stood up on a Saturday night was one thing. Running upstairs, slamming the bedroom door and bursting into tears because your father had just made an innocent comment about the length of a hemline or the prominence of cleavage was something else entirely.

And now he'd never be able to worry about it again. His eyes welled with tears as his mind strayed to the remembered sight of Emily's still body laid out on the marble slab of the mortuary. At times like this, carrying on with his own life seemed pointless. If he could have exchanged his life for Emily's he would gladly have done so.

He knew that Julia shared his feelings of utter bereavement. He hoped that in the turmoil of their emotions they might find comfort in each other, be able to use each other's strengths to counter their individual weaknesses. He hoped with all his heart that Julia would learn to forgive him for his fatal neglect of Emily on the beach that afternoon, that their love would overcome the tragedy that threatened to blight their marriage permanently. He knew rationally that the initial period of mourning would eventually stop. They would simply have to find a way of carrying on with their lives. Mike was already worrying what would happen thereafter. He suspected that Julia's mourning would not be over for a long time. And he knew exactly who would become the inevitable target of her rage and despair.

Oh Tom,

How I wish you were here with me now! It's Christmas — well, that's what the television and the newspapers tell me. Other people's houses are decorated with brightly-lit Christmas trees and the cash registers in the shops are ringing out the tune of that most sacred of all Christmas carols. Yet I sit here in a cold, dark house, because I haven't got the energy to turn on the central heating and the lights and because I feel halfway to being in the grave myself.

Last Christmas Emily and I spent hours and hours making decorations for the tree. Did I tell you Emily was amazingly artistic? It wasn't just her music that was so extraordinary. I struggled along in her wake and the men of the house stood back and admired. Now I haven't got the mental or physical strength to do anything about Christmas at all. The tree stands in its protective netting outside the back door, gradually shedding its needles because I haven't managed to find a bucket of water to stand it in.

The boxes of Christmas decorations are still in the loft. I can't bear to open them because Emily made them. And she isn't here to help me put them on the tree. Mike hasn't even asked me if he should put up the tree. Everything he does − or doesn't! − seems to rub me up the wrong way. Sometimes I think he has all the sensitivity of a double decker bus. I know it must be an art to find the right thing to say in this situation but he seems to find the wrong one all the time. That's why I wish you were here now. You'd know just what to say. Instead we face the prospect of a cold Christmas, each of us alone in this house.

And poor Jamie is stuck in the middle.

Oddly enough, on the surface I'm back to being Little Miss Sensible. I'm very well organised, always have been, haven't I? The house hasn't fallen apart. There is food in the fridge and clean underpants for the men in my life. I haven't scraped the car or blindly knocked over a pile of egg cartons in Waitrose. I show up for work each day in the West End on time (Railtrack permitting) and I get home in time to make dinner. Everyone compliments me on how well I'm doing to pick myself up after such a tragedy.

I want to scream at them, Tom, only I can't. I know the emotion is in there somewhere but it's buried so deeply inside me that it would take dynamite to uncover it. Instead I smile and I make small talk and I can see the other person is desperate not to set off some kind of chemical reaction in me by touching on the subject of Emily.

So I'm fine, I suppose. To all outward appearances life goes on and I'm a part of it. Jamie takes his GCSEs this summer and Mike is doing OK at the bank, although there seems to have been some turmoil in the south-east Asia markets this year and his annual bonus is down from last year's handout. He makes more from that bonus than I do in nearly a whole year's work once you take the tax off. And that's just supposed to be like a tip, isn't it? I used not to mind too much. The financial services sector is just better paid than a lowly administrator in music copyright clearance but now I sort of do resent it. I work just as hard as he does.

I seem to be finding fault with Mike all the time. We don't have rows. Maybe we're too English or just too middle-class for rows. But we get irritated with each other much more than we used to. We don't go out much any more, not even to the cinema.

I know Mike thinks I blame him for Emily's death and naturally enough he resents me for blaming him. The trouble is, I think I do blame him, though I try so hard not to. But I just don't think it would have happened if I'd been on the beach with Emily that day. Maybe I blame myself for taking that day trip to Capri. I think about this all the time.

And the weird thing is, I just feel numb. I had supposed that if you felt bitter and hurt it was a warm feeling, liable to explode into anger, but instead I feel like some great factory that is going out of business. I'm being asset-stripped. My emotions are being sold off and all that will be left of me is a shell of a body.

Maybe that's not entirely true because I can still experience emotion, but not the emotions I associate with myself. Last Saturday afternoon, soon after lunch, I was in the bathroom when I heard Mike shouting to Jamie that they were leaving. I called out to find out what time they would be coming home and Mike just barged into the bathroom. I don't think he meant to. I'm pretty sure he didn't because he looked so shocked. I'm afraid I was outraged. It's not an emotion I have felt for a long time and it makes me sound horribly middle-aged. I mean Mike is my husband but when he flung open the door and saw me sitting like that I felt utterly humiliated, as if it was a total stranger standing there. We used to share the bathroom all the time without the slightest problem, as you and I did. We never thought twice about it but I was just so offended to be invaded like that, I surprised myself.

As you've probably gathered, physical relations with Mike are not good. We do not touch, we do not kiss, we do not hold hands. Yes, we sleep in the same bed but that's maybe just because neither of us dares bring up the subject of sleeping alone.

In fact not only have we stopped touching each other, we've pretty much stopped talking to each other. Not nastily. It's not like we're in the middle of a huge row and we've retreated to the wings to lick our wounds. Nor do I mean this literally. Of course we still talk to each other in the sense that we exchange information but the conversations tend to be like Mike's telephone calls – brisk exchanges of essential information. I talk on the phone because the act of talking itself is the pleasure. I know Mike thinks I just babble on and don't say anything of significance but I've tried explaining that talking to my friends is therapy in itself but I know he doesn't get it.

Mind you, even these moments of pleasure are getting fewer. Sarah is the only one I really talk to. She works as a copywriter in an advertising agency in Cavendish Square, quite near our offices, so I get to have lunch with her at least once a week. After we got back from Ravello she moved into the house and stayed with us for ten days till the day of the funeral. I really don't know how I would have survived that time without her.

For years we shared our frustrations at a sense of all-pervading anxiety, a sense that we had let ourselves down somehow, that our options in life had narrowed so that the road ahead was predictable for both of us, which made it boring and unattractive, yet neither of us possessed the courage to do anything about it. Above all there was that feeling that attacks every woman I know. We never have enough time. We want so badly to be the perfect wife, the perfect mother, the perfect role model for our daughters. Well, that's all gone now. I've failed in the most basic requirement of all — keeping my child alive.

Funny how wrong you can be, isn't it? Who could possibly have predicted what has happened to me in the last five months? Now Sarah can't quite reach me any more. We don't share all the same emotions any longer and I'm wondering whether you're the only one that can. Now that I can't bear Mike to touch me physically I find myself living more and more in the past and the future with you. You're the only man I trust to understand my emotions, Tom.

You will be there for me, won't you?

CHAPTER FOUR

SARAH WAS DELIGHTED WHEN JULIA told her she was being sent to San Francisco on company business.

'What kind of business?'

'A concert recording — "Tony Bennett Sings the American Century". It's being televised by some big cable station out there and our company's got the rights to issue the CD.'

'Business class?'

'You must joking.'

'Hope you don't get economy long haulitis or whatever they call it.' Sarah blushed and wished she'd never said that. Somehow it was a reference to holiday travel and death. She wished she could have ripped the tongue out of her throat.

Julia knew exactly what her friend was thinking but wanted to change the subject so that Sarah wouldn't think she knew what was in her mind. It was embarrassing and hopeless. And it happened far too often.

'You're not going to miss that college reunion you were telling me about?' asked Sarah as quickly as she could.

'No. That's on the Friday night. I don't leave till the Monday morning.'

'That's going to be such a hoot.'

'What if I'm the worst one there?'

'The worst?'

'You know, the oldest looking, the heaviest, the one who never got on.

Don't forget, most of my year went into the City right in the middle of the Thatcher boom.'

'Well then, they're probably far too rich and successful to want to meet up with losers like you.'

'Thanks.'

'I was joking.'

The waiter arrived with their Caesar salads just in time for him to overhear Sarah's reference to her as a loser. Julia blushed, furious with herself for caring what the waiter might possibly think about her. She thought it unlikely that he would hurry back to the kitchen and tell everyone that the woman in the navy suit at table nineteen was a loser. No, she decided. That's exactly what he was going to do.

Across the table, Sarah was chasing a crouton round the plate with her fork. 'What's the weather like out there this time of year?'

'I think it's always pretty cold.'

'Really? I thought it was California. California's always hot.'

'This is northern California though.'

'But that view. That view of the city and the Golden Gate Bridge and all that.'

'I know. I can't wait. I'll send you a postcard.'

'Thanks. But you won't go without telling me about your triumph at the ball, will you?'

'What ball?'

'The Oxford Ball.'

'It's not a ball. It's a hundred women in a big hall, all talking at once.'

'Knock 'em dead, Julia!'

I wish, thought Julia wryly. She wanted to go to Oxford and blast the rest of the girls in her year straight between the eyes. It wouldn't happen of course. Susan Appleyard would be a QC earning £500,000 a year and Rosemary de Angelis would have married some international playboy and be flitting in for the evening from the island she owned in the Caribbean. She was totally convinced that everyone at the reunion would appear to be richer, thinner and more attractive than she was. What could she possibly do to strike a blow for herself? She caught the Piccadilly Line to Knightsbridge and fought her way through the crowds to the front entrance of Harvey Nichols.

Julia didn't go into the office on the Friday. She had still to pick up the traveller's cheques from her bank, a procedure which had suddenly been made unnecessarily complicated by the closing down of her old branch and its absorption into a newer, larger and considerably more frustrating one. She also wanted to collect the two dresses she had left at the dry cleaners the previous weekend and to compare them with the horrifyingly expensive but flattering red one she had purchased at a cost she could not bear to tell Mike about. He would find out when the Visa bill came but she hoped that by then he would have seen how gorgeous she looked in it and be in a more conciliatory mood.

All that afternoon she zipped and unzipped herself out of the simple, well-cut but frankly boring blue and black dresses she had worn for the past two years. None of the women who were going to be at St Winifred's had seen her in either but that wasn't the point. She had the chance now to make a terrific splash but to do so would also mean risking humiliating defeat. The red dress was eye-catching, the stylish cut flattering to her figure and the designer had just appeared in a Sunday newspaper colour magazine as one of the top five young designers. There was, however, one insuperable problem. The red dress needed confidence. And that was the very thing she lacked.

She decided to show Mike and Jamie, and went nervously downstairs. Jamie was watching *Neighbours* and couldn't have been more embarrassed if she'd walked into the lounge stark naked. Fortunately for her son the telephone rang for him (for the third time within the last hour, she noted idly) and he beat a welcome retreat into the hall. Mike was no more help. He simply dithered. It was new for a start and he didn't much care for change. He was used to her in the blue and the black ones and the idea of her on the loose in Oxford with a bunch of inebriated women, as they certainly would be by the end of the evening, was faintly unsettling. They were bound to be swapping stories about how awful their husbands were. What if he turned out to be the worst? Besides, many of them would remember him from his days at college and they were bound to make mischief. And it bothered him that she wouldn't tell him the exact price of the red dress.

'Do you like it?' Julia asked.

'I'm not sure. How much was it?'

'I keep asking you, what difference does the price make?'

'None. But if I'm paying for it I want to know.'

'Well, you're not. I'm paying for it.'

'I pay the Visa bill. You know perfectly well.'

'Out of our joint account.'

'So just tell me.'

'Fourteen ninety-nine.'

'Seriously?'

'Seriously. It was in a sale. Now do you like it?'

'It's stunning.'

'Really?'

'Really.'

'So I should wear it tonight?'

'If it's right for the occasion.'

She could have screamed. 'But that's what I'm asking you.'

'I can't tell you that. What does it say on the invitation?'

'Dress optional.'

'What a cop-out.'

'Exactly. Now tell me what you think.'

'What I think is if you go in your underwear you'll be better dressed than Helen Fairbrother.'

'You never liked Helen.'

'She was a dislikeable dyke.'

'She wasn't gay. She was just . . . a bit of a character.'

'She was a dyke.'

'How do you know?'

'Because I tried to kiss her and she nearly broke my nose.'

'You tried to kiss her?'

'It was very dark. I thought she was Sally Fox.'

'I didn't know you fancied Sally Fox.'

'Well, I certainly didn't get anywhere with her that night. Your friend Helen Fairbrother saw to that.'

'And that's why you think she's gay? Because she hit you when you made an unwelcome, unprovoked sexual assault on her?'

'No, I think she's gay because she wore leather trousers for three years, never went out with a bloke, smoked cigars, rode a Harley Davidson and made a pass at Barry Hall's very pretty blonde girlfriend.'

'I think you're a mass of prejudices.'

'Look, I don't care if she's a dyke, I don't care if she leaves a card in telephone boxes in Soho and I don't know why we're having this row.'

'I asked you whether I should wear this beautiful red dress.'

'Yes. I think you should wear it and I think you should staple the Visa receipt to it and see if anyone else can find one that looks as good for fourteen pounds ninety-nine pence.'

'Mike.'

'What?'

'I was joking about the price. It wasn't really in the sale.'

'No? Well, you had me fooled.'

She wore the black dress in the end. It had served her well for the past two years and it always looked good against her white skin, which was even whiter these days since she had decided to shield it permanently from the rays of the sun. The point was that the dress was unremarkable and that was precisely the way she felt. She was going in order to be invisible, to disappear into the varnished oak panelling of the college and watch everyone else.

She hadn't been inside her old college since the day she graduated seventeen years before. It appeared to be almost entirely unchanged. The students' pigeon holes had been moved from the Junior Common Room and the bar area had been expanded but that was as much as Julia noticed at first glance. The JCR was certainly shabbier than she remembered it. Indeed the college as a whole seemed a little more down-at-heel despite the impressive nature of the façade, which remained as imposing as ever. St Winifred's had always been one of the poorest colleges in Oxford and the intervening years had served only to widen the gap between those famous colleges rich in endowments and those like St Winifred's which struggled to compete.

The celebrations were to begin in traditional style with a sherry party in the Senior Common Room at 7.30 p.m. Each of the returning graduates had been allocated a college room in which to change, the undergraduates being at home for the Easter holidays. Passing each other on the stone staircase, Julia smiled pleasantly at a small Sri Lankan woman who disappeared into the room across the hallway from her. She looked very young and Julia couldn't for the life of her recall a Sri Lankan in her year. Then she glanced up at the name over the door, which read MENDIS.

Thankfully, she surmised that the woman was a postgraduate still in residence or even a terrified final year undergraduate who was so scared by the prospect of finals in two months' time that she had refused to go home for Easter. She was therefore twenty-one or twenty-two years old, not thirty-eight. Julia breathed a sigh of relief as she zipped up the black dress, took one last optimistic look in the mirror, shrugged off the disappointment that the face staring back was the same impostor she had been looking at for years, closed the door behind her and teetered slowly down the staircase on inappropriate high heels before clattering across the paved quadrangle in search of the Senior Common Room.

It was excruciating. She remembered nobody at all of the contemporaries she met crammed into the doorway and the dons who had taught her were nowhere to be seen. Instead they had been replaced by women of her own age, which Julia found logical but disconcerting. Most worrying of all was the presence of three male Fellows. The college had been one of the last to go co-educational and it was still an all-women college when Julia left. She hoped the men felt overwhelmed by their token status but she suspected they were rather enjoying it. She felt a tap on the shoulder.

'Hello. I thought I recognised you. You're Julia Cowan.'

Julia smiled, panicking. She didn't recognise the woman with the thick glasses who was staring so earnestly at her.

'It's weird. I've scarcely heard the name Julia Cowan spoken for seventeen years.'

'You didn't keep it for work?'

'No. I married soon after graduating and I rather liked the change of name. So everyone at work knows me as Julia Ramsey.'

'Are you still playing the violin? You were awfully good.'

'That's very nice of you but no, I just don't seem to have any time after work and the house and everything.'

'What kind of work do you do?'

Julia knew this was coming. It was bound to be one of the two key questions. The other one would relate to her family. The question facing her since she had made up her mind to accept the invitation was how much lying was she going to indulge in. She thought it was probably OK to embellish the c.v. a little. After all, everyone else was bound to be doing the same. It was bad enough that she wasn't a millionaire, with her name and photograph in the papers, on television or married to someone who filled all those requirements. She didn't think anyone would greatly care if, for the evening at least, she was a major player in the world of international rights and multimedia entertainment. It required a very small amount of liquid to polish her image for the evening. She took a deep breath and dabbed a little on for a spot test.

'I'm an executive for an international music publisher.'

'Oh, I say. That sounds rather high-powered.'

'It sounds a little more glamorous than it is.'

'Anything sounds glamorous to me. I'm just a housewife.'

Oh God. Typical, thought Julia. The one person I didn't need to try it on with in the whole room and I don't even know her name. I'd better ask quickly otherwise the conversation will be too far down the line. Before she could do so, though, the other woman continued apologetically with an explanation.

'I say I'm just a housewife but I'm more of a full-time unpaid nurse. My daughter was born with spina bifida and it's as much as I can do to get through the day. My husband's wonderful, though. He was really keen for me to come tonight. What about yours?'

'I . . .' Julia had no idea what was going to come out of her mouth. Fortunately nothing was necessary because at that precise moment a large gong was sounded. The high-pitched babble of conversation died away like the last of the air escaping from a punctured tyre. From somewhere at the far end of the room the familiar voice of Dame Margaret Hughes, the principal of the college, floated towards her.

'Ladies, you will all be delighted to know that you won't have to listen to me at length until you have been extremely well wined and dined. Let me say what a pleasure it is to see the matriculating class of nineteen eighty-two here in such distinguished numbers. If you can find your way into the main hall after so many years' absence you will be confronted with the table plan for the evening.'

Eighty-five women began to move slowly towards the hall and the two noticeboards which were to explain the nature of the evening that lay before them. Julia scanned the list quickly, noticing with some relief the presence of at least half a dozen names she recognised. She had just found her own when she was unceremoniously hauled out of the crowd by the short, powerful and still unmistakable figure of Helen Fairbrother.

'Oh, don't take any notice of that. You're sitting next to me. I don't care what that stupid board says.'

'Helen!'

'I'm certainly not sitting next to Linda Luscious Lips.'

'God! Is she here?'

'According to the seating plan. That's why I'm taking no notice of it. Now give me a hug.'

The two women embraced warmly despite the six inches difference in height. Helen barely crawled past the five feet mark while Julia felt embarrassingly tall at five feet seven.

'Come on. Let's get there first and cause a disturbance.'

Fortunately or unfortunately, Linda Lawson, whom nature had graced with particularly full lips, had failed to arrive by the time the duck terrine was served so the place next to Helen would have been empty. Helen was soon in full flow with her stream-of-consciousness thoughts about how the college had gone to rack and ruin since they had decided to permit admission to men. Julia only interceded when Helen revealed that she had just returned from San Francisco.

'I'm going there on Monday.'

'You'll have a ball. It's a great place. And you don't have to be gay to love it there.'

'I'm only going to be there a few days.'

'Hey! I almost forgot. Guess who I ran into when I was there?'

'I couldn't possibly begin—'

'A certain tall, good-looking American Rhodes Scholar, Balliol. Is any of this ringing a bell somewhere?'

A large hammer started knocking at the side of Julia's head from the inside. Julia pretended to search for the name.

'Oh, come on, Little Miss Perfect. I met him again.'

'Tom Johnson?' Julia's heart was beating faster.

'I was tempted to beat the crap out of him for what he did to you at the end but I decided not to. After all, he is over a foot taller than me and I'd have needed a stepladder.'

'You didn't need to do that on my behalf, Helen. It was a long time ago.'

'Maybe, but you really fell for him in a big way, the big prick. Does he have one, by the way? Not that I have the slightest interest in that sort of thing.'

'Where did you meet him?' asked Julia quietly.

'I was in San Francisco for the Annual Gay and Lesbian Orgy. Couldn't stand the speechifying, so boring, it was like the Lib Dem Party Conference, so I took off for the American Conservatory Theater. They were doing some buttock-clenching Tennessee Williams play which I'd never heard of. I was the second one into the bar at the interval. He was the first.'

'Oh?' said Julia, faintly. The room was beginning to swim.

'He was with a guy. Came as a surprise to me.'

'He's gay?' asked Julia disbelievingly.

'Thought the two of them were in town for the orgy for a moment but it turned out his male companion was his wine-maker.'

'He's still at the vineyard?'

'It must be doing all right. They were in the best seats.'

'What did you talk about?'

'You.'

'Me?'

'He asked me all about you. Seemed very curious. I suppose some people would say he's still quite handsome considering he must be forty. Can you pass the wine?'

Julia passed the wine with a trembling hand.

Helen took the bottle from her with a big smile. 'He gave me something else, too.'

'What?'

'His business card.'

'Oh.' For a moment, Julia was disappointed. Perhaps Tom was just being polite.

'For you, not me!'

'Oh. But did he say anything about ...' Julia was incapable of forming complete sentences.

'About his wife?' finished Helen.

'Well, I suppose so.'

'He's divorced,' Helen stated with an even bigger smile.

'Oh. I'm sorry.'

'No you're not.'

'I'm sorry for him,' protested Julia. 'He must be devastated.'

'Now look here, Missy, I'm probably the last person in the world to ask about men. The entire species is a complete mystery to me and likely to remain so but even I worked it out eventually.'

'Worked what out?'

'The poor misguided fool's still in love with you.'

CHAPTER FIVE

JAMIE SPENT THE EARLY PART of Friday evening preparing for the momentous events which were to follow by studying with furious concentration the dog-eared copy of *Asian Babes* he had been given by Rob Faulkner.

He knew he was supposed to find it arousing and it bothered him a little that he didn't really. On the other hand his head was always swimming with lustful thoughts about Leonie Williams, particularly during Maths II, but Rob had given him the dog-eared magazine with such a smirk he thought it must be the passport to some kind of sexual Disneyland.

Rob was his hero. Not like Tiger Woods or Sergio Garcia who were also his heroes but in the more circumscribed world of school and the south Hertfordshire teenage social circle in which he moved. Rob was a year older, he was in the Lower Sixth, and though he wasn't great at sport, which was the usual road to cult status at school, and quite frankly a bit of a tosser academically speaking, he just had that indefinable air of charisma that drew other kids, particularly girls, to him.

Jamie couldn't really define it. It was more than the *de rigueur* ability to belch and fart on demand which lots of boys could do, even if he couldn't. It was something to do with self-confidence really and Jamie had very little of that. It was odd in a way because out on the golf course he had such a strong sense of inner belief that he felt himself invincible. In a classroom of kids, though, he just wanted to be anonymous and usually he succeeded.

He was average in most of his subjects, average in sport (except golf), average in height, weight, build and looks. Girls didn't run screaming from him but they certainly didn't gravitate towards him as they did to Rob Faulkner. It was at times like these that he missed having a sister. It wasn't that he couldn't remember Emily but the picture of her which he carried around in his head was already starting to fade and it hadn't been a year yet since she had died. He knew her death was probably the cause of much of the tension between his parents.

His parents were decent people but they were so hopelessly out of touch. They behaved towards him as if he was still nine years old. He enjoyed being with his dad on the golf course, though he found his obsessive preoccupation with his son's golf and future career overbearing. Jamie liked the fact that his mum showed very little interest in his golf, preferring that he concentrate on his schoolwork. It meant he could play one off against the other. He was good at this manipulation and, as far as he could tell, neither of his parents was aware he was doing it.

Mum going to America was great news. As long as he did his stuff on the golf course, Dad didn't seem to mind too much what he did off it. If his putting or his driving were giving cause for concern then there would be a full-scale investigation but if he played as they both knew he could play he was spared any intrusion into his private life.

He never mentioned Leonie or Rob Faulkner to his parents. They thought he still had the same friends he'd had when he started secondary school at the age of eleven. Boys like Simon Turner and Alan Hilton had invited him to their houses for tea after school and his mum had picked him up there but that was in the first year and the only reason he had agreed to go with them was that they lived nearby and they had been at primary school with him. Friendship with either of them would do nothing to increase his street cred now. Rob Faulkner was a different matter.

He wasn't too sure how to gain Rob's confidence. Jamie harboured no craving for booze or dope or cigarettes, the generally accepted methods of social advancement, so it was with inordinate pleasure that he received the magazine from Rob one lunchtime.

'Hey, Ramsey, this is your life!'

Rob flicked the magazine horizontally at him. Jamie put up a hand to stop the magazine hitting him in the face, picked it up from the floor, saw what it was and turned bright red. There was a roar of glee from Rob and his gang. Jamie hastily stuffed the magazine into his school bag.

'You like Asian tarts then?' asked Rob loudly.

'Yeah,' shrugged Jamie as off-handedly as he could, calculating that this was the answer Rob wanted to hear.

'You wanna meet a few?'

'Sure. When?'

'Saturday night.'

'OK. Where?'

'In town. We'll let you know.'

Jamie was thrilled. In fact the call didn't come for nearly a month, during which time he continued to study *Asian Babes* as if it was his French vocabulary book and he was going to be tested on it by Rob and his gang – he had to be fully prepared. He knew all the poses, the parts of the body they revealed, he just didn't find it particularly erotic and it bothered him because he knew other boys did and he wondered why he couldn't respond as they did. He comforted himself with the thought that maybe they, too, simply wanted to belong to the gang.

Also there was the even more immediate problem of where to keep the magazine to avoid its falling into enemy hands. There had been a major battle just before Christmas when he had found his mother Hoovering under his bed. Both sides launched immediate full-scale artillery bombardments.

'What are you doing?'

'I'm clearing up your mess.'

'It's not a mess. It's just my things.'

'It's filthy in here, Jamie. This whole room is a health hazard.'

'Only 'cause you're in it.'

'The council could close it down, you know.'

'It's my room, Mum. It's the only place I've got to myself.'

'Then you should look after it better.'

'I will if you clear out.'

'Don't speak to me like that.'

'I'm nearly sixteen. I deserve some privacy.'

'You can have your privacy. You just can't incubate bubonic plague in here. And if you want to be treated as a grown-up you have to behave like one. And that means keeping your room tidy.'

His mother stamped out bad-temperedly, taking the Hoover with her. Jamie knew his victory was temporary. She would be suspicious of his demand for privacy and though she might be a little more circumspect about when she marched into his room next time, he knew another invasion was inevitable. Next time she'd know he was hiding something so he would have to be twice as cunning about concealing *Asian Babes*.

Every place he tried seemed to be carrying a red sticker emblazoned PORNOGRAPHY INSIDE HERE on the outside. His underpants and socks drawer was far too obvious, his school bag might be subjected to an impromptu strip search. When the magazine was tucked away under the mattress it afforded easy access at night but Jamie was never sure, even if he made his bed which he did whenever he remembered to do it, which day of the week his mother might suddenly choose to change all the sheets in the house.

He fell into conversation with Rob Faulkner about the iniquity of parental inquisitions in the style of an Ali G interview. Rob was instantly sympathetic.

'Know what mine's gettin'?'

'What?'

'One of them X-ray scanning machines they have at the airport to examine your hand luggage.'

'You takin' de piss, man.'

'Nah. She gonna set it up in de hall.'

'You ain't gonna be allowed into yo bedroom, man.'

'Right. She be gettin' those "checked by security" stickers.'

Jamie feared he would have to commit *Asian Babes* to memory. The back of his mind was the only place he could be sure his mother couldn't get into.

In the end he settled for his gym bag. There was an extra zip pocket on the inside into which he inserted the magazine after carefully wrapping a clean white T-shirt round it. Prodding the bag with her fingers, even if she found it buried under three pairs of trainers, his mother would feel only the outline of the T-shirt. If she unzipped the pocket she would see only the clean T-shirt.

It wasn't perfect but it was the best he could do and for the moment he was under the impression that he had triumphed. Now he let the magazine slip from his fingers as he lay on his back on the bed and anticipated the heady excitement of what was to come. That his mother should choose this night to stay away from home in Oxford seemed to him to add God's blessing to his induction into Rob Faulkner's wonderful new world. He knew Leonie Williams was part of Rob's crowd so he had been rehearsing topics to talk to her about all afternoon, even to the extent of writing them down on the inside cover of *Under Milk Wood*.

He told his dad he was going out but he knew he wouldn't face the usual interrogation he got from his mother.

''Bye, Dad,' he shouted as he ran down the stairs and across the hallway.

''Bye!' came the reply from the living room. After a pause Mike called out, 'What time will you be back?' but the pause was all the time Jamie needed to open the front door. The question was left trailing in the now vacant hallway as Mike reached for the paper to see if that night's episode of *Frasier* clashed with the end of the Nationwide League game he was watching.

The evening was both boring and fascinating. Rob and four other guys were there, along with Leonie and three other girls. Two of the boys were in the same form as Rob, but the other two Jamie had never seen before. Leonie and the three girls were sitting at a corner table sipping what he thought at first was water but which turned out to be vodka. Rob and the guys were at the bar. Jamie bought himself a lager but wished he'd been brave enough to order a pint of bitter. He was worried that he was more likely to be exposed as underage by the beer than the designer lager.

'Which one d'you fancy?' asked one of the boys Jamie didn't know.

Jamie was instantly faced with a major dilemma. He didn't know which of the girls 'belonged' to the boys. He couldn't say 'none' because it was a wimp's answer. He wanted to say Leonie but he was worried that one of the bigger lads had his eye on her.

'Leonie,' he said off-handedly. 'I'd give her one.'

He knew it was a mistake the moment he said it.

'Hey, Leonie, Shagger here fancies you!'

He could have died. Right there on the spot. He wished the earth would open up and swallow him whole. He was rooted to the floor with embarrassment. Leonie looked at him with what he thought was utter contempt and then leaned into the rest of the group and talked with great animation.

At least she's not walked out or hit me, thought Jamie as he turned back with seeming lack of concern towards the bar. He started to read the labels on the bottles on the shelf with enormous concentration.

Rob nudged him. 'Why did you say you fancied Leonie?'

'Said I'd give her one. Didn't say I fancied her,' replied Jamie, recovering some ground.

Rob ruffled his hair. 'She dumped Chris here last week. You'll be in there, my son. She's probably gagging for it.'

Jamie's heart was beating furiously. So that's why that idiot blurted it all out. He and Leonie used to go out with each other. He wondered about the exact nature of their relationship.

'What's all this?'

Jamie turned abruptly to face Leonie, his lager still in his hand. So abrupt was the turn that the drink spilled over the edge of the glass and onto Leonie's blouse. A wet stain spread across her left breast, highlighting the outline of her bra. She squealed and brushed ineffectually with her hand at the spillage.

'Oh sorry,' said Jamie, 'sorry, I didn't mean to . . .'

'Tosser,' said Leonie and disappeared into the Ladies.

Jamie was on an emotional roller coaster. As a gang they rolled out of the pub and down the hill to the multiplex. Jamie was flattered to be a part of the group and didn't mind so much that nobody talked to him. If anything, it was a relief just to be able to listen to the banter. As they stood in line to hand over their five pounds for the new Hollywood slasher/horror movie, the boys and girls began to intermingle for the first time. It looked like two packs of playing cards being shuffled into each other.

Jamie assumed he'd be the odd one out. He wondered if he could get the aisle seat, then he wouldn't feel such an alien. He was stunned when Leonie abandoned her friend Chloe and sidled over to him. As far as he could see, the lager stain had disappeared.

'I'm sorry about . . . that. I'll pay for a new one,' he said quickly, praying that it wouldn't cost him fifty pounds or something extravagant like that.

'Forget it,' she said shortly. 'It's old. I'll probably chuck it away tonight. Do you want to sit next to me?' she asked simply.

'Yes,' he said, as he would if she now asked him to eat the carpet they were standing on.

The conversation didn't get any more scintillating for the rest of the evening but she let him put his arm round her shoulder in the last fifteen minutes of the film and just before the end she turned her face to his and snogged him.

Jamie's previous moment of supreme elation had taken place after a hole in one at the par three 212 yard third hole on St Albans golf course when he was eleven years old. When the ball soared cleanly into the air, bounced once, kicked on and rolled at high speed across the green towards the flag and then disappeared from view into the hole, Jamie thought life could never get any better. He was wrong. This was much, much better.

Dear Tom,

I sat next to Helen Fairbrother last night at the college reunion. She gave me your business card with the word 'Hi!' scribbled on the back and told me all about your meeting at the theatre after the Tennessee Williams play. Quite a coincidence!

The reunion was the strangest experience, nothing like what I expected. For a start, I was relieved to discover that I wasn't the oldest looking in our year nor the least accomplished, and positively astonished to discover that Melanie Gordon (remember her? She was the girl with the permanently exposed navel who had seemingly slept her way through at least ten of the men's colleges, including yours) had become a born-again Christian! What I found very amusing was that she claimed not to have any memory of her previous existence and I, of course, was far too embarrassed to make any reference to it.

Shy, mousy Rosemary Dilworth is the big financial success story. She's already on the board of one of the major investment banks. Angela Fawcett – I'm not sure you met her, she was always in the library and she eventually took the top first in English in the university – is now a big wheel in the Foreign Office.

Suzy Holmes, the petite girl from Yorkshire with the Afro perm and the loud voice who lived in the room on the ground floor of my staircase and who wanted to burn the college to the ground, is now the New Labour MP for a constituency in the Home Counties.

She got very irritated when people tried to call her one of Blair's babes. I was delighted to see her after dinner trapped against a wall by the principal and the senior bursar who thought that Suzy might have it in her power to overturn the cabinet's current hostility towards the funding of Oxbridge colleges. Suzy was looking as though she had made a mistake in returning at all.

You must remember Jane Waterman; she lived next door to me in our second year and cried through most of it — she's now a stout, matronly-looking woman with a laugh like a braying horse. We talked about all those hopes and fears of twenty years ago and I said how pleased I was that so many of us had made the effort to come and then she mentioned Ali Baxter in a knowing sort of way. I remembered Ali only as the girl who sat her finals when she was three months pregnant and how we all envied her in a way because her boyfriend loved her, she was getting married after graduation and she seemed to have her life laid out for her. Apparently, she died of breast cancer five years ago. Jane said Melanie had told her that she had left a grieving husband and four kids and offered it as a reason for instant conversion.

So death has already claimed one of us from that bright eager bunch who gathered for our official photograph that brisk sunny October morning. You know, I'm embarrassed to say now I can't remember anything about Ali except that she was always smiling and since the middle of her second year madly in love with Tim Something, her handsome young engineer from Worcester College. If there was a possible advert for a happy married life, it was Ali Baxter. And she died at 33.

I thought as I drove home this morning that if I died in a car crash on the M40 on the way, what would I have left behind? A grieving husband; a world-famous golfer who was going to fail his GCSEs unless he spent more time on his homework and less on the driving range; the memory of a tragically lost daughter; a dozen compilation CDs of the best of American show tunes. And that's pretty much all, the sum total of nearly forty years on this earth. Not much to boast about, is it?

It certainly doesn't square with the hope and promise of that October morning. I wanted some proof that I had lived my life to the full. Where was the grand passion I was so sure was going to be mine? You left me, you bastard, you promised to send for me, wrote me that Godawful soul-destroying letter, and now I can't even bear to be in the same bathroom as my husband. What kind of a life is this?

After hearing about poor Ali I resolved to inform the rest of the women that my life was a major success. I reckoned the alcohol-fuelled nature of the evening was not the time for false modesty. Whereas nobody was terribly surprised that I hadn't gone on to become a concert violinist they were all seemingly impressed with my career choice. But then I suppose I did stretch the truth rather by telling everyone so much about Sondheim and Bernstein and the Gershwins, it must have sounded as though I popped over to have dinner with them most weeks.

By the end of the evening and fortified by the generous provision of madeira and claret, neither of which I had tasted for seventeen years, I had reached a state of mellowness that allowed me to think fondly of almost everyone I had ever met.

I was also surprised to discover that so many of them remembered Mike and remembered him fondly. Well, I suppose that was inevitable in a way. I mean, it would have been more surprising if they had slagged him off once they knew we'd been married for sixteen years. There were lots of divorced and separated women so I guess my marriage sounded to them like an oasis of blessed serenity. It has been a long time since I had thought of myself as so blessed. Mike must have made a better impression on our contemporaries than either of us recalled.

Was it just Emily's death that soured the marriage? Did I have too high an expectation of marriage? I wondered, I'm shocked to say, if even Ali Baxter's blissful union had been quite as blissful as they had always romanticised it would be. Maybe all marriages slump into a kind of lethargy after a few years, even Ali and Tim's. Nobody could reasonably expect to continue with the kind of romantic existence and frenetic sex life that seemed so normal in our early twenties. Yet isn't that what keeps us going when life is at its most frustrating — the prospect of someone dashingly romantic waiting for us just round the corner, a soul mate — a Tom Johnson?

Between midnight and one in the morning the party broke up and people drifted away to their rooms for the night. I walked down the stairs from hall and went outside into the brisk night air. In the far corner of the quadrangle I heard a peal of laughter and a tidal wave of nostalgia swept over me. This was the heady atmosphere I still associated with you. How many times did we clatter down the staircase after an evening making love and into just this atmosphere? You will always be associated with love and romance in my mind, just as Mike, I suppose, is associated with security and home and children and responsibilities and the bleak prospect of the years stretching ahead of me that I know will remain much the same until they carry me off in a wooden box.

Mike isn't a bad man, I know that, he's just ... not you. Yet you left me, you bastard, left me in such pain I thought I would never recover. You promised me, Tom, you promised me you would come back to me or send for me to come out to America and live with you. You were responsible for all those weeks and months of endless crying but it was Mike who was always there to comfort me, never imposing himself on me. I knew how much he wanted me but I just couldn't bring myself to do with him what we had done together. That would somehow have betrayed the perfection of my first love.

Well, in the end, I gave in, but that was your fault. You gave me no sign that you wanted to get back together. Later I checked with your college old boys' mailing list and I knew you had never left the vineyard but by that time I already had Emily and then Jamie and real life had taken over. You have always haunted me, returning whenever I feel low or listen to a particular piece of music, or then as I walked through First Court on a warm starry night, remembering the touch of your hand round my bare shoulder, the smell of you and the taste of you as we kissed in the corner of the cloisters.

I went back to my cold little attic room (I'm sure they've not changed the mattresses in twenty years) and fell into a restless sleep. I'm not sure if it was a daydream (if you can have daydreams at night) or a real 24-carat dream but I had the strongest sensation that something was going to happen on this trip to San Francisco I start on Monday.

In the dream, I'd just finished dinner with the company's American representatives and I let myself back into the hotel room which I believe is going to be a very comfortable one in Union Square to find a large bunch of red roses on the coffee table with an enigmatic note enclosed. I was puzzled but intrigued and hoped the next day would bring some kind of clarification. I took off my dress (the new red one because I wouldn't have all the anxiety that attended the reunion in Oxford once I'd arrived in California) and stepped into the shower.

It was while I was in the shower that you must have slipped the night porter a hundred dollar bill to let you into the room. All I know is that when I came out of the bathroom, towelling myself dry, you were there, sitting at the table in the upright chair with the shy but confident grin on your face that I'd first seen in a wine bar on the High. You rose to your feet as I stood there, beads of water still dotting my face and the back of my thighs (which had miraculously rid themselves of their cellulite). I don't think I can continue with this part of the narrative for fear of being arrested for sending naughty literature through the post.

When I woke up in the morning I was stabbed with disappointment that what had seemed so real to me during the night was once again merely the product of an overheated imagination. I drew back the curtains and peered out of the leaded window across the courtyard. I could just see the staircase where much of what I had dreamed about last night had actually taken place. You remember, I always preferred to go to bed with you in my own college rather than yours. After all, one of the benefits of snagging the handsome American was to parade him in front of my friends.

I tried to convince myself that I must get dressed, pack my overnight bag, have breakfast in hall and drive home. I've still got so much to do before the flight on Monday morning, but I couldn't seem to tear myself away from the window. Somehow this unchanging scene of seventeenth-century stone façade, stone-clad courtyard and lovingly manicured lawn had revived something in me that the previous seventeen years had suppressed. Even as I was lost in that cloud of nostalgia I was not sufficiently far gone to forget that awful time in my final year when only Mike's loving kindness had stopped me from jumping off the top of Magdalen Tower.

Seventeen years have passed since then. I've married, given birth to two children, suffered the torment of the damned, buried myself in work, continued to raise Jamie, looked after the house and kept my marriage together. I'm thirty-eight years old. In previous ages, in different societies, I would have been ready for the discard pile, maybe preparing to become an elderly wise woman.

Ha! That's a laugh. I feel no wiser now than the day I left college. Why haven't the passing years obliterated the memory of you, my first love?

Coming back to Oxford, particularly to St Winifred's, brought all those emotions streaming back into my brain. Handsome, smiling Tom, brilliant, witty, talented Tom, the first man to tease me into orgasm, the first man to introduce me to the wonder of Fred Astaire and Cyd Charisse in *The Band Wagon*, the first man to make me feel special in a way my parents, my teachers, even Jacqueline du Pré couldn't manage.

I started to cry. Nothing surprising there – I spent most of that last year looking at that view, in a similar state of emotional collapse. I asked myself why I was crying and I didn't know the answer. Was it for Emily? For me and Mike? Or for us, for what we had and what we lost? For the bleak years that now stretch out in front of me?

As I sit here at my desk in the bedroom I see before me my passport, my return airline ticket to San Francisco and that small three inch by two inch business card with the word 'Hi!' scribbled on the back. Put them all together and they mean only one thing. An airline ticket to romantic places, as you used to sing to me.

I can hear Mike and Jamie coming up the path, unloading their things from the car. I have to close now.

Do you really want to see me again, Tom, after all these years? Do you really? I wish I knew. Maybe I'll find out very soon.

CHAPTER SIX

JULIA WAS BOOKED ON THE eleven thirty flight from Heathrow to San Francisco on Monday morning. On the Sunday night she lay in bed debating with herself whether to initiate one of her infrequent attempts at lovemaking. She wanted to give Mike a going-away present rather like the casserole that now took up the whole of the top shelf in the fridge but she was afraid his response would be negative and the resentment between them would flare up again. She knew Mike felt that she had hurt him in this sensitive area since Emily's death so that he now rarely initiated any kind of physical advance himself. Although most of the time she welcomed the absence of traditional male pressure on her she also knew that the longer the interval between their sexual encounters grew, the faster their sex life would wither and die.

Still, she found his physical presence next to her comforting, and she knew that when she slept alone in the king-size bed which good American hotels always provide she would struggle to get to sleep because she would miss his familiar, reassuring company. So they lay together in the dark in a silence in which each of them knew what the other was thinking yet neither dared to make a move that might be open to misinterpretation. Julia wrestled with the conundrum until she heard the sound of Mike's rhythmic breathing.

If she left him she would miss him. If she walked out of the house she would lose her sense of security. Whereas normally she looked at the overgrown garden and the broken tiles in the bathroom and the ever widening crack in the bedroom ceiling with mounting despair, now she looked at her home with a desperate sense of potential loss. What if she met Tom out there and never came back? This was the centre of her existence. The maintenance tasks she was so worried about were minimal and irrelevant beside the sense of belonging which the house gave her.

What would happen to Jamie's school career? Would Mike fall apart at the seams? How would any of them cope if she never came back? What had she been dreaming of? She was a responsible wife and mother and the fact that she could barely tear herself away from her house, even to make a trip she had been so eagerly looking forward to, confirmed that she wasn't cut out for the reality of adultery, much as she might enjoy the fantasy of it.

By the time she arrived at Heathrow the hassle of travelling had driven all such thoughts from her head. There was an enormous jam on the busy arterial road round the terminal buildings and after she had been sitting in the back of the cab for twenty minutes as it inched its way forward from Terminal 2 to Terminal 3, Julia decided to take matters into her own hands. She paid off the taxi, wheeled her luggage along the road, choking with exhaust fumes, and eventually arrived at the check-in desk to find that only two of them were open and that there must have been a line of fifty or sixty people in front of her. She looked at her watch. The plane left in seventy-eight minutes.

There was less than forty minutes to take-off time when she arrived at the front of the queue, worried now that even if she didn't miss the flight her luggage might, thereby precipitating the nightmare of arriving at the hotel bereft of luggage and confidence. She was only partly reassured when the woman handed over her boarding card with the information that since the plane had been delayed for an hour and a half because it had been late leaving Frankfurt, her luggage would easily make it into the cargo hold.

By the time Julia had stuffed her carry-on bag into the full overhead compartment and prepared to face the boredom of an eleven-hour flight, she felt as though she had already been travelling for twenty-four hours.

Fortunately she had managed to book a window seat and once the plane had arrived at its cruising altitude and the captain had switched off the seat belt sign, she felt much of the tension of the last few days slip away. The screw-top bottle of white wine which she drank with her chicken and rice at lunch also sent a warm glow through her and as the other passengers settled down to watch the tiny screens fixed into the headrest of the seat in front, Julia willed herself into sleep. To aid her she swallowed one of the sleeping pills she had left over from an old prescription. It would probably have no effect at all but it might help to give her three or four hours of sleep.

She pulled down the small white window shade and tried to sleep but after shifting about in her seat for ten minutes she gave up the attempt, raised the blind again and looked out at the bright sunshine, the blue horizon of infinity and the thick carpet of white cloud. She knew perfectly well the reason why she couldn't get to sleep. It was burning a hole in her handbag. She unzipped the side pocket where it lay harmlessly, a small strip of printed card, three inches by two inches.

She withdrew it and read it again for the millionth time: 'Tom Johnson, President'. The letters started to dance before her eyes. Why had he given it to Helen? He couldn't possibly have known she would be coming to San Francisco. What was going through his mind? Was it simple curiosity, wondering what had happened to her? Was it old-fashioned courtesy, hoping she might wish to hear from him? Was Helen Fairbrother at her tricks again, trying to recreate an affair she had begun twenty years ago with a similarly casual introduction? Had he thought about her at all during his marriage? More to the point, had he thought about her during his divorce?

She tried to think back to how she must have looked to him twenty years ago – young, of course, sexy, presumably. Would today's 38-year-old woman be able to hold a candle to that bright sparky girl with the world at her feet in her first term at Oxford? She knew that despite her own deepest fears she probably looked OK, but OK didn't really cut it in today's world. Plus Helen had said quite categorically that he looked as handsome as ever.

The ageing process was so unfair. It seemed to favour men at every turn. For a start they didn't have to worry about recovering their shape after giving birth. If their hair turned grey, it was distinguished, it added a sexy gravitas. If a woman's hair turned grey, it was a disaster. Much as Julia scorned the use of artifice she knew well enough that if she were to let the grey hairs stand proudly untouched by hairdresser's wiles she might as well wear a sign shouting 'CLOSED'.

Tom wouldn't have that problem. He had been tall and slim and on that lean frame whatever excess poundage had been added over the years had plenty of space to hang out. In addition he lived in California where attendance at a gym was *de rigueur*, where healthy fresh fruit and vegetables were in constant supply fifty-two weeks a year, making it far easier to maintain your weight than in England where the weather in winter induced the inevitable comfort eating. If she saw him now she would be deeply envious that he had kept his figure and good looks. If he saw her he would be shocked at the way time had taken its toll on that twenty-year-old skinny body. So she wouldn't see him.

It was the only sensible decision. After all, if she remained out of touch, at least for a while longer, maybe he would pursue her, assuming that business card had been the opening shot in a new skirmish in a twenty-year-old war. If she came galloping over to his place a couple of weeks after he had casually given Helen his business card she could hardly maintain an air of mystery. Instead of CLOSED, her sign would read GAGGING FOR IT. She couldn't stand even the possibility of humiliation. Rather than subject herself to the certainty of rejection she would reject him before he could reject her.

After all, he was divorced now and divorced men were always trouble. Why did his marriage go wrong? she wondered. What terrible flaw of character had appeared that had made his wife flee? Was he so wedded to that vineyard of his, of which he had always spoken so proudly, that he had no time left for his wife? Maybe the fact that he was still so handsome had a downside, maybe he had turned into one of those vain middle-aged men who maintained their washboard flat stomachs at the expense of everything else, like a sense of humour and an ability to relate to the rest of the world. As soon as the first flush of romance had worn away she would be confronted by all these horrible vices.

She and Mike had managed to keep their marriage together for seventeen years – no mean achievement these days, especially as she surveyed the wretched marriages and broken dreams which had surfaced during the college reunion. Mike might be a pain in the backside sometimes but he was honest and he loved his son and they had built a life together. As far as she knew he had always been faithful to her and it would hardly be decent of her to repay his investment in the marriage by leaping into bed with a man she hadn't seen for eighteen years.

Yes, but Tom wasn't just another man. Tom was different from other men. She had never been able to rid herself of the mental image of him. Never. Even during those first years with Mike when she knew she loved him and she had a happy, contented family around her, the image of Tom Johnson was never far away. Sometimes when she was at the stove, stirring something slowly in a saucepan, Mike would approach her from behind, slide his arms round her waist and kiss the back of her neck. Her heart beat faster because it was a gesture she always associated with Tom. That was the way Tom had first touched her. And she'd nearly blown it then.

Her first instinct had been that she was being invaded. She had quickly dropped her hands to cover his to stop them travelling upwards. Unfortunately as she did so, the large wooden spoon she was using for stirring went with her and dropped boiling ratatouille on him.

'Jesus . . . H . . . Christ!'

'Oh God! I'm sorry, I'm sorry, I'm sorry! Shit!'

The spoon fell from her grasp and dropped onto the floor, sending boiling tomato across the linoleum.

'I'll get a J-Cloth.'

Julia doused the cloth in cold water and wrapped it round his burnt hands.

'Ouch! Thanks.' He winced bravely.

She sat on the floor at his feet holding his bandaged hands whilst he said nothing, the pain etched on his face. Fifteen minutes later she unwound the cloth to inspect the damage.

'There's nothing there!' she exclaimed, puzzled. She looked up at Tom who was unable to suppress his laughter. 'You weren't hurt at all!'

'I was surprised though.'

'I thought you'd be scarred for life, you bastard!'

'I might have been. In fact, I thought you wanted me to be. That's why I let you wrap the cloth round them.'

'Tom!'

'It was nice. I liked being looked after.'

'But I felt so guilty and you let me carry on feeling like that.'

Tom held out the wooden spoon to her. 'I'm sorry. *Batti, batti o bel, Masetto, la tua povera Zerlina*,' he sang.

'What?'

'*Don Giovanni*,' he explained.

'I ought to use this on you!'

'Thank you, Mistress,' he said penitently. He walked over to the kitchen stool and lay across it, face down.

'Now what?'

'I'm ready for my close-up, Mr DeMille.' He couldn't suppress a giggle.

'What's going on?'

'May I rise and approach the bench?'

'Oh, stand up, for heaven's sake!'

Tom told her very gravely that he had suffered from years of physical abuse at the hands of the evil witch and her trolls, who had kept him a prisoner in her cottage in the woods.

With some laughter and much relief she worked out that Tom Johnson was a magical storyteller, a fact she subsequently confirmed after many hours of hearing his deep seductive tones whispering everything from erotic stories of unimaginable athleticism to a quick precis of the reasons for General Gaultieri's decision to send armed troops to seize the Falkland Islands.

Tom was reading for a postgraduate degree in politics and she felt sure he was destined to become the President of the United States. He was so articulate, so well-informed, he could get a job with any politician or any political party. He was an instinctive Democrat, he claimed, because his family had always been Republicans. Reagan was the most popular President the country had known since George Washington so he knew there would be no chance of actually influencing anything until after the end of his second term in office which was still six years away.

Similarly in Britain, Tom chose to devote his time to the Social Democratic Party because he thought they didn't stand a chance of ever getting into power. He could therefore advocate almost anything in the sure and certain knowledge that he would never be held to account.

Although Julia had been raised at school to consider herself the equal of any man, she had always enjoyed the possibility that she might marry a man who would be successful in his own right as well as a veritable Rock of Gibraltar in his support of her chosen career. Tom was exactly such a man.

'You are so clever,' she said to him admiringly one day.

'Clever is as clever does,' he shot back.

'What's that supposed to mean?'

'I have no idea. My mom used to say it all the time. Drove me crazy.'

'You could do anything you set your mind to, couldn't you?'

'Nope.'

'Why nope?'

'I can't play that fabulous Beethoven Romance in F on the violin.'

'Does that mean you want me . . .'

'. . . You bet your ass, lady,' he said quickly, smiling broadly.

'And do I have to be . . .'

'Buck naked. Yep!'

'Oh, not again!' said Julia with mock exasperation as she started to unzip the front of her jeans.

For all his seemingly unquenchable libido, Tom was equally enthusiastic sitting in the front row when she was playing (fully dressed) in her string quartet at the various colleges around Oxford. He never stopped praising her, encouraging her to think of herself first, to ignore her parents' anxieties about whether she could support herself by her music alone.

'I can't, Tom. Not unless I drink only rain water.'

'I'll help.'

'How?'

'Financially.'

'You're as broke as I am.'

'I could be your groupie. Willing to offer sex just for the thrill of bedding a second violinist.'

'You don't need an excuse to offer sex,' she laughed.

Julia wondered if Tom was meandering towards a covert declaration of marriage but it was so covert that he never repeated it and the moment passed.

In the greenhouse of the intense eight or nine weeks which constitute a university term at Oxford, relationships form, blossom, wither and die in the space of it. A romance that lasts beyond the Christmas vacation is as good as a marriage and one that survives the four long months of the summer vacation is like a golden wedding anniversary. Julia and Tom lasted from the fifth week of her first term till the fateful blue letter day in September nearly two years later.

She couldn't rid her mind of the way it ended. It was a memory that she had tried unsuccessfully to bury for many years. When she thought of Tom for years after it had happened, all she could remember was the deep, intense pain.

He had finished his time as a Rhodes Scholar in Oxford at the end of her second year. He knew he had to return to America for the summer to tell his father that he had decided not to take over the family wine business. His intention was to return to Oxford in October and start teaching. His M.Phil. thesis had been an outstanding piece of work and there was no doubt that a bright career lay ahead of him in politics, philosophy or economics. He could survive for a year on his savings, together with the money he could make from tutorials and maybe speech-writing for the new Social Democratic Party.

Julia had even found a little one-bedroom flat above a health food store on the High. Technically she was supposed to live in college but as long as she paid her college bill, nobody really cared where she actually spent her nights. Her work was more than satisfactory and her relationship with Tom gave the authorities no cause for alarm. Ensuring that their careers meshed successfully the year after she graduated they both realised might become a problem but there was no doubt that the prospect of the year which lay in front of them promised nothing but bliss.

Then the envelope dropped through the letter box in Kenilworth. It was an ordinary blue air letter, one of those pre-paid ones which folded in three, allowing a great deal of writing space for a much cheaper price than a conventional letter. She seized on it as it lay on the carpet in the hall and raced up to her bedroom to read it. Apart from the pleasure it always gave her just to savour his attractive handwriting (it was her opinion that Americans must spend their primary school years practising nothing but penmanship) she knew that if past experiences were anything to go by most of the letter would be erotic in content.

This one wasn't. Tom's father had suffered a stroke and was in the hospital.

The whole of his left side was completely paralysed and the doctors doubted that he would ever fully regain the power of speech. Tom's mother, a flighty and somewhat impractical woman at the best of times, had collapsed on hearing the news and had taken to her bed. His older sister, Ellen, had flown in from Connecticut to help out temporarily but she had a husband and two young kids on the East Coast and she couldn't remain there indefinitely. Tom would have to stay and run the vineyard. The crops were being harvested. The next two months were the busiest and most important of the year because at the end of them they would know what sort of vintage they would be selling when it had matured. He would try to find a buyer but at the moment he just had to make sure he would be selling a going concern.

The letter was full of love and disappointment. It offered the possibility of future happiness but it was, at best, optimistic. They both knew that. Within two weeks another one arrived. This time it wasn't a blue air letter but the more expensive conventional sort. What Tom had to say in it was what she had dreaded from the moment she had carefully opened the blue one with the letter knife she had been given for her thirteenth birthday.

When she dried her eyes after three days of crying she wrote back politely enough. She was so physically and emotionally drained by the experience that she had no energy left to plead with him. Besides, she recognised the reality of the situation. There was no point. He was breaking her heart because his parents needed him. The decisive blow had fallen when he added that he didn't feel there was any point in her flying out at Christmas. She was young enough to put all this behind her, forget him and get on with the rest of her life.

He was right of course. In her more realistic moods she recognised that what he had to say in that letter was perfectly sensible. There was something impractical in attempting to continue the relationship at long distance. She had an important year left in Oxford. She was twenty years old. It was silly for her to stay in her room for a year and cry. Seen from that perspective Tom had behaved both honourably and sensitively, looking out for her long-term interests while at the same time obeying the dictates of his honour code. His parents needed him, the vineyard had been in the family for generations, he couldn't abandon everyone and waltz off to Europe to pursue his own pleasures. And yet, and yet . . . Julia believed that if the positions had been reversed she would never have abandoned the man she loved. She would have fought tooth and nail to keep the relationship alive. But then she loved him and he . . . She never wanted to finish the sentence or articulate the thought to anyone.

For most of her final year Julia felt like an amputee still experiencing the pain of a limb that was no longer there. Being stuck in Oxford didn't help. She still had to walk past that little flat in the High Street on her way to lectures, she had to sleep in the same bed in her college room where they had made love. She still knew his friends in Balliol and she saw them in the pubs they went to. She could stay away from the little art-house cinema in Headington where they'd snogged throughout the entire duration of an Ingmar Bergman retrospective but she couldn't avoid the Playhouse in the centre of town where she'd seen him acting in an OUDS production of Arthur Miller's play *All My Sons*.

'We are now cruising at thirty-seven thousand feet, ladies and gentlemen. If you look out on the left-hand side you'll see the southern tip of Greenland. We've caught up the few minutes we were behind and we aim to have you on the ground in San Francisco just about on schedule. The weather's much the same as it was in London – about sixteen degrees with cloudy skies.'

Julia woke up with a start, for the moment totally disorientated. So she had been asleep after all. She checked her watch. Another five and a half hours to go. They were only halfway there and she'd never be able to get to sleep again. She hauled her handbag up from the floor by the strap and checked that Tom's card was back in its zippered pocket. It wasn't. She experienced a hot flush of panic.

She unfastened her safety belt and squirmed around in her seat to find that precious card. Trapped in a window seat in economy class, she couldn't stand up and look round and was reduced to feeling for it with her hands in the side gaps. Nothing. If she didn't find that card, it would be a terrible sign that it wasn't meant to be. She jammed her head awkwardly against the window trying to peer down the side of the seat. It was there on the floor, staring up at her. She reached down with her arm but her fingers came to a halt six inches from the floor. Eventually by twisting her leg back at a painful angle she managed to tease the card into such a position on the floor that she could reach it with her fingers. She hauled it to safety and grasped it tightly as she committed the words and numbers to memory. Then she slipped it back into the side pocket of her handbag and zipped it firmly shut.

I'm totally obsessed with this card, she chided herself. What am I really expecting to happen at the other end? After all, he hasn't been checking the passenger lists on every flight from London for the past few weeks? Has he been sitting by the phone, the fax machine or his e-mail, waiting for some kind of communication from me once he knew Helen had given me the card? Is he going to be out there with a bunch of flowers when I wheel my trolley into the arrivals hall? Of course not.

Julia shuffled past the suspicious immigration clerk, collected her luggage, assured customs that she was bringing no citrus food or meat products into the country and marched into the arrivals hall, determined not to look right or left because she knew, just knew, that he wouldn't be there so why bother . . .

'Julia!'

She heard her name being called by an American man and swung round immediately in its direction, hope surging through all her veins that the fairy story had a happy ending after all. She saw the smiling face of Jimmy Reasoner, the company's West Coast executive for the Easy Listening department. She was never so disappointed in all her life and though she did her best to hide the fact, it was obvious to Jimmy that the woman he had driven for eight hours to meet was less than pleased to see him.

'Hey, who were you expecting? Tony Bennett?'

Julia smiled. 'No, of course not.'

'Did you forget I was driving up from LA to meet you? Here, let me take that.' Jimmy took possession of the trolley and started to wheel it towards the exit.

'To be honest, Jimmy, I had. I was just going to look for a taxi and crash out in the hotel.'

'You're at the Westin St Francis on Union Square, right?'

'Is it a nice hotel?'

'The best. Booked it myself. Perfect place to meet your fantasy lover.'

Julia laughed nervously. Was she really that transparent?

CHAPTER SEVEN

HE WAS IN LOVE. HE thought it must be love when she asked him to sit next to her and his heart started hammering so hard he wondered whether he might be having a heart attack. He was absolutely sure the moment he felt Leonie's tongue snake into his mouth. When he thought back over the events of that Tuesday night, he decided that it was love that made him invite everyone to the house. Love and the timing of the two phone calls.

'Jamie, I've got a late night this end.'

'Don't worry, Dad.'

'I'm trying to tie this deal up tonight but I'm waiting for the New York branch to get back to me and they're five hours behind us.'

'Dad, it's fine. I'll bung something in the microwave.'

'And go to bed at a sensible time. You're an athlete.'

'I will. I was in bed at ten last night.'

'Good boy. Ring me at the office if you need me.'

'I'm OK, Dad. Honest.'

Jamie had only just put the phone down and headed for the fridge when it rang again. He swore briefly. When would his dad learn that he was a grown-up now? He was so tempted to tell him about Leonie, not to ask his advice or anything embarrassing like that but just to get him to understand that he wasn't a kid any longer.

'Hello?'

'That you, Shagger?'

'Rob!' Jamie felt absurdly pleased by the nickname so speedily, if inappro-
priately, conferred on him.

'You on for tonight?'

'Tonight?'

'Yeah. Bunch of us is goin' clubbin' up West.'

'Bit short of squids.'

'Leonie's comin'.'

Shit! thought Jamie. He knew his dad was right about the need for sleep
before the tournament, which started the following Thursday, but he was
scared of losing face with the exciting crowd he was now mixing with and,
more to the point, he wasn't going to pass up a chance of snogging Leonie
again. His mind sized up all the alternatives like an internet search engine.

'Why don't you come round here?'

'Parentsville? You crazy, man?'

'They ain't here.'

There was a short pause as Rob broke away to decide Jamie's fate for the
evening. He wondered how much two six-packs of Carling would be at the
off-licence and whether that would be enough if Rob brought more than
himself, Chloe and Leonie.

'We'll see ya 'bout eight-thirty.'

'Great,' said Jamie trying to sound as off-hand as possible. Leonie was coming
to his house. His empty house. Could he get her into bed? That would mean
he would have to buy a condom and he didn't think the off-licence or the
Asian corner shop sold them.

On the way to the off-licence he thought he had better limit his target
for tonight. He could hardly take Leonie into his own bedroom. The walls,
despite the Britney Spears and Limp Bizkit posters, were still covered in the
same childish wallpaper he'd had since he was seven and his single bed was
already getting too small even for him. He was intimidated by the prospect of
using his parents' bed which in its own way was equally unappealing. He'd be

bound to feel his mother's outraged presence in the room even though she was six thousand miles away.

He bought a dozen cans of lager and six bottles of cider. He could always toss them out if they didn't get through them all, to forestall any parental interrogation. The cost pretty much cleaned him out. He'd have to start finding out where his post office savings book was if he was going to mix successfully with Rob's crowd. Knowing his parents, they'd probably locked money away for him, which he wouldn't be legally entitled to receive until he was fifty which was the age they might start to trust him.

Jamie poured the contents of one can of lager down the sink and left the empty can strategically placed in a crumpled heap on the coffee table to indicate that he had already begun a normal evening of hard drinking. He heard the car approach before he saw the sweep of the headlights across the living-room window. He got up to answer the doorbell, vaguely aware that the noise the three kids were making was quite loud. As he pulled back the catch he wondered who was driving since Rob was still sixteen. As he opened the door he found out. What appeared to be the entire teenage population of south Hertfordshire pushed past him, laughing and shouting.

The evening, which had given him two hours of blissful anticipation, turned rapidly into a living nightmare.

Mobile phones were used to summon yet more reinforcements. They stormed through the house, kicked over the milk bottles on the doorstep, burst into the living room, ransacked the fridge, overflowed into the garden where they began an impromptu game of football with an empty beer can, trampled the flowers, threw up on the living-room rug, locked the bathroom door whilst presumably snorting cocaine, filled the house with the sweet distinctive aroma of cannabis and used his parents' bed in exactly the way Jamie had decided not to do with Leonie.

Leonie herself wasn't even there.

'Where's Leonie?' asked Jamie desperately.

'Dunno,' said Rob who was snogging some girl Jamie had never seen before.

'Who are all these guys?' asked Jamie frantically, as the sound of glass breaking was followed by a drunken roar of approval. Rob, who was pretty much out of it, removed his face from the anonymous young girl and stared around as if surprised that anyone else was present.

'Dunno,' he said again.

'Well, where did they come from?'

It was too late. Rob was consumed by lust and could not be cajoled into a coherent answer.

Jamie opened the hall cupboard where his mother kept the dustpan and brush, grabbed them and headed off to the kitchen. No sooner had his feet touched the linoleum than they shot from under him. He landed in a puddle of sticky liquid. The floor seemed to be awash with wine or beer or juice of some sort. As he hit the floor with a thump, the sound of loud music came from the living room. It wasn't anything he recognised as his own or his parents' music. They must have brought it with them – as they had brought the copious quantities of alcohol – unless the ten cans of Carling and the six bottles of cider were the modern-day equivalent of the loaves and fishes of biblical times.

Jamie picked himself up and wrote off the kitchen as an impossible task. He went into the living room and turned down the volume control on the stereo.

'Neighbours,' he shouted as an explanation to nobody in particular. He no longer cared about the noise, for his attention was concentrated on the empty birdcage. His mother's birdcage. Ira the budgie was gone. Only a small plastic mirror, a tiny ladder and a residue of Trill, the food that makes budgies bounce with health, was left to indicate that Ira had ever lived in Waterford Drive, St Albans.

'Ira!' screamed Jamie. 'Ira!' He dropped to his knees and crawled round the room, shouting the name repeatedly, hoping to meet a small yellow bird three inches high hopping towards him. He crawled round the back of the sofa to be transfixed by the sight of a small bare female breast whose nipple was being licked into prominence by a boy with long unwashed hair and a two-day growth of stubble. The owner of the nipple opened her eyes, saw Jamie staring at her and shrieked. The boy with the enterprising tongue broke off briefly from his life's work and smacked Jamie in the face.

'Perv!' muttered the girl, closed her eyes and settled back into her former state of sexual abandon. Jamie scuttled away in embarrassment.

As he got to his feet he bumped into Leonie.

'Oh,' he said, completely thrown. Usually he liked to have time to rehearse what he might say to her. 'How are you?'

'What?' yelled Leonie. The music had been turned up even louder than it had been before.

'I said how are you?' shouted Jamie. Leonie just shook her head. Jamie, emboldened, grabbed her hand and pulled her out into the hall which had filled up in his absence. It was hazy with smoke, tobacco rather than marijuana. Jamie mentally calculated how long he would need to keep the doors and windows open to clear it before his mother returned. He concluded that it would probably have to be the whole week.

It took Jamie a few seconds to realise that Leonie had allowed him to seize her hand quite uncomplainingly.

'I've lost Ira.'

'Who?'

'The budgie.'

'Where is he?'

'I don't know. Someone's opened the cage and let him out.'

'Is he like a homing bird?'

'He's a budgie not a pigeon. He's never been outside his cage.'

'I know why the caged bird sings,' shouted Leonie.

Jamie was puzzled. 'Why?'

'No. It's the title of a book.'

'Oh.' Jamie was completely stumped. The conversation appeared to have arrived in a cul de sac.

'Where are your parents?'

'My dad's at work. My mum's in California. She loves Ira.'

'Is that your Dad's name? Ira?'

'No. Ira's the budgie. Like Ira Gershwin.'

'Who's Ira Gershwin?'

Jamie was about to explain when he was knocked flat by a boy who had slid at high speed down the banisters and crashed painfully into his back. He lay on the floor, groaning and winded. Leonie bent down to help him up. He allowed himself to become limp in her arms and, just as he had hoped, their proximity led to the start of an earth-shattering kiss. She opened her mouth to welcome him but pulled away, her ear cocked.

'What?' asked a frustrated Jamie, his raging hormones temporarily blocking out his sense of hearing.

'Cops!' yelled a distant voice and immediately they could all hear the unmistakable sound of a police siren.

The front door opened and the youth of south Hertfordshire raced out of the parentless house and towards the sanctuary of the black void of a cold April night.

Mike turned into Waterford Drive and saw the flashing blue light on top of the police car. His heart plummeted even as his gorge rose. He left the car and raced towards his house, knowing, without question, that the police were at his house and not his next door neighbour's. The devastation in his house was as nothing compared to the devastation he saw in his son's face.

The sergeant was very comforting. 'It's not your lad's fault, sir. We get quite a bit of this sort of behaviour.'

'They all had mobiles, Dad.'

'It's true, Mr Ramsey. They find a house with no parents at home and suddenly the word is passed on and the party starts in minutes.'

'Jesus!' said Mike, sighting the devastation through the open front door.

'Do you know who they were?'

Jamie shook his head. It was the only possible response. He couldn't even begin to explain. 'They took Ira.'

'Ira?' The policemen perked up. They didn't get many kidnappings on his beat.

'The budgie'.

'Oh.' The sergeant sounded disappointed.

'They killed him?'

'I don't know. He's gone.'

Jamie seemed on the verge of tears. His father put his arm round his shoulder. If there was any anger, it wasn't visible to a relieved Jamie.

'I saw the police car and I was so frightened, Jamie. I'm just so relieved you're all right.'

Jamie was slightly embarrassed that what could have been a major bollocking was turning into something quite different. 'There's a bit of a mess in there, Dad.'

'Just so long as we get it cleaned up before Mum gets back.'

'I'll do it now.'

'You can do it tomorrow. Tonight you need your sleep. You've got a tournament starting on Thursday.'

Jamie and Mike picked their way through the debris, Mike trying hard to contain his rage and his disgust. Jamie pointed to the dustpan and brush as symbols of his careful husbandry. Mike nodded and told him to run a bath. As Mike began the long process of cleaning up, Jamie lay in the bath recalling the sensational micro-second when Leonie Williams began to French kiss him. At the same time, Ira the budgie cautiously began his exploration of the next door neighbour's rhododendron bush.

CHAPTER EIGHT

THE CONCERT WAS EVERY BIT as exciting and satisfying as Julia had hoped it would be. Tony Bennett sang with evident passion all the songs that had made her want to take up her profession in the first place. From Irving Berlin's first big hit, 'Alexander's Ragtime Band', in 1911, through the great Porter, Gershwin and Jerome Kern standards to Kander and Ebb's 'New York, New York', they were all there.

Tony Bennett was anxious to steer clear of too many comparisons with Sinatra so he preferred not to sing 'Young At Heart', 'Witchcraft' or 'Come Fly With Me'. There had been some discussion about whether he should sing 'My Way'. It was generally agreed that although Sinatra had sung the definitive version it had been covered by so many artists that it would hardly be lese-majesty if Bennett sang it as well. It was only logical given the location of the recording in Davies Symphony Hall a dozen blocks from the bay that he should end the concert with the song that the world always thought synonymous with him – 'I Left My Heart In San Francisco'.

The audience started applauding when they heard the first two bars of the introduction, like the Viennese in the Musikverein on the traditional New Year's Day concert when they hear the first strains of 'The Beautiful Blue Danube' waltz. 'I Left My Heart' earned the singer a standing ovation lasting over seven minutes.

For Julia the highlight of the evening was his perfect rendition of 'Fly Me To the Moon' which he took as slowly as it was possible to do but he made out of the words a soaring poem. It had been the first song Tom had ever sung to her and she had never been able to hear it subsequently without thinking about him. She had carefully gone through her record and cassette collection when she started seeing Mike and given away any copy of the song.

It had cropped up in various compilations the company had released but she had gone out of her way to avoid listening to it if at all possible. When she thought about it she didn't know quite why she had maintained this rather childish total exclusion zone. As the years slipped away since the first heady moments of the love affair with Tom, it became increasingly hard to justify it.

If she was avoiding it because it reminded her of the break-up with Tom then that was particularly stupid since the song belonged to their early carefree days. It was now nothing more than an instinctive superstition and when she was sitting in the Time-Life Warner office in San Francisco discussing the running order of the concert she was confronted with the inescapable fact that unless she made an embarrassing exit in the middle of the second half she was going to have to sit there and listen to Tony Bennett singing 'Fly Me To the Moon'.

A famous line of dialogue flashed through her brain: 'Strange how potent cheap music is.' It was a line from a Noel Coward play, she thought, but it was ridiculously inappropriate. The talk in the room was of millions of dollars – not just the cost of setting up the concert, the money paid to the copyright holders, and the expense of the technical video recording of it for transmission on the Home Box Office network but the revenue they expected to acquire in overseas sales of the programme as well as the income generated by the CD. 'Cheap' was the one thing this concert was never going to be.

When finally its turn came, just after Cole Porter's 'Night and Day', her heart was beating with the irregular urgency of a pinball machine but to her surprise it was simply a pleasure to listen to. She thought it was like hearing from an old friend who had moved away and had failed to keep in touch. The gentle introductory music and the teasing lines of the first verse warmed her so that by the time Tony sent the phrase 'Fly me to the moon' soaring into the San Francisco night sky, her anxieties had all drifted away and she was left with nothing but warm memories and a renewed appreciation of Tony Bennett's technical command.

As he finished his song about love, in a poignant diminuendo, she knew without question that she had to see Tom Johnson just once more. This was their song. The coded message via Helen had provoked the possibility. Listening to 'Fly Me To the Moon' simply confirmed it.

After the concert they were all invited backstage to meet the great man himself, who was charm personified. He shook Julia's hand and whispered in that distinctively husky voice, 'Thanks so much for coming.' She was quite sure that he had no idea who she was but for the brief moment their eyes made contact she was definitely the most important person in the room.

The reception was relatively brief. Tony was booked on a flight to Vegas where he was appearing the following day. As soon as he left and the booze and canapes ran out, the numbers dwindled rapidly. Such had been the magic of the occasion that they were all still in a daze of good feeling and mutual self-congratulation as Jimmy Reasoner led his party of twelve across the Civic Center to Stars, the culinary temple of Jeremiah Tower, the famous superchef who, it was claimed, invented California cuisine. There, in the club-like atmosphere of one of San Francisco's top restaurants, they just managed to get themselves seated before a boisterous group tumbled in from the neighbouring Opera House. Clearly, the experience of sitting through four and a quarter hours of *Parsifal* had failed to dampen their spirits, or possibly their recent liberation had induced these feelings of exuberance. Whatever the reason, Jimmy found it incumbent upon him to apologise to his guests for the anti-social behaviour of the Wagnerian hooligans.

Julia was amused rather than offended and utterly relaxed by the success of the concert. She fell easily into conversation with the man sitting next to her, Larry Moss, an earnest thin young lecturer who was on the humanities faculty at the University of California at Santa Cruz. It didn't take long for Julia to become aware that his interest in her wasn't entirely restricted to a shared appreciation of popular songs. He wasn't unattractive in a slightly geeky way and he chose what Julia felt must be the only way left for a single man to chat up a woman in California, which was by railing against the social constrictions caused by current legislation designed to prevent sexual harassment.

'You ever see the David Mamet play *Oleanna*?'

'I don't think so,' admitted Julia, trying to recall dimly what the play had been about.

'Jim Crystal, my friend in the history faculty, he gave a female student a poor grade on an important term paper. So you know what this woman does?'

'Claims sexual harassment, I suppose is where you're going . . .'

'Claims sexual harassment,' echoed Larry Moss, who had obviously regarded his question as rhetorical.

'So what did this woman say exactly?'

'She just invents this whole saga of sexual harassment during a tutorial.'

'But if it's only her word against his . . .'

'Oh, but she'd thought of that. Her best friend, surprise surprise, corroborates the testimony.'

'Didn't your friend have his own character witnesses in the faculty?'

'Didn't matter. See what I'm saying?'

'I think—'

'Everyone knew the woman was spouting a crock.'

'Pardon?'

'A tissue of lies. A crock of shit.'

'So why didn't—'

'Because the university authorities are a bunch of chicken-shit scared yellow-bellies.'

'So what did they do?'

'They fired him.'

'I'm sorry.'

'Jim Crystal, one of the best teachers of Western Civ. in the state—'

'Did he get another job?'

Larry Moss looked at her. 'Whaddyou think?'

'I guess not.'

'You guessed right. Nobody wants to hire the guy. His life is over.'

Julia clucked her concern. She rather admired the outburst of passion even though she had no idea of the respective merits of the case he was arguing. Larry picked up on her interest and leaped spectacularly to the wrong conclusion.

'So you're in show business, right?'

'At quite a considerable remove.'

'But you like the free and easy atmosphere of the entertainment industry?'

Julia moved swiftly to block his predictable attempt to switch the focus of sexual interest to herself. She rather enjoyed the battle of wits. It had been some time since she had received even this much attention from an available man, and she found the fact that he was so clearly interested in her mildly comforting. It would require little effort on her part to invite him back to the hotel for a drink after dinner. It would then be socially acceptable to drop inhibitions. She could certainly get rid of him early the following morning and it would be unlikely that anyone would ever find out.

She knew, however, even as she explored the possibility of such a scenario that she was not going to let it happen. It wasn't so much that she instinctively disapproved of one-night stands but that she knew they weren't created for her. The mechanics of the act itself held no appeal for her. She enjoyed the few minutes during which she allowed Larry Moss to think there might be the possibility of future activity and marvelled yet again at the power women could wield when the interest was coming from the other side of the table but in the end she thought she ought to put poor Larry out of his misery. A hint as to the existence of a much loved husband and son at home and the need to return to the hotel to ring them before they left the house in the fast approaching English morning did the trick. Larry backed off.

At the hotel Julia picked up the telephone and did exactly that. It was early in the morning in St Albans and Mike's voice was still fogged with sleep but he seemed happy and pleased to hear from her. She raised the possibility, tentatively, that she might spend the next few days seeing the area around San Francisco. Mike couldn't have been more enthusiastic.

'I think that's great.'

'I'll probably come back on Sunday or Monday.'

'When are you expected back in the office?'

'Oh, not for a few days. They're all on that silly retreat in the West Country.'

'Where are you planning to go?'

'Jimmy said he'd show me around the city then I could rent a car and drive up the coast towards the Oregon border. Apparently it's amazing country up there.'

'What about Big Sur?'

'That's south.'

'I know but we've always talked about going there.'

'I met a professor at dinner. He's at the university in Santa Cruz.'

'Do you fancy him?'

'Oh Mike, for God's sake! He's barely older than Jamie!'

'So?'

'So he offered to show me around Santa Cruz and Monterey and Carmel.'

'Isn't Clint Eastwood the mayor there?'

'I don't know. Anyway I'm not going. I want to go north of here so I'll be out of touch for a few days. OK?'

'Sure.'

'How's Jamie?'

'He's fine. He'll also still be here when you get back.'

'Can I talk to him?'

'He's asleep.'

'Has he been working?'

There was a fatal fractional pause before Mike's affirmative reply. Julia leapt on it.

'He hasn't, has he?'

'I just told you he had.'

'Something's happened. I can hear it in your voice.'

'What you can hear in my voice is the result of being woken up from a deep sleep.'

'I know something's happened. Tell me.'

'There's nothing to tell.'

'I always know when you're lying.' Julia couldn't prevent the accusation escaping.

'And I always know when you're lying so we're quits.'

There was a tense silence whilst Julia thought about continuing with the verbal sparring but, as usual, she decided against it. There was nothing to be gained and she was anxious to calm any fears or resentments Mike might harbour about her driving off into the unknown. Whatever it was that had happened could clearly await her return.

'I'll be back early next week. Probably Monday morning. I'll give you a ring when I've booked the flight.'

'Do you want me to meet you at the airport?'

Julia paused. She couldn't work out whether she did or she didn't. She'd prefer the convenience and she didn't like paying the inflated taxi prices but on the other hand it somehow put her into Mike's debt and just at the moment that was one place she didn't want to be. She wanted her account with him to be in credit. She might not cash the cheque but she wanted to know the money was there.

'I'll let you know when I see which flight I'm on and what time it gets into Heathrow.'

'Fine. Have a good time.'

'Give my love to Jamie.'

'Sure. Talk to you soon. I'd better go or the M1 will be at a standstill.'

'OK. 'Bye.'

Julia put down the phone with mixed feelings. She was relieved that she was in the clear for the next few days but unhappy about the underlying tension which had permeated the conversation. Was he just trying to spoil her free time by making her feel guilty? She got so little of it, what with the demands of the job and the house and the family. All she wanted was a couple of days to herself . . . Her thoughts petered out. There was no point blaming Mike alone for these intermittent sterile conversations, she knew she was also to a certain extent responsible. And in the end, it all came back to Emily.

It wasn't just the trauma, it was something neither of them could control or even fully understand. It was like those other couples she felt so sorry for — the parents of that poor black teenager Stephen Lawrence who was murdered by racist thugs, only nobody could prove it in a court of law, and the Bulgers, the parents of the little two-year-old kid, killed by two ten-year-old boys in Liverpool. As soon as the immediate media storm was over, their marriages ended. The trauma was somehow too great for the relationship to withstand it. She understood. Maybe, instead of imagining their marriage to be weak, she should start thinking of it as amazingly strong, strong enough to have survived this length of time and that one overwhelming, soul-destroying tragedy. Somehow she couldn't quite make herself believe it.

She took a long hot shower, humming to herself as many of the songs as she could remember from the evening. She would enjoy shepherding this CD through to its eventual marketing and she hoped there would be enough people out there who shared her feelings. She even started on 'Fly Me To the Moon' but this time, away from the concert hall, she could only think of the song in terms of the man who had introduced her to it in Oxford twenty years ago. And tomorrow, for the first time in nearly twenty years, she was going to see him. Within twenty-four hours she would know what spring was like on Jupiter and Mars.

CHAPTER NINE

IT HAD RAINED HEAVILY DURING the night and the streets of San Francisco, far from being the location for a glamorous television series of the same name, were simply wet and difficult to drive on. When Julia pulled down the tight drawstring on the heavy curtains, they parted to reveal, just as Tony Bennett had sung the night before, that the clouds had rolled in across the bay and fog had chilled the air. If there were any little cable cars out there, they were certainly incapable of climbing halfway to the stars and even the massive presence of the Golden Gate Bridge lay wreathed in mist.

Julia had said her goodbyes to Jimmy the previous night and, without the obligations of work, she allowed herself the luxury of breakfast in bed. However, by the time the waiter had wheeled in the little table covered with two tablecloths starched to a whiteness that it would be difficult to find in a television commercial for washing powder, Julia was nearly ready to leave. She had showered yet again (she would never again, she thought, accustom herself to that miserable leak from the wall that British Gas had persuaded her was a shower in her en-suite bathroom in St Albans), dressed and was almost packed.

She had not slept well. At first she attributed this to delayed jet lag, then to a possible sense of anti-climax after the excitement of the concert, the programme planning and the party afterwards or even to the lingering dissatisfaction that accompanied her after the end of the previous night's phone call to Mike but in her heart she knew why she had been so restless.

She was going to see Tom Johnson and she was as nervous as a teenager before a first date.

She looked at herself in the mirror. There was no real change. She didn't quite know what she was hoping for other than perhaps some genie had miraculously spirited away Claudia Schiffer's body and slipped it painlessly over hers during the night. It hadn't happened. She looked much as she had done the previous night when she had performed a similar routine.

She certainly wouldn't call herself a narcissist. A narcissist, she believed, was someone who spent hours looking at her (or wasn't it 'his' in classical mythology?) reflection and falling in love with it. She did spend quite a long time each day looking at her reflection in the mirror but it was always with a distinctly critical, not to say jaundiced, eye which surely exonerated her of the charge of narcissism.

Now that she was in California, the home of the nip and tuck doctor, perhaps she should forget about Tom and pay a quick visit to a cosmetic magician. Or better still, a few hours on the magic table and off to find Tom after lunch. She wondered what could be improved for, say, two thousand dollars. Not much probably. Kim Basinger lips was about all she'd get for that and she wasn't at all sure it would be an improvement.

She peered into the mirror. She could certainly use a face lift, make the skin a little tauter. It was definitely sagging round the mouth and under the eyes. The crow's feet, the laughter lines as she preferred to think of them, the loose skin on her neck – well, it wasn't exactly hanging in folds but if the surgeon could remove it at the same time ... A liposuction would be a good idea too, she felt sure; it was almost routine out in this part of the world and that cellulite on her thighs was hardly fashionable now that Diana wasn't around to deflect the attention, plus perhaps she ought to have her boobs looked at. Looked at? That didn't sound right at all.

The telephone rang. The rental car was waiting outside, would Madam like the bell boy? Madam would.

She got into the car, wondering how the man who had driven it to the hotel was going to get home and how tall he was. She could barely reach the pedals when she sat in the driver's seat and spent an ungainly minute searching for the lever to edge the seat forward but found, initially, only an unwelcome dollop of some kind of grease. Eventually she slipped into the flow of the traffic with an exhilarating feeling of pure freedom. She had no idea where she might lie her head that night. If she had been with Mike and Jamie, such knowledge would have induced nothing but panic, but now it made her feel like a backpacking student again – a backpacking student, she noted wryly, with an American Express card, a full-size Buick Century and collision damage waiver insurance.

She headed off in what she had been assured was the direction of the Golden Gate Bridge but soon found the signs had completely disappeared and she was driving up and down the famous hills of the city. She stopped the car, bought a bottle of mineral water at a gas station and asked the woman behind the counter where the bridge was. She then discovered that she had been driving south for fifteen minutes towards San Jose; the Golden Gate Bridge lay in the opposite direction, which was why all the signs to it had disappeared.

The benefit granted by this detour was that by the time she did manage to find and cross the bridge in three fast-flowing lanes of traffic, the sun had burned through the clouds and Julia could see in the distance the East Bay and the green hills of Marin County. Frustratingly, she was driving away from what she felt sure was the spectacular sight of the city itself but fortunately, as she neared the end of the bridge (without having paid the toll she was expecting), she saw a sign indicating a vista point. She turned off to the right and pulled the car into one of the few remaining spaces. The car park was surprisingly full at this time on a weekday morning but she soon discovered why.

As she stepped out of the car and turned to face the city of San Francisco, she was confronted by a sight she would never forget. Although she'd seen it a hundred times in photographs, on television and in the movies, nothing prepared her for the full impact of the breath-taking panorama. Over to the left stood the impressive Bay Bridge linking the city to Berkeley and Oakland. Between the two bridges lay the island of Alcatraz on which the now disused prison stood. It was rumoured that no escaping prisoner had ever made it to dry land, so cold was the water that lay enticingly between him and freedom.

Beyond Alcatraz was the city of San Francisco itself with the skyscrapers of the commercial district dominating the skyline and behind them the green hills of the hinterland. The sea danced and sparkled on the shimmering water of the bay. It seemed impossible that such a stunning sight could be enjoyed by thousands of people who drove into the city to work every day. Julia wondered how they could possibly appreciate what she was looking at if they saw it on a daily basis the way she saw Junction 2 of the M1 motorway from the train as it approached Mill Hill station.

Julia had seen the Bay of Naples from Capri, Wall Street and the tip of Manhattan from the Statue of Liberty and Paris from the top of the Eiffel Tower but none of them compared to the sight that lay before her. Sir Francis Drake, she remembered dimly from her primary school history lessons, had been the first Englishman to sail into this bay, on his way to the mythical El Dorado. In which case, Julia thought, he'd found it. This must surely have been El Dorado, not the fabled city of gold.

If only he had stayed and invested in real estate instead of sailing away in the hunt for Spanish treasure, he would surely have died a happier man. Still, she concluded, maybe Elizabethan sea dogs weren't into real estate and at least Drake had lent his name to a road that passed through some of the most expensive property in northern California. For most Americans that was true immortality.

Reluctantly she dragged herself away and back into the car. She was puzzled by her own emotional reaction. Oddly enough, now that she was on her way to see Tom, she had started thinking about Mike, not just thinking about him but wishing he were here with her.

She didn't understand these feelings. She understood well enough that Tom, whom she hadn't seen for twenty years or so, represented the embodiment of romance and that the domestic war of attrition she now fought with Mike on a daily basis had robbed him of any sexual attraction for her, yet now, of all times, having been deeply moved by one of the most romantic sights she had ever seen, it was Mike she had wanted to share the experience with, not Tom.

She pulled out onto the 101, the main freeway that cut through the heart of Marin, Sonoma and Mendocino Counties. She turned off the freeway into Napa, the principal town of the Napa Valley, the area of California most closely associated with winemaking. It was by now a warm and sunny April morning with the temperature well into the seventies and Julia regretted that she had been intimidated by the fog and the chill of San Francisco into dressing in slacks and the warmest woollen top she had brought with her.

She parked the car just off Napa's main street and got out. She lifted up the boot and unzipped her suitcase, rummaging through it carefully until she found the summery yellow dress she had packed for just this eventuality. She slid it into a plastic bag and walked into the nearest department store where she slipped into a fitting room. She discarded the sweater and slacks and stepped into the cool dress. Much relieved, she dropped the old clothes back into the car before setting off for the tourist information centre.

Napa was quiet and unhurried after the cosmopolitan bustle of San Francisco. The sun shone out of a cloudless blue sky and the variations of climate which San Francisco was endlessly subject to seemed further away than the forty or so miles she had driven since leaving the city. Before she arrived at the information centre, Julia stopped at an internet cafe. She thought she ought to check her e-mail, feeling irritatingly guilty for having been out of contact with the office for the past three hours.

She waited quietly until one of the PCs seemed to be free and then edged towards it, waiting for the bureaucracy to intervene. 'Do I have to pay for this?' she asked the bored youth at the desk. 'Nope,' he replied, still bored. She logged on, glad that she had registered with one of the internet service providers whom she could track from any machine. To her great pleasure she saw that she had 0 new messages. Nobody wanted her. Her life was her own. She sent brief cheery greetings to Mike and Jamie and walked out free as a bird.

The tourist information centre was devoted almost exclusively to the wineries. Julia had to stop herself asking about 'vineyards' which seemed the logical name to give to the farms where grapes were grown and wine was manufactured. What surprised her initially was the sheer volume of such places. There were nearly three hundred of them in Napa and the neighbouring valleys. She picked up a map of what was called the Wine Country and looked immediately for the Johnson Winery. It took her some time to find it because it was far to the north and west of where she stood.

Julia collected the various brochures and sat down at a table on the pavement outside a cafe where she started to flick through them whilst waiting for her Caesar salad and mineral water to arrive. She found it interesting that the mushrooming of these wineries was so recent. She knew that the Johnson vineyard was started a hundred years ago, which must make it one of the oldest wineries in California. She was beginning to understand the pressures that might have been exerted on Tom to prevent his coming back to Oxford. She certainly appreciated the power of a family history in this area as compared to the rich retired bankers from San Francisco who had recently arrived and thought that running a winery might be a fun way to spend their retirement.

She finished the salad and ordered a coffee. Why, she wondered, was she so reluctant to get back in the car and drive straight to the Johnson vineyard? She had left the St Francis Hotel that morning with only one aim in mind

– to find Tom as soon as possible. Now she was dragging her heels, drinking unwanted cups of coffee, poring over the brochures of different wineries, none of which she had any intention of visiting, despite their blandishments. Should she give up now, drive back to San Francisco and just let herself be a genuine tourist?

Such a course of action had much to recommend it. It meant that when she flew home she could look Mike squarely in the eye. It meant she wouldn't risk the prospect of finding that Helen's description of Tom didn't match the reality, or that her account of Tom's interest in her was exaggerated or, even worse, that when he saw her he'd think she'd turned into a haggard old wreck. If she drove back now she need fear none of these things. It was the right thing to do, the sensible decision.

Eventually she returned to the car and found her way back to Route 29. At the T junction she could either turn to the left which would take her back to San Francisco or right which would lead up the Napa Valley. The traffic light turned to green. Julia sat there as if paralysed. When it became apparent to the farmer in the pickup truck behind her that she wasn't moving, he gave her a long and unnecessarily loud blast on the horn. Julia turned the wheel instinctively. She couldn't turn left because that would be dangerous as the light had already turned red again and it would mean driving almost into the cross traffic. So she turned the car to the right, along route 29 heading north towards Yountville, St Helena, Calistoga and Tom Johnson.

Well, she thought to herself as the Buick sped northwards, I could just visit the Johnson vineyard. I don't have to ask for Tom. He owns the place so he's not going to be the tour guide. He may not even be there. He could be anywhere. In San Francisco, in New York, maybe in the Loire Valley – she remembered the family prided itself on making a fumé blanc that could match any comparable wine in the Loire Valley. She could take the Johnson Winery tour and if she didn't see Tom she'd book into a motel for the night and then drive around the beautiful countryside tomorrow and head back to San Francisco at the end of the day.

It certainly was beautiful countryside, blooming yellow with a profusion of mustard flowers. She was surprised at how like Tuscany or Provence it appeared; she associated California with smog and Disneyland and the Universal Studios Tour, all of which, she recalled, were about five hundred miles to the south. You wouldn't expect the Highlands of Scotland to be too similar to London so why should she be surprised that the northern California countryside was so spectacularly different to its southern counterpart?

Every mile on the main road was dotted with signs indicating the turnoff for the various wineries, their guided tours and their (presumably free) wine-tastings. It must be possible to start at ten o'clock in the morning and be drunkenly incapable of proceeding by lunchtime. It was the civilised tourist version of a pub crawl. She could imagine the triumphant evening boast of a British Cabernet Sauvignon lout. 'I got through eight bloody wineries, then had a curry and threw up all over the Robert Louis Stevenson memorabilia in the Silverado Museum.'

At the head of the Napa Valley she drove into Calistoga which seemed to her to be scarcely a part of modern California at all but, with its wooden plank storefronts, fretwork and clapboard, more like a thriving town in a Wild West movie or a relic of the gimcrack towns which grew up in the wake of the gold rush of 1849. Julia soon discovered that Calistoga prided itself on being a spa town. Having been on an anniversary weekend trip to Bath and noted the distinctly green and unwelcoming waters which coagulated outside the Pump Room and the Assembly Rooms yet which were described with such admiration by Jane Austen, Julia thought she could easily avoid the enticements of the Calistoga mineral baths.

However, when she pulled up outside one particular motel which offered both room and treatments for a specially reduced combination price, Julia found the attraction increasingly seductive. A quick look in the driving mirror confirmed her impression that it could do her prospects no harm given the possibility of the meeting that might be coming up in a couple of hours.

There was, worryingly, she thought, no waiting for the treatment and within ten minutes of booking in for the night she was disrobing in a cubicle, before slipping her hair into a blue plastic shower cap and wrapping an enormous white towel round herself. A Hispanic girl came into the cubicle, smiled at her and led her along a well-used passageway that somehow reminded her of swimming lessons at school. They emerged in what seemed like a boiler room. Everything was outsize. The baths were large, the showerheads enormous, the gauges on the wall seemed to belong to a nuclear power plant. She was on the verge of fleeing when the girl, who introduced herself as Juanita but who otherwise spoke very little English, gestured for Julia to remove her towel. Not without trepidation, Julia handed it to her.

Juanita seized a huge wooden shovel which seemed almost as large as she was and began to stir the unappetising mud that filled the large enamel bath in front of her. When she had finished, making no difference whatsoever as far as Julia could see, Juanita gestured for her victim to clamber in. Recalling her old school prefect days, she told herself not to be such a wimp and she climbed over the side and inserted herself slowly into the mud. It was a slow process because the mud impeded all her movements, and it was a full five minutes before she could seat herself properly in the stuff.

It was hot and it was muddy. There is no doubt about it, Julia thought, I am paying sixty-nine dollars to sit in a tub full of hot mud. And I'm not even enjoying it much. She rested her arms along the outside rim of the bath. Juanita came back, jabbered at her in what could have been either Spanish or heavily accented and incomprehensible English, and physically forced both arms down into the hot mud. Julia smiled weakly and thanked her with instinctive politeness. Only her red face and blue shower cap were now visible above the mud.

She looked at the clock which was set on the wall in front of her. It wasn't a clock, she noticed on further examination, it was a kind of large oven timer. The timer she worked out had been set for thirty minutes. She had been in there for about two minutes and she saw absolutely no way in which she could possibly survive another twenty-eight.

Julia tried to shift her body to a new position, hoping that the air that might be manufactured in the movement would provide welcome relief. She couldn't move. This must be what it feels like to drown in quicksand, she thought, like the maid does in Wilkie Collins's detective story, *The Moonstone*. She wondered whether she could name the other Wilkie Collins novels, of which there must be half a dozen or so, but all she could remember was *The Woman In White* because she'd seen a rather feeble television adaptation of it one Christmas.

Julia always forced her mind to act like this when she was on a long motorway journey at night and was frightened of the prospect of falling asleep at the wheel. It was a panic reaction and she didn't think she should be panicking. 'Keep young and beautiful,' she hummed to herself, 'if you wanna be loved.' She looked at the oven timer. Nearly four minutes had passed. She felt like a Christmas turkey. In a minute Juanita would come along and stick a fork into her. She wondered which parts of her would be dark meat and which white.

By now it had become impossible for her to look anywhere but at the oven timer. There were stories of people dying like this, as if in an Alfred Hitchcock murder mystery and nobody could work out how it was done because the murderer alters the thermostat before the dead body is discovered. A stiff upper lip was one thing but rigor mortis was something entirely different. It surely couldn't be good for her general health if she spent her whole time during this relaxing and restorative spa treatment worrying about being murdered.

'Juanita,' she called apologetically. Juanita was nowhere to be seen. Maybe she been lured into some fiendish white slave trade as her mother had always warned her was likely? 'Juanita!' Julia shouted, her voice now tinged with more than anxiety. Juanita appeared, smiling, obviously pleased that the rich white woman was having her skin burned off and was paying through the nose for the privilege.

'It's very hot, Juanita,' said Julia slowly, trying hard to make it sound like a detached observation rather than a wimp's cry for help.

'Chaquenoarrivista out?' said Juanita. All Julia heard was the word 'out'. 'Out' sounded great to her. Any kind of out was preferable to being simmered, which was how she regarded 'in'.

Juanita hauled the mud-encrusted Julia slowly from her enamel prison and pointed her towards one of the showers. The water jetted out of the shower head but whereas she would normally expect to be clean again in a matter of seconds, it seemed at first to make almost no impact on her blackened skin. Eventually, with the aid of massive quantities of shower gel and some sharp work with her fingernails, she managed to scrape away enough mud to reassure herself that her skin, which she had so long taken for granted, was still where she expected to find it. But even frantic scouring failed to remove all traces of the mud which clung stubbornly to her in the most inaccessible of places, like sand in the bed after a day on the beach and two baths.

Juanita led her willingly towards the clean whirlpool bath. This looked much more like her cup of tea – it was basically nothing more than a private Jacuzzi. Her first sensation was pleasant. It certainly wasn't as cool as she might have hoped for but it wasn't like the awful cloying heat of the mud bath. Juanita set the oven clock again, this time for twenty minutes, and turned the whirlpool levers full on. Julia smiled bravely at the girl who settled the plastic cushion against the nape of her neck.

Good, thought Julia, this is nice. This is what I came for. Now I can relax in healthy water and think lovely romantic thoughts. I can think of walking through a dark green forest glade, where there is a shiveringly pleasant sensation of a private world enclosed by huge oak trees, and emerging from the chill into the bright warm sunlight to walk slowly, hand in hand, along the side of a swift flowing river of such crystal-clear water that I can see the fish swimming contentedly in it. Hello, the noonday sun must be high overhead now. It's getting hotter.

Julia opened her eyes with a start. She was back in the Calistoga spa clinic and the sweat was cascading from every pore. The whirlpool bath, far from being a gentle, relaxing meditative pleasure, was like a giant soup tureen. She looked at the omnipresent oven timer. Minutes had passed since she was walking through that cool forest glade. She wanted to go back there and screwed her eyes tightly shut but the forest had caught fire and burned down in her absence.

Now she was crawling on hands and knees across a desert towards an ice-cold drink in Alexandria. She flicked her eyes open. Five minutes gone. She couldn't wimp out twice, could she? Sweat dripped off her brow onto the tip of her nose and thence onto her neck. She had always believed that really hot baths were very bad for the skin and this was the hottest bath she had ever been in. Surely these people knew what they were doing. Some American woman with a healthy bank balance would otherwise have sued them into bankruptcy.

Julia didn't care about anyone else. She was having a miserable time and she didn't give a damn who knew it. She began to clamber out of the bath. Immediately Juanita was by her side. Was she genuinely solicitous of her welfare or did she just see her tip disappearing? Julia didn't much care. She padded after Juanita who had obviously dealt with wimpish white middle-class women like her before. She was led into the room that Julia was later to remember with such ecstasy. It was a small cubicle with reinforced plastic partitions in which stood a massage table. It was covered with two huge towels the size of a sheet for a double bed.

Julia lay face up on the sensuous towels, the cool air feeling like paradise on her burning flesh. All semblance of modesty had long since disappeared. She didn't care who saw her like this. The entire British Lions rugby touring party could file past staring at her intently and she wouldn't bat an eyelid. Juanita took the end of one of the towels and covered her body with it in a welcome gesture of reverence. Juanita slipped quietly away. Julia stared blissfully at the ceiling. Never had she felt so content.

Julia remembered dimly that her father had told her that this kind of treatment could be equally effectively achieved with a brick. If you kept bashing your head with the brick for long enough, it would feel like so much never-ending pain. Once the brick stopped coming into contact with the head, the resulting relief would be enormous. This, Julia thought, was essentially the philosophy underpinning the entire spa treatment business. She never dreamed it would have been possible to have reached this level of sensuous satisfaction merely by lying naked on a towel in a small, empty, damp but cool plastic cubicle.

By the time Julia emerged into the fading warmth of the four o'clock sun, she was feeling almost serene. She had paid in advance for the night's lodging in the adjoining motel so she was already relieved of the niggling anxiety as to where she would be laying her head that night — the freedom of the backpacking student had lasted about five hours before giving way to the anxieties of the thirty something mother and wife.

The journey north-west towards Healdsburg took Julia into the Alexander Valley alongside the Russian River. She assumed that the Russians had somehow landed here, perhaps on their way to Alaska, but it was an unlikely prospect. Once out of the highly developed Napa Valley, she discovered a new kind of wine country, one with plenty of wineries but sufficiently widely spaced to give an indication of what Napa must have been like before the rush to develop began in the 1970s.

She glanced down at the road map spread out on the passenger seat beside her, then at Tom's business card which lay flat on the ledge at the bottom of the windscreen. She could feel her heart beating faster. There was still a strong likelihood that she wouldn't see him but as the mileage counter ticked over on the speedometer, the moment of encounter was approaching with the inevitable possibility of two results – happiness or unhappiness. There was no point now in telling herself there was time to turn round. She obviously wasn't going to turn round.

North of Healdsburg she realised that the Johnson Winery was probably less than ten miles away. She glanced at the digital clock on the dashboard. It read 4.46. By the time it got to 5.46 she might well have seen him again. Not that long. Maybe ten past five. It was just under eighteen years since she'd seen him. Eighteen years since he'd walked through passport control at Terminal 3 at Heathrow Airport on a Pan Am flight bound for San Francisco. Pan Am! The airline didn't even exist any longer. That was how long ago it was.

There were the letters of course. She had written the first one on the day of her wedding but they had soon tailed off as her life with Mike fulfilled and absorbed her. Now, since Emily's death, Tom, or perhaps more accurately the image of Tom, had become increasingly important to her. Tom would know how she felt, Tom would understand exactly the turbulent emotions that were affecting her. He didn't need to read or possess the letters. That was one reason why she had never posted them, why they still remained in the red luxury chocolate biscuit tin in a cardboard box somewhere in the tightly packed loft. It had been eighteen years since she'd seen him but she knew in her heart that what they had created together in the early 1980s was so strong that just the sight of each other might be enough to reignite it.

Well, she might not look twenty-one any more, despite the best efforts of Juanita and Estée Lauder combined, but these emotions that she had felt then were still amazingly close to the surface. Even if Tom had changed, as she knew she must have changed, the love they had had between them was very special. It wasn't like the love she felt for Mike. Tom had always been a special person in her life and she owed it to both of them, she owed it to that mysterious bond that united them and, she was sure, kept them together in an unspoken way ever since, to see him again.

She looked at the road sign. She had overshot the turning over Lambert Bridge. She did an ungainly U-turn and headed back the other way down the road she had been driving along in a reverie of times past. This time she spotted the turning well in advance and left the main highway to head towards Wine Creek Road. This was it. And that, in the distance, must be Tom's place. As far as her eye could see, the land was covered with vines, their branches stretched out in identical fashion, the whole field looking a little like the endless symmetrical rows of white crosses on the First World War graveyards of northern France.

But it wasn't Tom's place. The sign over the gateway entrance told her it was the Ravanelli Winery. Tom's place must be at the top of the hill. Julia's heart gave a lurch of recognition. Rounding the bend in the road she could see the original Victorian house. Tom had kept a photograph of it on his mantelpiece in his room in Oxford. Sure enough, she soon drove past the sign that identified the turning to the Johnson Winery a hundred yards distant.

She could still go home, she told herself. She could just stop the car, do a three-point turn on the lonely dusty track and go on back to the 101 Freeway and into San Francisco. By the time she had thought about it for the fiftieth time the Buick had turned itself into the gate and come to rest in the car park opposite the entrance to the winery building. On top of the hill behind it stood the Johnson family house.

The car park was almost empty. She pushed open the door of the reception room to be confronted by nobody. Panic gripped her. Despite what she had been telling herself all day, she really hadn't driven all this way just to look at a wine pressing machine. A pretty young girl (Tom's daughter? Tom's illegitimate daughter??) emerged and smiled at Julia. Why do Americans smile like that? wondered Julia. Why don't they just greet you with surly insolence like they do in England? At least you know how you stand when you get that kind of response.

'Hi. Can I help you with something?'

'I was just wondering when the tour starts.'

'Oh, I'm so sorry. The last one started at four. We close at five. I'm sorry.'

And she was. She was genuinely sorry.

'Is there anyone here who can help me with some research?'

'You can take this brochure. It tells what kind of grapes we grow, what kind of wines we make. If you want to see round the place you could always come back tomorrow. We open at nine.'

Julia took the brochure, looking through it quickly for a photograph of Tom. There was one of the vineyards, one of the house, one of the bottling plant but not one of Tom.

'Who takes the tour?'

'Tourists. Hey, that sounds kinda dumb. Tourists. But it's true we get hundreds of tourists. You come back here in the summer. It's real crowded.'

'Sorry. I meant who takes them round. Who's the guide on the tour?'

'Oh, I see. It depends. Sometimes I do it.'

'And if it's not you?'

'There's a bunch of us from UC Davis. That's the nearest University of California campus. We're working our way through school and Mr Lacroix hires us to look after the store, serve the wine tastings and take the tour.'

'Who's Mr Lacroix?'

'He's the winemaker and the vineyard manager as well.'

'Is there a Mr Johnson of Johnson's Winery?'

'Oh, sure. But we don't see him too much.'

The girl was locking bottles in cupboards, clearly preparing to close for the day but too polite to hustle Julia away.

'If you come back at nine you could meet Mr Lacroix. He's usually here first thing. I'm sure he'll be able to answer any question you may have.'

They were so polite and helpful, these young Americans.

'Thank you.'

'You're very welcome. And Mr Lacroix is real cute,' she added with a shy smile. Julia stood by the open door and smiled back.

'And Mr Johnson? Is he real cute?'

'Oh, he's too old for me,' said the girl.

Julia laughed. 'Thank you. You've been very helpful.'

She walked back into the fading sunshine, unsure of her next move. She could go back to Calistoga where she had booked a room and return the next day as the girl suggested. This time she could blow seventy-five dollars on an Executive Facial or a full ninety-minute aromatherapy session, provided she didn't have to place herself in the dubious hands of Juanita once more. Could she summon up the mental strength to come back here a second time? She doubted it.

She looked up at the house on the hill. Dare she wander around where tourists were clearly not welcome? How could she just turn the car round now, knowing that Tom might be fifty yards away? She stood there, spirits plummeting, her body seemingly paralysed by indecision.

For all the mud wraps and the salt glow scrubs, she might as well not have bothered. She felt heavy and old and tired.

A pickup truck turned in off the dirt track and bounced to a halt across the car park. A young man leaped down from the passenger seat. He had a fine head of curly dark hair, stylish mirrored sunglasses, a Tommy Hilfiger shirt and smartly tailored jeans and cowboy boots. This had to be the dashing M. Lacroix.

She pressed the unlocking button on her laser key ring. The lights refused to flash in acknowledgement. Her bag slipped off her shoulder and fell with a splat onto the ground. Inevitably, the catch wasn't fastened and the contents went flying everywhere – lipstick, purse, keys, hairbrush, sunglasses, packet of Kleenex. She dropped to her knees and scrabbled around, trying to retrieve her belongings, hoping M. Lacroix had gone inside to chat up that besotted young girl. A hand dropped into view and picked up the sunglasses.

'I hope they're not scratched.'

She knew that voice. She would know that voice anywhere. She looked up to see Tom Johnson's smiling face looking down at her.

She had rehearsed this moment in her mind a thousand times. It always went something like Lauren Bacall saying, 'You know how to whistle, don't you, Steve?' or Ingrid Bergman reacting to Humphrey Bogart storming into the nightclub when he hears Sam playing 'As Time Goes By'. It all disappeared. She remained on her knees squinting up at him into the sun. He offered her his hand to help her to her feet.

'Shit!' she said as eloquently as she could. 'Sorry.'

'I've been kinda expecting you,' he said quietly and the years just rolled away. He loved her. She knew it from that one sentence. He loved her. He loved her still. And she loved him. Now and for ever.

CHAPTER TEN

MIKE AWOKE FROM A DREAMLESS sleep in the middle of the night with a raging thirst and a full bladder. He groped his way to the bathroom, tormented by the recurrence of his occasional hypochondria. Why was his bladder unable to sustain him through the night? Was there a blockage in the urinary tract? He thought, looking back on it, that he had been drinking and peeing rather a lot recently. Weren't these the first unmistakable signs of diabetes? Where was Julia when he needed her? She was always so good at exposing his groundless medical worries for what they really were – the fantasies of the worried well.

He went downstairs and opened the fridge, feeling a blast of cold air sweep over his defenceless naked body. He plucked a can of Diet Coke from the inside of the door, snapped it open and drank most of it in one gulp. His throat was so parched that two-thirds of it slipped down before he felt the effect. He took the can into the living room and slumped into an armchair but decided against turning on the television. The prospect of watching an Open University programme on War, Literature & Society whilst seated naked in an armchair with a can of Diet Coke was too odd to contemplate.

He looked with nostalgia at the battered old sofa which they had been meaning to replace for years. They had inherited it from the previous owner of the house and had found it so comfortable it became the site of their first sexual encounter, three days after they had moved in. The children were asleep upstairs and their bedroom was full of unpacked cardboard boxes. The living room was the only place that was reasonably clear and that was only because the television set stood at the far end of it and they needed space for a clear view.

Mike could remember the night very well. They had eaten fish and chips with their fingers on paper plates because Julia couldn't remember where she had packed the cutlery or the crockery and both children were desperate to eat anything — pizza for preference but fish and chips would do. After Jamie had been coaxed into the bed which he no longer liked because it reminded him of the old house and why couldn't he go back there to sleep, Mike and Julia opened a bottle of red wine and watched a wildlife documentary on BBC 1. Both of them were exhausted by the physical exertions involved in moving house and relaxed by the food and the wine, and when he put his hand on her knee, Julia had lazily opened her arms to him.

In the months since Emily's death, Julia's attitude to him had changed. After the first numbness and despair had worn off, Julia had simply slipped, or so it appeared to Mike, into wifely autopilot. The clothes were washed, the food was bought and prepared, the house was organised and managed with her usual efficiency but something had undoubtedly disappeared from the marriage — hope perhaps, passion certainly.

Julia had never blamed him for what had happened that day except once, when he had done something quite trivial. She knew it wasn't necessary, as he never ceased to flagellate himself. In an attempt to reset the timer on the boiler after the clocks had gone back that autumn, Julia had run a bath for herself early on the last Sunday night in October, only to find that there was no hot water. She had pulled on a dressing gown and raced downstairs to launch into a fierce, and as far as Mike was concerned, an entirely unprovoked attack.

'You never think. You never think about anyone but yourself!'

'I meant to turn it back but I turned it forward. I'm sorry. What can I say?'

'You think that's enough, don't you?'

'What?' Mike knew instantly where she was going with this one.

'Just saying sorry doesn't mean a damn thing.'

'I thought being in love meant never having to say you were sorry,' he smiled.

'Yes, well, maybe that's true. Maybe you can work it out from that.'

'I'll put the immersion heater on. I'll fill the kettle.'

'That's not what I'm talking about and you know it.'

'No?' said Mike slowly, knowing he was standing on dangerous ground. 'So what are you talking about?'

'I'm talking about you and your selfishness.'

'I told you, I didn't mean to turn the hot water off.'

'And you didn't mean to let Emily drown.'

'Julia, for God's sake—'

'You think ten minutes snoring on the beach is worth the life of your own daughter?'

'Julia, shut up, you've said enough.'

'There isn't a day, an hour, a minute that goes by when I don't think about her.'

'I don't—'

'No! No! There isn't! I loved her so much ...'

'You think I didn't?'

'Then why? In God's name, how could you lose her?'

'Julia, stop this. It isn't helping.'

Her face was red and tears were pouring down her cheeks as she attacked him with her fists.

'You bastard, you killed her, you killed my little girl!'

Her body was shaking with sobs. He tried to hold her, hoping to offer comfort and security, but she pushed him away so violently that the knot in the towel which she had draped round herself in the bathroom when she discovered the cold water coming out of the hot tap was jerked undone and the towel fell to her feet.

Mike stared at Julia's naked body, instinctively aroused and yet embarrassed by his own lust. This was not a deliberate act of seduction on Julia's part and she was equally quick to see that even in the middle of a row about the most terrible thing that had ever happened to either of them he could allow his mind to wander to the possibility of sex.

Mike moved as if to help her with the towel but she turned sharply away from him, rejecting his help but, by doing so, unavoidably offering him the fleeting sight of her bare bottom and the pendulous swing of her breasts. She fled from the living room and raced back up the stairs, slamming the bathroom door and jerking the bolt into place so fiercely that Mike could hear it quite plainly from where he stood in the living room.

If he looked at the couch and screwed his eyes up tight he could just remember the touch of Julia's velvet skin that night they had made love there for the first time. He left the Diet Coke can on the coffee table and returned to the cold and unwelcoming bedroom.

He stared at himself in the full-length mirror, worrying away at whether he had gone to seed or whether the sight that confronted him was merely to be expected in a man of his mature years. Although it was the body of a man approaching middle age, there was little surplus fat to be found. His belly was hardly as taut as it had been in his student days but it was solidly packed. He cast a critical eye over his thighs. They were as firm as they had ever been. He'd always been shyly proud of them and in the days when Julia's hands had visited them on a daily basis she had always remarked on their impressive physical condition.

Julia! Why couldn't he talk to the woman he loved so much about the act of love? He did love her. He was quite sure of that. It wasn't that he didn't find other women attractive. He had always found other women attractive even when they were first in love and he was totally besotted with Julia. He regarded it as rather odd but he didn't feel it was a discussion that Julia would be particularly anxious to pursue so he never raised it with her.

He was sad that he spent night after night, lying beside her, thinking how much he wanted to stroke her and being too intimidated to do it because he knew her response would be one of irritation. He thought wryly of how it had been between them, how they had discussed whether they should be in the *Guinness Book of Records* for the number of mutual climaxes they had given each other when they had spent all day making love and drinking white wine in a pension in Provence during the month after their graduation.

How did they get from there to here, where he knew she accepted his embraces mostly on sufferance? He couldn't begin to conceive how society had once believed it was normal for a husband to feel that he owned his wife and she knew she was legally and morally obligated to submit to him whenever he desired her. That didn't appeal to Mike. What he wanted was the reciprocal loving which he felt Julia had denied him for too long. He certainly had no intention of ringing the numbers posted up in telephone boxes all over London advertising sexual services. What he was looking for you just couldn't buy. But was this yawning void in his life all he was going to have to look forward to till the day he died or as long as the marriage lasted? — whichever came the sooner.

Walking home from school the following afternoon, Jamie experienced a similar feeling of emptiness. Unable to talk to his mother — not that he would have done anyway even if she had been in the country — unwilling to share the confidence with his father, and scared of how his friends might react if he opened up to them he decided to talk to Emily about it.

Sitting on the front seat upstairs on a green double decker hurtling along the quiet Hertfordshire road to the cemetery, Jamie wondered why he had so scrupulously avoided coming before. He got off at the bus stop and walked past the flower stall outside the wrought-iron gates which guarded the entrance. It would never have occurred to him that at any point in his life he would spend his precious pocket money on something as completely useless as flowers. He was fifty yards past the stall when he realised that this was the day when it would happen. He knew that Emily wasn't going to spring out of the grave and confront him if he arrived flower-less, but it would have felt like arriving at a friend's birthday party without a present.

He retraced his steps towards the stall and stood in front of the array of flowers, confused by the variety of choice. A white-haired lady with a kind face finished serving a customer and gave Jamie a few moments to come to a decision before asking, 'Would you like some help?'

'Yes, please. I'm visiting my sister's plaque and I don't know what to buy.'

'Do you know what her favourite flower was?'

Jamie shook his head and wondered why he didn't know.

'How old was she?'

'She was fifteen. She drowned. We were on holiday in Italy.'

'How sad. I'm so sorry.'

The woman leant over and plucked a bunch of short-stemmed yellow roses from a black plastic bucket. She held them out for Jamie to sniff but far enough away for the water to drop from the stems on to the ground rather than on to Jamie's shoes.

'How much are they?'

'These are seven pounds fifty.'

Jamie looked horrified. The woman realised that perhaps this might be beyond the financial resources of a schoolboy and recalculated.

'How much would you like to spend?'

Jamie took all the change out of his pocket. There were two pound coins and a small amount of silver.

'I've got two pounds thirty-five.'

The woman took half the roses out of the bunch and replaced them in the bucket.

'I think your sister would like these very much.' She picked one of the pound coins and two ten pence pieces from Jamie's open palm, dropped them into her pouch, and handed over the flowers.

'Thank you very much,' said Jamie, aware that the woman's maths didn't make any sense. Either she had given him a very good deal on the flowers or she couldn't count. Either way Jamie was too embarrassed to prolong the conversation.

In the Garden of Remembrance Jamie took the wilted flowers out of the metal vase that hung in front of Emily's plaque and refilled it with fresh water from a nearby free standing tap. He unwrapped the fresh yellow roses and dropped them into the vase, replaced it on the plaque and stood in front of it reading the inscription over and over again.

He cast a quick glance around. He was grateful he was alone because he wanted to speak to Emily aloud and he would have felt foolish had people been near him. Slowly at first, and then with increasing confidence, he poured out his troubles. He complained about Julia's constant monitoring of his activities as if he were still six years old, about his father's late nights at the office, and the smouldering tension between their parents. He really missed Emily. She would know exactly what to say about their mum and dad. Now that he thought about it he vaguely remembered Emily talking about their parents' relationship. He just couldn't remember anything she had specifically said.

When it came to the business with his friends he became a little more circumspect. He knew that nobody could hear him, especially not the person to whom his comments were addressed, but it was still awkward for him to talk aloud about the money problem and the drinking thing and the longings and yearnings he was starting to experience for the first time. He found it ironic that he could talk to Emily, in whom he had never really confided during her life, about matters he could not broach with a living soul.

He concluded with a short account of the disastrous impromptu party of which he could now just about see the funny side, and of his fears for the golf tournament which was about to start. 'The problem is Dad. I know he thinks I'm going to be this great champion one day, like Tiger Woods, but I'm not. I know I'm not. I mean even if I'm an exceptionally talented Under Sixteen in south Hertfordshire that's just one county, half of one county to be exact. Then if I turn out to be just an ordinary good golfer and not a great professional one, is Dad going to look at me for the rest of my life like I've disappointed him? I know he doesn't realise he's putting this pressure on me. He probably thinks he's just being encouraging or something but I do wish he'd leave me alone to play the game the way I want to play it. Mum's away this week so he thinks this is our big chance to cover ourselves in glory. Trouble is, it's all down to me. I'm the one standing on the tee with the club in my hands. He doesn't have to hit the shots. I do. I think I'd rather go out drinking with Rob Faulkner and that lot but I'm not sure if they like me and I'm not sure if Leonie really likes me either. What do you think, Emily?'

Jamie stood in quiet contemplation for a few minutes as if straining his ears to catch the words of his sensible sister as they were borne on the wind towards him. His concentration was broken by the arrival of a family whose loud and cheerful conversation seemed distinctly out of place in the setting. Jamie whispered a soft goodbye and his thanks for her help to his sister, along with a promise of further visits. He walked back towards the bus stop with his problems unsolved but distinctly less weighty than they had been when he arrived. He was cheered that something as simple as visiting the Garden of Remembrance could help to fill the emptiness in his heart he had felt since Emily's death and the visible disintegration of his parents' relationship.

Mike's chance to fill the void he felt in his life came sooner than he anticipated. One of the major American telecom companies was looking to acquire a smaller British company operating in the same field and had sent Melanie Katz to work with Mike's team at the bank as they explored the various options. Melanie was a New York Jewish divorcee, smart, sassy and with a specifically Manhattan air of sophistication that Mike found extremely attractive.

On Wednesday, the other members of the team had left at seven thirty but it was past 9 p.m. before Mike turned off the computer with a sigh. He had rung Jamie to tell him he wouldn't be home till after ten but when Melanie suggested a drink before he set off he was only too willing to accept. They made their way to one of the many City bars that seemed to be populated by young people in their twenties.

'Feeling old?' shouted Melanie above the noise of the crowd, gesticulating in the direction of a party of young people with very little hair but much facial jewellery.

'Yes! You?'

'Let's get outta here,' and they tumbled out of the hot noisy wine bar with relief.

'I'm so sorry . . .' started Mike.

'What are you apologising for?'

'For in there.'

'Why is that your fault?'

'I don't know. I think I felt responsible for the country showing its less attractive face.'

'Do you always apologise for things that have nothing to do with you?'

'Constantly. I feel guilty for our treatment of blacks and Asians and gays . . .'

'All your fault?'

'Entirely my fault.'

'Princess Di?'

'I should have told the driver to lay off the booze.'

'Women?'

'Pardon?'

'Since you're feeling guilty about all the persecuted minorities . . .'

'Oh, well, sure. I feel very guilty that Posh Spice is so thin and that Vanessa Feltz can't be the shape she wants to be.'

'That's a reassuring thought to carry home in the taxi.'

'Would you like a lift?'

'A ride? Oh, sure. You have a car?'

'Yes and I feel guilty about that too but the company provides the parking space. I just pay the tax on it. Where do you live?'

'I have an apartment in Cumberland Terrace.'

'Regent's Park?'

'You know it?'

'Of course.'

Melanie saw the look on Mike's face. She smiled and touched him lightly on the arm. 'My company's paying for it.'

Mike smiled back. He liked the touch of her hand on his arm and made no attempt to remove it.

In the car on the way to her apartment Mike found a distinctly warm, almost maternal side to Melanie's character which he hadn't suspected lay beneath that brittle Manhattan exterior. It was a warm, balmy night with clear skies and a cluster of stars.

Melanie wanted to know all about Jamie and Julia but Mike found himself reluctant to convey too much information, as if the knowledge would be sufficient to render him less sexually attractive in her eyes. Instead he turned the conversation to the subject of her divorce which he believed Americans were only too ready to discuss in intimate detail.

'He was a rat fink. He screwed around once too often so I eighty-sixed him.'

'Is that some American corporate finance term I'm not familiar with?'

'No. It just means I kicked his ass.'

'How long have you been . . . free?'

'Free? You know what my charge out rate is?'

'I meant available, divorced, I was trying to find the right word. There doesn't appear to be one.'

Melanie laughed and grabbed at his arm again. 'You British guys are all the same.'

'Really? How's that?'

'I figure it's your school system screws you all up.'

'Well, at least we haven't yet reached the number of shootings your schools specialise in.'

'Touché.'

'We're just fucked up in a different way.'

'You can turn into the park at the next entrance. You want to come up?'

All the way through the West End Mike had been worrying about his response to this question should it arise. Melanie's voice, outside the office, had taken on a different and much more attractive timbre. There was a throaty giggle where previously there had been a stern and hectoring tone. The perfume she was wearing was intoxicating. In the confines of the car's leather interior it inflamed his feelings.

Melanie was a grown-up. If she invited him up for a drink it wasn't going to involve a declaration of love. He wouldn't have to divorce Julia. Melanie was just an attractive and probably lonely woman who would appreciate an evening with male company and probably be grateful for it. In many ways she was the perfect companion for his own bruised ego.

As the car turned into Park Square, he imagined the scenario as he followed her swaying backside up the thickly carpeted stairs of the ornate Nash terrace house. She would open the front door, toss her coat onto a chair and lead him into the living room with its stunning views across the park. He would take off his jacket and follow her over to the window. She would turn to look at him, smile and then run her fingers through his hair with that sly come-hither stare that strips his conscience bare, that's witchcraft. Shit! It was a lyric! It was one of Julia's bloody Frank Sinatra romantic ballads! Bugger!

'I'd love to but it'll be nearly eleven before I get home and I like to talk to Jamie at the end of the day. Do you think me awfully rude?'

'No,' smiled Melanie, 'I think you're an awfully nice man.'

Mike leant across to open the door for her. She kissed him briefly and platonically on the cheek, then climbed out.

'Sorry about the drink. Let's take a rain check?'

'Absolutely. A rain check is a great idea,' replied Mike and drove back home, delighted to have been given a rain check and another chance which he knew, without question, he would blow next time round just as emphatically.

Instead of following Melanie's flowing buttocks, he climbed the stairs to Jamie's bedroom a little wearily. Still, he knew he'd made the right decision and he did, genuinely, enjoy shooting the breeze with his son at the end of the day.

'Hi!' he said brightly. 'Sorry I'm late. The house looks great. Mum'll never know.' Jamie was sitting in bed reading a golf book he had given him for Christmas. 'How are you?'

'Tired. Night, Dad.' Jamie snapped the bedside light off and snuggled down under the covers.

CHAPTER ELEVEN

JULIA LIFTED THE MUG OF tea to her lips with a trembling hand. She had no idea why she had asked for tea. She was sitting in the large and immaculately designed kitchen area of one of California's oldest and best known wineries and she was drinking a cup of tea.

Tom had smiled when she had made her request. 'You wouldn't prefer some of the local produce?'

Julia looked at him blankly. Her mind had seized up. She couldn't for the moment think what he meant. Produce? she thought. Did he mean peas? Did he grow his own vegetables? Oh God, the grapes, the wine, I'm such an idiot!

'Of course,' said Tom quickly, 'it's five o'clock. What else does an English-woman drink at five o'clock?'

'Remember what your tutor at Balliol said to you, first time you met him?'

'Of course. Now, how did it go? "Ah, Johnson, bit of a problem here, five forty-five, too late for tea, too early for sherry." I sure knew I was in a different country.'

Julia nodded happily. Her heart was beating at triple speed and she was terrified she would be unable to speak in complete sentences.

'I'm sorry it's Liptons. There's not much choice out here.'

'San Francisco?' Julia was delighted she could summon up the name of the nearest large city perfectly but she knew she couldn't put it into a sentence.

How long would this last? she wondered. Would she spend the rest of her life with Tom talking like a recent immigrant who had only just started English lessons and hadn't learned anything but how to ask directions to the railway station? Tom seemed unfazed by what might otherwise appear to be this startling regression towards infancy.

'Oh sure. You can get anything there if you know where to go. You can probably even get that stuff you used to buy. Typhoon?'

'Typhoo. I only bought that because my mother used to buy it. And I think she only bought it because her mother bought it too.' She knew she was babbling. And he was just being kind. For Tom it must be like meeting a very ancient relative, an aged woman in her dotage, ninety years old at least. He's making me a cup of tea because that's what you do with old people. You make them tea and cut them a piece of sponge cake because they can't eat biscuits as their teeth aren't strong enough.

'Sorry I don't have those chocolate cookies you liked either, what did you call them? Choccy biccies? I loved those.'

'Well, I can't eat choccy biccies any more either.'

'Why? You lost all your teeth?'

Julia blushed. How did he know? She ran her tongue round her teeth surreptitiously, just to make sure they were still there.

'No. I'm on a diet.'

She wasn't but she felt she ought to let him know that she was still looking after her figure. Unless that meant that he would now think that she thought she was fat, in which case he would obviously think so too. She knew she was overweight, certainly by her own standards and undoubtedly by the standard of whatever weight he remembered she had been in the early 1980s – before the Falklands War, for God's sake. This whole situation was too unreal. She had to get hold of her thoughts which were running through her head like a cassette rewinding at high speed.

'Why are you on a diet?'

'Because otherwise one day I'll be so fat I won't be able to haul myself out of the bath. I'll just have to sit there till they send an enormous forklift truck up the stairs into the bathroom to transport me from the house to the television studio where Oprah Winfrey will make people applaud sympathetically because I've lost a hundred pounds in five months and my weight is down to twenty-five stone – that's three hundred and fifty of your American pounds.'

'Will you be naked?'

'What?'

'Will you have time to get dressed before they deposit you on a chair opposite Oprah or will you be buck naked?'

'Does that matter? I'll be so gross I'll be fit only for a freak show.'

'I'll watch if you're naked.'

'Tom! That's disgusting.'

'Well, I don't normally catch Oprah, so you're probably safe anyway.'

'I wasn't being entirely serious, you know.'

'Really?' He took a swig of tea and put down his mug with a grimace. 'Sorry. Shouldn't have made it in the microwave.'

'I wondered why you did that.'

'I just make everything in the microwave. Since Candice left I don't think I've turned on the oven.'

There was a silence. Did Tom want her to ask about Candice? Was he still crazily in love with her? He seemed to be pleading domestic ineptitude but then, unlike Mike, he was never particularly handy round the kitchen, Julia remembered, so it could be a simple statement of fact.

'How long has she been gone?'

'In reality about nine months. In spirit about ten years.'

Julia's heart leaped. She simply didn't have the strength to pretend to herself. She was glad that Tom had suffered in a bad marriage. She was delighted that he had tried to stick it out even though Candice obviously hadn't cared for him. Dare she hope that one of the reasons for the failure of their marriage had been Tom's memory of his romance with her?

'I'm sorry,' she lied, 'that sounds miserable.'

'It was mostly my fault. I guess I'm not cut out to be a husband.'

Now what the hell did that mean? Every little clue Tom dropped about his life was racing through Julia's computer searching for a link. Was he not cut out to be a husband because he's a wife beater? Because he's a drunkard? Because he feels fated to choose women who don't appreciate him? Or was it a direct reference applicable only to his marriage to Candice? Was she the drunk? Was she promiscuous? What?

'Depends what kind of a husband your wife was looking for.'

'Julia, we haven't seen each other for nearly eighteen years ...'

Seventeen years, eight months, three weeks, thought Julia, having worked it out on the drive out of Healdsburg.

'... I don't want to start again by discussing my ex-wife.'

Start again? Did he really say start again? Did he really mean start again? Julia shed twenty years and as many pounds in the space of a single sentence.

'Now you're here I think we should just accentuate the positive.'

'And the negative?'

'Eliminate it entirely. And whatever you do ...'

'Don't mess with Mr Inbetween,' they chorused happily.

'Listen, I don't know what plans you have for this evening but I'd really like to take you to dinner. Do you have to be back in the city at any particular time?'

'Calistoga.'

'Where?'

'I'm not staying in San Francisco. I'm staying in Calistoga in the Napa Valley.'

'I know where Calistoga is. I just wondered why you were staying in that Disneyland cowboy town.'

'Because I got a great deal on a motel and mud bath.'

'You get to sleep in the mud bath?'

'The treatments. The facials and the spa treatments. They sounded interesting.'

He looked at her, smiling. He was always smiling. That's what she remembered about him. Nothing seemed to faze him. He was always cheery – unlike Mike and his moods. Unless he was laughing at her. Surely not. She knew she must sound like a basket case but surely he didn't think she was a figure of fun.

'It's quite a short drive. I could choose somewhere to eat between here and there. Would you like to have dinner with me?'

That was easy, of course she would.

'I'd love to have dinner. Where did you have in mind?'

'There's a really smart place in the plaza in Healdsburg. It's run by a friend of mine and, just by coincidence, he serves almost nothing but wines from the Johnson Winery. If you don't want to taste it neat here, perhaps I could persuade you to try a sip over dinner.'

'I won't need persuading. I should have had some instead of the tea.'

'Yes, I'm sorry about that.'

'No, really, that wasn't a criticism of your tea. I just wasn't thinking wine at this time of day.'

'Quite right but in fact I could probably offer you a wine that would match whatever time of day you could name and whatever kind of spirit you were in and whatever kind of food you had just eaten or were about to eat. Even that old creep at Oxford, whose name I've blanked, wouldn't have a reason to refuse.'

'What time did you want to go? I need to get back to the motel and shower.'

'I have everything you need. You want to clean up right now?'

'Sure, if that's OK with you.'

'Follow me.'

*　　*　　*

Although the house was Victorian in origin it had been rebuilt twice, once in 1917 when it burned down and again in 1968 when Tom's mother decided that for all its architectural grandeur it didn't have a waste disposal in the kitchen or a window that didn't leak when the winter winds and rains lashed against it. She saw no reason why she should continue to live in what was to all intents and purposes her mother-in-law's house – particularly as her mother-in-law had only been allowed to rebuild it under the critical eye of her own mother-in-law.

Candice – presumably Candice – had decorated during her tenure with the eye of an interior designer. Apparently, it was Tom's habit to invite key buyers all over the country for weekends when a new vintage would be unveiled. To that end they had built three particularly attractive guest bedroom suites which, Julia noted with wry amusement, owed much to the brief success of Laura Ashley in America during the late 1980s. The wallpaper and furnishings nevertheless were particularly apposite to a house which was Victorian in structure and atmosphere but modern in technological convenience.

Tom showed her into one of the suites with evident pride. Julia gushed over it with genuine enthusiasm.

'Oh, Tom, this is stunning.'

'Come and look at the view,' he said, marching over to the window. Julia obeyed and stood quietly beside him, enjoying the five inches difference in their heights, feeling small and petite and protected as she had those many years ago. 'That's Mount St Helena you can see out there.'

'Looks pretty big.'

'It's bigger than anything you've got in jolly old England.'

'Oh yeah?'

'Yeah.'

'So how big is it?'

'Twelve, thirteen thousand feet.'

'OK, but isn't it also a volcano?'

'Yes, I think it is. But it hasn't been active for hundreds or thousands of years.'

'Hang on,' said Julia puzzled. 'I remember seeing pictures of it on TV volcanoing away like billy-o.'

'It's gonna take me some time to get used to the way you speak again . . .'

Did that mean he was going to make the effort, that he was talking about seeing her again, for a long period of time? Or was it just a reference to the conversation over dinner?

'. . . but I think you might be remembering Mount St Helens. That erupted in Washington State about ten years ago.'

'Must be. I'm feeling old but I think hundreds or thousands of years is probably an exaggeration. Besides, we wouldn't have had a TV hundreds or thousands of years ago.'

'No, but if you had, just think how cheap the monthly cable charge would have been.'

She smiled, buying time to think of a witty response. Tom looked at her as he had looked at her in Oxford.

'I'm so pleased you came, Julia. I can't tell you how pleased I am.' Then he took her into his arms and kissed her gently. She pulled away instinctively.

'I'm sorry,' he said. 'Put it down to over-enthusiastic American hospitality. I'll let you shower, and get cleaned up. Everything you need is in the bathroom.' He turned and left the room, closing the door gently behind him.

'Everything except you,' thought Julia, as she sat on the bed staring at the closed door.

CHAPTER TWELVE

HE HAD OBVIOUSLY SHOWERED TOO. When she walked downstairs into the living room she saw the back of his head as he sat reading a book. His hair was still wet from the shower. If Prince Charles can be Camilla's Tampax then maybe I could be Tom's soap on a rope, she thought. Julia had been irrationally pleased to find something as tacky as soap on a rope in an otherwise immaculately decorated bathroom and bedroom. It struck an incongruously false note and she assumed it was Tom's revenge on his ex-wife's exquisite good taste. Tom had always been more interested in books than artefacts, in feelings rather than outward appearances. It was one of his most attractive features.

He laid the book on the large mahogany coffee table as he heard her approach – it was a heavyweight analysis of the state of the American economy; she was glad to note his intellectual interests clearly hadn't shifted too far from his Oxford days – and stood up to greet her.

She had done her best, considering the fact that her clothes, with the exception of the ones she stood up in, were still in two suitcases in a motel in Calistoga. She particularly regretted the lack of the short black dress which was appropriate for almost any kind of social engagement. Julia hoped that Tom might regard her pale, translucent skin as distinctively sensuous. In Britain during the winter when everyone was pasty-faced and deprived of sunlight, she blended in. Here in America, in the golden state of the permanent tan, she felt worryingly conspicuous.

Tom had also shaved and the hint of expensive aftershave which she detected acted powerfully on her senses. He was wearing a clean white shirt, so clean that she could see the folds, which meant it had either come back from the laundry or it had been ripped out of its original packaging. She guessed the latter.

He held out a glass of wine. 'We've only just started growing this.'

'You're growing wine glasses? That sounds difficult.'

He smiled. 'Sauvignon Blanc. We've been planting Cabernet Sauvignon and Merlot for nearly twenty years but Henri only figured the hillsides were warm enough a couple of years ago for this grape to prosper.'

Julia raised the glass to her lips and took a little sip.

'What do you think?'

'About Henri?'

'Not about Henri.'

'Who is Henri?'

'Henri Lacroix is my winemaker and vineyard manager.'

'Can one man do both jobs?'

'Yes but you will never meet him.'

'Because he's cute?'

'Because I shall strangle you if you don't tell me what you think of the wine.'

Julia sipped again. It slipped down as smooth as velvet. 'Wonderful.'

'Really?'

'Really wonderful.'

Tom smiled with relief. Julia was absurdly pleased. It obviously mattered to him what she thought of his wine, like a child bringing home something he'd made at school. She had no understanding of wine. He must know that surely. When she bought wine it was generally from the supermarket and whereas she knew that anything that cost less than five pounds was unlikely to be much good she resented spending more than £7.99 for a normal table wine. I guess he's like an artist, she thought, a performing artist. He just needs to be told he's wonderful.

She sipped again.

'You can probably tell the classical proportions of ripe, vivid berry flavours which are ideally mixed with the graceful tannins in the wine.'

Julia nodded.

'Was that just what you were going to say?'

'Yes, though I wouldn't have phrased it quite like that.'

'And how would you have phrased it?'

'I think it doesn't taste like wine.'

'Excuse me?'

'You have to remember that the wine I tend to drink, when I drink it at all, usually comes from Waitrose.'

'Nothing wrong with that necessarily.'

'No, I mean this doesn't taste anything like the wine you can buy from Waitrose. This tastes like something infinitely better but I don't know how to say it.'

'You just did.'

She glowed inwardly at his approval.

'I've made reservations for seven.'

'People eat early here, don't they?'

'They also get up early. We're farmers.'

'Somehow I don't see you as a farmer.'

'We're in the agribusiness, we are dependent on our crops and on the weather and what the market will bear. What else are we then but farmers?'

'I suppose I just have a different image of farmers.'

'Grain silos, cornfields, combine harvesters, that sort of thing?'

Julia nodded.

'That's us.'

'Oh, come on.'

'Really. You can see the vines developing out there. We harvest them in July and August. We crush them through to early October.'

'You still tread the grapes?'

'Not exactly. That kind of went out with the surrey with the fringe on top.'

'Sorry.'

'Don't apologise. It's amazing the number of people who still think we round up the peasants to trample the grapes. I guess it makes for a more romantic image.'

'Doesn't look like you get too many peasants in this part of the world.'

'Not in the wine country. We tend to get more management consultants than peasants in this area.'

'So how do you turn the grapes into wine?'

'We have enormous pressing machines and then we store the wine in large tanks to ferment for eight to nine months. After that it's bottled and stored for eighteen months if it's a white wine, another year after that if it's a red.'

'So you know pretty soon if you're going to have a bonanza year ahead?'

'In theory. But we tend to take the negative route. When we taste the wine in the summer we know if we can afford the heating bills in two winters' time.'

'Why so gloomy?'

'Experience.'

'You seem to have done pretty well for a penniless farmer,' said Julia looking round at the large well-furnished room with its landscapes of the American south-west hanging on the walls.

'You want to see my mortgage?'

'You want to see ours?'

'I'll show you mine if you show me yours.'

'There are some secrets English people will take to the grave – the size of their mortgage being one.'

'I thought you Brits had changed. Now you're all touchy feely since you started throwing flowers at Princess Di's hearse.'

'I wasn't one of them. I thought she went off in a ridiculous blitz of media publicity. Very undignified. It was the sort of funeral that might have been designed by *Hello!* magazine if she'd pre-sold the rights to them.'

'Ouch! Sorry. I seem to have touched a nerve.'

'Not really. I didn't realise I felt so strongly about it.' Julia knew she didn't. The raging emotions of the day, the climax to eighteen years of wondering, were obviously causing her to behave in an unpredictable fashion. She sipped a little more of the wine, reluctant to indulge too much too early, not knowing what the evening might hold in store for her, fearing at worst a long drive back to the motel in Calistoga. She didn't know what drink-driving laws were like in America but she suspected that logic dictated that the California Highway Patrol was particularly keen to breathalyse any car with a rental agency's sticker on the bumper.

Tom gently took the glass from her. 'Perhaps we should leave a little room for dinner.'

'I didn't want to be rude.'

'You weren't. Anyway I prefer you to be rude rather than pissed before we leave the house.'

'Pissed? Is that an American term?'

'I've always said pissed since I got back from Oxford. I'm too old to change now.'

'Old? You?'

'We met at nine . . .' Tom started.

'Did we really?' she replied.

'I was on time.'

'That's true. You always were,' said Julia, deliberately suppressing Tom's attempts to play their old lyric game.

'You're right,' he admitted, 'but at least I'm younger than Chevalier.'

'And I'm a damn sight younger than Hermione Whatsername.'

'Gingold. You sure are,' Tom agreed, staring at her face, then dropping his gaze. 'Younger than springtime are you . . .'

'Hey, don't start that or we'll never get to the restaurant.'

Tom picked up his dark blue jacket from the back of the chair on which he had draped it and slipped it on. It was immaculately cut and accentuated the slimness of his build. Instinctively she compared him to Mike who was a year younger but much thicker all over. If only Mike could absorb the romantic qualities that Tom possessed and recycle them for his own use, it would completely change their marriage for her.

'Did you eat out much in San Francisco?'

'Oh yes. In fact, only last night I was dining at Stars.'

'Stars, the culinary temple of Jeremiah Tower?'

'Yes, next door to the concert.'

'You were at the Tony Bennett concert?'

'Of course, that's why I'm here, why I came to California. My company's got the recording rights. We're putting out the CD.'

'I was there. We could have been sitting a few rows away from each other. Well, don't look so shocked. You know I love that kind of music. I taught you about it, for Christ's sake!'

'I'm not shocked, just surprised I didn't see you.'

'Were you looking for me?'

'No, of course not. I was just thinking what a wonderful way to meet each other again if we'd been given tickets next to each other.'

'A meet cute.'

'You mean a cute meet?'

'No,' he said, guiding her out of the front door with the lightest of touches on her shoulder, 'a meet cute. However crazy the syntax, that's what Hollywood writers always called the contrived situation when the boy meets the girl.'

'Like when the girl's sunglasses fall out of her handbag and the boy picks them up?'

'Exactly like that.'

She turned to look at him as he smiled at her. That smile drove her crazy. She could hardly tell him to stop smiling but it was churning up her insides. She had dreamed about it so often, it was disconcerting to see it again in the flesh. It was all very well, dozing off on the commuter train from St Albans or fantasising in bed in the dark, but this was different. It was now for real and how she handled herself and the situation in the next few hours might determine the future course of her life.

He held the passenger door open for her.

'Fasten your seat belt, it's going to be a bumpy night,' she said to Tom as she pulled on the seat belt cord.

'Why?' he said as he helped her find the seat belt connection in the dark interior of the car, not recognising the quotation from an old Bette Davis film. Tom's special subject was strictly the musical. 'This car's got the greatest suspension in the world and the road to Healdsburg's practically deserted.'

She switched tack. 'I mean it brings back a night of tropical splendour.'

'Ah,' he sighed happily as the engine fired almost noiselessly and the car rolled out of the gates, 'and this brings back the sound of music so tender.' He pressed two buttons. The roof slid slowly back to reveal a darkening evening sky carpeted with stars. On the CD player came the unmistakable sound of a Cole Porter ballad. On the lonely valley road the fierce shaft of the car's headlights which briefly illuminated the passing hedgerows and spreading vines was the only evidence that there was still life on earth.

Tom's fingers snaked across the leather seat and found Julia's compliant hand, waiting softly in her lap. The years rolled away and they were twenty again, with all their need for romance and heedless of the casualties it might bring in its wake.

CHAPTER THIRTEEN

JULIA COULDN'T REMEMBER THE LAST time she had been out to dinner with a man. The previous night certainly didn't count and if she extracted from the list all encounters which were also business meetings and all the dinners she had had with Mike, of which there had never been very many in any case, she was left puzzling as to when the last time had been.

She revelled in the unaccustomed luxury. Tom opened doors for her and generally looked after her in a way that wasn't patronising but spoke of genuine solicitude. It wasn't that Mike didn't do these things so much as that neither of them really cared whether he did or he didn't.

Though Julia considered herself a feminist, at least to the extent that she had grown up with the idea that men and women should be educated and paid similarly, she was also a realist and she didn't care greatly that Mike didn't play the assiduous lover any longer. Frankly, it would have been strange if he had behaved in such a manner after so many years of marriage and her instinctive suspicion would have led her immediately to the conclusion that he was trying to compensate for some aberrant behaviour which she had not yet discovered.

She resolved to eradicate the memory of Mike from her brain just for the evening. She wouldn't enjoy it if she was constantly assailed by images of her husband and, so far at least, nothing had happened that she could not relate to him in every detail. Every detail, of course, other than the reason for her presence here at all. If Mike knew that she had driven north to find the one man in the world of whom he was probably still jealous, it would be irrelevant that nothing had so far 'happened'. They would both know that the mere fact of her being in the same room as her old lover was proof of her intentions.

It wasn't just the warmth of Tom's attention that she was basking in, it was also the unaccustomed feeling of energy. For as long as she could remember she had been tired. Life just took it out of her. The commute on Thameslink, the hot and sweaty London Underground, the general sense that nobody in the company cared a damn what she did, that her whole working life was one huge irrelevance — and that was just the working week.

Then there was life at home which had been an echoing void since Emily's death. Her son was a lovely boy but he was fifteen. The growing up and growing away process had already started. He never buried his head in her waist the way he did when he was little and she was standing at the kitchen sink doing the washing up. He never crawled onto her lap when she was sitting in the armchair in the living room trying to read. She supposed that few fifteen-year-old boys confided much of what was really happening in their lives to their mothers but because she wasn't getting much of an emotional charge from Mike either, she knew only too well how barren her life was.

Jamie was a teenager and as such he obviously didn't need the cuddles and the physical affection that she still craved. His passion was shared with his father on the golf course and though she knew, or thought she knew, how he felt as a little boy, since the day of his tenth birthday when he told her he was too old to be bathed by her, that was no longer the case.

It wasn't as if Jamie was a rebellious boy. He wasn't smoking dope in his room or getting drunk in the pub every weekend. She never found discarded needles or porn mags when she Hoovered under his bed, though she thought deep down that perhaps she ought to find some mildly risqué material, and as the months went by and there wasn't even the sight of a well-thumbed copy of *Playboy,* she began to worry that perhaps there ought to be some evidence of teenage heterosexual activity, but if there was, she never found it.

He went out on Saturday nights but was always home by eleven thirty which was his curfew and on the two occasions when he had missed it there was a perfectly good explanation which related to the unreliability of the Thameslink trains which she appreciated only too well. He was a really good boy. The vast majority of parents would love to have a fifteen-year-old boy who caused so little trouble.

Jamie's passion seemed to be reserved for the golf course. Mike's passion was there too and that left Julia precisely nowhere. Where was her passion? She couldn't conceive of slipping out of the office early to hold hands under the table with some guy in a wine bar near King's Cross station – if there was one. King's Cross was noted for its winos rather than its wine bars. She wasn't built for deceit, the lies she would have to tell, the discomfort they would cause and the catastrophe when she was found out as she knew she would be eventually.

She remembered what her primary school teacher, Mrs Vaughan, had once written on the blackboard after some poor boy had been found to have stolen fifty pence from the pocket of a raincoat in the girls' cloakroom. TRUTH WILL OUT. She wrote it slowly in chalked capital letters. It was one of the more frightening experiences of her life, like being present at the announcement of a 'Guilty' verdict at the close of a murder trial when the only possible sentence would be death by hanging. Julia didn't consider herself any kind of holier-than-thou moral person but she had never knowingly hurt anybody and she couldn't bear the thought of being categorised as someone who did. The public humiliation and the private contrition would be far too great.

She had done nobody any harm, she had contracted a respectable marriage, stayed faithful to her husband, lived for her children, cleaned the house, shopped on Saturdays at Waitrose. Was this it? When Jamie left home and Mike disappeared to follow him on a golf tour or slumped into a depression because Jamie hadn't made it as a professional, what then for her? What life did she have to look forward to? What kind of life had she had?

Please, she begged herself silently, please let me enjoy this evening. Let me turn off and not think about home or work. Let me just enjoy being with this man again. If something seems to be developing, I'll think about the dangers then. I want to feel free of all that stuff. I just want to be loved again.

The restaurant offered valet parking. A short, swarthy Mexican (Juanita's brother?) in a smart red waistcoat opened the door for Julia as Tom drew up outside. Julia stepped out and watched as the man replaced Tom in the driver's seat and roared away. Julia knew he was simply taking it to the car park which was presumably at the rear of the building but it did look for the moment as though that was the last they would ever see of Tom's expensive car. It clearly didn't bother Tom who waited patiently for her eyes to return from the disappearing tail lights before guiding her into the warmth and chatter of the restaurant.

'So,' said Tom, snapping a bread stick in half, 'I never asked you what you thought of the concert.'

'I couldn't really enjoy it as a spectator. I was too worried about the recording and the marketing and the ratings on HBO and the reviews in the trade press and whether we should hold back the release till Christmas.'

'Do you like your job?'

'I like the music.'

'That sounds like a "no" to me.'

'No, it means I like the music but I was never cut out to be a company person.'

'So why are you one?'

'We need two incomes.'

'That's not quite the answer to the question I asked.'

'I couldn't become a professional musician, I suppose.'

'Why not? You were good enough.'

'I was good enough to play in the second violins in a less than first-rate orchestra, always travelling, never settling down, unable to raise a family, never earning enough to feel secure.'

'Nothing to do with your folks?'

'My parents? I don't think so.'

'Are they still alive?'

'My father died about ten years ago. My mother moved in with her sister. They have a cottage in the West Country.'

'That's Gloucestershire, right?'

'A little further west. It's in Cornwall. It's a long drive. We don't see her much.'

'Oh, but they've built roads and freeways and stuff surely.'

Julia paused for a moment. She didn't care much for the path the conversation was taking. 'I suppose the truth is that we don't see each other because we don't want to,' she said with what she hoped was an air of finality.

The waiter hovered. They made their choices and the waiter snapped the menus out of their hands with an alacrity that suggested they were wanted urgently by another and much wealthier party in the furthest, most distant part of the restaurant. The wine waiter immediately took his place, showed the label on the bottle to Tom who nodded and smiled.

As the waiter expertly removed the cork and poured a modicum into the bottom of Tom's glass, Julia couldn't help remembering the last time she and Mike had had a bottle of wine with their dinner. The top three-quarters of the cork snapped off leaving the bottom quarter exposed and rotted through, clinging with no conviction at all to the neck of the bottle. Mike's painstakingly careful attempt to reinsert the corkscrew resulted only in the cork breaking up and floating about just under the neck, a visible reproach to their ineptitude and their ignorance of wine. Eventually, Julia poured the wine into the glasses through a tea strainer. She didn't think Tom would be too impressed as he explained to her the provenance of the wine they were to drink tonight.

'What shall we toast?' he asked as the wine waiter departed and he raised his glass towards her. 'Old times, a bright new future, the revival of the American popular song?'

'To us,' said Julia simply and clinked her glass against his.

'To us,' Tom repeated happily. 'Thank you for taking the trouble to come all this way to see me again.'

'Was that why you gave Helen your card?'

'I guess so. It was kind of a regular thing to do, you know? You see someone unexpectedly after a long time and you give them your business card because it places the onus on the other person then to get in touch with you.'

'You never liked Helen, did you?'

'I guess I never really thought about her.'

'Did you know she was a lesbian?'

'Of course. But that wasn't why.'

'Then why?'

'Because I was in love with you. I didn't look at another woman for the two years I was in Oxford.'

The chilled gazpacho arrived before Julia could follow up such a leading statement. It seemed to take an age before both starters were served with appropriate condiments and the wine glasses topped up.

'And afterwards?' said Julia quickly as soon as the waiter's back was turned. 'Did you forget about me?'

'I've never forgotten about you. I meant every word I ever said to you in Oxford. I also meant every word I wrote explaining why I couldn't come back.'

'You put your family before us.'

'My father had a stroke. My mother couldn't cope. My sister, Ellen, lived in Connecticut. What choice did I have?'

Julia looked down at her gazpacho.

'Julia, look at me. I'm sorry. I'm as sorry now as I was then. I wouldn't dream of hurting you. Then or now.'

'You didn't invite me to come out here.'

'Your graduation was a year away. I didn't expect you to live like a nun for twelve months.'

'I would have done anything for you, Tom.'

'I thought we should end it – for both of us. I was an asshole, right?'

Julia looked up. Her eyes had filled with tears.

'You're crying!'

'Not yet. I think I can hang on if you talk about something else.'

'The weather?'

'In California? What's to talk about?'

'How beautifully blue the sky/The grass is growing very high/Continue fine I hope it may/And yet it rained but yesterday.'

'What on earth was that?'

'*The Pirates of Penzance.*'

'I forgot you loved Gilbert and Sullivan.'

'Best thing ever to come out of England. With one exception.'

'Tom!' she said warningly. 'I don't know why I'm quite so emotional. There's so much I want to say to you but I'm terrified I'm going to burst into tears. Everyone in this restaurant will then jump to the wrong conclusion and the restaurant will cancel its order to your vineyard for millions of bottles of Chablis so for both our sakes let's just talk about politics or religion or something else equally uncontroversial.'

'Great. Suits me. What do you make of George Dubya over there? You know, this wine is even better than I remembered. We really do make some great stuff. I think I undercharged them. Jesus!'

'What?'

Tom inclined his head towards a family two tables away. There were grandparents, parents and children making the sort of noise most families make, particularly Italian families who enjoy eating out together. One of the kids had knocked over a glass of red wine and the concerned babble was getting louder as a tolerant waiter ran towards them with a napkin.

'Why do people bring little kids to a classy place like this?'

'Maybe they like your wine.'

'If they do, they can't appreciate it with those kids racing around. Honestly, parents with kids can be so thoughtless. I hope you don't behave like that.'

'We go to TGI Friday's.'

The rest of the dinner passed off as unremarkably as Julia could have wished. They talked about music and art as well as politics and the midterm elections. Tom seemed impressed when Julia mentioned Jamie's prowess as a golfer but she didn't feel comfortable talking about her family, not yet anyway, and he allowed himself to be steered away into the calmer shoals of tabloid TV. Tom was amazed that every tacky American talk show could now be seen on British television. They shared a nostalgia for a time when British television was demonstrably superior to its American cousin. Tom professed himself sad to see how far it had declined.

He settled the bill quickly, signing the credit card receipt and slipping it back into the large leather folder that reminded Julia of the one her mother had used to protect (from what act of aggression? she wondered) each week's copy of the *Radio Times*.

As they emerged into the cool night air, the Transportation Captain, as he was called on the badge he so proudly displayed on his waistcoat, asked for their valet parking ticket.

'I think we're just going to take a stroll first. The young woman hasn't seen our fair city.' He turned to Julia. 'You OK for a walk to aid the digestion?' he asked innocently.

Julia nodded. Where could be the harm? If he wants to kiss me he could as well do it in the car or the house as on the street. And if he wanted anything more he was certainly not going to do it in the road. Besides, Tom was a gentleman and 'anything further' was now at her discretion, she knew perfectly well.

'The plaza's the best thing about this town. I think they copied it from the one in Sonoma itself.'

'So why were you so keen to show me the sights?'

'I didn't want the evening to end. Not yet.'

'OK. So tell me about Healdsburg.'

'It's kind of winery central for this part of Sonoma County. See that store there?'

'Kendall Jackson Wine Country Store,' read Julia with difficulty. The square wasn't particularly well-illuminated.

'You can taste wines there from all over the state, not just the valleys round here but as far south as Santa Barbara.'

'I didn't realise they made wines as far south as that.'

'Listen, they make wine everywhere these days – eastern Europe, South Africa, even the UK's joined in.'

'Not so you'd want to drink it though.'

'You'd be surprised. It's a technical business these days, all done by men in white lab coats with MBAs from Stanford and Harvard. My grandfather would have had a fit if he'd seen the way the business has developed.'

'But California wines have improved out of all recognition since his time so that must be good for your business.'

'Sure, but so have wines from Chile and Bulgaria. They can be imported now as cheaply as we can make them, whatever our savings in economies of scale.'

'So why stay in the business? It's not like you have to keep it going for your family any longer, is it?'

'I might moan about it but I love this business. It's what I've always said to you. My great-grandfather started the Johnson Winery in eighteen ninety-three. I'm not going to betray that trust.' Tom stared blankly ahead. Julia reproached herself for unwittingly leading the conversation back to the moment of their break-up. They were in a deserted, darkened street, she couldn't see his face. She sought his hand and squeezed it. He squeezed back.

They walked on in silence. Then he stopped and she halted obediently by his side and waited.

Hesitantly, like on their first walk across Christ Church meadow, he moved his face down towards hers. She had plenty of time to move and avoid it, but she didn't. She wanted the touch of his lips on hers and when it came it was extraordinarily fulfilling.

She had fantasised for so long the feel of his naked body on hers and now here she was like a twelve-year-old schoolgirl finding a full measure of satisfaction in the chastest of kisses. She felt the pressure of his tongue but she kept her lips firmly shut and he retreated. Tom gave no indication that he took her rejection to heart. Still, she needed to say something that would keep the atmosphere light.

'Was that regular or decaffeinated coffee we had?'

'I guess it was regular. We didn't ask for decaff.'

'I'll be up all night now.'

'You always have decaff?'

'In the evenings, otherwise I can't get to sleep till after midnight and we have to be up by seven.'

She could tell he was struggling with something. She tried to ease the conversation along by bringing up the topic as casually as she could.

'I've got the motel room key in my car. How long will it take me to get back to Calistoga?'

Tom didn't answer immediately. Then he said, 'I would like it much more if you didn't go back tonight, Julia. You've seen the guest bedroom. It would be a pity to let it go to waste. My room's way across the hall. I can promise you an untroubled night.'

She thought about it for only a second. It was exactly what she'd hoped he'd say.

'If you're sure it would be no trouble.'

'It would be my pleasure.'

'Then I'd love to stay. For tonight.'

CHAPTER FOURTEEN

IT WAS AS IF THEY had been riding their horses together across the open countryside, come to a fence or a river and both their horses had stopped abruptly and refused to move another step. Julia had thought that if they built up enough steam, the horses would leap effortlessly clear but now that they had come to a dead stop she was starting to question why she had made the journey in the first place.

I've got to go back sooner or later. I'm not going to stay out here and never go home again, she thought, so let's dismiss that fantasy. I'm not really a one-night stand sort of a girl either, even if it could be argued that I'm just in a weird long-term relationship with an enormous hiccup — one that has lasted eighteen years. So what the hell am I doing here?

Tom was doing his best, smiling and polite as always but almost certainly puzzled because if she didn't know what she was doing there, how the hell could he? The car turned into the driveway with only the porch light gleaming in an otherwise black desert. The nearest human being was in the neighbouring estate at least a mile away. As Tom held out his hand to help her out of the car, a meaningless but appreciated gesture, she grasped it more tightly than she needed to — as if she trusted the pressure of her fingers to convey the subtleties that her words could not.

There was a quarter-moon visible above Mount St Helena. It looked like a cut-out for a school play, a paper moon sailing over a cardboard sky. It seemed at once to emphasise the stereotypical situation in which they found themselves, lulled by the music on the CD player, the warmth of the powerful car heater and the mellifluous qualities of Tom's carefully chosen wine. Wine for him, music for her.

They stood there together on the porch, gazing at the magnetically attractive night sky. Tom put his arm round her shoulder. It made her shiver and she turned her face into his chest. He folded both arms round her, enveloping her in an embrace. She lifted her face to be kissed. He obliged. There was plenty of romance and passion in the kiss but no force, no urgency. He was still letting her make the decisions.

'Do you want me to wake you in the morning?'

'What time do you get up?'

'Around seven?'

'Isn't that late for a farmer?'

'It's kind of normal in the agribusiness.'

'I forgot you don't have cows to feed. Except me.'

He laughed. 'You don't feed cows. Usually you just milk them.'

She laughed too.

'It's getting cold. Want to go inside?'

She nodded. He opened the front door and they left the night sky and the paper moon behind.

As they were crossing the large open hallway, she slipped her arm through his. She loved the smell of his aftershave. It wasn't what she had remembered but it was intoxicating. She wanted to run her fingers through his thick silky hair.

'Thank you for dinner,' she said. 'Really. It was lovely. And it was lovely seeing you again.'

'I feel the same way.'

He walked her to the door of her room, the point of no return. She turned her face to his for the traditional salute. He bent down and, still tenderly, kissed her on the lips again. And then she felt it. A surge of sexual electricity coursed through her veins. She opened her mouth to meet him. His tongue responded eagerly, almost choking in its raging desire to explore her.

He pulled her tightly to him. She could feel the outline of his rapidly hardening penis stiffen against the inside of her thigh. She pulled back slightly. It was enough for Tom to take the hint.

'Sorry.'

'There's nothing to apologise for.'

'I'll see you at seven.' He turned to go.

'You haven't changed.'

'Bit older, bit fatter.'

'Not so you'd notice. But what I meant was you taste the same.'

'You can remember?' He was amazed.

'Sure. It's only been eighteen years.'

'Well, that's kind of what I mean.'

'It's been eighteen years but only one other man. That's what I mean.'

'Want another memory chaser?'

She smiled and nodded.

Somehow they had both relaxed sufficiently to enjoy the kiss this time. The uncertainty of how they felt about each other was gradually thawing. There remained, for Julia at least, the major problem of where they went from here, but just for the moment she was content to remember herself pressed up against the railings of her college as part of a row of girls lined up at five minutes to midnight to extract the last drop of passion from their boyfriends before the gates banged shut at midnight.

'I want you,' he murmured as his tongue burrowed its way teasingly around the lobe of her ear. She shivered in response. It had been a long time since anyone other than her GP had shown an interest in this part of her anatomy but Tom clearly remembered how sensitive she was there. She wondered if he would recall her other significant erogenous zone and felt with pleasure the touch of his hand as it unerringly found the back of her knee. He had remembered. She kissed him again, this time with gratitude as well as passion.

'I know,' she said, her lips touching his in a series of butterfly kisses, 'but this is so sudden.'

'Twenty years isn't a long enough introduction?'

'You know what I mean. I don't know if I'm ready.'

'I am.'

'I know you are.'

Julia suddenly felt emotionally liberated. All those erotic dreams over so many years and at last they were to be given physical expression. This wasn't some tacky one-night stand, some toyboy lover, office romance or housing estate affair. This was Tom, the man to whom she had first given herself, the first and possibly the only true love of her life.

'Have you been thinking about me, Tom?'

'You know I have.'

'I don't mean since five o'clock. I mean since nineteen eighty-three.'

'I don't quite know what you want me to say.'

'I want you to tell me the truth.'

'Yes. The answer is yes.'

'Often?'

'Julia, I've been married since we last met, I've been unhappy since we last met, I've sought comfort in the arms of other women since we last met. If you're asking me if I've done nothing but think of you since nineteen eighty-three it wouldn't be true but I loved you then and I think it's starting all over again.'

She kissed him again. She appreciated the truth, or at least his partial version of it, but it wasn't exactly the passionate declaration of love she had been hoping for. This time she kept her mouth closed and as she pulled away from him Tom knew, with sinking heart, he had been handed an informal notice to quit.

'Thank you for coming to see me. Thank you for coming to dinner. It's really wonderful to see you again. You make me feel so young.'

Julia smiled in acknowledgement. She knew where he was going with this one. 'And you make me feel like spring is sprung.'

'OK, listen. Special treat, for both of us. I've got a bottle of nineteen forty-seven Châteauneuf-du-Pape. I'm going to open it.'

'Tom, it's nearly midnight.'

'I've been keeping it for about ten years. Candice kept asking me why and when I was going to open it and somehow there was never a time.'

'Well, why now? Why waste it on me?'

'Because it wouldn't be a waste. Precisely because it is you. C'mon.' He took her hand and pulled her towards him. They walked hand in hand through the house to the door of the cellar which was protected by an additional burglar alarm. With the hand that wasn't holding on to Julia, Tom pressed the buttons and the door swung open more like the vault of a bank than the cellar of a house.

He turned on the light and guided Julia down the stone steps into the cellar which was entirely covered by wooden wine racks stretching from floor to ceiling.

'Good God! How many bottles have you got down here?'

'I don't know how many exactly. Thousands, I guess.'

'Are these just for you?'

'Sure. I get through about two entire wine racks a week.'

'Tom!'

'It's an investment. Like paintings or porcelain. I love wine. I collect it because it gives me pleasure and because every year it increases in value.'

'Aren't you ever tempted to drink your investments?'

'Would you paint over a Van Gogh?'

'But what are we doing now?'

'We are celebrating you coming back into my life. We're celebrating finding each other again after twenty years.'

'Seventeen years, eight months, three weeks.'

His eyes were searching the racks looking for the vintage Bordeaux. He dropped her hand when he saw the object of his search and seized it eagerly from its dust-laden resting place.

'How do you know where to look?'

'There's a system.'

He blew the dust away and his eyes sparkled as they devoured the printing. Julia could see the pride of ownership in his eyes as he turned to show her his prized possession. In the poor light and with much of the label still covered in the accumulated dust of ages, she could barely read it. Tom pulled her into his arms.

'A jug of wine, a loaf of sourdough bread and thou beside me.'

'Omar Khyyám?'

'O Mein Papa.'

'Are you sure you want to do this?'

'Julia, what I want to do is impossible in the limited space down here.'

'Tom!'

'I mean I haven't got the room to pull the cork out with the dramatic flourish the occasion deserves. Also, I don't have a corkscrew.'

'Oh sure!'

'Didst thou think I meant country matters?'

'That's a fair thought to lie between maids' legs.'

'I can't beat you at anything.'

'Why do men think the world is a competition to be won?'

'Because it is.'

As they emerged from the cellar, Tom relocked the door with the security code and took Julia into the living room. It was a comfortable room with that indefinable air of reproduction Victoriana, as if all the furniture and artefacts had been purchased in a huge warehouse called Victorians R Us. It wasn't that it was tacky or cheap. Indeed it was probably the result of Candice having worked closely with an expensive interior decorator but the final effect, to Julia's eyes, was something that remained obstinately American rather than Victorian. Then she realised with embarrassment that the look probably accurately reflected turn-of-the-century Americana. There seemed no logic why she should have expected Candice to have re-created a south London Victorian mansion in 1893 – particularly one with a stereo and CD stack discreetly placed in the corner.

Her thoughts were punctured by an explosive sound as Tom withdrew the cork from the most expensive bottle of wine in the world and decanted it into a cut-glass container before setting it on the table.

'We'll let it breathe for a bit.'

'Tom, I'm very flattered by this.'

'I just wanted to show you how much you mean to me. I couldn't think of a more appropriate way.'

'Just saying it would have been enough.'

'No, I wanted to show you. To show you how much I want you.'

'I know how much you want me.'

'I don't just mean physically. I mean the works.'

'How romantic!'

'Julia, please, don't give me marks out of ten. I'm a little out of practice at this.'

'I'm not exactly a professional myself.'

They were sitting on the deep, comfortable, high-backed couch together. He took her hand and examined it minutely.

'What can you see?'

'An extraordinary vision. I can see two people, one old and decrepit, the other young and beautiful.'

'How decrepit is the woman? Does she have use of her legs?'

'No. It's the man who is old, the woman is young and beautiful.'

'Indeed. And where are this odd couple?'

'It looks to me . . .' he screwed up his eyes, 'it looks to me as though they are sitting on a couch. Yes, that's it, a couch.'

'And what are they doing?'

'The old man is holding the hand of the fair young maiden and kissing it.'

'Are you sure?'

Tom took lifted her hand to his lips and pressed it against them. 'Quite sure.' He lifted her other hand and performed a similar gesture.

'Is that all that's happening?'

'No. He wants to kiss her but he thinks she'll reject him because she is so young and fair and then he would have to throw himself off the castle walls.'

'Oh no!' Julia touched her lips against Tom's. 'He mustn't do that. She cares for him but she doesn't know how much he cares for her.' Julia snuggled up against Tom, her face resting on his shoulder. Tom bent down and kissed the top of her head, inhaling the mingled fragrance of perfume and hair conditioner which acted so powerfully on his senses. He held her face between his hands and looked at her directly in the eyes.

'Julia, it's not been an easy life. Maybe I've become a little cynical. It's certainly harder for me to open up emotionally than it was when I was twenty-one but I do love you, you know. I guess I haven't thought about you every day because what would be the point? I let you down, I knew how much I must have hurt you, I didn't know how I could apologise. I knew a wonderful woman like you wouldn't be alone for too long. And then it was too difficult to meet you again. But, boy, am I glad you came out here today!'

Julia was choked full of emotion. She had waited eighteen years to hear those words. So many times she had played that speech in her head, knowing that he did love her, that he did still care for her, that something was stopping him making that declaration of love. There had to be a reason she had been carrying the thought of Tom around in her head all these years. 'The very thought of you,' sang the husky voice of Al Bowlly to her once more.

As Tom kissed her, Julia lay back on the couch. Fortunately it was a large and comfortable one. It was a kiss that seemed to be an end in itself. It wasn't the perfunctory precursor of sex but an entire lovemaking experience that continued until she ran out of breath. Then it began again. She felt herself slipping ever surely but quite willingly into Tom's power, ceding to him the right to explore her as he felt the need. She ran her hands up and down the back of his still firmly muscled thighs.

'It's not too late,' whispered Tom. 'It's not too late for you to pull away and go back to your room. I won't pursue you and I won't pressure you. I just want you to know how much I want you.'

'I do know, darling Tom, I do know. And I want you too.'

'Do you want to come to my bedroom?'

'No, I want you to come to my bedroom.'

'Mine's bigger.'

'But mine's mine. I want to show you how much I want you. I want you to know I'm making the choice.'

'Like going back to your college room not mine?'

'Exactly.'

'You haven't changed.'

'I'm not nineteen any longer, Tom. I won't be the way you remember me.'

'But you are. You are exactly the way I remember you – shy and beautiful and clever and full of life and very proper like a proper English lady.'

They were at the door of the bedroom.

'Do you want to go in and do things?'

'What sort of things?'

'Whatever women do in this situation.'

'Usually they need a man to do it with.'

'Right. You're right.'

She opened the door and her hand searched for the bedside light switch. She found it. She sought Tom's hand and drew him slowly into the room. He caught her round the waist and began devouring her with kisses as his fingers sought the zip at the back of her dress. He drew it slowly down until it came to rest in the small of her back.

Tom helped the dress slither to the floor. His hands ran eagerly up and down her bare skin, hindered only by the strap of her bra and the panties which were perhaps not the ones she would have chosen had she been completely sure when she got out of bed in her San Francisco hotel that this would be her situation when she removed them. This was the moment of truth that she had long desired and dreaded with equal fervour. As much as she had wanted to feel Tom's arms around her once more, she had feared his judgement on her 38-year-old body.

'You're beautiful, Julia, just as beautiful as ever you were.'

She fell back against the bed and pulled him down onto her in a deep and grateful embrace. It didn't matter if he was lying through his teeth. They were the words she had wanted to hear. When they paused for breath he detached himself slowly from her and this time she watched as he began to lick gently the lobe of her ear, her neck, and her nipples which were clearly showing an interest in what was happening to her. She kissed the top of his head and breathed in deeply the indefinable aroma of his shampoo which was now mixed with the mingled smells of the restaurant. Her senses all felt sharp as if they were coming back to life again after many years of hibernation.

It was as if she had been locked up in a tower like a princess in a fairy tale for years and years so that she was covered in cobwebs. Now the man she had been dreaming about was ripping off the locks and chains, bursting through the door of her room and tearing away the cobwebs that had covered her to find that she was quite unchanged. Tom's enthusiasm for her might, she supposed, be attributed to what he claimed was the paucity of his own sex life so that he might find almost any woman attractive but she was so attuned to rejection, and so acutely sensitive to the slightest modulation in his speech that she doubted that this was the case. His enthusiasm for her body appeared to be entirely genuine.

The way Tom touched her felt unutterably wonderful. Her body was the same one that had lain next to her husband for seventeen years but it was responding in an entirely new way. It was as if her body was a violin and had been picked up by Yehudi Menuhin after years of being scraped by a teenager in a school orchestra.

Not even eighteen years ago did she remember it being like this with Tom. He must have been to a seminar or taken a course in it. Americans were always keen on self-improvement books. She thought Tom must have done more than read a few — he must have written one of them. Maybe he travelled America giving lectures on 'Women — how to touch them — a series of thirty-six lectures — with illustrations'. He began stroking the sensitive insides of her thighs. All the doors and windows to her soul which had been blacked out and sealed up were being flung open again and warm sunlight illuminated every crack just as Tom's tongue finally found her clitoris. He had been taking her on a guided tour of her own body and saved the best till last.

Now she was ready, now he had repaired the damage of nearly two decades. She couldn't be the woman taken in adultery because it was all too perfect for that. If Fate hadn't intended this, all those forks in the road she had been confronted with would not have led her inexorably to this place. When Tom entered her it wasn't just the ultimate connection with the lover she had been waiting for. It was a connection with some missing part of herself. She loved this man, she had always loved this man. Julia felt whole again.

CHAPTER FIFTEEN

THEY TALKED UNTIL THE DAWN broke. To Julia, Tom had always been the epitome of masculine certainty. She had supposed that it was one of the features she had always found so attractive about him. He seemed uniquely centred. He was a year older and an American living in a foreign country. Maybe that helped to produce the impression of maturity she found so appealing. Now she was learning that there was an entirely different side to Tom.

'I'd blame my folks, only it makes me sound like a wuss.'

'Blame them. That's what parents are for.'

'I mean I was a Rhodes Scholar, for God's sake.'

'Parents aren't like a dissertation.'

'Anyway, Candice turned out to be as intractable as my parents were. It was fine until they clashed. Then it was like the Iran-Iraq war.'

'And when they did clash, whose side did you take?'

Tom looked away and Julia knew the answer.

'I need to tell you about Candice.'

Candice had worked for a high-powered firm of international management consultants based in San Francisco. The hours were long enough to cause her to stay in town from Sunday night to Friday afternoon. It was entirely consistent with her long-term career goals that she also enjoyed the fact that she had married into the well-known Johnson Winery family. Much of the rapid growth in the wine country in the 1970s and 1980s had been driven by the desire of the wealthy elite of the business community to spend their final years making another fortune in a new and sexy field.

'To her the winery was like a weekend cottage.'

'That's OK, isn't it? For you it's work but for her it's like a vacation coming here. What's wrong with that?'

'She used to invite work colleagues and prospective business clients here all the time.'

'Well, I can understand that. It's a beautiful place.'

'But she showed no interest in the work we did here, I did here. She made me feel like the hired help.'

'Did you tell her about the history of the place like you talked to me?'

'Yes, but it made no difference. She didn't understand. She had no feeling for the land the way we have. It was like a stud farm or a ski lodge in Aspen to her.'

'She must have been impressed with the way your family built up the business, though. After all, she was a management consultant.'

'And presumably still is.'

Julia blushed. She shouldn't have made it sound as if Candice was dead but Tom raced on, seemingly oblivious to the deeper meaning of his correction.

'The winery's turnover is peanuts compared with the billions of dollars she deals with on a daily basis.'

'What about children?'

'I knew she didn't want any when we got married. She was quite upfront about that.'

'And you?'

'I wanted kids, sure.'

'So why did you marry her?'

'I loved her,' he said simply and Julia cursed herself for asking a question whose reply caused her so much pain. 'A young American career-orientated woman in nineteen ninety was bound to say she didn't want children. I figured as the biological clock started to tick on she'd change her mind.'

'What a typically male piece of reasoning.'

'Or she'd bang her head on the glass ceiling and figure bringing up kids was easier.'

'Tom, that is so arrogant!'

'But it's honest.'

'I suppose so,' said Julia grudgingly.

'Anyway, what the hell, it didn't work out. It's hardly front-page news, is it?'

'Did you talk about adoption?'

'She wasn't infertile, Julia. She just didn't want kids, however they came. I did. I couldn't envisage a future without them. I guess now I'll have to.'

At the back of her mind Julia recalled those odd comments he had made about the Italian family in the restaurant – how they had no right to bring little kids there. She wondered for a moment how Tom would have raised their children but he was already deep into his explanation of how his wishes for children were always thwarted by others.

'My folks certainly wanted us to have kids.'

'For grandchildren?'

'For legal beneficiaries.'

'What about your nieces, Ellen's kids?'

'Alice and Beverley have grown up in the East. They fly in for the family Thanksgiving every fall and sometimes they come out for a week in the summer but they always complain because there's nothing to do here.'

'Yes, but they're kids now. When they grow up . . .'

'I don't think they're going to miraculously develop a sudden urge to take over a winery from their uncle and spend the rest of their lives in Dry Creek Valley in Sonoma County worrying about grape yields.'

Julia could see how upset Tom was and rolled herself into a position in which she could put her arms round him. In response he snuggled down and laid his head across her breasts. She felt a stirring and saw that Tom did too.

'How was the sex between you?' she asked quietly, knowing she was setting out across a minefield but she was determined not to let her physical relationship with Tom fall into a black hole as it had recently with Mike. They had to talk about it. The more they talked about it, maybe the quicker the tension would ease.

'Candice approached sex like she approached her work and the prospect of kids.'

'Doesn't sound very nice.'

'I just mean there was a kind of fierce intellectual passion about her.'

'That doesn't sound too pleasant either.'

'Oh, but it was. I found it real stimulating.' Tom looked up at Julia who was lost in thoughts of their own times past. 'It was different, Julia. She was very different from you. She was different from all the girlfriends I'd ever had.'

'How different?'

'I always thought I was OK in the sack.'

'You were great. Still are.'

'Not great but certainly OK.'

'It was great with me.'

'Candice told me I was lousy.'

'And you liked that?'

'No one had ever said that to me before.'

'Maybe no one needed to say that to you before.'

'I liked her telling me I was lousy. Does that sound weird?'

'A bit.'

'It was kind of a turn-on, you know? I'd always gotten great reviews from the women in my life but Candice was something else again.'

'What did she do? Tie you up?'

'No. Nothing like that. She tore the clothes off me as if they were held together with Velcro.'

'Sounds expensive.'

'She took the initiative as if she were still issuing commands in the office.'

'You do office work too.'

'Yes, but I work at a much slower pace and a much lower level of intensity.'

'But she was only here at weekends, you said.'

'That's why I started travelling into the city at least twice a week.'

'Bad for business.'

'But great for the marriage. Or so I thought.'

'So what went wrong?'

'Things got a little over-excited.'

'You had a heart attack?'

'I had a mind attack. I started to wonder where Candice had developed her own fertile erotic imagination but she just smiled at me whenever I asked.'

'Were you jealous?'

'I thought what we were getting into was unhealthy.'

'How long did that take?'

'A couple of years after we got married I started to worry.'

'And it was just about sex?'

'The sex was part of it. But it was everything. Everything I'd found attractive about her started to worry me.'

'Like what?'

'Like the hours she worked, the fact that if I wanted to see her during the week I had to drive into San Francisco.'

'But you drove in willingly. You just said.'

'At first. But you know ... when the sex thing wears off ...'

'Sure.' Julia didn't want to stray too far down this path. Not yet anyway.

'She wasn't changing her mind about having babies, she showed no interest at all in what was happening in the winery. Some weekends she was too busy to come out at all and when she did she spent most of the time working or entertaining. So we started fighting.'

'Did you try therapy? Couples therapy?'

'We talked about it briefly. Neither of us was too enthusiastic.'

'I thought all Californians went to a therapist.'

'Well, if you want to know, I figured most of the problems came from her. I thought I'd already made all the compromises but she wanted to be the dominant one, in and out of bed, and I thought it should be more like a partnership of equals. I knew she wasn't going to change her behaviour, so what was the point?'

'So you just gave up on it?'

'No. We staggered on for years. When we left the area, went on holiday, to the Caribbean or Europe, it always improved. She stopped working, I stopped worrying about this place, the sex was exciting again ...'

'And children?'

Tom shook his head sorrowfully. 'She wouldn't move on that one.'

'Did you keep trying?'

'All the time. She just shut down whenever I raised the issue. When we were first married she would always call me when she got back to the apartment in the city. When it started to go belly up she stopped calling and coming out here.'

'You must have been lonely.'

'Well, no, I wasn't and that's when I realised we were in trouble. I started to like it when she wasn't here and we didn't talk. It meant no more fights.

And my folks were getting old and it was just easier for everyone if she wasn't around.'

Julia gently kissed the top of his head. 'When did your parents die?'

'My dad went first. He'd never really been the same since that first stroke in eighty-three. It just took ten years for it to kill him. He kept having strokes all the time. Each one left him weaker. In the end it was a relief when it happened.'

'And your mother?'

'She'd been the strong one. She had to be, for Dad. But when he went she just seemed to give up. She died nine months later.'

'Without seeing her grandchildren.'

'No, she saw Ellen's kids.'

'I mean yours.'

'Yes. I guess I felt resentful that Candice denied her that pleasure but it wasn't much of a reason for her to have kids if she didn't want them.'

'So you've been on your own ever since?'

'There's been the occasional interlude when I've had company.'

'Good reviews again?' Julia smiled.

'Strangely enough, after Candice, I didn't much care what they thought. So probably I got crap reviews.'

'Till tonight.'

'You're sweet. And beautiful.' He kissed her again. Slowly. Lovingly. Julia revelled in the warmth and tenderness. She couldn't help thinking that the perception of Tom's marriage she had held had been completely wrong. She could not believe how wrong she had been. The man she had imagined to be almost invulnerable was as flawed as anyone else and in as much pain as she was. She didn't know how it had happened but this new knowledge made him even more attractive. She pulled him towards her.

'I've never talked about myself like that to anyone,' said Tom, after he had made love to her for the second time.

'Don't give me that,' said Julia, running her hand softly through the matted hair on his chest. 'Americans discuss their feelings with the milkman.'

'We don't have milkmen in this state. We have grocery stores. And you really wouldn't want to discuss your marriage with some spotty college kid who can't work out how to scan the barcode, even in Berkeley.'

'I'm glad you told me. I feel very close to you.'

'I feel like we've never been apart.'

'What time is it?'

Tom looked round the room. 'I've never spent the night here. I don't know if there's a clock. Does it matter?'

Julia shook her head and kissed him.

'Now tell me about you.'

'I'm just a housewife.'

'You were never "just" anything.'

'What's to say? My life is equally full of shit.'

'Let's analyse this for a moment. Do you have a job?'

'You know I do.'

'Do you have a nice house?'

'Needs painting outside.'

'Not the question.'

'Well, it's not exactly up to your standard . . .'

He slipped his hand between her legs and tickled her. She squealed and thrashed around under the duvet as if to expel the intruder but in fact succeeded in trapping his hand precisely where she wanted to feel it without appearing to have sought it.

'OK, OK,' she admitted, 'it's a nice house.' His hand paused temporarily.

'And you are still married to the same guy after more than sixteen years?'

'I don't think this is the right time . . .'

His index finger continued its journey, trying to tickle her.

'Oh! All right, I'm not divorced, I'll grant you that.'

'Good job you're confessing. Otherwise I might have to punish you.' His finger worked its way further inside her.

'You wouldn't dare.'

'No? The marriage might have gone kaput but I learned a thing or two from Candice.'

'Am I going to find out what they might be?'

'Almost inevitable, I'm afraid.'

'Ooh! Sounds exciting!'

'So you have a good job, a nice house and a marriage that's lasted nearly seventeen years.' His finger continued its exploration.

'I'm going to say anything you want if you continue to do that.'

'And your children?'

'Tom, I don't . . .'

He pushed his finger in her firmly.

'No!' Her tone of voice changed completely. Tom recognised the shift and withdrew his finger rapidly.

'I'm sorry. I was only playing . . .'

'It's not that. I can't talk about the children.'

'Why? You've got one who's going to be the new Tiger Woods. And what about the others?'

Julia didn't reply. Instead, she turned her head on the pillow and looked away. Tom had never seen a woman change so rapidly from sexual excitement to the depths of despair. Obviously he had made some terrible faux pas, but he didn't know what it might be. Was one of them handicapped in some way? He couldn't leave it like this.

'I'm sorry, Julia. I can see I've upset you. But I don't know what I've said to make this happen.'

Without turning her body to him, Julia stretched out her hand, seeking his. He gave it to her willingly. 'I find it difficult to talk about.'

'Then don't.'

'But I want to. You're the one person in the world I want to talk to about her.'

'Her?'

'Emily.'

Tom didn't say anything. He had broached the subject, now it was up to Julia. He knew instinctively that the less he said now, the better. It was up to her to do the talking. The best thing he could possibly do was to listen. He gave her hand an encouraging squeeze.

'She died. Eight months ago.'

He stayed silent, now too shocked to speak, and waited for her to find the words.

'And I wasn't there.' Julia paused. 'We were in Italy. We were sharing a house in Ravello with some friends.'

She stopped again. The memory was so painful, it was like some kind of internal blockage. Tom had been to Ravello with Candice who had been sent to Rome to meet representatives of Alitalia. One balmy starlit evening they had travelled down the coast to hear a wonderful concert in the grounds of the romantic Villa Rufolo. He continued to wait.

'We just wanted to see Capri.'

Her body was wracked by silent sobbing. He tried to cuddle her by shifting his body as best he could over to her.

'It happened so fast. When we got back she was dead.'

The tears were pouring from her, cascading down her cheeks onto the pillow. He felt wretched for her. Whatever miseries he had suffered in his life were meaningless beside this.

'How?' he asked softly.

'She drowned. She got cramp. Nobody saw her.'

'Oh God, Julia, I . . .' Words failed him. What could he possibly say now? How did you even get up in the morning knowing your child was dead? He couldn't conceive of such an emotion.

'Oh, Tom, I miss her, I miss her so much.'

'I'm so sorry, Julia.' It was paltry and inadequate but what could he do?

'She was going to be the musician, you see. I was going to give her all the support I never got. The Suzuki violin, piano lessons, the flute. I played her Mozart and Gershwin when I was pregnant. She was the baby I always wanted – the baby I wanted with you.'

He kissed her and tried to lighten the conversation. 'I'd probably have made a rotten father.'

'But you said you wanted kids.'

'I do – did – in the abstract. I don't know about the twenty-four-hour care and attention they all seem to need. That's what Candice was always warning me about.'

'You'd have liked my children.'

'Sure I would. I'd love anything that was part of you.'

'Anyway, you've got plenty of time. Men can go on having children till they're seventy.'

'I don't see how you can push a pram if you need to keep both hands on your Zimmer frame.'

'What kind of kids would we have had?'

'A butch lesbian performance artist and a gay accordion player.'

'Tom!'

'What are you? Anti-gay?'

'I was thinking of a beautiful chanteuse, singing in smoky nightclubs . . .'

'Sorry, against California state law. No smoking in any public place.'

'I suppose you'd want a million-dollar baseball player.'

'Only a million? Listen, these guys earn ten million a year. A million a year – don't insult our child.'

'Our child. Wouldn't that have been great?'

'We've got each other. After all these years, we've found each other again. Let's just be happy for that.'

'We won't ever be apart again, will we?'

'I love you, Julia.'

They were the last words she heard before she drifted gratefully into a deep slumber with Tom's arms wrapped protectively around her.

CHAPTER SIXTEEN

FOR THREE DAYS THEY NEVER left each other's side. The romance they had found in Oxford was only a distant relation of their feelings for each other now. The whips and scorns of time had matured them to an extent that they no longer sought the uncomplicated first love of their remembered youth but the solace of instinctive understanding. To them that was love.

Between the talking, remembering and a great deal of singing there were silences so delicate, so delicious that Julia thought her heart would burst. How different these silences were to the ones she knew with Mike when they had simply run out of things to say to each other.

All her senses were now fully functional again. It was as if she had been carrying two large bags of shopping around with her. Every time they had an argument Mike would put another large packet of frozen vegetables in the bag and she would continue on her way, resentfully staggering under the load. It was as if they were playing some demented television game show that was destined never to end. Tom had simply relieved her of the grocery bags and dumped the contents in the dustbin. She was free.

It wasn't that she didn't think about Mike and Jamie. She eventually talked about them to Tom, just as he talked about Candice and his parents. He was a product if not a prisoner of them just as much as Julia knew that her husband and son were a constant fact of her life and were not going to disappear just because she had found Tom again.

Most of all though, and it both surprised and pleased her that she didn't find it humiliatingly superficial, she loved touching Tom and the way he touched her. Sometimes it was sexual, sometimes it was not. It always felt right and she revelled in the feel of his hands on her hands, of his skin on her skin, of his face on her face. She liked the certainty with which his hand found hers as they walked along, no longer young lovers, considering they now had a combined age of eighty, but unashamed at the public demonstration. Julia was consciously relieved, however, that this was taking place as they were exploring Napa and Sonoma Counties together. She doubted if she would have had the courage to stroll hand in hand with Tom into Marks and Spencer in St Albans town centre.

Far from diminishing his reputation as a man, Tom's confessions of his increasingly dysfunctional sexual relationship with Candice seemed to enhance his appeal in Julia's eyes. It made them more equal and she felt comfortable in squeezing Tom's buttock cheeks through his black Calvin Klein jeans. She couldn't imagine doing the same to Mike on their walk through Verulam Park and she noticeably didn't do it when they were walking along the crowded streets of San Francisco, but when they were relatively alone she loved the freedom she now felt she had to touch Tom whenever and wherever she wanted, knowing that in so doing she was giving pleasure to them both.

Tom was predictably a thorough and knowledgeable guide to northern California. He showed her a side of San Francisco she never knew existed – a hundred elderly Asians performing their ritual early morning t'ai chi in Washington Square, followed by an amazing breakfast in the Buena Vista Cafe on Hyde Street on the Northern Waterfront and then the view across the bay from Coit Tower with its extraordinary murals.

They drove back across the Golden Gate Bridge into Marin County but this time turned left towards the delightful small towns of San Anselmo and Mill Valley, suburbs which wore their wealth lightly. They strolled along the streets casually window shopping until Tom pulled her abruptly into Chadwicks of London, a high-class lingerie store.

'Why are you bringing me in here?' whispered Julia, slightly intimidated by being with a man in such a determinedly female atmosphere.

'I want to buy you something. Anything. Then I want you to model it for me.'

'And where will the catwalk be?'

'My bedroom.'

'I see.' Julia looked at the range of bras, panties, slips, teddies and nightdresses in a variety of light pastel shades and delicate fabrics. 'Why here?' she whispered, noting with alarm some of the prices.

'Because it's the best.'

'How many girls have you brought here?' she asked suspiciously.

'Candice came here all the time and she had great taste. Chadwicks of London dominated every Visa bill of hers I ever saw. Besides, they're English and so are you.'

'Not necessarily. They could be American. Maybe they think being English is classy out here.'

Tom strode towards a short, thickset man with thinning hair who was bent over a desk at the rear of the store examining invoices.

'Sir, may I ask you a question? Are you Chadwicks of London?'

The man looked up, a little bemused. 'This is Chadwicks of London.'

'No. I mean are you British?'

'Of course.'

'And are you from London?'

'My wife and I are from a little town just outside London.'

'Yeah? That's great. So is my friend. Julia, c'mere!'

With reluctance Julia dragged herself away from the white lace knickers she was examining with interest.

'This is . . . Mr Chadwick, right?'

'Right.'

'Julia lives just outside London. Where exactly?'

'St Albans.'

'Mr Chadwick is from the same place.'

'St Albans?' Julia panicked. How could Tom have been so foolhardy? Mr Chadwick looked rather embarrassed.

'Manchester actually.'

Julia looked relieved.

'We came here about fifteen years ago. We thought Chadwicks of London sounded more appealing than Chadwicks of Manchester.'

'Doesn't Manchester have all that great music and a great soccer team?'

'Yes it does. It has two great soccer teams, to be accurate. But we thought that as far as Mill Valley is concerned, our customers would respond better to London.'

'And have you really been established since eighteen ninety-three the way it says on your sign outside?'

'Sure. At least that was when my grandfather started in the business.'

'That's an incredible coincidence. My great-grandfather started our winery business in eighteen ninety-three. We have a place north of Healdsburg.'

'Yes? We're just about to open another store in Healdsburg.'

'You must come out and visit.'

'We'd love to.'

'So tell me about your grandfather.'

'He came from Russia to England and he worked in a branch of the clothing industry with the rest of his family. They called him a Nochschlepper. But we thought Chadwicks of London sounded better than Nochschleppers of Manchester.'

In the end Julia chose the white lace panties and their sister in powder blue and canary yellow, along with a white silk nightgown with a tiny pink bow on the front which felt sensuous against her skin.

'This won't get you into trouble, will it?' asked Tom after he had watched Mr Chadwick running his gold card through the machine.

'How so?'

'Well, will Mike notice you've suddenly acquired a dazzling new lingerie collection?'

'Mike has no interest in my underwear and even less in what's in my underwear drawer.'

'He's a jerk,' said Tom dismissively.

Julia said nothing. She was assailed by a surprising prick of loyalty. If Mike was a jerk, and he was sometimes, it was her right to be contemptuous of him, not Tom's. He was her husband and Tom had never even met him. Plus why did he think she had married him in the first place?

They left and went back to the car.

'Is the weather always fine and warm like this?'

'No. We're lucky. Can be quite cold this time of the year.' Tom pressed a button and the top of the convertible parted company with its metallic hold and slowly whirred into place, bunched up above the back seat.

They headed back towards Shoreline Highway, the famous coastal route. The warm breeze fanned their faces.

'This feels heavenly. Like a summer's day in England.'

'Don't give me that crap. I know your English summers, remember?'

'What's wrong with them?'

'The rain and the cold mostly.'

'Not in the summer!'

'May I remind you of our attempts to watch McEnroe at Wimbledon during your so-called summer?'

'Why do Americans always say Wimpoleton?'

'Excuse me?'

'Everyone says it out here. Wimpoleton.'

'What are you talking about? Wimbledon's Wimbledon.'

'Not the way you say it.'

'You're crazy. How do I say it again?'

'You say it like all the Americans say it. Wimpoleton.'

'Are you through here?'

'Yes.'

'Good, because I'm going to pull the car off the highway at the next exit and kiss you.'

'I don't suppose I have the right to refuse you, do I?'

'That depends.'

'On what?'

'On whether you wish to exercise that right.'

'Of course not.'

'In that case you have it.'

That particular quasi-sexual interlude was short-lived. Hardly had Tom's left hand begun to explore the contours of Julia's right breast than they were both startled by a knocking on the window. A California highway patrolman in regulation dark glasses was standing by Julia's door. She frantically pushed the button to lower the window without realising that Tom had turned off the electricity supply with the ignition. So she opened the door to allow the policeman freedom to talk to them and succeeded in catching him a sharp blow on the knee.

They were duly chastised and drove away like naughty teenagers caught necking in Lovers Lane. Their embarrassed silence lasted a full thirty seconds before they both burst out laughing.

'You think he's going to call my mother?'

'I'm older than he is. When did I get to be older than the cops?'

'I'm going to be grounded, you know. I'll have to knot the sheets together to climb out of the bedroom window.'

'I'm not sure you can do that with fitted sheets.'

The scenery north of the city was not as magnificent as Route 1 heading south through Big Sur but it was impressive to Julia nonetheless.

'I take all this stuff for granted,' Tom apologised.

Julia's eyes swept across the seascape. 'How could you? It's glorious.'

'I still find Oxford glorious. The Cotswolds and Blenheim Palace . . .'

'God, you sound just like an American tourist.'

'And you sound just like a British tourist.'

'Touché.' Julia laughed her apology and squeezed his arm harder than she meant, causing Tom to swerve to avoid the oncoming traffic.

'Hey! What's that all about?'

'Sorry. It was a gentle squeeze of affection. There was nothing remotely admonitory.'

'Admonitory. Christ, I never hear words like admonitory in the wine trade.'

'Don't hear much of words like that in the Easy Listening department either.'

'I guess it's because it doesn't rhyme too well.'

'Admonitory. Hmm. How about promontory?'

'Not bad but when would you ever use promontory in a romantic verse?'

'Bet Larry Hart could.'

'Larry Hart also wrote "Blue Moon".'

'Genius.'

'Incomparable.'

Route 1 turned to go inland for twenty miles and only rediscovered the coastline in Bodega Bay.

'It's creepy round here,' said Julia, puzzled. 'The atmosphere's so different to what it was in Marin County.'

'You don't recognise it then?'

'Have I been here before?'

'A little art-house movie theater just outside Oxford?'

'The Moulin Rouge in Headington?'

'That's the one.'

'What's that got to do with where we are?'

'What did we see there on our first anniversary?'

'Wasn't there some kind of season going on? Truffaut, was it?'

'Close but no cigar.'

'Hitchcock? That's right, it was a Hitchcock.'

'Which one?'

'Oh heavens, you can't possibly expect me to remember that. It was a long time ago.'

'I can remember,' said Tom simply, a little hurt by her casual dismissal of what was for him still such a vivid memory.

'*The Birds!*' said Julia suddenly. 'That's what we saw. I was terrified.'

'I remember. You were too shaken to have sex with me.'

'You were very sweet and comforting.'

'There wasn't much choice.'

'I still don't get . . . Here? This is where it happened?'

'Rod Taylor and Tippi Hendren and a million crows in Bodega Bay.'

'Crikey,' said Julia, twisting in her seat as if straining to catch a glimpse of Taylor and Hendren as they walked to their trailers. 'And what's that?' she asked pointing to a lush piece of land jutting out into the ocean.

'That's the Marine Biology site – it's part of the University of California.'

'No, not the building, the land.'

'That's just Bodega Head.'

'No it's not. It's a promontory!' Julia declared ecstatically.

The discovery of the promontory seemed to act like the missing piece of a jigsaw. Somehow it washed away any doubts Julia might have had about what she was doing. It was perverse logic but it was intuitive and in a typically Julia sort of way it was the more convincing for being such a specious piece of reasoning. Tom caught her mood exactly. He stopped the car and kissed her.

'Is the policeman following us?'

Tom checked the rear-view mirror. 'All clear.' He kissed her again.

'I can feel the sea luring me towards its treacherous depths.'

'We call it the ocean, honey. The sea is what you have in England. We're big boys out here. That's why we have oceans.'

'I'm going to paddle in it.'

'Julia!'

But she had already opened the door and was running away from the car. 'Look! Seals!' she shouted, seemingly as excited as a child by the sight of the indolent creatures sunning themselves on the rocks. She picked her way down to the shore and stooped to slip off her shoes then ran across the sand towards the seals.

'Jesus!' said Tom, unsure whether to follow her or not.

'Come on!' shouted Julia.

Tom took off his shoes and socks, tossed them in the car and followed suit. 'Aaaaagh!' he yelped as his bare feet came into contact with small sharp stones.

'Look at them,' whispered Julia in amazement. 'They're so tame!'

'Hollywood seals. They're probably on vacation, just swum up the coast from Malibu.'

'Cynic!'

'Naif! Honestly, Julia, these are C-list celebrity seals, probably paid for by the California State Tourist Authority.'

'How can you tell?'

'Because they're just lying there waiting for you take a photograph.'

'I wish I had my camera,' said Julia as she inched her way nearer the mother seal.

'I wouldn't get too close.'

'They're harmless. They don't attack people.'

'They've got big teeth.'

'How do you know?'

'I saw a Disney documentary on them.'

Julia laughed. 'For a farmer you don't know too much about animals, do you?'

'I'm not that kind of farmer. Anyway, aren't they mammals? Besides, the only thing to do with things that live in the sea is put them in a pot and boil them.'

'Tom!'

'And serve with a chilled Chablis or Sancerre.'

The mother seal clearly took offence at this for she rose grandly to her full height, honked at Tom, waved her flippers at her children and the whole family waddled across the beach and flopped lazily into the water.

'Do you think I upset them?'

'With your talk of boiling them in a pot and serving them with a dry white wine?'

'They couldn't understand what I was saying, could they?'

'Well, possibly. They're very intelligent creatures, seals.'

'That's dolphins.'

'I'm sure they're related.'

'Should I apologise, do you think?'

'If you don't want your vineyard to be attacked by vast armies of angry sea urchins.'

'How are they going to get from the beach fifty miles inland to the winery?'

'Like me, I suppose.'

'In a rental car?'

'Exactly.'

'OK, I'll apologise.'

'Well, you can't do it from here.'

'Will you come with me?'

'Sure.'

Hand in hand they ran across the deserted beach and waded out into the ocean until the water came up to their waists.

'I'm very sorry, seals,' bellowed Tom. 'It was a joke. I didn't mean to hurt your feelings.'

From the depths of the Pacific Ocean came the sound of a chorus of honking seals.

'Does that mean they've forgiven me?'

Julia nodded, smiling. 'Your vineyard is safe.'

Oblivious to the fact that they were still standing waist deep in water, they started to kiss. The kiss became more passionate as the urgency they each felt transmitted itself to the other. Julia broke off.

'I need air.' She gulped a large breath.

'Ready?' asked the eager Tom.

Julia nodded and kissed him again.

Deeply entwined with each other as they were they couldn't see the large wave that was gathering menacingly twenty yards away. Even if they had, it was unlikely they would have been able to do much about it but inflamed with passion as they were, the wave gave literal meaning to the expression swept off their feet.

Julia went first as the cold wave smacked her fiercely on the back of the head, knocking her forward into Tom who had no chance of releasing her as the combination of the wave's force and Julia's body momentum caused his feet to leave the sand and both their bodies to splash about in the water, gasping for breath and spitting out salt water.

'Oh my God! Are you all right?' asked Tom, worried, as he regained his feet and hauled Julia to hers.

Julia couldn't speak for laughing although Tom's earnest solicitation interpreted it initially as a struggle for air. Julia clung to Tom as she gradually regained her composure.

'I'm fine. Just fine.'

'Jesus, I was worried for a moment there.'

'Really, Tom? Why? I mean we're standing in three feet of water here.'

'Because I love you,' he said simply.

CHAPTER SEVENTEEN

AFTER THE EXCITEMENT OF TUESDAY'S impromptu party, nothing else of significance happened till late on the Friday afternoon. It was the last week of the Easter holidays and because they had known for some time that Julia would be out of the country, Jamie had persuaded his father to allow him to enter the qualifying event for the England Amateur Open Championships that would take place later in the summer. It would be great experience and he'd be bound to miss the cut for the last two rounds which took place after the second round on the Friday evening. That meant that he'd be home for the weekend before starting school again on the Tuesday morning. Jamie also promised faithfully to have completed all his revision for his GCSE exams before the tournament began, and to help his father repair all the damage caused by Tuesday night's fiasco.

The reappearance of Ira the budgie, discovered on the patio when Jamie woke up on Wednesday morning, seemed to them both to be a harbinger of better times ahead. Jamie was clearly motivated to give the tournament his best shot.

Mike didn't need much persuading because his mind had already been wandering down that fairway. Since Julia was going to be away he didn't need to obtain her approval which was a major relief and it was about time Jamie tested himself against the cream of England's amateur game. His only reservation was that Jamie was unlikely to play as badly as he was predicting and since he feared that Julia might decide to fly home that weekend there was a chance that they would be on the famous golf course in Lytham St Anne's when he should have been at Heathrow Airport.

On the Thursday night there seemed little chance that there would be a conflict of interest. Jamie had had one of those days when he hadn't been able to sink a putt longer than two feet. On half a dozen greens he had three putted, and since he had driven wildly off the tee on maybe another six holes, only some sterling recovery shots had kept his score down to a reasonable five over par. Already, however, he was eight strokes behind the leader and if he dropped another two shots or the leaders sprinted away they would be heading back down the M6 a very miserable pair indeed. The lowering grey skies, the swirling drizzle, the enveloping mist and the biting wind which whipped up off the Irish Sea all conspired to mirror their mood.

They spent the night in a small guesthouse just off the sea front. Jamie was moody and withdrawn, unable to explain to himself, let alone to his father, why he had played so poorly. Mike decided it was time for the relationship to shift to another footing. Instead of sitting in the bedroom watching the twelve-inch television set balanced precariously on the small chest of drawers, Mike took Jamie from a Chinese restaurant to the Rose and Crown where he ordered a pint of bitter for himself and left the decision to Jamie as to what he would order. He settled for a half of lager. They took their glasses to a corner table and watched two old men playing darts.

It was Jamie who broke the silence.

'Sorry, Dad.'

'What are you sorry for?'

'Playing like a spas.'

'I don't like that language.'

'Playing like a twerp.'

'You think Tiger Woods has never three putted? You think Sergio Garcia's never driven into the rough?'

'I've blown it.'

'You haven't blown anything.'

'I'm eight strokes behind!'

'So you shoot birdie on the first hole tomorrow, Greenhough and Tattersall both take bogey, suddenly you're only six shots behind and you've got the momentum.'

'What if it's the other way round?'

'It will be if that's the way you're thinking.'

'Sorry.'

'Never mind sorry. What's the most important distance in golf?'

Jamie smiled. His dad had been saying this to him since he was three years old or at least for as long as he could remember.

'From ear to ear,' he parroted, drawing an imaginary line from one ear up and across his head and down to the other ear.

'And don't you forget it. Now drink up. You can still get a good night's sleep. You'll need all your energy tomorrow.'

When Mike pulled back the curtains the following day and looked out, he was dazzled by the bright sun which shone out of a blue sky decorated with cotton-wool clouds like a coloured illustration in a children's book. Jamie seemed to have taken heart either from the chat and the half-pint of lager or from the lightening of the climatic conditions.

The first hole was a par four with a series of deep bunkers guarding the entrance to the green. The previous day Jamie had plugged the ball into the extreme left-hand bunker. Today the ball floated high above them, pitched within twelve feet of the hole and spun back to stop six feet short. The putt dropped into the hole with a comforting rattle and it was the perfect start. They looked up at the scoreboard. Greenhough and Tattersall had both begun badly. Jamie was only six strokes behind them. He was on his way.

It wasn't a course record as Mike had fondly imagined. For a start, too many outstanding golfers had played the famous old course but Jamie finished with a highly impressive round of 66, six under par, one under for the tournament, and only three strokes behind the leaders. That meant Jamie had qualified to play the final two rounds, creating the slight problem of how they would explain their whereabouts to Julia if she chose to come home over the weekend.

With some trepidation Mike rang the answering machine at home to hear Julia's buoyant voice announcing that she would be catching the Sunday night flight from San Francisco, arriving at Heathrow Airport, Terminal 3, at midday on the Monday. Mike was relieved. Jamie could concentrate on his game without fear of incurring his mother's displeasure and he could concentrate on Jamie without the aggravation that he had learned to expect from Julia.

The weekend was different again from the atmosphere that had permeated the first two days. There had been a great deal of widespread nervousness at first but it pretty soon disappeared as the players struggled in the difficult weather. On the Friday much of the competitive flavour left the competition as those who were going to make the cut easily and those who were never going to make the cut at all played just for the enjoyment.

On the Saturday morning as Mike and Jamie drove in through the main gates, they were astonished to see a large crowd making its way down the first fairway as the leading pair teed off. Ordinary people had actually come to watch this competition as opposed to the motley group of long-suffering parents who were usually the only audience. Mike felt his heart leap. At last a real competition. Now he'd see what Jamie was made of. He cast a sideways look at his son. There was no visible response. As usual Jamie maintained that imperturbable phlegmatic outward appearance.

It would be lunchtime before Jamie started because he was in one of the last pairings. That gave him plenty of time to get changed, go to the driving range, then onto the putting green before eating two bananas, an orange and a high-glucose drink which Mike's researches had determined was the best possible food before a round of golf. Jamie added of his own volition a king-size

Mars Bar which he surreptitiously bought from the vending machine in the pro shop when his father thought he had gone to the toilet.

The first shot always told Mike what sort of mood Jamie was in. The first shot in front of the clubhouse with strangers idly standing around and watching is usually all the pressure that is needed to make most normal golf club members feel physically sick, wind up for a huge drive and smash the ball fifty yards off to the left into a thicket of gorse bushes. What follows is invariably four hours of torment interspersed with some inventive swear words.

But Jamie wasn't a normal golf club member and as the starter called his name to a smattering of polite applause from the twenty or so people who had gathered around the first tee, Mike could see that his eyes were completely focused. Mike was temporarily in awe of his son. Jamie looked as though he had done this sort of thing every day of his life.

And that was how he played. Mike could see that he hadn't teed the ball up very high, the usual sign of a nervous golfer who didn't care about the yardage and just wanted to avoid the embarrassment of a rotten shot off the tee, or, calamity of calamities, an air shot in which the club swung frantically at the ball and failed to make any contact at all. Jamie's swing was as smooth as normal, the metal wood made good contact, with a satisfying ping, and the small white ball sped two hundred yards into the air, landed in the middle of the fairway and bounced on for another fifty yards. Mike's heart soared.

It wasn't a spectacular round, unlike the previous day's major surge, but it was solid enough – a 70 compared to the previous day's epic 66. It was the round of a professional, someone who wasn't fluctuating wildly between great shots and terrible shots but the round of a young man who was quite certain of which club to use and which shot to play. As Mike had always suspected, his son was a champion in the making.

Jamie's certain progress put the wind up both Tattersall and Greenhough who were making mistakes under the pressure Jamie was exerting on them. At the end of the day Jamie was tied for the lead with a total of 212 shots since Thursday morning. He came off the last green, having just sunk a vital eight footer, with a grin as wide as the English Channel. Mike couldn't help wondering what his face would look like in twenty-four hours' time.

Before they changed their shoes and drove off for an early dinner they both looked at Johnny Watkinson, the young man who had shot a 65 to finish level with Jamie. They would be going out as the last pair on Sunday afternoon. Watkinson was a student, in his last year at St Andrew's University, perhaps not exactly coincidentally chosen since the Old Course in that Scottish east coast town was known the world over as the home of golf. Watkinson was apparently dead set on turning professional as soon as he could. When Mike and Jamie caught up with him he was busy chatting to three young girls. Clearly, he had decided to make an early withdrawal from his superstar account.

Mike thought a Chinese restaurant and a good night's sleep would be the best combination for what he presumed must be Jamie's fluttering nerves. The boy didn't look particularly nervous and Mike was unwilling to broach the issue for fear of inculcating nerves that did not exist.

They were waiting for the Peking duck to arrive when a man in his twenties came over to their table. Mike thought he looked vaguely familiar.

'Mr Ramsey?'

Mike nodded. The man set a business card down on the table.

'My name's Tim Lloyd. I'm a sports reporter for the *Lancashire Evening Post* and I also contribute the occasional piece to Red Rose Radio. I saw this young man's closing holes tonight.'

'I thought I recognised you from somewhere.'

'May I sit down?'

Tim told them how impressed he had been by Jamie's performance and was keen to write an article about him.

'If he wins tomorrow, you mean?' asked Mike sceptically.

'No. I just think your son's got it. You could be the new Tiger Woods,' he said, looking directly into Jamie's eyes. The boy felt uncomfortable and averted his gaze.

'I just want to be the old Jamie Ramsey.'

'You know what I mean.'

Mike knew what he meant. At last he was getting proof that his dreams for Jamie were being given some credence by the opinions of others, outside his corner of Hertfordshire.

'Have you seen Watkinson play?' he asked.

'He was at Birkdale a couple of years ago.'

'How did he get on?'

'Similar position at the end of the third round but he blew it on the back nine. Couldn't take the pressure. I think he finished fifth or sixth. You can take him, Jamie.'

'He's a few years older than me.'

'But he hasn't got your temperament. That's what'll win it for you. If you can get to the fifteenth with the scores level you'll blow him out of the water.'

It was exactly what they both wanted to hear. Tim took his pocket tape recorder out, pressed the red button and set it on the table between Mike and Jamie. The son looked at the father in a silent question as Tim started the interview. Mike nodded back.

'So, Jamie Ramsey, fifteen-year-old superstar in the making, how long have you been playing golf . . .'

If it ever went out on the radio, thought Mike, the interview wouldn't have people tuning in from all over the north-west. Jamie was stilted and self-conscious, barely managing more than a monosyllabic response to anything that Tim asked. He wasn't being deliberately uncooperative but it was his first experience of the media spotlight and he didn't much care for it. For Mike, it was a staging post. If Jamie was this hot at fifteen, what would he be like as an eighteen-year-old with a few titles under his belt? That is, if he and Tim Lloyd were right.

*   *   *

On the Sunday afternoon the weather turned back to what it had been like on the Thursday. The wind blew in raging gusts and seemingly never from the same direction for more than ten seconds at a time. It would have played havoc with a field of hard-bitten old pros but it devastated the young amateurs.

Watkinson had the skill to counter the conditions, Jamie the temperament. Watkinson dropped a shot at the second with a wild swing off the tee but regained it at the fifth when he chipped in from a greenside bunker. Jamie made a steady par at both holes. None of the others in the field had made any headway on the leading pair so by the time they came to the last four holes it was apparent to everyone that the title was going to whichever one held his nerve the longer.

One of Watkinson's girlfriends was certainly making her presence felt. She was wearing an anorak over a mini skirt in an attempt to cheer on her hero and avoid the worst ravages of the wind. By the middle of the afternoon her knees were roughly the same colour as the dark red anorak covering her dyed blonde hair. Her shouts of encouragement were helping neither golfer and after the ninth hole when Watkinson three putted she was firmly told to keep her opinions to herself. After the tenth hole finished all square, she ostentatiously crossed the green, running as elegantly as she could in the tight skirt, back towards the clubhouse but whether it was the drizzle or tears that were besmirching her face it was hard to tell.

The two contenders were still level when they came to the fifteenth. Tim Lloyd's words were ringing in Jamie's ears as he drove off the elevated fifteenth tee. If he could just keep it steady over the last four holes . . . Allowing his concentration to slip like this was just sufficient to cause him to slice his shot and the ball clipped one of the oak trees that lined the right-hand side of the fairway.

When they found the ball it was lying so close to the tree that he had no room to play a proper shot. All Jamie could do was to chip it sideways twenty feet out of the forest of trees and back onto the fairway. It meant he could manage nothing better than a five. An exultant Watkinson took the regulation four strokes and he went to the sixteenth one ahead of Jamie but then played that hole so badly that he did almost exactly what Jamie had done on the fifteenth. That meant they were all square and there were now just two holes left.

Watkinson started to panic. Jamie bisected the fairway with his drive but Watkinson, in a desperate attempt to regain the lead, decided he could out-hit Jamie. Unfortunately for him, although the ball travelled past Jamie's, it also went twenty yards further left than he had intended and found a sand trap that had been placed there for that exact situation. The ball was lying cleanly on top of the sand but it still finished twenty yards short of the green after his approach shot.

Jamie, on the other hand, found the green safely enough but it was a large one and he had left himself nearly thirty feet for a birdie. Watkinson's third shot was a chip straight for the flag but it rolled agonisingly six inches past on the left and caught the slight downslope at the back of the green, coming to rest on the apron ten feet beyond the hole.

'What d'you think, Dad?'

'What do you?'

'Left to right slope. I'm aiming for the left of the cup.'

Mike just nodded. It didn't matter what Jamie said. The important thing was for him to work it out for himself and not be deflected by his father's opinion, which wasn't necessarily right anyway. 'Just get comfortable and don't putt till you're ready.'

Jamie stood over the ball for an age. Mike knew the demons must be playing havoc with the inside of his head but if ever there was a time for the boy to come good . . . From the moment the ball left the putter, there was only one place it was going to finish. As the ball disappeared from view, the freezing, windswept spectators roared their approval. Jamie felt as if he'd won the Open. Mike was just about holding himself together. What he wanted to do was run to his son and kiss him. What he had to do was to stay very calm and wait politely for Watkinson to putt.

If Watkinson sank the putt, Jamie would have only a one-stroke advantage, but if he missed . . . The ball rattled into the hole before Mike could work out the ramifications. From somewhere Watkinson had found nerves of steel. As they walked to the eighteenth and final hole of the championship, Jamie was in the lead by one stroke.

'Just think par,' said Mike to Jamie as he wiped the putter before replacing it in the bag. 'If you take a four you'll make the bugger shoot a birdie to force a play-off. He's not going to make an eagle. You just can't lose.'

Mike's heart swelled fit to burst as he watched his son drive off the last. This was the moment he'd been waiting for. 'The mate that fate had me created for,' he sang to himself as he remembered one of Julia's Frank Sinatra CDs. Why couldn't he get them out of his head? As the winner of the previous hole, it was still Jamie's honour to drive first. The boy was coming good just when it mattered, as Mike had always hoped and prayed. There was no way Jamie was going to lose it now.

This thought had dominated Mike's thinking from the moment the ball left Jamie's putter on the seventeenth green to the moment it flew off his driver on the eighteenth fairway and into the thick rough down the right-hand side. Watkinson couldn't repress a brief smile as he watched his young opponent wilt at the last. It had been a tough contest but the kid was still a kid and finally his nerve had broken.

On the advice of his caddie, Watkinson exchanged his driver for a two iron. He was playing safe, smart golf – ironically, the very opposite of what Tim Lloyd had predicted. He cracked his drive two hundred and twenty yards down the fairway, slightly left but the green was well in his range for his second shot. He picked up his tee and marched after it, the applause of the crowd ringing in his ears.

Jamie betrayed no emotion but deep inside he was fighting back the tears. As he walked alongside his father he saw Tim Lloyd making a fist and urging him on. He looked at his dad.

'OK?' asked Mike, feeling instinctively that what Jamie needed was as few words as possible.

'Sorry.'

'No sorries. Not now or ever. Just do your best.'

His best, however, was an uncontrolled hack out of the undergrowth. The ball rose into the air but, almost as if an unseen hand had punched it, the ball started to swerve to the left, entered a thick coppice twenty yards short of the green and disappeared. With it went Jamie's last chance, felt Mike, who was quickly getting his head around the certainty of defeat and the best way to pick up his son from what would be a desperately disappointing collapse after having victory in sight.

Watkinson could barely stop himself from whistling. He lined up his approach shot and hit it well enough if not perfectly. It landed on the green, made soft by the incessant drizzle, about twelve feet short and died on impact. He had a good chance of holing the putt from there even though it would be downhill and harder to control. A par was probably all he needed. It was doubtful if Jamie even had a shot at the green.

He didn't. To his horror his ball had come to rest at the base of the trunk of a huge oak tree. It was trapped between two exposed roots and so close to the tree that he couldn't get a swing at it even though he could see the flag a tantalising twenty-five yards away through the trees. Mike's heart sank. Jamie might need three or four shots to get out of this. He might not even finish second.

Jamie looked at it very calmly and then asked for his two iron, a straight club with minimal loft. It made sense to use it if he was just trying to keep the ball low, below the height of the overhanging branches, but Jamie couldn't even get a swing at this one. Mike handed it to him silently. Jamie stood next to the ball, confirming his fears that he couldn't swing the club in his natural right-handed stance. He turned round and stood closer to the tree and addressed the ball left-handed.

Mike knew instantly what he was going to do. He'd be hitting it with the back of the straight iron but at least he could get a swing at the ball. It was a trick shot he'd recorded on video when Sevvy Ballesteros had played it once in similar circumstances. But Jamie had never tried it in a championship.

'It's all I can do, Dad,' said Jamie apologetically.

'Just knock it onto the green,' replied Mike, knowing that it was a near impossibility. Only Mike, the course marshall and half a dozen spectators including Tim Lloyd saw what happened next. With minimal backswing Jamie clipped the ball left-handed and with the back of the club as if he'd played that way all his life.

The ball shot through the air about two feet off the ground, passed through a three-foot gap between the trees bordering the fairway, bounced once just off the green and caught the top of the bank which took all the pace off it. The ball rolled down the bank across the green, heading straight for the hole. A huge roar started as it travelled the last ten feet; the momentum of the ball was dying but the crowd's gathering roar seeming to keep it in motion.

Jamie, Mike, Tim and the others had come bursting out of the coppice after the ball just in time to see it clip the top of the bank. As it started on its way towards the hole, Jamie was running onto the green. When the ball rolled its last circumference and dropped into the hole, the crowd's roar could have been heard in Blackpool five miles away.

If only Julia had been here to see this, thought Mike almost immediately. Now she'd know for the first time what I've been living for these past ten years. It was one of the greatest moments ever seen on the Old Course.

Poor Johnny Watkinson was devastated. Jamie's incredible heroics had given him the title. Even if Watkinson now sank his own awkward birdie putt, the best he could do was to finish second, a stroke behind. He couldn't believe it. There was no way that kid could have holed that stroke from the dense trees to the left of the green. No way. He felt he should ask the marshall if the boy took a drop and incurred a penalty stroke but he knew in his heart that he hadn't. His mind seized up. As he putted he saw his angry girlfriend waiting for him under the cover of the doorway of the starter's hut.

Watkinson underhit his putt and finished three feet short of the hole and six inches wide. He tried to refocus but couldn't. The next putt stopped on the lip of the hole and he tapped it in. Five minutes ago he was on the verge of winning the championship. Now he had finished three strokes behind a fifteen-year-old kid. It was utterly humiliating but he knew the etiquette. He picked his ball out of the hole, thanked his caddie, touched the rim of his cap to acknowledge the crowd's applause and walked across the green to where Mike was giving Jamie a huge bear hug.

'Well played.' He offered his hand. Mike put Jamie down.

'Thanks. Great game.'

Mike shook hands ritually with Watkinson and his caddie and the course marshall but before he could turn back, Jamie was surrounded by a triumphant crowd who bore him aloft on their shoulders.

'I have to sign my card!' yelled Jamie unavailingly. 'I have to sign it otherwise it's not legal. I haven't won if I haven't signed it!'

Eventually the crowd deposited him in the starter's hut. Mike could see in the distance Watkinson and his girlfriend in the middle of what their body language indicated must be a blazing row. His thoughts turned once again to Julia. Surely she would be proud of her son after this astonishing and significant triumph. Maybe this would be the beginning of a wonderful new period in all their lives.

In the car on the way home Jamie let his head loll back against the headrest and tried to sleep. Mike concentrated on his driving. The M6 was bound to have some terrible contraflow traffic jam at some point near Birmingham; it always did, even at this time of night. He kept the radio on low, hoping that the late-night sports news might possibly say something about Jamie.

Just north of Birmingham Jamie woke up, turned to his dad and squeezed his arm. 'Thanks, Dad. You're the best dad in the world. I couldn't have done any of this without you.'

Mike didn't reply. He couldn't. He was too choked. He wished yet again that Julia was with them. If she could only have been there with them to have shared that supreme moment of triumph then she would know why he was so obsessed with the thought of turning Jamie into a champion. She would have been so proud of her son, so proud of both of them, surely.

He soon realised that there was no way of contacting her even if he had been sitting by the telephone at home. He looked at the illuminated digital clock on the car dashboard and tried to calculate the time difference and work out what she was doing right now. Must be just after lunch, he eventually concluded. In that case, thought Mike, it's a good job I'm nowhere near her. She's almost certainly struggling with her luggage on the way to the airport or stuck at the back of a dispiriting queue at the check-in.

CHAPTER EIGHTEEN

'I'M NOT GOING TO LET you go back.'

'I have to go back.'

'I love your back. And your front.'

Julia and Tom lay naked on the bed, the covers kicked off, stroking each other gently.

'But do you love me?'

'You mean if you had neither a back nor a front?'

'Well, that would make it more difficult.'

'I'd find a way of loving you whatever shape you were.'

'Why? Why do you want me so much?'

'Isn't it obvious?'

'Can you avoid answering my question with another question?'

'Only by doing this.' He kissed her again as if he could keep her in his bed by the force of his passion for her. 'Julia, this is a turning point in both our lives. God brought you back into my life for a reason.'

'I thought you didn't believe in God.'

'Well, I don't believe in a supreme being, a great oneness, the creator of the universe, the first cause of all things.'

'Then what do you believe in?'

'A very old man with a long white beard sitting on a cloud dressed in a white coat.'

'Sounds like a National Health Service dentist.'

'I think He also has dental qualifications.'

Julia laughed, kissed him firmly on the lips and rolled out of bed. She walked towards the bathroom, enjoying the sense of his eyes devouring her naked body. Tom made her feel as if she had suddenly lost twenty pounds. If she didn't feel supermodel thin then she certainly felt at least like an attractive newlywed. She turned back to face him.

'I'm not a Van Dyke painting, you know.'

'Sorry, it was the moustache and the goatee beard that made me think you were.'

'I mean I can feel your eyes following me round the room.'

'Well, who are you going to believe? Me or your own eyes?'

Tom sprang from the bed and pressed himself against her, running his hands from the middle of her shoulder blades slowly down her back until they reached her bottom. 'Come back to bed,' he whispered into her ear.

'I've got a plane to catch and I haven't even started packing.'

'I'll help you. We've got hours.'

'And I need to take a shower,' she protested, half-heartedly, as she felt herself once more submitting to Tom's sweet irresistible force.

'Me too,' said Tom, guiding Julia into the shower cubicle without taking his lips from hers. They parted with a sudden screech as the water descended in a freezing torrent.

When they emerged, the atmosphere in the room had changed. They knew they now had not much more than an hour before she had to leave to drive to the airport. They had postponed coping with the reality of such a painful parting until this moment.

'I don't want you to go.' Tom hoped it sounded like a lover's entreaty. He feared that it sounded more like the whine of a spoiled teenager.

'Please help me, Tom. Don't make it worse.'

'When am I going to see you again?'

'I don't know. Can't you see I'm as lost as you are in this situation?'

'I love you, Julia. You are the lover I've been waiting for.'

Julia smiled. 'I know. The mate that fate had me created for.'

She opened the large fitted closet and took out her smart suitcase which Tom had rescued from the motel room in Calistoga. She laid it on the bed, unzipped the top and began to take the clothes off the hangers in the closet.

'What would happen if you didn't go back?'

'I'd lose my job.'

'You could get another one here.'

'I'd lose my husband.'

'Ditto.'

'I'd lose my son.'

'He's fifteen, Julia. You're going to lose him soon anyway. Then what have you got?'

Tom went out to the kitchen and started mixing eggs in a bowl, leaving Julia to recover from the shock of his remark. It had pierced her heart.

It was true, of course. That's why she had deliberately avoided asking herself the question. As long as Jamie was a schoolboy there was always the chance that he needed her, that golf would turn out to be just a phase he was going through. In September he would be in the sixth form, he wouldn't have to wear school uniform and he would be staying out late at parties every weekend, possibly with a girlfriend, if he ever found one.

In her bleakest moments Julia felt that Jamie was all that was keeping Mike and her together. She was only thirty-eight years old. Tom was offering her a whole new life in the California sun with him, a man whom she had adored for nearly twenty years. Was she crazy flying back to that dull Hertfordshire town when she had only to look out of the window at the stunning landscape or across the king-sized bed at Tom's still lean body to find happiness?

When Julia entered the kitchen fifteen minutes later, the table was set for a large brunch with freshly squeezed orange juice in glasses, cut halves of grapefruit, a plate of strawberries and sliced canteloupe and the smell of fresh coffee in the cafetiere. There was also, inevitably, a bottle of white wine in the cooler at the side of the table, as if they were in a restaurant.

'I'm sorry,' said Tom simply. 'I shouldn't have said that. I didn't mean to hurt you. I never want to hurt you. I guess I'm frightened because you're going. I feel like I'll never see you again.'

'Oh, you don't get rid of me that easily,' smiled Julia and turned her face to his to be kissed. Tom obliged with such passion that she had to pull herself free just to be able to breathe. She turned her attention to the breakfast table.

'This looks wonderful.'

Tom raked his eyes over her as he stood by the stove scrambling the eggs. 'So do you.'

Julia sat down abruptly. She didn't like the new atmosphere. She wished Tom would help her by being superficial and jokey rather than heavy and emotional.

'OK if I sit here?'

'I'm afraid that place is reserved.'

'I'm sorry?'

'It's reserved for the most beautiful woman in the world.'

'Is that supposed to be me?'

'I don't know. Do you have any ID on you?'

'You mean like a driving licence or a credit card?'

Tom took the pan off the burner and slid half the eggs onto the plate in front of Julia. 'No. I mean like this.' He bent down and kissed her softly on the lips and smiled. 'My apologies, madam, this must be your reservation.'

Julia picked at her food.

'You don't like?'

'Oh, I like OK. It's great.'

'Wine?'

'Can I take it on the plane with me?'

'I don't think they're keen on that. It puts their suppliers of screw-top bottled alcoholic dishwater out of business.'

'Is that a reference to anyone in particular?'

'Some of the big boys in the Napa Valley. They just can't wait to get their Chardonnay onto those plastic trays.'

'They're in business. You can't blame them.'

'I prefer to make wine for occasions like this.' He took the wine out of the cooler, expertly withdrew the cork and poured a full glass for Julia. She looked up at him. 'It's wonderful. Trust me.'

'I do. It's just that I have to drive into San Francisco. I'd like to make it to the airport and not career off the Golden Gate Bridge.'

'That's real difficult to do even if driving while inebriated. Just taste a sip.'

She did. He was right. It was delicious. She tried to eat the eggs but they turned to ashes in her mouth. She set the fork down and pushed the plate away. Her eyes were starting to fill with tears.

'I've got to go.'

'You've got another half-hour at least!'

'Please, Tom. Just help me out here. I have a husband and a child waiting for me in England. I love them. I've got to go.'

'And me?' he asked, clearly hurt. 'What am I? Just a holiday romance?'

'You know what I think about you, Tom. I've shown it over and over again these last few days. I've got the difficult bit to do. I don't know how things will turn out between us but please try to help by being completely unselfish. I love you, I really do.'

He smiled at her. That old devastating hymn to American orthodontistry. 'Sure. Just leave the food. I'll put it in the freezer. You can have it when you come back.'

That was it. That was exactly what she needed to hear at the moment — light, inconsequential, a sense that she could always return but he wouldn't make things difficult for her.

He carried her suitcases to the car and placed them carefully in the boot. Julia turned to him and prepared herself for the final kiss. Tom tightened his grip on her waist and held her to him, their lips barely touching. Suddenly he broke off.

'I'm coming with you.'

'Tom, don't be ridiculous.'

'Just to the airport.' He turned and ran back to the house, set the alarm and shut the door, disappearing inside.

A few seconds later Julia heard the sound of his car starting, the garage door raised itself slowly and Tom backed out. He touched the device which he kept attached to the sun visor and the garage door began its mechanical descent, as did Tom's car window.

'I just remembered. I need to check my air miles.'

'Wouldn't it be easier to use the phone?'

'They keep you on hold for hours. Plus are you sure you can find your way to the airport?'

'I've got a map.'

'Women can't read maps. It's in their DNA, or rather it's not in their DNA.'

'Chauvinist pig.'

'If you want, you can take your car back to the rental agency and then struggle onto those buses which always leave just as you're taking the luggage out of the trunk. This way you get a guide to the airport, a lift to the check-in, a porter to carry your cases and a linguist to translate from the Spanish if you need to talk to anyone in the golden state of California.'

Julia smiled. 'You won't drive too fast and lose me, will you?'

'You want to take all the fun out of this?'

'No, but—'

'Then let's go!'

Tom roared out of the gate. Julia gave a little shriek, got into her car, tried to start it but couldn't get the key into the ignition. By the time she had managed to get it moving, Tom was out of sight. She tore round the first bend to find Tom waiting for her, both indicators flashing, grinning mischievously.

'You are such a bastard!'

'But a real lovable one, don't you think?'

'Just drive! Slowly!'

'Yes, ma'am!'

For a mile he drove at a pace fit for a hearse until Julia lost her patience and overtook. Immediately he was on her tail, headlights on, waving inanely at her from his car. She looked at the apparition in the rear-view mirror and thought that though this might be the silly behaviour of a teenager, the fact was that she hadn't felt so alive, so vibrant in years. Tom had awakened something she thought must have died within her, her sense of self-worth, she supposed it must be, maybe just her sense of humour.

He overtook her again as they approached the 101 Freeway that would take them back to the city. Although she had only been there four days, already she felt a sense of belonging in the wine country. In part it was because the landscape reminded her so much of Tuscany where she and Mike had spent so many summer holidays.

They approached the Golden Gate Bridge for the last time through the typically California developments of strip malls and discount warehouses which looked as though they had been designed by architects who had drawn the basic shape on a table napkin with the use of the restaurant's book of matches. The sun was disappearing early as the clouds inevitably rolled in across the bay. She knew that Tom in the car ahead was humming the same lyric that she was. She could hear Tony Bennett starting the famous verse, 'I left my heart . . .' before the audience applause drowned it out.

The disappointment of being deprived of 'the view' across the bay as they rumbled over the stately bridge was masked by a lurch of panic as she realised she didn't have the three dollars in change ready to hand to the guard at the toll booth. Tolls were a stupid system. Why didn't they have a road fund licence like the British? Fancy having to pay up every time you crossed Waterloo Bridge.

She flashed Tom with her headlights but he must have thought that she was still playing games because he refused to acknowledge her distress call. When her car drew level with the guardhouse she rolled down her window and started to apologise. The guard, behind his entirely unnecessary dark glasses, waved her through, irritated by her pause, as a result of which the traffic behind her had started to back up immediately.

'Guy in front paid, lady, keep moving,' he said briefly.

Julia felt a surge of gratitude and kept moving.

To her surprise, the farewell at the airport was actually easier than it looked like it was going to be at the house. Somehow the presence of so many other people, all of them with similar tales of emotional distress to tell, no doubt, inhibited their behaviour. Tom guided her expertly from the car rental building round the one-way system and into the car park. He wheeled her luggage over to the airline terminal and waited with her in line until she was officially recognised as a subhuman with the issue of her economy-class boarding card.

The pace of their walk to passport control was slower than she would have liked. For all her love for Tom she knew she had to get her mind reset to meet Mike and Jamie. Tom was hanging on to her for every available second. Finally she turned to kiss him goodbye. It was scarcely more than a peck.

'I'll be in touch,' she promised and scooted into line, her passport and boarding card held out in front of her. Only when she had passed the point of no return did she turn to look at him again. He hadn't moved. It was if his shoes had been nailed to the industrial carpet. If she flew back into San Francisco International Airport at any point in the next twenty years she felt sure he would be in the same position, his eyes fixed on her retreating body.

'I love you,' she mouthed silently but with sufficient movement of her lips to render the words decipherable. He smiled back as if he was a father watching his eldest son marching off to war and certain death. Julia turned for comfort to the anonymous embrace of the departure lounge and the brightly lit, highly scented aisles of the duty free shop.

Julia was struggling with her emotions. She loved Tom, she had always loved him, so what was she going back for? These few days with Tom had confirmed her belief that her marriage, though pleasant enough in its way, was moribund, devoid of all genuine passion. Neither Mike nor Jamie appeared to need her, yet here she was leaving a man who was available, who did need her, a man who adored her, who made her feel good about herself. It made no sense.

These thoughts tormented her throughout the long and wearisome flight. They took off at six o'clock and because they were flying east the sky was dark before the dinner was wheeled down the aisle. After the trays had been collected, the overhead lights were turned off and most of the cabin settled down with a thin blanket and tiny pillow to try to sleep till they arrived at Heathrow.

Although the flight was only eighty per cent full, Julia was one of the unlucky ones who was seated in the middle of a configuration of three. Although she couldn't be described, even by herself in one of her more self-deprecating moods, as a big woman, she found the lack of leg room extremely uncomfortable. There was no more room in either the aisle or the window seats but there was a psychological sense of not being hemmed in by the rest of mankind. She couldn't move, she couldn't sleep, all she could do for ten hours was to think about Mike and Jamie and Tom and Tom and Mike and Jamie in endless conflicting combinations.

By the time the first window shutters were raised to find the early morning sun streaming into the cabin and the stewardesses wheeling their microwaved eggs and bacon with a fierce determination to deliver them and collect the empties inside twenty minutes, Julia had come to a conclusion of sorts.

She was a married woman. She had always taken her marriage vows seriously. She felt, by her own admittedly subjective rule of morality, that she had 'deserved' this interlude with Tom but how was she to see him again? Where was this relationship going? And was it fair to Mike? All right, maybe Mike hadn't been a great romantic husband but how many men were? It didn't help matters that he and Jamie were so close that she felt excluded but if she wasn't so defensive about it maybe she'd be able to see the benefits. Few teenage boys felt the need for a maternal presence in their lives – they needed food on the table and clean clothes to wear. Why should Jamie be any different?

And she was grateful to them both. Jamie was a good kid, and Mike had provided a good standard of living for the family, he had been generally supportive about her job, he hadn't, as far as she knew, been with any other woman. Would she have cared if he had? It was a question that had often bothered her. She didn't think she ever rejected his advances outright but she knew that she didn't exactly welcome them these days. Their sexual intimacy had diminished but it couldn't be all her fault. Look how she had been with Tom. That playful, uninhibited Julia had been the real her, so she obviously still had a sex drive, which life with Mike had recently made her doubt.

Julia had a splitting headache. She thought it must be the result of a combination of the lack of sleep, the rotten airline food, the discomfort of her seat as well as the emotional turmoil. Would she be able to cut Tom out of her life and return to the mundane boredom of her long-standing marriage? Could she learn to live on the memory of four golden days for the next twenty years?

Would Tom start calling her at home or would she inadvertently leave clues so that Mike would find out? And if he did find out, would that be it? The end of their marriage? It would make her free to be with Tom of course, but how could she live with herself, having destroyed her marriage and abandoned Jamie?

Perhaps the approach of Jamie's GCSEs was something to be welcomed in this new situation. He would certainly need her to be supportive, to be a sounding board, to be an academic coach. She remembered how important organisation was in the taking of exams, dividing the time available precisely by the number of questions to be answered to ensure that he didn't get to the end of the exam and find that he'd only answered three-quarters of the questions. She and Mike were both good at exams. She knew she could be a help to her son.

By the time the plane touched down on English tarmac a surprising twenty minutes early, Julia had resolved nothing. Maybe, she thought, seeing Mike again after this extraordinary week would enable her to rekindle the flame of passion for him. How convenient that would be! Could she take something from her love affair with Tom, however brief, and somehow apply it to her marriage?

Would it be better if Tom were to rent a flat in London so they could see each other on a regular basis? All right, it was an affair but it might allow her to juggle things at home for a while longer. And hadn't men been doing exactly this throughout history with no feelings of guilt? A woman at home to look after the family, a woman at work to help him feel young and attractive.

Normally she experienced nothing but contempt for such men but now, torn in half as she was, she wondered whether her judgement had been too harsh, too easily arrived at. She just didn't know how long she could carry on without seeing Tom again, without feeling the touch of his hand on hers, the smell of his flesh as he leaned in to kiss her.

She decided she was going to act as if she was pleased to see Mike waiting for her beyond customs because she felt instinctively that if she was glad to see him, he'd be glad to see her. She'd be tired when they got home but if she kissed him with a certain degree of intent then maybe he'd start to relax and the potential tension in the household would never materialise. Anyway, maybe he'd missed her and was looking forward to seeing her again. Positive thoughts, she kept repeating to herself, positive thoughts.

The portents were excellent. She was feeling surprisingly fit and fresh as she smiled at the stewardess and she revelled in the freedom of getting her limbs moving again as she pulled her smart zip-up bag on wheels the length and breadth of the airport, following the reclaimed baggage sign. The wait at immigration was almost non-existent although she noted that the American man who had been sitting next to her on the flight was at the back of a frighteningly long queue for those unfortunates not equipped with EC passports, and the moment she got to the carousel her bags came bursting through the hanging strips of heavy plastic that separated the baggage handlers from their traditionally angry victims. The four customs officials who were supposed to be manning the green channel were involved in what must have been an engrossing poker game played for very high stakes and by the time she emerged into the scrum of waiting humanity she was feeling a whole lot better.

She scanned the faces as she pushed her trolley along the protected passageway that led from the customs hall. No welcoming sight awaited her and her heart plummeted. He had abandoned her. All that positive self-exhortation had been pointless. He hadn't even bothered to come to meet her. Julia didn't have any English change so she reversed the charges to ring home. There was, as she expected, no reply. She didn't feel comfortable reversing the charges to Mike's office so she sat down at the meeting point and tried to gather her thoughts. She had a credit card. She could use that to take a tube to Watford and then take a taxi and stop at a cashpoint. Maybe there was a cashpoint in the terminal for just such emergencies. She stood up to find out when she heard her name being called.

'Julia!'

She turned to see a florid, flapping Mike running towards her, dodging the crowd. He flung his arms round her and kissed her awkwardly on the side of the face. He had been moving too quickly to allow Julia to get her lips into the right position to receive his embrace.

'I'm sorry, your plane arrived early and that threw my plans and then there were road works from Junction Three and all down the approach road and

I had to go up five floors in the multi-storey before I found a place to park. Anyway you're here. How was the flight?'

In the time it took to gabble out his excuses, Julia knew her marriage was fighting a losing battle. It wasn't so much that she didn't love him. Indeed, there was something comfortingly familiar about Mike. It was just that he didn't arouse anything inside her. Her heart didn't thrill to the sound of his voice, her face didn't tingle when he touched it, she didn't long for his touch the way she had with Tom, she didn't want to feel his arm round her waist almost crushing her ribs. Mike took control of her loaded trolley and started to push it towards the lift whose doors never seemed to open.

As the familiar flat scenery of the northern rim of the M25 sped past the car window Julia listened to Mike's euphoric retelling of the legend of Jamie's final shot that won him the championship. She couldn't help contrasting the dull landscape with the lush beauty of Marin County, the endless vistas of Dry Creek Valley, the magnificence of San Francisco Bay. She tried hard to grasp the significance of Jamie's triumph and respond to the excitement in Mike's voice but she just wanted to talk to Tom. Tom would understand exactly the feelings she was currently experiencing.

Before driving to Heathrow that morning, Mike had been to Waitrose. He had filled the fridge with the fruit and salads and pasta sauces that he knew Julia liked. And again her emotions lurched so violently she wondered if she might be experiencing the menopause ten to twelve years early. Mike, she told herself, had met her, he'd taken the trouble to make the house ready for her even though he and Jamie only got back at midnight last night. Would Tom be trying that hard after nearly twenty years of marriage?

It was the last day of Jamie's school holiday so he was out of the house when they arrived home. He came back, predictably, when he was hungry but he was pleased enough to see his mother again. Julia thought he had grown in the week she had been away but maybe it was just the effect of his great victory the previous day. If he hadn't grown physically in height he had certainly grown in stature and confidence. Maybe Mike was right. This golf lark was going to be the making of him. If he could only translate this new-found confidence into exam performances, she thought, but he showed no interest in her wanderings down this path and at the mention of the word 'exams', he excused himself abruptly and went upstairs to his room.

Mike went off to work and said he'd be home late from the office since he was going in late. With Jamie busy e-mailing his friends from his bedroom computer Julia suddenly found herself intensely lonely. The day dragged past. As afternoon turned to evening, she rang Sarah who was too busy cooking dinner for her family to spare time for anything more than a cursory chat. Jet lag crept over Julia. All she wanted now was a hot bath and her own bed. She knocked on Jamie's door to say goodnight and in response got a hand waved vaguely in her direction.

What had happened to that curly-haired, gap-toothed little boy who would fling his arms round her neck and hold her so tight she thought he might strangle her? If only she still had his sister, another girl to chat to, to confide in, to help over the inevitable boyfriend problems.

She ran her bath and dribbled some bath salts into the fierce jet. She stepped out of her underwear and checked her body in the full-length mirror. Oddly enough, it seemed to have slipped back into its former state of incipient obesity. It was either the glass or her brain that couldn't cope. She wanted the mirror in Tom's bathroom, the one that told her how beautiful she was. She didn't like this lying English reflection and slipped quickly into the hot water in whose comforting embrace she only just stopped herself from falling asleep.

The cool sheets and the firm mattress of her own bed caressed her aching limbs. Dimly she heard Mike's car crunch to a stop in the driveway. She didn't want to talk to him. She figured if she could get to sleep in the next few seconds she would be bound to be dreaming about Tom. The car and the garage and the conversation of what was only twenty-four hours ago was still vivid in her memory.

But it was a dreamless sleep she found and she was aware of nothing until she heard a bang and the sound of swearing. Mike had tripped over something in the dark and was clearly angry about it. He clambered noisily into bed, dragging the covers away from Julia towards himself, leaving her covered by sheets that were suddenly cold. Damn it! she thought. I'm awake. How can he be so selfish!

Mike tossed and turned. Julia pretended to be still asleep and sent forth what she hoped was convincing regular breathing. It wasn't a snore but it certainly wasn't the breathing of a woman who was wide awake and hoping for her lover's embrace.

She got it anyway. A hand slipped under her ribs. She had carefully ensured that her back was turned to Mike but his hand started dragging her back towards him. He had obviously missed her. Normally she wouldn't mind obliging him but at the moment his touch and his urgency simply reminded her that he wasn't Tom. In California Tom was probably sitting on his front porch overlooking the valley, sipping a glass of chilled white wine and thinking of her, of Julia, of what they had done together, of what they meant to each other. Mike's insistent embraces were destroying her fantasies. She couldn't lie here and take this. She had to get out of the room, away from Mike. She pushed him off her and scrambled to her feet.

'Sorry, I'm jet-lagged.'

'Well, hadn't you better stay here and get some sleep?'

'I'm hungry,' she explained briefly, grabbed her dressing gown and fled the room.

Mike had been hoping that a happy Julia, refreshed by her holiday and anxious to be part of her family again, would respond to his amorous advances with enthusiasm. He sighed and tried to get to sleep.

In the kitchen Julia blinked under the harsh glare of the overhead fluorescent light. Now that she was downstairs she did feel hungry. She poured herself a bowl of muesli and noted that there was only regular milk in the house. Mike's shopping list hadn't extended to her non-fat skimmed milk. She remembered the breakfast Tom had prepared for her so lovingly, the sliced fruit and the scrambled eggs, the heavenly aroma of freshly made coffee and the chilled white wine. She wanted to cry.

Instead she went upstairs to check that Jamie's light was out and that Mike was asleep. He was snoring in that remorseless pattern that she remembered well enough to decide that he wasn't faking. Julia went downstairs again and looked at the clock on the mantelpiece in the lounge. It was 1.45 a.m. She made a quick calculation. That meant it was quarter to six in the evening in California. It had been thirty hours since she had driven out of the Johnson Winery. She picked up the phone and dialled.

'Hello?' He answered on the first long ring. It was as if he was waiting for her. She didn't know what to say. Should she put the phone down, no harm done? Did they have 1471 over there? Could he trace the call? Or didn't it work with overseas calls?

'Julia?' He knew.

'Yes,' she whispered as if Mike was in the next room.

'I've been waiting for you to call. I haven't left this room all day.'

'They're asleep. I've got jet lag.'

'Are you OK?'

'Yes.'

'You don't sound OK. What's the matter, sweetheart?'

Julia felt a huge choking sob take possession of her. She couldn't have answered the question even if she'd had full control of her senses — which she didn't. Tom filled in the silence.

'Listen, I've been thinking. I've been thinking ever since I left you at the airport. I'm in the middle of a deal with Château Deschamps. There are still some things to be ironed out. I have to make a trip to the Loire Valley to see them. Soon. Maybe next week. Will you come with me? Or meet me there? Or maybe we could meet in Paris. Please, Julia, please say yes. I love you so much.

I need you so much I'm almost incapable of getting out of this chair. Please say yes.'

Julia couldn't speak.

'Does that mean yes?' asked an anxious California voice.

'Yes,' Julia whispered. 'Yes, darling. I'll come. I promise. I love you too.'

She put the phone down and burst into tears. When Mike found her in the morning she was curled up on the couch with a raincoat over her body while a girl in a leotard went through the full burn of aerobic contortions on the television set in front of her.

CHAPTER NINETEEN

'So, HOW WAS IT?' SARAH couldn't have been more intrigued. A week in San Francisco paid for by the firm, five-star hotel, room service, no husband, no kids. The whole scenario just made her mouth water.

'It was great.'

'That's it? Just great?'

'What did you expect?'

'Details, I suppose.'

'It was a wonderful hotel. I could see the Golden Gate Bridge from the bedroom window. I sent you a postcard.'

'And was it foggy, like you told me it would be?'

'A lot of the time, yes. But it cleared up now and then.'

'How was the concert?'

'Truly wonderful.'

'And did you meet him afterwards?'

'Who?' Julia blushed slightly. What on earth had she said to Sarah before she left?

'Tony Bennett of course!'

'Oh, yes!' God, she thought, it all seemed so long ago now. 'Well, briefly, anyway. He had to leave to catch a flight to Las Vegas. He was opening in a show in one of the big hotels there the next day.'

'Did he look into your eyes and sing?'

'No, but as the waitress came round with a tray of nibbles, he shook my hand with his right hand and grabbed the last cheese and pineapple chunk on a stick with his left hand.'

'Any other major romantic interludes?'

Julia had known this was coming and still hadn't worked out an answer. Should she confide everything in Sarah? She thought she could certainly use a friendly sounding board just at the moment but what if Sarah was dead against her seeing Tom again? What if she mentioned something to John and John said something to Mike? It was too risky. But then again, she would probably need someone to cover for her. If she was going to continue to see Tom she was bound to need the help of her best girlfriend at some point. Was it better to spill the beans now or wait till the moment of need was at hand?

'San Francisco is the gay capital of the universe.'

'So no romantic interludes?'

'Nothing to write home about.'

'Well, you'd hardly write home about a romance if you were having one, would you?'

Julia smiled and changed the subject. 'Remember the college reunion?'

'Of course. Are you going to finish that salad?'

Julia pushed her plate into the centre of the table. Sarah skilfully speared three slices of tomato with her fork and transferred them to her own plate.

'I met Helen Fairbrother again.'

'Oh yes, I remember you telling me about her. Isn't she the butch dyke?'

'Sarah!'

'Sorry.'

'She'd been there about a month earlier.'

'Where? Oxford?'

'No. San Francisco.'

'So?'

'She ran into my old boyfriend. Well, my first boyfriend.'

Sarah dropped her fork melodramatically. It clattered onto her plate. 'Tom?'

'Oh, did I tell you about Tom?' asked Julia innocently.

'Are you kidding? This is me – Sarah. You first mentioned him about twenty-five minutes after we met in the maternity ward. You were still in love with him.'

'No, I wasn't!'

Sarah stared at her. 'I'm not stupid, Jules.'

'I'm sure I never—'

'You saw him again? This trip?' Sarah's eyes were sparkling. Julia wondered if that's what her eyes did when she talked about Tom. She might be about to find out. She slid both her hands across the table and covered Sarah's in a grip born of desperation.

'If I tell you everything, will you still be my friend?'

'What are you talking about? I am your friend.'

'No. I mean will you please not judge me? Will you help me if I need help? Will you try to empathise and see it all from my point of view?'

'You've always told me everything. I know all about your relationship with Mike. What could you possibly say that would surprise me? You're not a spy, are you?'

Julia smiled and shook her head.

'A porn star?'

'Not unless Tom's got a hidden camera.'

Sarah's eyes widened. 'Omigod, you have! You've started seeing Tom again.'

'Not just seeing him.'

'You know what I mean.'

'You remember your promise?'

'It's in the vault, Julia. I promise.'

'And the combination to the safe?'

'Swallowed. Look!' Sarah pitted an olive, popped it in her mouth and swallowed it straight down, nearly choking as she did so.

'I hope that's not a bad omen,' said Julia as Sarah quickly seized her glass of Perrier and helped the olive on its way.

'Sorry. Tell me everything, omitting no detail, no matter how small. He still loves you?'

'That's one of the biggest details. I'm not likely to omit that one.'

Julia plunged in. Sarah was right. She did know everything about her, about her relationship with Mike and her sense of boredom with the marriage, her love for her children. Sarah had been there when Emily was born and she was there when Emily died. There was no point in trying to deceive her. Oddly enough, despite the deception with Mike, both in the recent past and the imminent future, Julia actually felt as though she were coming clean, owning up, revealing her true emotions as honestly as she could. In the end she was glad she'd confided in Sarah.

Sarah sneaked a glance at her watch.

'Sarah!'

'I just wanted to see if I needed to start inventing an excuse for taking a two-hour lunch break.'

'Oh God! I hadn't noticed.' Julia checked her watch and gave a startled yelp as she saw it was nearly ten past three. 'OK. I'm your important client and you're mine.'

'Sounds good to me.'

'So what do you think?'

'You really need me to say anything after what you've just told me?'

'But I'm torn, can't you see? I'm a married woman. This isn't me.'

'Of course it's you. That's what you've just spent an hour and a half telling me. Finally, this is you. You're unhappy with Mike.'

'I never said that.'

'All right, put it this way, you're blissfully happy with Tom. I don't see the dilemma here.'

'I should just go off with Tom? Abandon my marriage, my son? Just like that?'

'That's not necessarily what's on offer. You meet Tom in France. Maybe outside his own territory he'll be different, not quite so appealing. Then you can come back home with a nice little adventure under your suspender belt. Don't tell me he likes stockings? I've never understood what men see in them.'

'He did buy me some expensive lingerie.'

'Stockings and suspender belt?'

'Knickers and a nightie.'

'Won't Mike notice?'

'Would John?'

'Only if they were being modelled by Claudia Schiffer.' Sarah asked the waiter for their bill.

'So you think I should have my fling?'

'Do you think you deserve it?'

'Yes.'

'That's your answer.'

'But aren't you supposed to be the sensible friend? The one that tells me "East, west, home's best".'

'That was the one part of The Wizard of Oz I never liked. I always wanted Dorothy to stay in Oz much longer. The colour was better. And no, I'm trying to do what you asked. I'm not judging you. I'm trying to help you fly.'

'It's only a few days. Mike'll probably be glad to get me out of the house again.'

'You don't think he . . .'

'Sometimes I'd like to think he does have someone. It would make me feel less guilty, that's for sure. Anyway, doesn't everyone have the right to a decent sex life?'

Sarah looked at her with amused detachment. 'Why do you think they do?'

'It's just something I started feeling strongly about the moment I decided I didn't have one. I mean, how is it for you? I notice you haven't mentioned John once in this whole conversation.'

They paid the bill and Sarah started to gather her things together. Julia did likewise.

'You know exactly what I feel about John. But my first boyfriend wasn't the romantic type. Not like Tom anyway.'

'You've never told me about your first boyfriend.'

Outside the restaurant Sarah waved at a taxi which signalled its acknowledgement and veered dangerously across two lanes of traffic to get to her.

'We did it standing up in an alley behind a club off Tottenham Court Road. A dog came along in the middle of it and weed on my tights. I haven't been carrying this romantic image around in my head for twenty years.' She pecked Julia on the cheek and opened the taxi door. 'Can I give you a lift?'

Julia shook her head. 'I want to walk back to the office. I need to think. Thanks for lunch – and everything else.'

'Call me if you need to talk. Any time.' Sarah stepped into the taxi and banged the door.

By the time she got back to the office Julia had the whole plan in her mind. The company was very much in favour of expanding its commercial ties in Europe. She had been thinking about a CD of French love songs to include Maurice Chevalier, Edith Piaf and Johnny Halliday for some time. As she felt the first drops of rain on her head, her mind flicked from the realisation that she wasn't carrying an umbrella to a memory of the colourful poster for the classic French romantic musical film *The Umbrellas of Cherbourg* with its tuneful score by Michel Legrand. Since her job was to clear rights she felt she would certainly be able to find a plausible reason to go to Paris to unknot some tricky copyright problem. And she just might have to stay a day or two longer, preferably walking hand in hand with an American man along the left bank of the Seine before returning to their charming little hotel off the Boulevard St Germain to make love all night.

'Eric Neville, her boss, almost beamed at her when she suggested it and Julia knew exactly why. He would of course take the credit for the idea of the French love songs and it could lead to all sorts of European multimedia tie-ups. Eric had grand plans for his future. He had already mentally designed the business card which indicated that he had offices in New York, Paris, Milan, Berlin and possibly Sydney – European and worldwide connections. Julia didn't care about a scuffle on the corporate ladder – she had other things to look forward to now.

Eric had been remarkably pleasant to her since they had returned from their separate journeys. The retreat had gone very well for him. He and the president of the marketing division had won the three-legged race designed to encourage teamwork. He rather fancied a promotion to marketing – more opportunities for worldwide travel, new media and so on. And the general feedback from the West Coast office on Julia's Tony Bennett trip had been good as well.

Eric was feeling in a generous mood. She could go to Paris. He didn't even need to refer it upstairs. It could come out of the budget for which he had sole authorisation, which had been increased at the last review. He felt like a bigshot. Let her have a couple of days in Paris. Keep the troops happy. That's what rising young executives were supposed to be good at. More to the point, maybe she'd feel suitably grateful on the next trip which might be a joint one if he felt she was going to be co-operative. He'd always liked the shape of her behind and fantasised about uncovering it since the day he'd first interviewed her. And if not, well, for a young man like him on the rise, the world was full of available women. Not today, admittedly, but soon, really soon. Surely?

Julia returned to her office, buoyed by the ease with which she had slipped this one past the oily Eric. She had felt the disgusting slob mentally undressing her as she sat in his office and leering at her as she left but he no doubt had a stack of lurid magazines full of naked women with large breasts in his desk drawer and he could content himself with them. She was going to make her daily call to Tom.

She was quite comfortable now with the idea of telephoning Tom from the office. Their conversations were strictly strategic and in the unlikely event of their being monitored, any terms of endearment could be construed as gentle office banter between friendly colleagues who were making arrangements to meet up in Paris for business purposes.

It took three long days of organising and plotting before the final plans were laid just before Julia left the office on Friday evening. As she had anticipated, Mike wasn't exactly heartbroken at her going away again but he was working hard at being understanding. They had come to an agreement about Jamie who was going to attack his schoolwork and the imminent start of GCSE exams with diligence.

In return for this promised dedication Julia had agreed that he could play in the qualifying tournament for the Open Championship in Scotland in July. Unless he actually won the Open, which would be no easier than taking off and flying round the bedroom, he would then stay on to take A levels in his three best subjects. He wasn't committed to the school's sixth form, though. They decided to postpone the discussion of whether he should study A levels at a co-educational sixth form college until after his results came through at the end of August.

It was sheer good luck that Jamie and Mike were on the golf course when the phone rang on Saturday afternoon. Tom was planning to leave that day to fly to Paris where he would change planes for a flight to Lyons. A car would be waiting to drive him to the chateau in the Loire Valley where he was staying. Business would be concluded by Tuesday night, leaving three working days and the weekend for the lovers to revel in their Parisian freedom. Julia was Hoovering the lounge and anticipating the gastronomic and sensuous delights awaiting her at the same time on the following Saturday when she picked up the phone.

Her initial thought was that Tom had taken an unacceptable risk to ring her at home, presumably to tell her that he was in Paris or Lyons or even at the chateau. She soon found out he was still in California where it was seven thirty in the morning.

'I'm sorry, Julia, I had to call.'

She could hear the anxiety in his voice. 'What is it?'

'I can't come. I can't come to Europe.'

Her heart sank like a stone. 'Why?'

'I've got a major problem here.'

'What?'

'Pierluigi Mancini's coming to the coast.'

'Who?' Julia was irritated. At first hearing it sounded as if Tom was turning her down because he'd got tickets for a concert by some Italian tenor she'd never heard of.

'He's the owner of Domenico's.'

'What's that?'

Now it was Tom's turn to sound faintly annoyed. 'Domenico's. It's the best, most expensive Italian restaurant in New York City. It's like Le Cirque. You must have heard of it.'

'I live in St Albans with my family, Tom. I told you already, our idea of an evening out is TGI Friday's.'

'OK. I get the picture.'

'So what's the big deal about this place?'

'They're opening a Domenico's West in San Francisco and I think I've got a shot at Mancini to take our stuff.'

'I'm sorry, Tom, I still don't understand.'

'It's the most prestigious restaurant in the continental United States, Julia. It's just amazing that he's even considering us. Every winery in America's been chasing this guy.'

'So why can't you come after that?'

'I can't leave town. I just can't. I don't know when he'll come, how long he'll be around for, whether he'll stay here. It's just too big and too exciting.'

Certainly bigger and more exciting than I am, thought Julia ruefully. 'But what about Château Descartes?'

'Deschamps.'

'They can wait.'

Me too, thought Julia again.

'That's an ongoing deal. This is different. To be sole provider for Domenico's West would make this the most respected winery in California. Suddenly everyone else would want us too. We could go from ten million dollars annual turnover to a hundred million dollars a year. Just on the back of this one deal. You've got to see how important this is, Julia.'

There was no response from St Albans.

'You can, can't you?' he asked, a little more anxiously this time.

'Sure,' she said briefly, unable to disguise the hurt in her voice. All those dreams of life with Tom, all those memories of what they were doing only a few days ago were being washed away in a stream of red wine. It was just like 1983 all over again. The damned winery had come before her then and it was coming between them again. She hated it with a passion.

For the first time she was beginning to wonder whether Candice had some justification for what had appeared to be her unreasonable behaviour towards Tom. Julia had assumed that Tom was always the victim of Candice's selfishness but now, for the first time, she was beginning to speculate about Tom's attitude towards her. Could anyone who was so clearly obsessed with his business ever have time and space in his life for a wife, let alone a family? Maybe there were reasons for his not having children that Tom hadn't articulated to her. Maybe it wasn't just Candice's selfishness. Maybe she had spotted something in Tom's character.

'Listen, darling, I'm disappointed too but we can still do Paris another time. Meanwhile you can come out here again. When can you travel, d'you think?'

'Tom, you must be kidding. Have you any idea how difficult that would be for me?'

'Julia, please, I'm desperate to see you again. Please come out here.'

'To California?'

'I can wire you a ticket.'

'For three days?'

'If you can. Please say yes.'

'Is there any point?'

'Any point? I love you. Isn't that the point?'

'I was being a little selfish and subtle at the same time.'

'Huh? Oh! Of course there's a point. I'm not going to be with Mancini twenty-four hours a day. At least I hope not.'

'So I would get to spend some time with you.'

'Of course. Why else would I ask you? Please come. I need you so much.'

And I need you too, I know that, thought Julia who was now feeling dizzy. All those plans, all those phone calls, all the plotting and planning had come crashing to the ground. She couldn't go through that again. But she'd have to. If she wanted to see Tom again, she'd have to. And she wanted to. She knew that for sure now.

'No. I'll have to do it from here. It's too complicated, too risky if you do it. I'll still leave on Wednesday as I arranged and I'll have to be back Sunday night. I'll make some phone calls and ring you back.'

'OK, fine. Whatever. Just buy yourself a mobile phone. One that works in France and the US. Give your husband the number and he'll never know where you are.'

'Why didn't we think of that before?'

'Didn't buy the handbook on adultery, I guess.'

'You're a genius.'

'And you're my girl.'

'I'll call you later.'

Julia was cheered by the thought of the mobile phone. She had been meaning to buy one for months, but until Tom's phone call, she had lacked the motivation. She had a phone in the office and a phone in the house. She had not particularly wanted to join the ranks of incessant babblers on the St Albans to King's Cross train. Yet now she thought what a Godsend to women seeking sexual fulfilment it must be. She reckoned she had two hours or so before Mike and Jamie came back. She needed every minute because she couldn't use the joint credit card to pay for the new ticket and only by relentless badgering and quoting her Frequent Flyer number did she manage to persuade the airline to confirm her booking over the telephone with a promise to pay before midday on Monday with a personal cheque.

She was back on the phone to Tom when Mike's car turned into the drive. She said a swift farewell to Tom and replaced the receiver, glad to have bought herself one of the long-distance pre-paid cards which enabled her to ring Tom without any trace of it appearing on the home bill. By the time Jamie came bursting through the door to stick his head in the fridge and mumble the traditional question about what time dinner was, Julia had recovered her composure.

She even managed to summon up the conviction to kiss a disgruntled Mike when he came in, complaining with justified bitterness of Jamie's delinquency in leaving him to hump both the heavy golf bags from the boot of the car. Falling in love again with Tom was making her a better wife to Mike, she thought to herself, quite surprised by the perverse revelation.

The atmosphere in the office was positively glowing on Monday morning. Half-yearly profits had just been announced to the financial press and the City had reacted positively, sending the share price up a significant few pence. Eric was speculating on acquisitions and mergers, about which Julia knew little and cared less even though Mike, who worked in corporate finance for one of the foreign banks in the City, spent much of his time discussing such strategies.

It was so spectacular a profits forecast that it made the chances of the Easy Listening department being asset-stripped almost an impossibility. If anything, the company's merchant bankers would be looking to acquire a rival to put it out of business and asset-strip it instead. Nobody worried about Julia slipping out for an early lunch to buy a mobile phone at the carphone shop and pick up an airline ticket to romantic places.

That moving, poetic lyric pounded through her head, conjuring up a series of Art Deco 1930s still photographs: a cigarette that bears a lipstick's traces, the airline ticket to the Seychelles, or in her case San Francisco, mixed with the image of Tom in a white dinner jacket and black tie, looking impossibly handsome, staring at her across a candlelit table as a waiter discreetly pours Johnson Winery Cabernet Sauvignon into heavy cut-glass goblets. The very thought of it gave her a warm glow all the way down Regent Street.

That night she lay in bed waiting for Mike to come in from the bathroom. He hadn't attempted to touch her again sexually since the first night she arrived back from California. She had, she felt, been very nice to him since Saturday when she had decided to go back to see Tom again and she was sure he would respond to this new warmth in their relationship by making an explicit advance.

Nothing, however, had happened for three nights but since she was leaving in the morning she expected an attack to come now — they would have five days apart for the wounds to heal. She wondered why she was thinking of their sex life as if she was a pioneer crossing America in a covered wagon, hearing the war cries of Indians, knowing that one night they would come. She knew perfectly well it wasn't really like that. Mike was not an insensitive lover.

When Mike did come in from the bathroom, she had turned out the reading

light and the bedroom was in darkness. She fell instinctively into her regular
habit of pretending to be asleep, leaving him to make the advance, if he dared.
She braced herself for the hand as it ruffled the duvet and made its way towards
her breast. She had decided she wouldn't reject him but she wouldn't go out
of her way to make things easy for him.

In the end the assault on her covered wagon never happened. Mike tossed
and turned but he kept his hands to himself. And now, perversely, Julia felt
sorry for him. As far as she knew, there was nobody else in his life, certainly no
Tom-like female equivalent. Mike was a decent man and she knew he deserved
something better than what she was offering him. She was a terrible wife — but
there was nothing she could do, for tomorrow she would be in the arms of her
lover and her heart raced and her body melted at the prospect.

Everything about the journey proceeded as planned. She was only going for a
few days and as far as everyone except Tom was concerned she was going to
Paris so it caused very little disruption or anticipation. With her new mobile
phone she could call home and Mike couldn't trace the call. If he called her,
he wouldn't know that she wasn't in an office off the Champs Élysées and if he
called her during the Californian hours of darkness, he would find the phone
turned off and the voice mail would operate automatically.

Tom had told her he would meet her at the airport but since he was
expecting the elusive Signor Mancini at any moment she wondered how
this was going to be possible. When she came out of customs and looked
for him she panicked when she saw that he wasn't there. Then she spotted
a uniformed chauffeur in a dark jacket and peaked cap holding up a card with
her name written on it in bold black ink.

The chauffeur introduced himself as Jim, wheeled her trolley ahead of her
rapidly and she trotted gamely in his wake. She couldn't help thinking that
this was what Mike probably thought he was reduced to when he met her at
the airport.

She had spent considerable time planning her return journey which presented more problems than usual. She had to be back in the office first thing on Monday morning and she therefore had to find a flight that would get her back to Heathrow on Sunday evening about the same time that a plane from Paris would be landing so that Mike could meet her. It meant having to fly the red eye from San Francisco to New York then take a daytime flight from JFK to Heathrow. She'd be truly knackered when she got back home but she was convinced the effort would be worth it.

It certainly seemed that way as she sat in the back of the limousine speeding along 101. Jim had run through the manifold delights of this supreme example of triumphal consumerism so quickly that all Julia could do was to nod and say 'Thank you', being unwilling to admit to never having travelled in such luxury before. She believed that if Tom had gone to the ridiculous expense of providing her with luxury, the least she could do was to act as if it was an everyday occurrence.

The telephone rang. Startled, Julia turned to lift it off its hook behind her right shoulder.

'Hello?'

'Is this Julia Cowan, movie star?'

'Old movie star.'

'You're the same age as Michelle Pfeiffer.'

'I know. We remark on the fact all the time.'

'How's the limo?'

'What, this old jalopy's a limo?'

'Cost me two hundred dollars.'

'I could have caught the airport bus.'

'To me what you're riding in is the airport bus.'

'Really?'

'Sure. I see a limo, I figure four kids whose parents have fifty bucks each to send them to the high school prom.'

'Well, I feel a bit like a prom queen.'

'How's that?'

'A little unsure of myself.'

'That's not a prom queen. A prom queen is figuring how she can dump the jerk she's come with and pick up the cute guy from LA with the floppy blond hair who's come as someone else's date.'

'Sounds like you know more than you should about teenage girls.'

'Yeah. I'm coaching the cheerleaders right now.'

'And Signor Mancini?'

'Later. Maybe tomorrow. Who knows? He's an asshole!'

'Will you be able to make a little space in your diary for me?'

'You'll see when you get here which should be . . . in around fifty minutes. Enjoy the limo. 'Bye.'

'Thanks, Tom,' whispered Julia and hung up the phone.

She opened a cupboard to find a drinks cabinet, discovered a tiny bottle of orange juice and poured it into a glass. She picked up the remote control and clicked it at the television screen that was cleverly inserted into the panel that separated the passengers from the driver. An old episode of *I Love Lucy* sprang to life.

She clicked again. A woman was telling Jerry Springer how she had managed to disguise from her boyfriend the fact that for the first twenty-seven years of her life she had been a man. She now realised she had made a mistake and wanted to reverse the operation. This information was so intimate and personal that she had decided to impart it to her boyfriend on national television. Julia clicked off the set and looked at the Golden Gate Bridge as it loomed ahead. Ever since she had met Tom again the bridge had become the symbol of her own liberation.

As the sleek limousine turned noiselessly off the road and through the gates of the Johnson Winery, Julia saw that he was waiting for her on the porch, the ubiquitous bottle of white wine in a cooler on the table. It was only a few weeks since she had driven into the car park for the first time. Now she felt as if she was coming home.

CHAPTER TWENTY

The four days passed in a blur. Signor Mancini was giving Tom the runaround, pointedly refusing to take or return his phone calls. Tom bravely disguised his disappointment and contented himself with being extremely attentive to Julia. Although delighted to have Tom all to herself, she couldn't help thinking that she was the more vulnerable one of the two of them and yet she was the one who was making all the sacrifices — just for the sake of the Johnson Winery.

These cavils were intermittent. The rest of the time Julia revelled in Tom's company. He drove her up and down Route 1 from the astonishing redwoods in Muir Woods all the way up the coast to the Point Arena lighthouse. When they had exhausted the coastal route, Tom took her the length and breadth of the beautiful Russian River Valley, making a point of ignoring all the wineries, which he dismissed as inferior because they specialised in sparkling wine, or 'grape soda' as he called it.

On their travels Tom explained more about his business which, to her surprise, Julia found interesting. Originally, back in their Oxford days, it had been an irrelevance, out of sight and out of mind. When they broke up she held the winery responsible for the destruction of all her dreams for the two of them but now, with Signor Mancini apparently removed from interfering in their limited time, the winery had brought them back together again. As such it was no longer the enemy and she found herself warming to Tom's tales of his family history.

She knew the business had been started by his great-grandfather around the end of the nineteenth century and was one of the oldest wineries in the business. Most of the California wine trade was really less than thirty years old. As Tom described the struggles of his grandparents to keep the winery going in hard times, Julia began to understand more than ever before why this patch of land exercised such a remarkable hold over Tom.

It was an estate rather than just a winery. It had always grown its own grapes, a process not shared by many of its rivals who could import grapes more cheaply than they could grow them. Their profit margins were therefore greater but the Johnsons despised the wine made from such sources.

It was a matter of family pride that they maintained the old wooden gravity flow winery building. By keeping as much of the winemaking process unchanged over the years but adding recent technological advances which he considered improved the traditional wines, Tom felt he had managed the difficult trick of keeping the winery's prices competitive in what had become an overcrowded market and at the same time ensuring that his Cabernet Sauvignon and Chardonnay in particular remained distinctive and outstanding.

It was Tom's proudest boast that if his grandfather, who had effectively built the place himself after his own father died suddenly of a heart attack in his early forties, came back to earth and tasted a glass of Johnson Sauvignon Blanc, he would think it was a vintage from his own days. Tom's grandparents nearly went under during the twenties when Prohibition virtually destroyed the embryonic wine industry in California. They survived only by selling small amounts of sacramental wine to local churches and operating largely as a supplier of fruit to the tiny widespread communities which dotted Sonoma County. That was an additional reason why Tom was determined never to import grapes from other estates no matter what cost savings it might produce.

In the late 1930s the vines were attacked and almost destroyed by phylloxera, a microscopic voracious insect that had been unwittingly imported from

Europe. Just as the Okies were trekking along Route 66 from the dustbowl ravages of the Midwest, so the vineyards of northern California were being wiped out by phylloxera which made its way along the Sonoma and Napa Valleys on the feet of animals, on the wooden boxes used for transporting grapes, or on the ocean winds lifting over the Mayacamas.

The Johnsons pulled through by the skin of their teeth. For all the trials and tribulations the estate had caused them, it was inconceivable to them that they would do anything else with their lives. Julia saw that Tom's professed desires to move into the world of politics had been only a flirtation. Dry Creek Valley exerted a pull as strong as anything Scarlett O'Hara ever felt for Tara.

On the Friday afternoon they walked slowly to the top of the hill behind the house, pausing only to admire the spreading panoramic view and each other.

'See that land from the lake to the road?'

'What about it?'

'Bought it about twelve years ago. You know, I feel differently about those acres than the rest of the place. They're mine. They were just dead fields. I made them grow. I don't know of a satisfaction like it.' He looked at her. 'Well, maybe one.' He kissed her. 'Could you live here?'

'I sort of am living here.'

'I mean permanently.'

'It's very tempting. Is the weather always as nice as this?'

'No. And if it rains in August, just as we're picking the grapes, we're all in trouble. But you're avoiding my question.'

'Tom, I'm not avoiding it. It's just too big to give you a snappy answer, so let me ask you something. Could you give all this up?'

His eyes narrowed. 'How do you mean?'

'I mean sell it, invest the balance with Goldman Sachs, come and live off the profits in England.'

'But what would I do? Where would I live?'

'You'd do something else and buy a flat with me in Hammersmith.'

'Why Hammersmith?'

'OK, not Hammersmith, but you get my drift.'

'It's a pretty big step.'

'Exactly. So let's just nurture what we have. For the moment.'

'I love you, Julia. I couldn't bear to lose you again.'

'You'll never lose me, Tom. I'll always love you.'

'But at a distance of six thousand miles.'

'We're not twenty-one any more. There's a lot of emotional baggage now.'

'I still feel twenty-one when I'm with you.'

'You make me feel so young . . .' Julia started.

'Let's do it,' said Tom urgently.

'Let's fall in love,' sang Julia automatically.

'Not the goddamn lyric! I mean let's do it here, now.'

'Have sex?'

'That's it.'

'On top of Old Smokey?'

'Any reason why not?'

'I've never done it al fresco,' she said doubtfully.

'This isn't al fresco,' said Tom, unbuttoning his shirt, 'it's more al Frisco. Or, if you point yourself in that direction, I suppose you'd call it al Fresno.'

Before they could proceed any further a mobile phone rang. Julia instantly reached for her phone, supposing it was Mike since it was too late for the office to be calling, but in fact it was Tom's cell phone which he was carrying even into the bathroom with him, so anxious was he not to miss the elusive Signor Mancini's telephone call.

Julia could see from his total concentration on the caller that this must be Mancini. Any thoughts of lovemaking had vanished from Tom's mind as he sprang to his feet and walked away from her, the phone clamped to his ear. She sat on the ground, hugging her knees, wondering if he exhibited similar intensity when she called. Somehow she doubted it. He snapped off the phone and turned back to her, pulling her to her feet and embracing her excitedly.

'He's coming. The sonofabitch is coming here.'

'I thought you said you'd lost it and he was never going to come.'

'Who knows? Who cares? He'll be here within the hour.' He started running down the hill with her. Julia tried to steady the pace.

'Hey! I'm not as fast as you. Can we go a little more slowly?'

'Listen, you've got to excuse me, this is real important. You just take your time, come down at your own pace.'

Julia didn't know if she was to be permitted to meet the all-powerful Mancini. Was she an asset or a liability? She washed her face, repaired her make-up, changed into a simple shift dress and awaited further instruction.

Tom was talking rapidly to Henri Lacroix when she emerged into the living room. She hung back, unwilling to interrupt what was clearly an important conversation, hoping Tom would turn round and smile. Before he could do so, Henri pointed to the window. Julia could see an expensive car rolling to a stop outside the main entrance. A short, dark man in a white linen suit and with a receding hairline stepped out of the back seat.

Tom turned and raced past Julia with a brief 'Hi' and ran out of the door to greet his distinguished visitor. Henri smiled briefly at her and followed his employer. Julia felt decidedly uncomfortable. In the end she decided to wait in the living room. If Tom was going to give Mancini a tour of the premises she had nothing useful to add and she would clearly be in the way. If he brought him into the house, which he must do at some point, she would be in the right location. If Tom wanted to send her to her room at that point, she would happily find an excuse and slink away.

It was nearly an hour before Tom and Henri returned with Mancini. Julia rose to her feet and smiled at him. Tom seemed briefly baffled, as if wondering why she was there, but Mancini exuded enough oily charm for the ten minutes of small talk to pass easily enough. Julia talked about her job and the Tony Bennett concert and the fact that she and Tom were old friends from college days. It all sounded incredibly innocent and she couldn't believe that Mancini would have grounds to doubt any part of the story but she could sense immediately that Tom wished she had not steered the conversation in that direction. Upset, she decided to make her excuses and leave.

When Tom came into the bedroom to find her reading one of the many art books which decorated the house, he wore the broadest smile she had ever seen.

'Did you get it?'

He lifted her up and hugged her. He was so transparently happy she could do nothing but hug him back.

'He wouldn't say. He's got other places to visit but we did well.'

'When will you know?'

'Could be a month but, honey, I think we have a real shot at this thing.'

'I hope I didn't get in your way out there.'

'Well, I was kinda puzzled. I didn't know what you thought you could add to the conversation.'

'I thought I might be able to help you.'

'What could you say? You want to talk to Pierluigi Mancini of Domenico's about your wine from Safeway?'

'Waitrose.'

'Wherever.'

'I didn't want to be rude.'

'You weren't. You couldn't be. And, honey, you could be looking at . . . no, I don't want to talk about it. It means too much to me. Let's make love instead. I have an urge to express myself creatively.'

Afterwards a terrible feeling of foreboding seemed to clutch at Julia's stomach. It was partly the knowledge that this visit was almost at an end and partly the realisation that she was no nearer to knowing where she and

Tom would go from here. She didn't like the lying and the deception; she knew that sooner or later she would have to tell Mike about Tom. She shuddered at the thought of his finding out inadvertently but then she couldn't bear to face the prospect of the pain she would be deliberately inflicting on all of them by telling him.

Tom spent the last hours just holding Julia in his arms. There was nothing he could say. He, too, knew there was no real solution in sight if Julia couldn't summon up the strength to leave Mike and Jamie and their life together. All he could do was to repeat quietly that he loved her. It wasn't a solution but it was what he needed to say and what she needed to hear.

'Just enjoy what we have,' said Tom as he kissed her on the lips, her eyelids, the tip of her nose and the lobe of her ear.

Julia didn't answer.

'Are you feeling guilty?'

'Of course. Aren't you?'

'Why should I? I love you. It's an entirely unselfish guilt-free emotion.'

'Why can't I be like you?'

'Oh God, no. I just want you to be like you. I want to spend the rest of my life with you not with me. You make me want to live for you. You make me feel unbelievably unselfish.'

'Tom, why didn't it work out all those years ago?'

'You know why,' he said shortly, a look of irritation clouding his face for a moment.

'Tell me again.'

'My father had a stroke. My mom couldn't cope. My sister lived back East. If I hadn't been here, stayed here, we might have lost the winery.'

'Might? Not would, just might?'

'OK, would. We would have lost the winery. And it would have been my selfishness that would have done it.'

'Nothing to do with me?'

'Of course not. You were . . . beautiful, you still are.'

'That's not what I mean. Did I, did our relationship, our future life together have any bearing on it?'

'I loved you, Julia, but you weren't pregnant and we were both young.'

'Meaning?'

'Meaning I hadn't left you a ruined woman. I hadn't left you stranded in the middle of the desert. And,' he paused before painfully extracting the words, 'I was a coward.'

'That may be a little hard on you.'

Tom shook his head. 'I was. I didn't look forward to the fights with my parents, with your parents, to proving them wrong. Maybe failing and proving them right. So I chickened out and stayed here.'

Julia kissed him softly on the lips. 'Thank you,' she said simply.

He nodded in acknowledgement. 'Besides,' he added cheerfully, 'I knew a woman like you wouldn't stay single for long. You were still a junior in college, an undergraduate. There'd be somebody else for you the next term.'

'And there was. There was Mike.'

'So I was right. Good old Mike.'

'He is good old Mike, you know.'

'Excuse me?'

'Mike's a good man.'

'Yeah, sure he is. But is he a great lay?'

'Well, I'm not exactly the most erotically adventurous woman you've ever met, am I?'

'I think you have the potential to be exactly that,' said Tom carefully. 'Want one last adventure?' He was kissing her ear and running his tongue around it. She felt herself shivering with pleasure.

'Yes, please,' she said, her eyes sparkling again.

Tom's embraces were wonderful. She felt so protected by them, so enveloped in his passion and his knowledge, in the sweet seductive air of the winery, in the glorious landscape which surrounded his comfortable house that now almost felt like a second home to her. They stood together in the shower for the longest time, their arms locked around each other's neck, eyes closed, just letting the warm jet of water spray off their bodies.

Neither of them was anxious to be the first to loosen their grip so they stood as they had twenty years ago at the end of their first Oxford Ball as the band played a slow version of the old Beatles hit 'Michelle'. Julia had slipped off her shoes and was holding them by the straps, her arms slung round Tom's neck. Tom had his arms wrapped securely round her bare back exposed by the low-cut ballgown.

As she packed her suitcase, Tom lay on the bed not taking his eyes off her. Julia felt a horrible stab of pain in her stomach, nothing remotely as bad as she had felt when Emily died but a sense of desertion, of desolation that certainly evoked memories of that tragic time.

'Don't look at me like that,' she said.

'Like what?'

'Like I was abandoning you.'

'Aren't you?'

'I'm going back to my family, Tom. Don't make it harder for me.'

'I'm sorry. I didn't mean to. I just wanted to remember you after you've gone. I want to memorise everything about you.'

'You're going to lie there fantasising about me packing?'

'Sure. That and other things.'

'What do you want from me, Tom?'

'I told you. I want you to leave your deadbeat husband and come and live with me here.'

'Mike's not a deadbeat.'

'I'm only repeating what you said.'

'I never called him that. I wouldn't. And I couldn't just leave him. I couldn't leave Jamie. I've told you.'

'It's not too late to have a baby with me.'

'You're being silly.'

'Why?'

'It's hard work having kids. You don't know. I do.'

'We can hire help – you can have whatever you need.'

'That's not really the point, Tom. I still love Mike.'

'What?'

'I never said I didn't love him.'

'Of course you did.'

'Oh God, this so complicated.'

'No, it's not, it's easy. You tell him you love me and you come and live here. You're complicating everything.'

'I've invested in seventeen years of marriage, Tom.'

'We all make bad investments. It's time to cut your losses, sweetheart.'

At that moment the doorbell chimed and Jim the chauffeur entered.

'I thought you were taking me to the airport,' said a surprised Julia to Tom.

'I wanted to give you a send-off in style.'

Jim picked up Julia's suitcase and exited with it discreetly. Julia and Tom embraced with the desperation of parting lovers.

'We'll see each other soon, won't we?' said Julia yearningly.

'Just as soon as I can get over there.'

'It won't be eighteen years this time, will it?'

'It won't be eighteen days. Trust me.'

It was an odd thing for Tom to say, perhaps an odder sensation for Julia to feel. She wasn't sure that she did trust Tom, not completely. Yet Mike, who would never say that, she did trust – completely. Of course she was comparing Tom's emotions to Mike's domestic reliability which wasn't very fair but as she kissed him for the final time, the image of stolid, reliable, dependable Mike, standing outside the customs hall at Heathrow waiting for her, sprang sharply into focus in her mind.

*　　*　　*

Her New York flight landed in London two hours before Mike was due to arrive to pick her up off the plane from Paris she had supposedly been booked on. In the intervening time she ripped off the luggage tags, tore the boarding card and ticket into a thousand pieces and rescued the French bread and slices of Camembert and Brie cheese from the bottom of her carry-on bag. Tom had provided her with the name of a delicatessen in San Francisco which specialised in French food. Although such delicacies were easily obtainable from the local Waitrose it had remained a ritual of theirs over the years to bring back French bread and cheese whenever they went to France. Mike would expect it and would comment if she didn't have them.

Julia spent an anxious half an hour scanning the arrivals screen in Terminal 2. She had pushed her trolley across from Terminal 3 very aware of the fact that if Mike got there before the flight disgorged its passengers he would be able to see that she hadn't emerged from customs but from elsewhere. Julia was relying on Mike's hatred of hanging around anywhere. He liked to time everything to the minute, including theatre performances, film starting times and, more worryingly, train departures. Her knowledge of Mike's behaviour patterns stood her in good stead.

He was mildly surprised to see her waiting for him when he arrived only fifteen minutes after the Paris flight had landed but he didn't question her explanation of being first off the plane because she had been sitting near the rear exit door and baggage handlers who wanted to go home as soon as possible had tossed the luggage onto the conveyor belt in record time. Julia found she was genuinely pleased to see Mike again, grateful for the stolid virtues he represented.

She had imagined that their house would look small, ugly and cramped when she got home. That had certainly been her reaction the last time she had flown back after being with Tom. This time, though, the house was the right size and it was comforting rather than frustrating. She looked forward to a long soak in her own bath. Showers were a pleasant change but nothing could beat a soothing hot bath with a glass of white wine balanced on the side of the washbasin and the sound of Gershwin on the radio.

Instead of being resentful, depressed or remote, as she feared he might be, Mike was actually warm, smiling and delighted to see her. Had something happened? It rather worried her at first, then she thought that maybe much of her dissatisfaction with Mike actually stemmed from her. Maybe he was this way most of the time but her own problems prevented her from seeing it.

Jamie was already in bed when they got in, although Julia thought she detected his bedroom light snapping off as she opened the front door. Mike didn't bother to eat either the cheese or the bread. Well, it was late, she admitted. She slipped the cheese into the fridge and tossed the bread into the rubbish bin. There was nothing worse than stale French bread and it had done its primary job anyway.

Mike had taken the trouble to remake the bed with clean sheets and had lit one of her scented candles. He was sitting up in bed reading the Sunday paper as she entered from the bathroom.

'This is so nice, Mike.'

'Doesn't compare with a four-star hotel.'

'Three star.' Julia didn't want Mike to think she had been living in luxury.

'Still . . . I wanted you to be glad to be home.'

'I am.'

And she was. She felt safe and secure and protected. She climbed into bed. There was nothing to compare to the comfort of her own bed. Mike waited till she had finished rubbing the lotion into her hands then leaned over to kiss her. Julia pecked at him briefly then picked up the remote control and turned on the late-night film on television. She no longer knew whom she was being faithful to and whom she was betraying.

Julia was back at work the following day, just as she would have been had she indeed been in Paris the previous week. She was deeply involved all day in meetings to discuss the launch and marketing of the Tony Bennett CD. She could tell that Eric was becoming increasingly irritated because she was being regarded by the head of marketing as the key person in the room but she was enjoying the experience and refused to let Eric depress her.

In fact it was a day of unexpected delights all round. The lawyers for the Richard Rodgers estate had finally agreed to the reissue of a compilation CD Julia had been planning in time for the centenary of his birth in 2002. She greatly preferred the somewhat cynical early Rodgers and the songs he produced in partnership with Larry Hart to the saccharine but undeniably memorable songs he wrote later with Oscar Hammerstein. The co-operation promised by the estate would enable her to select from the entire range of Rodgers' work, doubling the potential amount of music they could release and the potential profits. Even Eric could scarcely forbear to smile as he wrestled with the problem of how to present it to the board as his own triumph.

Before she left the office Julia picked up a message saying Mike had called. She was oddly pleased to hear from him, though she was still surprised by her emotional response, given the fact that she was engaged in a full-blown affair with another man. She rang him at the bank but he had gone. She rang the mobile but it was switched off. She'd catch him at home later, she thought, so she called Tom who was soon talking grandly of reinstating his trip to the Loire Valley within a couple of weeks. He asked Julia to work out when it might be politic for her to re-schedule her Paris meeting. This long-distance love affair was working out all right, Julia thought. Everyone seemed to be happy.

The six thirty-three left King's Cross on time, always a welcome surprise, although the crowning glory of the day was the man in the pinstriped suit who rose gallantly to his feet and silently gestured towards the seat he had vacated. Julia flashed him a dazzling smile and sat down quickly before he could change his mind or the young woman standing next to her could interpret it as an invitation for her.

Julia regarded this succession of good fortune as a positive sign, but she didn't know how long she could keep this balancing act going. At times she felt as though she was giving ninety-eight per cent of her energy to her family, to Tom and to her job, leaving herself with very little, and at other times she thought this was a small price to pay for the happiness she was preserving.

She opened the front door to hear the familiar strains of the signature tune of Jamie's favourite television soap opera. He was allowed to watch it before going back upstairs to his bedroom to finish his homework. Julia dropped her bags on the floor, took off her coat and hung it on the hook in the hallway. She went into the kitchen to warm up some soup before going into the lounge to see Jamie and Mike.

Mike wasn't in the lounge. He was in the kitchen, sitting at the table, waiting for her with a look on his face as if he had been struck on the back of the head with a large block of wood. There was a split second in which Julia thought that if she maintained her bright smile of welcome she could restore Mike to a similar state. It was only a split second. That look of his chilled her to the marrow. There was no point in seeking comfort in smiles or lies. Mike knew. He knew everything.

CHAPTER TWENTY-ONE

'HOW DID YOU FIND OUT?'

Julia had opened a bottle of white wine she had found in the fridge, checking the label in case it should be, of all the bizarre chances, a bottle from the Johnson Winery. It wasn't.

'I wanted to take you away for our anniversary.'

'Thank you.'

'I don't think so.'

Julia waited.

'I was going to use the air miles. I knew how many we had. I checked yours. You had twelve thousand more than you should have done. I rang your office to get the name of your Paris contact. I rang him and he said you'd postponed the meeting. You never went to Paris. You went to California.'

'I see.'

'That the best you can do?'

'I'm sorry.'

'I'm sure you are. How long has this been going on?'

Julia couldn't suppress the rueful smile. It was a line from a Gershwin lyric. How was it possible that these damn things kept cropping up in conversation all the time?

'What's so funny?'

'Nothing. There's nothing remotely funny here at all, Mike.'

'Who is he?'

Here it was. The question she had been dreading. It was one thing to have done what she had done. There was, in her own mind at least, some kind of justification which Mike, once he'd battled his way through the pain and anger, might possibly recognise had some validity. The identity of the other man was something else entirely. The revelation that it was Tom Johnson would destroy Mike utterly. She was tempted to lie, make up a name, he wouldn't know, wouldn't care. His argument was with her not with him, whoever this fictional him might be.

Even as she thought about it she knew she couldn't do it. She simply couldn't go on lying. What if they managed to stagger across this bridge and then he found out who it was? That would certainly be the end and it would be even more painful than the agony they were both suffering now.

'Tom,' she said quietly, not looking at him.

'Tom Johnson?' he asked, clearly horrified.

Julia nodded and ran out of the room and up the stairs. Dare she go into the bedroom? Where was her refuge now? Should she leave? What would she say to Jamie? What would Mike say to Jamie?

Then she heard it. It was the cry of a man whose heart had been torn out of him. No, not a man, it didn't even sound like a human kind of agony. It was more akin to the scream of an animal that had been caught in a man-made trap and knew it was soon to be clubbed to death. It tore through the house and through Julia's soul. Faintly she heard the sound of the lounge door opening as Jamie ran into the kitchen. Julia flung herself face down on the bed, burying her head in the pillows, longing for the earth to open up and swallow her whole.

She tried to force the good images into her mind – Tom's smile, the blowing away of the cobwebs that had been clinging to her since Emily died, the rebirth of her sexuality. It was no use. The terrible feelings of betrayal were too strong for the puny opposition erected by her falling in love again with Tom. She didn't know whether to reactivate the awful conversation or to leave it to Mike to find her when he wanted to talk. Should she pack a few things and go to a hotel? She had never been in this situation before and she didn't know the rules. Were there rules? What would she tell Jamie? How could she do this now of all times, with exams starting in ten days? How could she ever have been so selfish?

She got into her nightdress, climbed into bed and scrambled under the covers. She prayed for the merciful release of sleep but it didn't come. She could hear Jamie playing music too loudly in his bedroom. In the normal course of events she would go straight into his room and tell him to turn it down or off and to get on with his work or have a bath or read something worthwhile but now she didn't have the right any more – she had forfeited the natural authority that stemmed from being his mother and behaving like a proper mother. She had behaved disgracefully. She needed to be punished; she wanted to be punished.

Eventually she heard the slow, heavy tread of Mike's footsteps on the stairs. What should she do? Sit up and smile? Pretend to be asleep? They'd each done that to the other so often it would hardly be original. In the end she decided that the best thing she could do would be to lie in the dark on her back with her eyes open and leave the decision to him. Mike opened the door, picked his pillow off the bed, grabbed one end of the top blanket and pulled it off. He dragged it out of the room and shut the door behind him.

Julia didn't feel the cold caused by the removal of the top blanket. Her whole body was covered in sweat. Her nightdress was damp. She thought about penance, the sort of penance a nun might have expected, some kind of ritual flagellation that would purge the soul. All the justification she had used to persuade herself of the moral rectitude of her case had suddenly deserted her.

She fell into a troubled sleep shortly after one o'clock and woke with the dawn chorus at four thirty. For a moment she knew she was awake and she knew there was a problem of some kind but she hoped, as she regained her senses, that it would turn out to have been the dream she had just had. The full knowledge swept over her a second later. She decided to get dressed. It was something to do and it gave her a tiny advantage if any discussion were shortly to take place.

She put on her work clothes, made the bed and threw her damp nightdress with the debris of last night's undressing into the dirty clothes basket. She went downstairs to see if Mike was still there. She feared he might have gone off to a hotel or a friend's house. She wanted desperately to talk for a couple of hours or more before Jamie got up so that when he came down to breakfast he could see the two of them at least behaving almost normally.

Julia crept past Jamie's bedroom although she knew that he slept so soundly he didn't hear his alarm clock most mornings. She went downstairs into the lounge, then into the dining room, finally into the kitchen. There was no sign of Mike. She ran quickly back upstairs into the bedroom he used as a study. He was lying in a huddle on the floor, curled up in as near to the foetal position as he could manage, having wrapped himself awkwardly in the blanket.

'Mike?' she whispered. There was no response. 'We need to talk. Please.'

She sidled awkwardly into the small room. Mike's six feet of perfectly still body length took up a disproportionate amount of space in it. As she stood over him she noticed with a small shock that his eyes were wide open and dull with pain.

'Fuck off,' said Mike.

Julia flushed and shivered at the same time. Mike rarely swore but if he did it was always in anger. This was different. This was spoken with implacable cold hatred. Julia felt the tears filling her eyes at the hopelessness of the situation. She closed the door quietly.

She rescued her mobile phone from her handbag, picked her coat off the rack in the hall and walked into the cold mist of the early morning, closing the front door softly behind her out of habit. She could have used the mobile indoors of course but she felt in the circumstances it would somehow defile the house. She pressed the buttons and heard the sound of the American phone ringing. Tom answered on the second ring.

'Hello?'

'Tom.'

'Hi, honey! I was just thinking about you. In fact, all I do—'

'Tom, he knows. Mike knows.'

There was a terrifying silence on the line.

'Tom! Did you hear me? I said Mike knows.'

'Sure I heard you, honey. I was just thinking of the right thing to say.'

'Tom, I'm so frightened.'

'I'm coming to London. Just as soon as I can get on a plane. I've lost the deal for Domenico's West. That Mancini is a real bastard. I am so pissed off about it.'

Julia gritted her teeth. Why was he talking about his bloody winery now? Hadn't he heard what she had just said?

'Tom, he hates me. Mike hates me.'

'Sweetheart, calm down. We knew this would happen one day.'

'One day maybe. Not today, though.'

'Nothing's changed. I still love you. You still have problems with Mike.'

'No, Tom, everything's changed.'

'You've stopped loving me?' His voice was remote, a dull monotone.

'Please, Tom, this is about me, just for this moment. Me and Mike and Jamie.'

'So what do you want to do?'

'I don't know. I'm totally flummoxed.'

'How do you feel?'

'Devastated.'

'Julia, I think it's for the best.'

'Oh really? How do you work that one out?'

'You had to confront Mike sometime. Now you can cauterise the wound.'

'Tom, I can't hurt him any more. No matter what he's done.'

'Julia, you haven't killed anybody. You haven't been a wicked person. You haven't stolen money or dealt drugs. You just fell in love. Not even your New Labour government has criminalised that yet.'

'Tom, I've got to go.'

'Hey, don't go like this.'

'I'm walking along our street. I can see the milkman on his float coming towards me.'

'You still get milk delivered? You can't buy milk in grocery stores yet?'

'Look, this isn't the time for this conversation.'

'I love you, Julia. And I'll be in England by the weekend. If you need someone to look after you and take care of you I'll be there for you. We've found each other again. Let's not screw it up this time. OK?'

'Thank you, darling. I'll call you later.' She clicked off the phone.

Julia called in sick to the office. If the voice mail timed the call they'd find out it was made at 5.50 a.m. — conclusive proof, she thought wryly, that it was a genuine illness. She got into her car and started driving aimlessly to clear her mind, but her mind, like the roads, not only refused to clear but instead got steadily more congested. To get away from the rush-hour traffic she turned right at the next traffic lights since all the traffic was going left, and found herself on the old A40 heading towards Oxford.

It seemed somehow appropriate. Oxford was where her relationships with both Tom and Mike had begun. Could she find something there that might help her through this new crisis in her life? If she had been religious she would have visited a church or at least prayed but any vestiges of faith that had lingered from her childhood had been eradicated by Emily's death. If there was a spiritual answer it was not going to be the conventional religious one.

As she drove north-west, Julia gradually became aware that it had turned into a wonderful May morning in early summer. Bright sunshine dappled the meadows; it was a land of bluebells and cherry blossom, among the beechwoods covering the surrounding hills were green-gladed places, full of paths, mossy banks and sparkling streams running down to the river. A long-forgotten sonnet looped round her mind:

> Full many a glorious morning have I seen
> Flatter the mountain-tops with sovereign eye,
> Kissing with golden face the meadows green,
> Gilding pale streams with heavenly alchemy . . .
> Yet him for this my love no whit disdaineth;
> Suns of the world may stain when heaven's sun staineth.

Then she remembered where she had first heard that Shakespearean sonnet. Tom had recited it as he punted her down the Isis.

She drove across the ring road, ignoring as she always had the factories and houses of Cowley, and through Headington, passing the street on which the art-house cinema, the Moulin Rouge, had stood – the one Tom still referred to with such affection. As the honey-coloured stone, the immaculate lawns and spires of Oxford loomed into view she felt as if she was returning to the womb.

When she had come back for the reunion it had been a dark and cold April night and she had been too obsessed with whom she might meet and how she would feel about them to be influenced by the charms of the city. Now she left the car beyond the University Parks, off the Banbury Road, and walked back into town. The streets were full of students, many of them carrying that distinctive look of anxiety that presaged the approach of finals. She wanted to sit them down, to take the worry away, to tell them it didn't really matter what they wrote about either Beowulf or Sir Gawain and the Green Knight. In three weeks' time neither name would crop up in conversation again.

She turned off St Aldate's and walked through the majestic college of Christ

Church and into the meadow behind. This was where her life had begun. That pale provincial girl had started her life just as the Prime Minister of the time, another ex-Oxford woman with problems, had begun destroying everyone else's. I want to start again, thought Julia as she saw the students lining the banks of the river, some of them reading, some of them sleeping off the effects of last night's party, some of them pretending to work or abandoning the pretence and simply canoodling with each other.

It seemed such a time of innocence, before marriage, before children, when this great institution of learning had opened her eyes to the possibilities that lay before her, when the future, even the Thatcherite future of one of the university's less honoured graduates, seemed pregnant with the boundless possibilities that life offered. What would her eighteen-year-old self have said to her had she been granted the luxury of time travel? Would she have been disappointed that nearly twenty years on she hadn't achieved much, devastated by the death of Emily, traumatised by her current agony? Or would she have revelled in a life surrounded by music, in a son who might yet set the world on fire in a way she could never have dreamed of, in her two men, her two lovers, both of whom loved her, needed her, wanted her.

She walked slowly along the river, back through the Parks, and sat down when she was tired to watch a cricket match being played in front of the old pavilion. Now it really did appear as if time had stood still. The game was as slow and boring and repetitive as she remembered but in its unchanging rhythmic rituals she found a small measure of comfort and security.

When the players went off for lunch, the shirt-sleeved crowd which numbered not much more than fifty all stood up and applauded in a desultory sort of way. The younger ones departed swiftly and the rest, mostly old men and retired couples, opened sandwich boxes and began to unwrap their picnics. Julia continued with her walk, now passing through the colleges, studiously avoiding her own as if she might meet Helen or somebody who would ask whether she ever met up with Tom Johnson again.

It was two thirty before she realised that she hadn't eaten since the day before. She had been so traumatised by events that her brain had simply failed to transmit the message that she was hungry. It was a wonderful way to diet, she thought wryly. The pounds must be dropping off her as she walked. She recovered the car and drove out of the city, stopped at a village pub and ordered a ploughman's lunch and a Diet Coke.

When the bread and cheese came, she wolfed it down hungrily. This was no time to worry about weight. She was losing her marriage as she had lost her daughter and the knowledge was ripping off the scarcely covered scab of that old deep wound.

Was she really losing her marriage? she asked herself. She was no nearer to resolving her dilemma. She felt now that she had obligations to all the men in her life – to Tom because he had reawakened her and seemed to be preparing to demonstrate his commitment, to Mike for the history they shared, and to Jamie who was her son and still a kid for all his potential as the world's greatest golfer. How could she reconcile all these conflicting needs?

When she got home Jamie was back from school and sitting in front of the television with his feet on the coffee table, his shoes and blazer in an ungainly heap on the carpet. He was watching a cartoon and eating an enormous sandwich which he had clearly hacked out himself. It was so large it required great dexterity just to get it into his mouth.

'Hi, Mum. You're back early,' he said, his eyes not leaving the screen for a second in case Scooby Doo should do something unexpected.

Jamie appeared to be entirely unfazed by the events of the previous night, or else he was putting on a terrific act. Julia felt sure it was the former and a wave of relief swept through her. Mike had clearly said nothing to him, otherwise there must surely have been some evidence of distress. She couldn't believe that Mike had forgiven her but she was optimistic that because he hadn't bad-mouthed her to their son it meant he was still thinking rationally. When he got back from work they would be able to talk to each other like two civilised human beings.

But Mike didn't get back from work. He didn't ring and Julia dared not call his mobile. He always called her if his plans changed. If he hadn't called her, there was a good reason and she knew she mustn't interfere. He obviously needed space, just as she had needed her time in Oxford.

What an irony if he'd done exactly the same thing – called in sick and driven off to Oxford to think. The prospect of their bumping into each other in Blackwells bookshop would have been funny if it hadn't been so sad. She found herself listening for the sound of his car turning into the driveway, the engine being cut, the car door banging, the sound of his key turning in the lock of the front door – harmless sounds she had heard every day of their lives together for years but now suddenly invested with a new significance by their absence. She didn't know if she missed them because of this new significance or because they were part of a comforting routine.

She made dinner for Jamie and herself, a mechanical procedure which followed traditional lines. As she cooked, Jamie watched *Neighbours* and *The Simpsons*, then wandered into the kitchen to devour his dinner before going upstairs to his bedroom to do his homework. He was wearing his usual vacant expression and a baseball cap.

'Take it off at the table, please.'

'Why?'

'Because it's rude to eat with it on.'

'Who says it's rude?'

'I do.'

'That's stupid.'

'You can't eat with that thing on your head at the table.'

'All right. I'll eat in the living room.'

He started to rise to his feet with his plate.

'Jamie!'

Julia's voice almost shattered the water glass. Jamie sat down quickly. He wondered what had caused his normally phlegmatic mother to snap like that, but thought, on balance, it was probably better not to inquire. The meal terminated swiftly as Jamie sought refuge in his bedroom computer.

By ten o'clock Mike had still not shown up. Was he with another woman? What if he had gone out drinking? She couldn't confront him then. For Julia everything depended on Mike being calm and rational. She decided to have a bath and go to bed.

Pleased as she was to remove the grime of two days she wasn't in the mood to enjoy the bath. She couldn't play the radio as she liked to do, listening to *The World Tonight* or *A Book at Bedtime* on Radio 4, because she wouldn't be able to hear the sound of Mike's car arriving. In the event he didn't come home while she was in the bathroom so she got into bed and turned on the television, remote control on the pillow beside her, ready to turn it off should she hear him. She would receive him sitting up in bed reading rather than passively staring at Jeremy Paxman relentlessly hounding a junior government official.

She fell asleep and woke only briefly during the closing music of *Newsnight* to snap off the bedside light and the television. About an hour later she heard the front door opening and then the sound of movement downstairs. She got out of bed and pulled back the curtain. Mike's car stood on the driveway. Was he coming upstairs?

He was. She sat up in bed, heart pounding, waiting for the opening of the bedroom door and the long, silent, accusing stare. She resolved to be as passive as possible, not to speak unless spoken to, to let him do the talking, let the bile and the suffering pour out of him. But he never came in. She heard him open the door of his study and close it again. She knew his pillow and blanket were still there. When she returned from Oxford their bed had been made but Mike's pillow and the top blanket were still missing.

After so many weeks of agonising over Mike slipping into bed beside her wanting sex and then dropping off into a snore-filled sleep when she didn't, she took no pleasure now in her sole occupation of the double bed. She wanted to go next door and talk to him but she felt sure it was a pointless exercise.

Next morning she lay in bed, listening to the sounds of the house as Mike came out of the study, used the bathroom, made himself breakfast, then slammed the front door shut. Julia sprang out of bed, ran downstairs to examine the usual places they left messages for each other in case Mike had written her a note because he couldn't face talking to her. Nothing.

She made breakfast for Jamie, explaining that she might have to go away again on business. Jamie showed absolutely no interest in her movements. She might as well not have bothered telling him anything for all the emotion he exhibited. After he had left the house, still enumerating rock formations for his geography exam, she called Sarah and asked to meet her for lunch.

'I have to go to Oxford Street.'

'Why?'

'I have to return a purple top I bought there last week.'

'Purple's not your colour.'

'I know but this one's more of a mauve. Anyway it looked hideous when I put it on at home. John said he'd divorce me if I didn't take it back so I'm taking it back.'

Julia felt a quick stab of jealousy. John cared enough about Sarah to have that sort of easy conversation, something Julia thought she'd destroyed for ever with Mike. They could joke about divorce – Julia couldn't.

'Please, Sarah.'

Sarah caught the urgency in her voice. 'What is it? Does Mike know?'

'I'll tell you later.'

'Oh my God! He does! Oh, darling, I'm so sorry!'

Julia looked so awful when she arrived at the office that she was treated with great consideration by everyone, including Eric. She was urged to go back home as soon as possible since she had palpably returned to work too soon.

She struggled on to lunchtime. Sarah made it by one fifteen looking flushed but carrying a Marks and Spencer bag.

'Sorry, darling. Left work early to avoid the rush but of course I didn't.' She drew the mauve top out of the bag. 'What do you think?'

'I think John's probably right.'

'He frequently is. Very frustrating.' She paused, waiting for Julia to open up. 'How did it happen?'

'Mike checked the air miles.'

'God, who could have guessed! What rotten luck.'

'It had to come out sooner or later.'

'Always better later, always.'

'How would you know?'

'You think you're unique?'

'Sarah!'

'Oh listen, it wasn't so bad and John never found out or if he did he just kept quiet about it.'

'Who . . . I mean why?'

'Do I really need to tell you?'

'No, of course not. I'm just surprised.'

'Why? You think I don't want romance in my humdrum life? You think this job and cooking for the kids and washing and changing the sheets and getting five minutes how's your father once a month makes me feel like a princess?'

'Who was it?'

'Let's just say he was disgracefully young and fortunately living in Milan with no plans to move to north London.'

'That's why you were so sensitive, so unwilling to judge me.'

'I'd like to think I would have been anyway. I mean, you're my friend. Why wouldn't I be there for you?'

'I don't know. I guess I'm so appalled at what I've done that I expect to have a scarlet A branded on my forehead.'

'Do you love Tom?'

'Of course. At least I think so.'

'Just think so?'

'I love him.'

'And do you love Mike?'

'Well now, this is the really weird bit.'

'Try me.'

'I love Mike too. I still love Mike.'

'Why's that weird?'

'Because I'm in love with two men at the same time.'

'And you think this makes you unique in human history?'

'I . . . I don't know. I would never have believed it was possible.'

'Oh, it's possible.'

'You too?'

'Answer me this. Has Tom dumped you?'

'No. He's coming to London. He'll be here tomorrow.'

'So what are you going to do?'

'I don't know. I was rather hoping you might help me.'

'You can stay with us if you want.'

'Well, I think I'll have to stay with Tom. I mean he's coming all this way.'

'Have to? You feel obliged to sleep with your lover?'

'I didn't want a lover.'

'Don't be silly. You didn't want the complications. You sure as hell wanted a lover. And that's not all your fault so will you please stop beating up on yourself.'

'Sorry.'

'And stop apologising for everything.'

'Sor— OK.'

'I have only one piece of advice.'

'Go on.'

'Listen to your heart. Your heart knows.'

'Sarah,' said Julia impatiently, 'what are you? Some wise old Eastern mystic?'

'Sure. A wise old mystic from Mill Hill East. I mean it. You'll know it when it happens. It's just like falling in love.'

'Meanwhile?'

'Burn no bridges. And pay the bill. I've still got to get back to M and S.'

Julia smiled as Sarah clattered away using her shoulder bag to clear a passage for herself by the cashier's desk. How she wished that the most important thing in her life right now was to get a refund for £29.99 from Marks and Spencer. Yet she knew that most of the women in this very restaurant would be envious if they were expecting their first great love to be flying in from California for a night of passion and a lifetime of love.

The moment Julia saw Tom again the following evening after work, she felt her heart surge with joy so she supposed that Sarah had been right. When she knocked on the door of his hotel room he was obviously still asleep. Eventually, he opened it dressed in the thick white towelling robe provided by the hotel and rubbing the sleep out of his eyes. Unshaven and with tousled hair, he looked amazingly handsome.

'Sorry. Didn't mean to disturb you.'

'I didn't realise I'd be so jet-lagged.'

'Got the energy for one last embrace?'

He nodded, smiled and enveloped her in a huge bear hug. 'I love you, Julia Cowan.'

'I'm starting to get used to that name again.'

'Do you want something from room service?'

Julia shook her head. 'Just you.'

Their lovemaking this time was slow and gentle. It might have lacked the urgency of their first meeting but it reflected their current mood which was rather sombre. They were both conscious of the major decisions that were still to be made.

Afterwards, Julia walked across to the window and looked down over Hyde Park. She remembered when the hotel was built her parents telling her there had been a big scandal because the top-floor guests would be able to look into the garden of Buckingham Palace. This would presumably interfere with the Queen Mother's topless sunbathing.

As she looked into the grounds of one of Great Britain's most hallowed institutions, all she could see were two men examining a heap of scaffolding. They must be erecting a marquee for a garden party, she thought. Julia couldn't understand why the Queen should object. People would only see that she had builders and scaffolders banging away outside the bedroom window just like the rest of the country.

Tom walked over to her, slipped his hands round her waist and pulled her to him.

'Thank you for coming into my life again.'

'Thank you for coming to London when I needed you.'

'It was no problem. I had to meet Jean Pierre Deschamps sometime. Monday's as good as any other now that asshole Mancini's out of the picture.'

Julia turned to look at him. 'Is that the only reason you came?'

'Of course not. I came as soon as you called.'

'Would you have come if there hadn't been a business reason to fly to Europe?'

'I don't know what you mean. You've known about this meeting with Jean Pierre for weeks.'

'Yes,' said Julia doubtfully. Her emotions kept shifting like the ground before an earthquake. Every time she thought she knew how she felt about Tom, how Tom felt about her, something made her unsure again.

'Can you stay here tonight?'

'I'm trying not to provoke Mike.'

'But you're not sleeping with him?'

'No. He's still sleeping on the floor of his study.'

'So he's hardly going to know—'

'Of course he is.'

'But why should he care?'

'And there's Jamie.'

'For God's sake, Julia, the kid's fifteen years old. You're treating him like he's five.'

'You don't think this is traumatic for a child at any age? Particularly one who's in the middle of exams?'

'Hey! I didn't fly all this way for a fight.'

'I'm sorry.'

'Me too.'

'Let's do something we can't do over the phone.' He took her hand and led her slowly back to the bed.

She lay on her side, her head resting on his chest, his arm round her shoulders. He was lifting the strands of her hair and kissing them. If only she could lie here for ever, naked in the arms of her lover, and not have to worry about anything else. They could live off room service and the mini bar and when they had reached the financial limit set by their credit cards they would be found by the rest of the world as they were now, wrapped in each other's arms in an eternal embrace.

But in two hours' time Julia knew she would be on the M1 heading north towards Junction 6, following the tail lights of the rush-hour traffic. Tom was here, in London, with his arms round her but she knew now that his arrival was not in itself going to solve anything.

CHAPTER TWENTY-TWO

MIKE HAD NOT FELT so energised for years. Julia's betrayal and the wild fury he felt about her and Tom was being recycled in the most positive way.

He had always known that Julia had loved Tom in a different, more romantic way than she had loved him (if she had loved him at all, he sometimes felt) and he had resented it from the moment they met and she had told him about the recently departed Tom. He felt bitter, too, about the way Julia had punished him with silent reproach since Emily's death. He had his own guilt to deal with, a guilt that would stay with him every day for the rest of his life.

Was this her revenge? She had taken a lover and not just any lover, this wasn't an office romance or a one-night stand with a 25-year-old man to make her feel better about the ageing process; she had deliberately sought a romantic love affair with the one man in the world she knew he could never tolerate.

The depth of his anger had somehow sustained him in the week since she'd been back from California. Normally when he got angry with Julia he did so for an hour or two, maybe overnight if it was a particularly bad row but then they made up. True, they didn't make up on the carpet in front of the gas fire in a tangle of discarded clothes as they had in the early days but they laughed and kissed and hugged.

Jamie knew they rowed but he didn't seem to be upset by it. Julia was always worried that he might be, remembering the frequently frosty atmosphere in the house where she had grown up. Mike had always been less concerned because he knew what a self-contained lad Jamie was. He had seen it on the golf course from a very early age. Deprived of that vital insight, Julia would never understand Jamie as he did.

Mike made a point of leaving the bank early to be home when Jamie got in after his first GCSE, which was French oral. Julia had an important meeting in town, or so she said, and couldn't make it. Mike glowed inwardly. Wherever she was he was sure her mind would be straying towards Jamie. He knew her so well. Let Tom Johnson deal with the pull-back, the distracted air, the blank face and the indefinable sense of boredom that could emanate from her at such moments during the act of love.

Mike was unloading the dishwasher when Jamie walked in, a broad smile on his face.

'How d'you feel?'

'Starving.'

'Tea and sandwich?'

'Cool.'

'How'd it go?'

'*Comme un dream.*'

'You didn't say that?'

'No, but I've been talking Français for *vingt quatre heures* now and I can't get out of the habit.'

'So what came up?'

'Not the restaurant.'

'*Sacré bleu.*'

'It was the French pen pal, holidays in France, the EU and I managed to get him talking about Jean Van der Velde.'

'Brilliant.'

'Though I say so *moi-même.*'

'Great!'

'He was very impressed. I could see.'

'Parental occupations?'

'Right at the start.'

'You still had me down as a postman?'

'Yeah, Mum too.'

'What?'

'Dad, it's so much easier.'

'You don't think he suspected?'

'I think he probably felt sorry for me.'

'I need to talk to you about Mum. Here's your sandwich.'

While Jamie silently munched his way through the sandwich, Mike did his best to explain what was going on without bringing Tom into the equation. He told Jamie that he and Julia still loved each other but they'd been married for nearly twenty years and there were always bumps along the way in a long marriage. That was all they were going through. They both wanted him to do well so the best way he could help matters was to concentrate on working hard for the exams.

It was plausible enough. A lot of it was true. As an explanation it lacked one crucial element but at this stage Mike didn't feel that was relevant to Jamie.

'Are you and Mum going to split up?'

'Did I say anything about splitting up?'

'Dad, get real. It happens all the time. Ten of the kids in my class went through it, five more live with a new mum or dad.'

'No, Jamie. We're not splitting up. Mum's still here, isn't she?'

'She looks so unhappy. Both of you do.'

'We'll get over it. What's tomorrow?'

'English One'

'What's that?'

'*Julius Caesar, Under Milk Wood* and *Lord of the Flies*.'

'You need me to test you on the quotes?'

'What quotes?'

'You haven't learnt any quotes? I don't believe it!'

Jamie smiled. 'You sound just like that old bloke in *One Foot in the Grave*.'

'Very funny. Go on upstairs and get going. Dinner'll be ready at six thirty.'

'Is Mum coming back?'

'Later.'

Mike was in his study working when he heard Julia's key in the front door lock. He continued to work steadily through the data printout and type the relevant figures into the computer which in due course gave him the projections he needed but his mind was elsewhere in the house. He could visualise Julia putting down her bags, looking for Jamie, seeing the mess in the kitchen, padding lightly up the stairs, knocking on Jamie's bedroom door, going in and getting the repeat broadcast of the French oral experience.

He wondered whether it was time to open negotiations for a peace treaty. He could afford to demand stiff penalties; after all, he was the injured party, she could hardly contest that. Still, it couldn't be entirely like the Treaty of Versailles. He couldn't demand reparations in case it led to the rise of Hitler and the outbreak of the Second World War. Nevertheless, it was important that she recognise his right to demand reparation payments even if he intended to display his magnanimity. There was a knock at his door. He swung his chair round from the desk to face the door.

'Come in,' he said, his heart beating, hoping it was Julia. It was.

'We have to talk, Mike.'

He nodded in agreement. She sat down in the armchair. She glanced at the neat pile of his bedding with the pillow perched on top. She looked up at him.

'We can't go on like this.'

Mike wasn't too sure about this opening. He wasn't clear where it was leading unless she was going to collapse spinelessly in front of him.

'Tom's in England.'

Mike's mouth went dry. He didn't like this conversation at all.

'Jamie's upset and I don't think I'm helping by staying here. Tom's asked me to move in with him.'

No! thought Mike. No! This wasn't what was supposed to happen. 'Are you going to?' he croaked with some difficulty through parched lips.

'What do you want?'

'Since when did you care what I wanted?'

'Mike, that's unfair. I was hoping we could have a sensible talk and see what's best for all of us.'

'I've been waiting for you to say something for the last week.'

'I didn't know what to say. I was hoping the situation might resolve itself when Tom got back.'

'Got back from where?'

'He's been in the Loire Valley.'

'I see. That sounds familiar. Did he manage a weekend break in Paris as well?'

'Mike, please, let's just concentrate on our situation here.'

'So what's he offering?'

'He's negotiating to rent a one-bedroom apartment. I can stay there when he goes back to America.'

'Whereabouts?'

'Hampstead.'

'Very nice. Very expensive.'

'And very small.'

'But very cosy.'

They stared at each other. Although they were talking they weren't attacking the main issue. Too much hurt had damaged them.

'You don't mind running out on Jamie in the middle of his GCSEs?'

'I'm just trying to create an atmosphere where he can do his best work. I'm not running out on anyone.'

'You're running out on me.'

'I'm not! I'll stay if you want me to but you obviously don't. I know how much you hate Tom. And I know I've hurt you by what I've done.'

'But you were in the grip of a violent passion and you couldn't help yourself.'

'I suppose in a way that's true, though it sounds trite.'

'Well, it isn't bloody good enough. You've behaved like a total selfish bitch . . .' Mike's voice spluttered away, he was so angry. He wanted to hurt Julia the way she had hurt him but he couldn't so in frustration he picked his small transistor radio off his desk and hurled it across the room. It smashed into the foot of the bookcase and shattered into three large segments. Julia looked at him sadly and rose to her feet.

'I'm sorry, Mike. I'd better go. It'll be best for all of us, just for the moment.'

He got up as she went out and closed the door quietly behind her. He wanted to scream at her, 'Go on, you bitch, go back to your boyfriend. And don't come back here. Ever. That's it, Julia, that's it. It's all over. No money, no Jamie, no house.'

Of course he said none of these things. Instead, he sat slumped in his chair at his desk looking at the computer screen but not seeing any of the figures on it. He heard Julia go into Jamie's room. He thought about racing in and throwing her bodily out of the house but he wanted Jamie to adjust to the new situation as fast as possible and he knew in his heart that Julia did too. Whatever she was saying to Jamie would be important in keeping him calm and focused – the two words he always used about Jamie's golf game – calm and focused.

He waited till he heard her slam her car door and drive away then he went down into Jamie's room and sat on the edge of the bed. Jamie was reading a heavily underlined copy of *Julius Caesar*.

'Need me to test you on anything?'

Jamie shook his head. 'Mum came in. Said she's going away for a few days but she'd ring me every night and every morning before I go to school and she'd talk to you about what to do at weekends.'

'It's just temporary, Jamie. We're just seeing what to do for the best.' Mike felt the tears coming into his eyes. Damn it. He was supposed to be the strong one in this situation, not Jamie. He could either stay and collapse on the bed, which would be no use to anyone, or he could get the hell out as fast as possible and save both their faces.

'I've got to go to the toilet.' He walked out briskly as if it was true.

It was true in a way. He went into the bathroom, locked the door, sat down on the toilet and burst into tears. He pulled violently at the toilet paper, tore off too much, blew his nose and tried to stem the flow of tears. When he thought the sound of his sobs might penetrate the walls of Jamie's bedroom, he pulled the chain to drown them.

He felt utterly desolate. The thought of Julia sexily undressing and doing to Tom Johnson what she had avoided with him for so long had already sent him spiralling down the ice-slicked slopes of jealousy. Now her departure left him feeling bereaved. He wanted to go back into Jamie's room and hold him and kiss him, not because he thought Jamie needed the comfort of his father but because he needed the physical comfort of being close to his son.

Instead he ran himself as hot a bath as he could stand. Somehow the burning, tingling, shivering sensation caused when his flesh came into contact with the hot water felt appropriately painful. Gradually he eased the rest of his body into the lacerating heat.

When he got out of the bathroom half an hour later, Jamie's light was off and his bedroom was in darkness. He didn't go in to check on what he hoped was his sleeping child. It was time they all behaved like grown-ups, starting with himself.

It was easier said than done. He got into bed and tried to read but the ineradicable image of a naked Julia lying in a pose of wanton abandon soon put paid to that. Traditionally that would be fuel for his own fantasies but now he felt as though he had somehow forfeited them. In some horrible, unjustified way Tom Johnson had stolen his fantasies as well as his wife.

He searched for the remote control which he usually had to reclaim from under Julia's sleeping body, another painful reminder of what he was missing. When he found it, the television set conveyed all the images he was seeking to erase from his mind. How was it possible that there was a soft porn movie on every channel? He wondered whether he should write to Mary Whitehouse and complain. He hastily turned to the sports channels where he could choose between Indy car racing, WWF wrestling and a race round the Isle of Wight by tall-masted schooners.

This was obviously some kind of Divine Test. Just as God sent his biblical characters into the wilderness to test their faith in Him, so in some weird way Mike felt he was being tested too. If he could get through the next few weeks, show his strength and his maturity, it wouldn't matter what Julia did. He knew she wasn't a triumphalist by nature or a mean-spirited person who would revel in his distress so it probably wouldn't help his cause if he reacted emotionally to the terrible provocation he was being subjected to. He would simply rise above it, be aloof and make her see that he and Jamie could survive very well without her. If only he could be sure she was consumed with guilt and that she and Tom were having a miserable time it would make his life so much more bearable.

The days passed in a kind of surreal blur for Mike. He made breakfast for Jamie and himself, did the frantic last-minute history, geography, chemistry and biology questions followed invariably by the prognostication that whatever the gap in Jamie's knowledge, it was unlikely to come up in the exam — a blatant lie but one which they both needed.

He tried to get home from work as fast as he could but it was rarely possible to be back when Jamie got home around 5 p.m. A major client on whose account he had worked for the past three years was contemplating a hostile takeover of a rival firm. It was a deal worth millions of pounds to all parties and however pressing the need to be at home with Jamie, it was frequently impossible until after nine at night.

Most of the time Jamie was quite content to grab a frozen meal for one out of the freezer, puncture the film a hundred times with the carving knife in a frenzy of delighted violence, toss it in the microwave and eat the result ten minutes later. It seemed to him a perfectly reasonable way to cook the evening meal and he couldn't understand why neither parent was happy for this state of affairs to continue indefinitely.

Julia spent at least one night during the week at home trying to cook dinner for herself and Jamie, which Mike didn't much care for but could not in all conscience do much to prevent. She always did the best she could to make sure she left before Mike arrived but it wasn't always possible.

One night Mike arrived at seven thirty although he had left a note for Jamie telling him he wouldn't be home before nine. With a start, Julia heard the car swing into the drive. How many times had she heard that sound over the years? How could she ever have imagined that one evening she would hear it and feel trapped like a burglar caught unawares – an odd thought with a spray bottle of Dettox in one hand and a sponge in the other, but at least she was wearing rubber gloves so there would be no fingerprints.

Mike had obviously seen her car outside so he was prepared for the confrontation, but of course, as they were two English people trying desperately to behave properly, the chances of the conversation being punctuated with flying plates was remote.

'Hi.'

'Hello.'

'Sorry. I was just leaving.'

'The six-thirty meeting was cancelled at the last minute.'

'You don't have to apologise.'

'I didn't mean to embarrass you. I should have rung.'

'It's your house, Mike. You don't have to ring to see if the coast is clear.'

'Jamie told me you were coming tonight.'

'How did today's go?'

'He didn't have one today.'

'I thought it was English language.'

'Tomorrow.'

'Oh.'

Mike looked in the fridge, not because he was particularly hungry – in fact he hadn't been hungry since he rang the airline to check on the air miles – but because he couldn't look at Julia without seeing Tom Johnson's grinning 23-year-old face superimposed on it.

'I rang this afternoon and there was no answer. That's why I thought he must have been sitting the exam.'

'Well, he's upstairs working now.'

'How do you think it's been going?'

'The exams?'

'Yes.'

'I suppose that's the only safe topic we've got to talk about, isn't it?'

'Mike, please don't be hostile. I'm very . . . fragile at the moment.'

'Well, you can go back to your boyfriend now. I'm sure he'll be able to stiffen you up a bit.'

'He's not here. He's in the Loire Valley on business.'

'So you're alone in Hampstead?'

'Yes.'

'Do you want to stay here tonight?'

'What do you mean?'

'It's not that difficult a question, is it?'

'I mean where would I sleep?'

'Oh, for Christ's sake. In the bath. I don't care. Wherever you want to sleep.'

'I think I'd better be getting back.'

'Fine, fine. Do whatever you like. You always do.' Mike slammed the microwave door shut, programmed the instructions and pressed 'Cook'. The plate began to rotate.

Julia hadn't moved. She wanted to tell him about the money, the twenty-pound note she felt almost sure Jamie had stolen from her purse, but she couldn't. She knew Mike would deny it strongly as if it were somehow a reflection of his inability to parent. He didn't look at her. She turned and left the room.

Mike regretted his momentary impatient outburst. He wanted to talk to Julia about Jamie. He had discovered on two separate occasions that money had gone missing from his wallet. He didn't know how much because he rarely bothered to count the money he had in his wallet until he knew he was getting short.

He suspected that Jamie had taken it but in the middle of exams he couldn't possibly broach the matter. He wanted to talk it over with Julia but just to come out with it in that strained situation in the kitchen would have been pointless. Either it would sound as if he couldn't handle things on his own, and he wasn't going to give her that satisfaction, or she would regard it as an attack on her for deserting the family home and neglecting her remaining child. He had hoped she might stay for a few hours and after a glass of wine . . . no, not wine, he couldn't even think about grapes now, let alone wine, without feeling his resentment rising.

It was most unlike Jamie to take money without asking for it. Julia and he had arranged on his thirteenth birthday that he, like Emily, would have his own bank account into which an agreed weekly sum would pass from their joint account so he would learn to be responsible for a budget. They would still buy his clothes and cover most of the big items of expenditure but if he wanted to go to see a film with his friends at the multiplex or rent a video or hang out at McDonald's, he would have to spend his 'own' money. For the past two and a half years the system had worked very effectively. Maybe the emotional pressure of the exams and Julia's departure and the atmosphere in the house was getting to him. Now wasn't the time to ask if he had become a pickpocket.

The GCSE exams finished at the end of June. There were technically another two and a half weeks before school broke up for the summer holidays but everyone knew that there were no more lessons. Apart from the last day when they were supposed to return their textbooks and listen to some pontificating words from the headmaster, they were not expected back at school until September. That left nearly three months for golf.

The most important amateur youth tournament of the golfing year took place in August. It was open to everyone under the age of twenty-one who wasn't being paid to play golf for a living and it was usually won by a university student like Watkinson whom Jamie had defeated so memorably at Easter. For the past three years Jamie had been making steady progress up the field, finishing sixty-fourth when he was thirteen, thirtieth when he was fourteen, and tenth last year. This year Mike knew he stood a good chance of winning it and if he did, or even if he finished in the top five or six, it would be time to consider playing in the qualifying tournaments for the Open Championship itself next July.

But for all the joy of the tournament win during the Easter holidays, Jamie himself was becoming increasingly less attracted by the prospect of a life that contained golf and nothing else. It was all very well for his dad to think he was the new Tiger Woods or Sergio Garcia but frankly what if he wasn't? What kind of a life was he facing then? He could have talked to his mum about such worries because he knew she had always been sceptical about his turning professional but now that she had buggered off, there was no one to turn to. He didn't dare talk to his dad about this.

The exams had induced in Jamie a schizophrenic response. He knew their importance in the general scheme of things. His mother in particular had talked about them practically every day for five years, so it was ironic that she wasn't there when they finally started. His dad viewed them more as an escape route in the remote possibility that his golf didn't pan out. For Jamie the GCSE exams were the gateway to a grown-up life – sixth form, no uniform, girls, drinking, a car and the wonderful sense of independence it would bring. He was totally fed up with being good. He had been good his whole life and the result was that his sister had died and his parents were splitting up, so what had been the point? It was about time he did something for himself.

Unfortunately Jamie found that if he wanted to be part of the pub/club scene he had to buy his round like everyone else and four or five pints meant that pretty much his whole week's pocket money was gone in that one order. The agreement with his parents had always been that the weekly standing order paid for everything. He could hardly ask for a rise and present as an explanation the new underage drinking society he had joined so he was forced to steal the occasional twenty-pound note from his dad's wallet or his mum's purse. He wasn't exactly proud of it but he felt he had no choice.

He tried to persuade his dad to put back his curfew but Mike insisted on eleven thirty.

'Why?' complained Jamie, bitterly but rhetorically.

'Because you're fifteen years old. When you're sixteen it'll be midnight.'

'All my friends are fifteen and none of them has a curfew.'

'None of them?'

'No.'

'What about Barry Morley? I know he's got one. I spoke to his father about it.'

'Yeah, but it's one a.m.'

'Bollocks!'

'That's what he told me.'

'What about that nice boy, Andrew?'

'Andrew Wharton?'

'No. The other Andrew. Whatsisname?'

'Andrew Grieves?'

'Yes. Him.'

'His parents are in bed at ten o'clock so they don't know what time he comes back.'

'It doesn't really matter about the others, Jamie. I'm concerned about you.'

'But I'm just like everyone else so why shouldn't I be treated like everyone else?'

'Because you're not like everyone else. If you want to be a professional sportsman you need to show you can live a disciplined life. Better still, a self-disciplined life.'

'All right, make it half past midnight then.'

'No. It's staying at eleven thirty.'

Jamie settled on midnight in his own mind. It would show his father he couldn't be bossed around. Mike soon tacitly accepted the compromise because he felt that it showed he was still winning the overall war. Or so he thought at first. Over the course of one week there were three nights when Jamie staggered through the door at between midnight and half past. Mike let the first two go, unwilling to provoke what he feared might become a major confrontation over twenty minutes or so, but on the Friday night Mike was sitting up in the living room getting increasingly concerned as the clock ticked over towards quarter to one.

Ten minutes later he heard the scratching of the key and Jamie opening the front door before shutting it with a bang loud enough to have woken him had he been asleep in bed. He went out into the hall with a look of grim determination on his face. Jamie was slumped on a chair in the hall, the chair on which he ritually slung his school bag when he came home every day. His face was a deathly shade of white. Mike's incipient anger was rapidly replaced by concern.

'Jamie, are you all right?'

Jamie just buried his face in his hands.

'Jamie, what the hell . . . ?'

Mike pulled Jamie's hands away and saw that the boy was about to vomit. He dragged him towards the downstairs toilet but they failed to make it in time. Projectiles hurtled from his mouth over the walls, the carpet, the sanded floor, behind the toilet bowl, over the lid of the toilet bowl and, Mike feared, over the coats that were hanging there. He shut the door on his son in disgust.

He went into the garage and found an old bucket he used in the summer for carrying soil around the garden. He took it back into the kitchen, rinsed it out, then filled it with hot water and the strongest bleach detergent he could find, dropped a large hard scrubbing brush into it and took it back into the downstairs toilet where Jamie lay in a horrendous heap of his own making. The smell made Mike want to gag and it was all he could do to hang on to the contents of his own stomach.

'Here,' he said brusquely, 'clean it all up, then take off your clothes and leave them to soak in the sink in the garage overnight. Then have a bath and get into bed. We'll talk about this in the morning.'

Mike felt sure he was doing the right thing. This was no time to be understanding. This was the time to impose parental authority. Jamie had been provoking this for days and Mike wasn't going to back down, otherwise it would lead to anarchy.

Mike lay in bed thinking about his own adolescence. He wasn't much of a boozer so he had never been through a parallel experience but he did remember his first week as a freshman at university and imbibing too much hospitality from the various societies who wanted him to become a member. He had felt light-headed and ill in equal proportions but he soon learned to control his alcoholic intake. He hoped Jamie would be making a similar resolution right now, though remembering the look of utter wretchedness on his face as he lay miserable and helpless on the floor he suspected that it might well be one of a lifetime of total abstinence.

The morning conversation went exactly as Mike would have wanted. Jamie lay passively on his back as Mike stood in the doorway of his son's bedroom and tore him off a strip. Jamie confessed to the alcoholic binges and asked for the thefts from his dad's wallet and his mum's purse to be taken into consideration when sentence was passed.

Mike was so pleased with himself that he genuinely considered ringing Julia to tell her what had happened and recount his own parental triumph but then the image of her and Tom flashed into his mind and he decided not to risk damaging the positive image he currently had of himself by making such a risky call. Indeed, Jamie's adolescent behaviour precisely matched that of his wife — they were two of a kind, though in Jamie's defence he genuinely was an adolescent whereas Julia was just behaving like one.

Mike was quite sure that Jamie was now under control once more, which was why he was shocked beyond belief when he opened the front door at eight o'clock one evening the following week to find a shamefaced Jamie standing on the doorstep next to a uniformed police constable.

CHAPTER TWENTY-THREE

JULIA WAS STUNNED WHEN MIKE rang her with the news.

'Drugs! Jamie?' She couldn't speak in whole sentences. This was Jamie they were talking about, her Jamie, her little baby boy Jamie. It made no sense.

'Well, it's just dope. It's not heroin or crack and he wasn't dealing or anything like that so they're not going to prosecute.'

'What'll they do?'

'He's going to get some kind of formal caution.'

'But how—'

'I still don't know the details. The headmaster uncovered some sort of ring, some fourteen-year-old kid, the year below Jamie, broke under interrogation and named names. Jamie was one of them.'

'Why didn't the head just cover it up and tell the parents? Let them deal with it in private. It hardly reflects well on the school, involving the police.'

'You know what he's like. He doesn't believe in hushing things up. He'd bring back National Service and flogging if he could.'

'That's no reason to involve the police. Just think of all the lives it could ruin.'

'Well, as far as he knows the smoking didn't take place on school property or during school hours so he thinks it's our problem not his.'

'So why didn't he just stay out of it altogether?'

'The dealing was probably going on in the playground, in which case he probably felt he had a legal obligation to inform the police.'

'How did Jamie get involved in the first place?'

'He's been coming in later than he should. I thought he was just going to the pub with his mates but apparently there's a gang of them, passing round dope and getting pissed and showing off to some of the girls from the convent school.'

'The convent!'

'Slags, apparently, according to Jamie.'

'What can I do?'

'I thought you should come with us for the formal caution.'

'What happens?'

'I think we just stand in a room and Jamie gets a stern lecture in front of us. The idea is to humiliate the parents so he won't do it again.'

'I didn't know he was doing it now. Did you?'

'Of course not.'

'Mike?'

'What?'

'Is this my fault?' Julia waited for his reply with trepidation. If ever there were a moment when Mike could put the boot in, it was now. He must know that guilt was never far from her mind these days and this was the perfect opportunity to make her feel truly wretched.

Mike was torn by much the same emotion. He was wounded by her desertion, by the sexual humiliation she had subjected him to by running off with Tom Johnson. He could really hurt her now, maybe consume her with such guilt that it would overload the relationship with Tom.

'No,' he said quietly. 'It's not your fault. No more than it's mine. We mustn't overreact. Either of us.'

'But it's drugs, Mike.'

'Can I remind you of certain parties we went to at Oxford? Certain musician friends of yours who couldn't open their lips without inserting a joint between them?'

'We were older.'

'Fifteen now is not much different to when we were nineteen.'

'I don't think that's a valid comparison. It was such a different social situation.'

'You telling me you never stole sweets from the newsagents when you were a kid?'

'I don't think so.'

'Oh Julia, for God's sake. You must have done something like that.'

'I think we occasionally took a lipstick or something from Boots without paying for it.'

'And I used to specialise in travelling on public transport without buying a ticket, just to see if I could get away with it. It's not the end of the world.'

'OK, OK. I get the point. I feel awful. How's Jamie?'

'Probably worse, which is what should halt his descent into a life of crime.'

'Where is he?'

'At the driving range.'

'Sure?'

'Took him down there myself.'

'Still . . .'

'You weren't here to see the look on his face when he came home last night. Believe me, his criminal days are over.'

Julia couldn't get back to the house until Friday evening. Life at work had changed beyond all recognition. Creepy, greasy Eric Neville had thankfully won the promotion to the marketing department he wanted and she had taken his place in overall charge of Easy Listening, Nostalgia and Spoken Word.

It meant a substantial increase in salary – Julia was amazed to discover that the company had thought Eric worth £10,000 a year more than she had been but she soon grew to appreciate that the work, though in her eyes less creative, was ultimately more burdensome. Her workload effectively doubled because she found it difficult to delegate by conceding her former territory and so she was faced with combining Eric's old job with hers to create an impossible new one.

Nevertheless, she would have been enjoying the challenge were it not for other events in her life. Her release was her weekly lunch with Sarah, now restricted to sixty minutes maximum since she couldn't afford to be away from the office for much longer than that.

Sarah, of course, didn't want to talk about work. She wanted to talk about Tom.

'Why? Why are you so obsessed with Tom?' protested Julia.

'I'm not the one obsessed with Tom. You are!'

'But that's all you ever want to talk to me about now.'

'Well, I would think it was a major event in your life. Why wouldn't I want to talk about it?'

'Because it's a major event in my life, not yours. I'm sorry, that came out wrong. It wasn't supposed to be hurtful.'

'Oh Julia, why don't you think I have exactly the same feelings?'

'But you don't. You told me you don't.'

'When?'

'You said that the first time you did it a cat peed on your tights.'

'You're taking me far too literally. You've done what millions of women would like to do.'

'What?'

'Sacrifice all for love.'

'But I don't want to. I don't want to sacrifice everything. Everyone just gets hurt.'

'You want to give up Tom, never see him again, go back to fantasising about him, playing the events of those few days in California over and over again in your mind?'

Julia couldn't reply.

Sarah poured the jug of cold skimmed milk into her coffee and stirred it slowly. 'Julia, do you think you're the only one who thinks about recapturing that first heady taste of romantic love? Do you honestly think you're the only woman whose thoughts of romance have been replaced by work and commuting and school runs and shopping and washing and ironing?'

'No, of course not.'

'Well, I'm one of them. If it can work with you and Tom, maybe there's hope for all of us.'

'Why do you think it's hope to leave your family and your home and run off into the unknown?'

'Precisely because it is hope and it is unknown. I know what's here. I don't know what's out there. It might be wonderful. I just haven't got the bottle to try and find out and I hate myself for it.'

'And that's why you want to know about Tom?'

'Every gesture and every word. That's why you went, isn't it?'

'Of course. But I wasn't searching for a vague someone, any tall, dark and handsome someone who turned me on and wanted me. I needed Tom in my life again. I felt like I've needed him ever since he left. That's why I kept writing to him.'

'Julia!'

'It's all right. I never sent the letters.'

'How long has this been going on?'

'That's just what Mike said.'

'He knows?'

'Not about the letters, no. They're hidden away in the loft.'

'Isn't that dangerous?'

'Not really. Nobody could find anything up there.'

'Then why keep them?'

'Sort of like a safety net. They're my diaries. They tell me I'm more than just a wife and mother.'

'Well, no more letters, missy. You've got him now. So what are you going to do with him?'

Julia paused before answering. She wondered whether she should maintain the illusion with Sarah because it might help quell the doubts she was starting to harbour. In the end she decided to come clean.

'I haven't got him. He comes in for a few days at a time every other week. The travelling is killing him. When he arrives he's jet-lagged and before he's recovered from it, it's time for him to get back on the plane again. He always travels economy, like Bill Gates does, I'm told, which I can't understand because I'm sure they can both afford to fly business, so he arrives struggling against cramp and bad temper as well as jet lag.'

'This is not good. This isn't the romantic dream I thought you were living.'

'Well, it's the forty-year-old's version of the romantic dream. It's called transatlantic reality.'

'So it's a crock of shit, this whole romantic shenaningans?'

Julia shook her head and smiled. 'No. Because when he looks into my eyes I know he loves me and when he makes love to me I feel alive.'

'Very nice but that could be sex with anyone.'

'What!'

'Oh, come on, Julia. You remember when I told you about Gianfranco. That's exactly how I felt. I just didn't love him. So you're cheating. You're missing out the key component.'

'Which is?'

'Do you love him?'

'Haven't I always told you I do?'

'Didn't count when you were fantasising about him on a Thameslink train. Now he's real. Tell me. Yes or no.'

At that moment the waitress returned with Julia's credit card and the receipt. 'I couldn't possibly give you a snap answer in this situation.'

'Yes or no isn't a snap answer. It's just a short one. If you can't answer the question with regard to Tom, what about Mike?'

'The more I think about this the worse it all gets.'

'Want a piece of advice?'

'Desperately.'

'Flip a coin.'

'Sarah!'

'I'm serious. It always works. Trust me.'

'Don't be silly. I'm not going to make a decision that will affect the rest of my life on the toss of a coin.'

'It'll work. I promise you.'

Julia gathered her things together. 'Look, I've got a meeting that starts at two thirty. And there's a taxi just letting out over there. Can I give you a lift?' She was relieved to see the shake of Sarah's head and ran into the road to claim the idling taxi before it could depart. As she tried to settle into the uncomfortable seat of the cab, she wrestled with Sarah's parting advice. What on earth did she mean by that casual remark? How could she possibly toss a coin to decide the fate of four lives?

On the Friday Julia managed to leave the office early enough to catch the five forty-seven train from King's Cross, which meant she was at the house in St Albans just after six thirty. For one frightening moment, as she scrabbled in her handbag for the keys, she wondered whether Mike had changed the locks but her key turned smoothly and she was greeted by the slightly distasteful odour of the decaying flowers on the hall table. She knew that both Mike and Jamie never 'saw' the flowers she painstakingly placed in vases scattered about the house, although she wondered how they could possibly have been oblivious to the bad smell.

She was outside the back door dumping the remains of the orange salmon Queen Elizabeth roses into the dustbin when she heard the front door slam.

She darted back inside. Jamie had his head in the fridge. It was such a welcome, familiar sight — although it used to irritate her because he kept the fridge door open so long before deciding what to eat — that she just wanted to scoop him up in her arms and cover him with kisses, but at five feet eight and heading for ten stone, this was no longer an option.

Jamie closed the fridge door with a broken-off hunk of cheddar cheese in his mouth before he saw his mother. For a split second Julia saw the sudden fear in his eyes before he regained his composure with a studiedly indifferent greeting.

'Hi, Mum. Is there anything for dinner?'

She realised the fear must be occasioned either by his anxiety as to what she might say about his experiment with marijuana or by the worry that her presence might mean another seismic shift in the life of their family. Although he had been outwardly cool and seemingly unaffected by her departure, she was convinced that inside he was full of churning emotions. She also knew her son well enough to realise that he wasn't going to volunteer how he felt.

'I can make an omelette and I think there's some sprouts and potatoes in there.'

Jamie screwed up his face. 'Can't we get a pizza?'

'Is that what your father does?'

'Yes,' he said defiantly, daring her to complain so he could accuse her of abdicating her responsibilities and therefore disenfranchising herself from having a vote in what they ate for dinner.

'In that case you certainly need more vegetables. Is that a new spot on the end of your nose?' She walked towards him. He turned away. 'Have you been putting the acne cream on?' she called out to his disappearing back but all she heard was the sound of his footsteps running up the stairs and the slam of his bedroom door. Familiar as it was, it didn't offer much in the way of comfort.

She made as much of a Spanish omelette as she could for herself and took a Marks and Spencer chicken and pasta bake meal out of the freezer. She went upstairs and knocked on Jamie's door. There was no reply.

'Jamie?' she said softly. She looked under the door. There appeared to be no light on. No sound of life came from his stereo. She opened the door carefully. Jamie was lying on the bed staring at the ceiling. It was still a fine summer's evening but the sun had disappeared and the trees in the garden cast a shadow over the house which reached into Jamie's bedroom window at the end of the day.

'Darling, can I talk to you?'

'Why?'

'Do I need a reason?'

'Yes.'

'I want to know if you want me to put the chicken and pasta bake into the microwave.'

Jamie shrugged.

'Is that yes?'

Jamie turned his face towards the wall.

'Do you want me to go?'

No response.

'Do you want me to go for ever?'

'Yes!' he hissed fiercely. 'Fuck off and don't come back!'

Julia stood there transfixed. He had never spoken to her like that before. Ever. She had to do something. If she left now she would have made a critical concession; it would be tantamount to admitting that his accusation was justified. She sat on the edge of his bed.

'Jamie!'

He continued to stare at the wall.

'Jamie, look at me!'

He turned slowly but kept his eyes fixed on the ceiling. She decided not to push it.

'I know you're angry with me and I understand how you feel.'

'No you don't.'

'What?'

'You don't understand how I feel. You never have.'

'Never?'

'Well, maybe when I was little but not for years.'

This wasn't the time for self-justification. 'OK. Why don't you tell me how you feel?'

As she feared, the question was met with total silence.

'If you don't talk to me,' she said simply and without hostility, 'how will I ever know?'

'I love you, Mum, I just don't like you very much.'

'Why not?'

'Because . . . because you treat me like I'm still a little kid.'

'How do I do that?'

'I've still got a curfew and most of my friends haven't, my pocket money allowance is about half what they all get and you come shopping for clothes with me like I don't know what fits me and what looks good on me. I do.'

'OK. And this . . .' She struggled to find the right words. 'Well, me living in London during the week, this isn't a problem for you?'

'No. I prefer it.'

'Why?'

'Because I don't like you living here. Because you and Dad are always rowing.'

'We aren't.'

'Always.'

'No more than any of your friends' parents . . .'

'Seems like it to me. That's why I want to be out on the golf course all the time.'

He couldn't see, because he wasn't looking at her and by now the room was gloomy anyway, but she had started to cry. This was so cruel, coming from Jamie whom she loved and adored so unconditionally. She didn't know how to counter it. But Jamie wasn't finished yet.

'I just don't think you love me.'

'Oh Jamie, I do love you, I love you so much I could—'

'Just leave me alone, Mum. Go back to your toyboy.'

'My toyboy is older than I am.'

'You know what I mean.'

'Please, Jamie, let me explain to you.'

'I don't want to listen to you.'

'But you've made all these accusations. You should let me defend myself.'

'It's not a courtroom, Mum. It's my bedroom and I wish you'd fuck off out of it.'

Julia stood up. It was time she acted like the parent again. 'Please don't use language like that, Jamie.'

'It's the only thing I know'll get through to you.'

'I never knew you hated me, Jamie.'

'I don't hate you, Mum. Just go away. Stay away and leave us alone. Me and Dad'll be fine. We'll work things out.'

'But this drugs charge—'

'Oh, for fuck's sake, Mum, that's just what I mean.'

'But the police—'

'Listen, I've smoked a joint or two with some other kids at a party on Saturday nights. I'm not shooting up with heroin using dirty needles in some filthy alleyway or blowing fifty quid a night on coke. I'm all right. Now just fuck off and leave me alone!'

He turned away from her again to stare at the blank wall which he obviously found a more congenial sight than his mother. Julia decided it was pointless if not impossible to argue with him. She almost staggered out of the room, her limbs numb with shock. She saw Mike's coat draped over the knob at the foot of the banister. It was a sight she had always hated. Instinctively she picked up the coat, opened the cloakroom, placed it on its hanger and hung it up. When she went into the kitchen she saw Mike pouring himself a whisky.

'Hello, Mike.'

He looked at her but gave no smile of welcome. He tossed back the glass and recoiled from the afterburn. 'You been interrogating the suspect?'

'Not exactly. If anything he's been interrogating me.'

'What's he been saying?'

'Oh, pretty mundane stuff, like he wishes I'd fuck off and leave him alone, he doesn't want me here, I've never understood him, just the usual sort of mother-son banter.'

'I'm sorry.'

'Who for?'

'You. Well, all of us really. We all seem to be in a bit of a mess.'

'I don't know how we got into it.'

'Maybe he's just in a state about his golf. He's got this England Amateur Under-Twenty-one tournament coming up next month.'

'He's been in tournaments before.'

'His game is in trouble, Julia, and I don't know that it's going to recover in time. I'm thinking I should withdraw him but I'm worried that he'll lose confidence if I do and that'll only make things worse. On the other hand if he competes and plays badly and misses the cut, then what?'

Julia looked at him helplessly. 'I don't know, Mike. I don't know anything.'

The tears started to escape despite her best efforts to control them. Julia wasn't trying to gain Mike's sympathy. She was just overwhelmed with feelings of helplessness. She desperately wanted Mike's comforting arms round her at that moment but she knew she dared not ask. This was the first major tragedy they had not faced together — Tom's first desertion, the nightmare of their parents and the wedding, the estrangement from her mother, Emily, Jamie's school problems — they had shared them and done the best they could as a unit. Now she had turned Mike into the enemy. It was never her intention but suddenly everything about him, his idiosyncrasies, his predictable habits, they took on for Julia a new and desirable appearance.

She had never felt so helpless since she had first learned of Emily's death. It was a shocking sensation. She was one of life's copers — practical, sane, reliable, both at home and at work. Now everything had gone wrong and it was all because she had, or thought she had, met once more the only true love of her life.

How odd, she thought, that she didn't really want to go back to Hampstead to await her lover who was flying in that night from America. She wanted to stay here and sort things out with Jamie. Mike would know what to say. He knew that boy so well, he was such a good father. Would Tom know what to say to Jamie? He wasn't too great with kids, no matter what he claimed. And he kept telling her Jamie was grown up and should be left to get on with life on his own. Well, he wasn't grown up. He was still a vulnerable teenager.

'Can I stay here tonight?'

'Where?'

'In the house.'

'No. I mean where in the house?'

'I can sleep in the study if you like.'

'Would you mind?'

'It's your house.'

'Oh, don't be so ridiculous. It's our house. Sleep where you want — as long as you tell me then I can sleep somewhere else.'

'In that case I'll sleep in the study.'

'You know you can't just walk in and out of the house whenever you feel like it, Julia.'

'I'm sorry, Mike. I'm just a bit lost.'

'You want a drink?' He indicated the bottle of whisky.

Julia nodded. 'When was the last time you had a whisky?'

'The last time I got done for speeding.'

'Oh no! You didn't!'

'Bloody video camera.'

'Where?'

'On the Watford Road. Just before the turnoff for the M1.'

'How much?'

'Sixty quid and three points on the licence.'

'I'm sorry.'

'I'm livid.'

'What were you doing?'

'Fifty-four miles per hour in a forty zone.'

He slid the glass over to her. She sipped at it. She smiled briefly.

'What's the joke?'

'I was just remembring. When the kids were little and we got stopped in Headington. And you tried to blame it on Emily who'd got out of her car seat and was trying to get into the front to sit on my lap.'

'Oh yes. And you wanted the cop to book Emily as well.'

'I wish he had. We'd have had such fun.'

'We did, didn't we? Sometimes?'

'Of course we did. Lots of times.'

Mike paused. He knew it was hurtful but he couldn't resist it. 'Before you went and destroyed everything.'

Julia felt as if she had received a punch to the solar plexus; it knocked all the wind out of her. She resented the unnecessary insult. She was offering her hand, making a gesture of conciliation; how could he possibly think that everything was her fault? If he hadn't . . . well, there had been lots of things to complain about, particularly recently, no wonder she went looking for Tom.

Julia had no response. In the eloquent silence they heard the sound of Jamie's bedroom door opening and his feet come thumping down the stairs. Mike darted out into the hall to intercept him.

'Where are you going?'

'Out,' said Jamie sullenly.

'Where?'

'I don't have to tell you where. I just have to be back at eleven thirty.' He tried to open the front door. Mike interspersed himself between his son and freedom.

'I want you to apologise to Mum.'

'After what she's done?'

'You don't talk to her like that whatever she's done. She's still your mother.'

In the next room Julia glowed inwardly at these words.

'Why not? You hate her just as much as I do.'

'I don't hate her.'

''Course you do. Else you're stupid too.'

'Jamie!'

'The two of you fucking well deserve each other. I hate both of you. Now let me go.'

'You stay here, I'm going to get your mother. You don't talk to us, either of us, like that.'

As Mike walked back into the kitchen Jamie took the chance to make his escape. They heard the front door slam shut.

Julia was puzzled. 'Why did you let him go like that? You didn't have to come and get me.'

'I wanted him to go. If he'd stayed we'd have got into a terrible fight. All of us. This way he'll go out for the night, slag us off to his friends, they'll all tell him he's a martyr and describe their own appalling parents. In the morning we can, I can, start again. It's still a recoverable situation.'

'You should be bringing peace to Northern Ireland.'

'I'd settle for peace in Waterford Drive, St Albans.'

'When you talk to him . . . can you tell him I still love him as much as I ever did.'

'I already have.'

'He didn't seem very impressed.'

'I know he's usually a quiet kid but as you just heard, he feels all this deeply.'

'He said upstairs he doesn't care, he says lots of kids in his class have got divorced parents, he says I should go back and stay with my toyboy.'

'Can you blame him? Honestly? Forget the swearing.'

'I suppose not.'

Mike stood up. 'I'm going to make something to eat. Do you want anything?'

'I'm not hungry.'

She knew exactly what Mike was going to do. He did it every time he made dinner for himself. First he put the kettle on and made a cup of tea with two tea bags. She had complained often enough that they got through packets of tea bags at a ridiculous rate. He would always apologise but he never altered his habit of using two tea bags. She didn't know anyone else who did that, not in a single mug anyway.

Sure enough, he lifted two tea bags out of the canister and dropped them into his favourite mug — the one he had bought for her inscribed with the words 'I am a natural blonde — please talk slowly' on it. Julia had been unimpressed with the sentiment although she had laughed when he first showed it to her, and Mike had taken possession of it himself. She would never have believed that she could ever find the familiar prospect of Mike's making a cup of extra strong tea in that old mug such an emotional event. Could she ever sit on the back porch in Sonoma County and find Tom's withdrawing the cork from a bottle of '94 Chablis equally moving? She doubted it.

But neither could she see how to tell Mike all this. Events had moved on and she feared that, despite what Sarah had said to her, she had indeed burned her bridges. Her actions had hurt Mike dreadfully, and he had found out in a particularly cruel way, though how she could ever have sat down and told him that she had met Tom Johnson again and fallen in love with him without devastating him, she had no idea.

As Mike squeezed both tea bags against the side of the mug, she realised the implication of what she had just told herself. The revelation that she had fallen in love with Tom would have devastated Mike because he loved her. If he didn't love her still, in spite of what she'd done, if Jamie didn't love her, would the atmosphere be so tense? She wanted to reach out to Mike, reassure him that she still cared for him despite everything that had happened.

She touched his arm. 'Mike . . .'

'Do you want a lift?'

'Where?'

'Back to your home. To Hampstead.'

'I thought I was going to stay here tonight.'

'I think you should stay away from Jamie a bit longer. I'll need time to calm him down.'

'Shouldn't we do this together?'

'Julia, for God's sake, make your mind up. You can't switch lives just when you want to. Tom's not here so you want to play housewife and mother. Tom arrives and you want to be his eighteen-year-old girlfriend. For God's sake, make a decision and grow up.'

His words hit her like a bucket of cold water. He was the mature one. She was the indecisive ninny.

'Is your car here?'

She shook her head.

Mike turned away and picked up the phone. 'Hello. Could I have a taxi at number fifteen, Waterford Drive, to go to Hampstead in north

London ... No, I'll be paying cash here before the driver leaves ... As soon as possible, please.' Mike put his frozen meal into the microwave, jabbed at the controls and walked out of the room. Julia made no attempt to follow.

CHAPTER TWENTY-FOUR

SHE SAT IN THE BACK of the minicab with a heavy heart. She knew this constant shuttling between Tom and Mike could not continue indefinitely. It was fair to neither of them and since she frequently felt just as wretched about it as they did, she accepted that a decision had to be made soon.

The night was unseasonably cold and before they had reached the motorway the darkening clouds which had lent such an oppressive air to Jamie's bedroom produced a miserable drizzle that entirely matched her mood. The taxi driver flicked on the windscreen wipers but the drizzle was so fine that all they succeeded in doing was to smear the windscreen with grime and obscure his vision still further. It was like her life.

Instead of being thrown into focus by this exhilarating affair with her longed-for lover, her life was being overlaid with a film of confusion. She remembered when she first fell in love with Tom how everything in her life had been heightened — how the colours were more vivid, her taste buds sharper, her brain keener. He had awakened all her senses.

He had done something similar this time round but now, instead of breathing the clean air of a pine forest, she smelled the stale odour of rotting vegetation; instead of looking at the world and finding only joy, she was finding nothing but pain.

The minicab drew up fifty yards past the flat because the parking in Hampstead was so difficult. Well, it wasn't really Hampstead. She had told Mike it was Hampstead because she knew it sounded better but in reality it was down the scruffier end, towards Gospel Oak where the residents' cars lined the narrow road on both sides, making parallel parking a highly prized skill.

The flat was dark and cold when she got in. Tom was catching the Friday overnight flight from San Francisco and would be arriving at Heathrow early in the morning. It was still a surprise to Julia to open the front door and find everything exactly as she had left it. For years she had got used to the mess that children made, to Mike's dropping his coat and briefcase in the hall, to the kitchen liberally spattered with the remnants of Jamie's rudimentary sandwich-making and Mike's endless cups of tea. For years she had bemoaned the fact that she couldn't keep the house tidy for more than an hour. Now that she was living in a flat where, most of the time, she was the sole resident, she found the solitude creepy and unsettling rather than liberating and restful.

She climbed into bed and hauled the covers over her head.

Was sensuous pleasure to be the root of her downfall? If she were to be punished for eternity on account of those few brief moments of sexual pleasure, it would be no more than the fate of so many women down through the ages. The cast of literary fallen heroines passed before her eyes as if they had been sewn onto an enormous tapestry. From Cleopatra to Tess of the D'Urbevilles they had loved and been destroyed for it. Was Tom Johnson's reappearance in her life to be the harbinger of similar disaster? What was disaster anyway? Losing Tom or losing her home, her marriage and her family?

In the house on Waterford Drive, Mike tossed the remains of his dinner into the kitchen bin. He had eaten it straight out of the plastic carton so he had managed to reduce his entire dishwashing exercise to one fork. He didn't seem to need much food these days. He was being fuelled by righteous anger at Julia's betrayal.

He opened the newspaper but he couldn't concentrate. He picked up the remote and flicked through the channels, none of which managed to hold his attention for the five seconds he allotted each of them. He snapped off the television and went upstairs. He stood by the window on the landing and looked out at the drive. Why had his mind seized up like this? He had to do something, anything, to unfreeze it. He decided to tidy the loft.

He hauled himself carefully off the top of the stepladder and sat on the floor of the loft wondering idly how he was going to get into the loft when he was sixty-four. The space was, as he feared, in total chaos. He opened the first cardboard box and discovered a pile of assorted carpet clippings. Why on earth had they been saved? The next box was even more puzzling a collection of ancient and rusting kitchen implements. He expelled both boxes through the trapdoor and they landed with a satisfying thump on the landing floor.

After half an hour of absorbing work Mike had imposed some sort of order on the unruly collection of crates and boxes. He felt purged. The physical exertion had done what he wanted. He opened one last box and discovered a red biscuit tin, probably an uneaten Christmas gift from many years ago. He lifted off the lid and found, instead of the mouldy family assortment, a collection of handwritten letters. The light was too dim to read by so he stuffed them in his pocket and manoeuvred himself out of the loft and back onto the stepladder.

He sat on the edge of the bed and stared in horrified fascination at the letters. They were written by Julia, the first one starting on their wedding day. The enormity of the betrayal possessed him utterly. All the way through the years when he thought they were happy together she had been writing to that bastard. He forced himself to read the intimate details because he thought he might discover some clue as to why his marriage which he had thought just fine until the tragedy of Emily's death, had disintegrated with such disastrous haste.

The more he read, the more he was puzzled. She must have cared for Tom, why else would she bother writing? But as he continued to read, intrigued and appalled at the same time, he realised that unless she had painstakingly written out an exact duplicate, the letters had apparently never been sent. Encouraged, he read on.

When he had finished he stood up, his back aching, his mind racing. Despite all those protestations of love for another man and the criticisms she had levelled at him he felt a curious measure of relief. Besides the significant fact that the letters had remained in a biscuit tin hidden away in the loft he recognised that some of her grievances were valid. He knew he didn't have the romantic soul that Tom allegedly possessed but he knew too that Julia understood that he had other qualities, that he was caring and reliable and a good father, whatever his deficiencies as a husband.

He wished Julia had been able to say to him what she had so clearly felt able to write (if not send) to Tom. Then he feared that maybe she *had* said these things, in that curious coded language women use when they wish to be provocative. And he had failed to hear.

Now that he had stumbled on the secret code book he felt that there might still be a chance for the marriage. Except, of course, he'd just blown it. She'd come back tonight, tried to hold out an olive branch, and he'd packed her into a taxi and sent her back to her boyfriend. What could he do now? There had to be something he could do.

An hour later he was still lying on the bed fully clothed no nearer the answer when the telephone shrilled into his ear.

They slept until nearly midday. Tom was the first to awake. He gently disengaged himself from Julia's trailing arm and flung the curtains back. A shaft of bright sunlight flooded the room.

'The threatening cloud has passed away, and brightly shines the dawning day,' he sang from the closing chorus of *The Mikado*.

'Oh, not now,' moaned Julia burying her head under the pillow.

Tom quickly ripped it away as he continued in fine voice. 'What though the night may come too soon, we've years and years of afternoons.'

'Come back to bed,' smiled Julia as seductively as she could. 'You make me forget everything when you're next to me.'

'Do I have to stop singing?'

'I'm afraid so.'

Tom climbed back into bed and pulled the covers over them. Julia felt as though she wanted to stay there for ever — just her and Tom, with the rest of the world blotted out completely.

As long as he was with her and not separated by the width of the Atlantic Ocean and the continental United States, she felt anything was possible. All the problems with Mike and Jamie seemed to diminish. Her love for Tom seemed as strong as ever.

Two hours later after a hasty brunch they were tramping hand in hand across Hampstead Heath towards the grounds of Kenwood, the Georgian mansion in north London whose woods and lawns had long been a magnet for city dwellers who wished to experience the charms of rural England while still being within walking distance of a good delicatessen.

The sun was directly overhead as they walked up the long hill from the Gospel Oak entrance to the heath. When they reached the top they turned and looked at the London landscape which was dominated by the Post Office tower to the west and Canary Wharf way off to the east. Between them the soup tureen lid of St Paul's Cathedral seemed small by comparison.

Tom flung himself onto the thick grass and offered his hand to help Julia down to lie beside him. There were plenty of other couples in skimpy clothes already engaged in sunbathing or decorous embraces although Julia thought that most of them were fifteen or twenty years younger than they were.

It didn't take long for her to feel a similar age. His hand felt for hers and raised it slowly to his lips.

'I think I'm the luckiest guy in the world.'

'Why? Did you win the lottery?' whispered Julia. She could never have too much of Tom talking like this.

'I sure did. But you're the only prize. Shit!' Tom sat up with a start. A tennis ball had dropped onto his stomach and bounced up to hit him on the nose.

Julia sat up abruptly too. Tom scrambled after the ball as a six-year-old boy came running towards it. Julia could see where a father and two other boys were playing cricket and waiting for the ball to be recovered. Tom was in no mood to throw it back.

'Sorry!' came the six-year-old's cry.

Tom hurled the ball with as much violence as he could muster away from the boy in the direction of Canary Wharf. The little boy stopped, unsure of what to do, never having seen a grown-up stranger behave like this.

'I'll get it, Paul. You come back here,' shouted the father, running after the ball which was gathering pace on its journey down the hill.

'Goddamn kids! Why don't they look what they're doing? They shouldn't be allowed to play here.'

'They have as much right to be here as we do,' said Julia mildly.

'We don't throw things at them. They shouldn't be allowed to throw things at us.'

'They weren't throwing things. They're just little boys. I've got one myself,' she said, remembering the countless occasions when she and Mike had had to retrieve Jamie's ball from some socially awkward place.

'Ruined the atmosphere,' complained Tom. 'And just when I was building up to my big moment.'

'What big moment?' asked Julia, intrigued.

'Tell you later,' said Tom, hauling her to her feet.

They turned off the heath and through the gate in the railings that surrounded Kenwood House.

'You know,' said Julia, desperate to recapture their formerly easy and relaxed mood, 'the remarkable thing about this heath is that it is not possible to enter or leave the place without getting lost. No matter which exit you find on the way home, it's never the one you think it is.'

'Where's the palace then?'

'It's not really a palace.'

'But it was that place in *Notting Hill*, right – where Hugh Grant meets Julia Roberts for the second time?'

'Yes.'

'Well, it sure looked like a palace to me.'

'Blenheim's a palace. This is just a Georgian country house.'

'In the middle of London?'

'Not when it was built. It was still in the country in the nineteenth century. There it is,' she finished as the path emerged from the overhanging trees to reveal the full glory of Kenwood House.

'How do they keep it so clean?'

'Lots of Dickensian boys in rags and big caps are released from the workhouse every day to clean it.'

'Do they sing?'

'Just the songs from *Oliver*.'

'So where are they today?'

'They don't work weekends.'

'Union rules?'

'Exactly.'

'Got a penny?' Tom clearly wasn't interested.

Julia rummaged in her purse. 'Just a five pence piece.'

'Can I have it?'

'Sure. You can't buy anything for five pence though.'

'Do you think this lake's a lucky lake?'

'A lucky lake?'

They had arrived at the bandstand where on Saturday evenings throughout the summer English Heritage destroyed the tranquillity of the surroundings by launching into full-scale renditions of the 1812 Overture and other pieces of a similar decibel level. Between the bandstand and the house lay a small man-made lake of shallow water which now looked positively enchanting in front of the green lawns sloping down from the classical cream-fronted house.

324 FIRST LOVE, SECOND CHANCE

'What are you going to do?'

Tom held up his hand for silence, closed his eyes, mumbled to himself and tossed the coin into the lake. 'Remember *Three Coins in the Fountain*?'

'Sure. That was the Trevi fountain in Rome, not the lake in Kenwood.'

'But I'm not seeking happiness. I've already found it.' Tom dropped to one knee.

Julia was horrified and delighted at the same time. 'Tom, you're not going to propose to me here!'

'Why not? A beautiful English girl, a beautiful English landscape on a beautiful English summer's morning. It's perfect. You're perfect.'

'Tom, it's Saturday morning.'

'So what? You're not Jewish.'

'Tom, everyone's looking.' She tried to pull him to his feet but it was a hopeless task. He was determined to remain on one knee in a pose of exaggerated formality. Meanwhile a crowd was starting to gather.

'Excuse us, folks, I'm just proposing marriage. Just walk on by.'

'Tom!' hissed Julia, embarrassed. The crowd was increasing.

'What's that man doing?' demanded a four-year-old girl.

'He's asking that lady to marry him,' laughed her mother.

'Why?'

'Because he loves her.'

'Why?'

'Because he thinks she's beautiful and he wants to spend the rest of his life with her.'

'Why?'

'Because that's what happens when people love each other.'

The little girl thought about it for a moment. 'How long does he have to stay like that for?'

'Till she's said yes.'

'When will that be?'

'I don't know, darling. She might say no.'

'Tom! Get up!'

'You heard the little lady. Now what's it to be?'

'OK. OK. Just get up.'

'She said yes, folks. Show's over.'

Everyone cheered and applauded. A teenage boy high-fived Tom who was smiling and holding his hands over his head like a boxing champion. A small group of fascinated spectators had just gathered round Tom to congratulate him when Julia's mobile phone began to shrill. She rummaged in the bag, withdrew it and clicked it on but there was no response from the other end.

'Hello?' she said again, annoyed at the idea that a heavy breather was ruining this romantic moment.

'Dirty phone call?' asked Tom, separating himself from his admirers and amused by the inappropriate timing. 'What does he want you to do?'

But there was a frown already creasing the brow of his intended. All Julia could hear was a series of strangulated sobs.

'Mike?' she asked in alarm. 'Mike, is that you?'

'Julia . . .' The words were almost inaudible beneath the heavy sobs.

'Mike? What? What is it?' Her heart and head were both hammering so hard she could scarcely hold the phone.

'It's happening again . . .'

'What? What's happening? Oh God, Mike, please, just tell me. Where are you?'

'Hospital.'

'Is it Jamie?'

There was no response.

'*Mike!*' she screamed. 'Is it Jamie? What's happened?'

The pause seemed to last an eternity then she heard Mike's voice, frighteningly weak and fractured.

'There's been a car crash.'

'*No!* Please God . . .'

'He's still alive . . .'

'Oh God! Oh God, please!'

'You'd better come.'

'Where? Which hospital?'

When he told her she clicked off the phone and turned to Tom, who had stood there throughout the conversation, helpless as his world crashed around him.

'He's in the hospital,' she said and started to run, wildly, without any idea of where she was going.

'Julia!' shouted Tom, racing after her. 'Come back!'

But Julia just kept on running.

CHAPTER TWENTY-FIVE

JULIA RAN FROM KENWOOD ALL the way back to the flat in Gospel Oak to find that her car was blocked in by a large grey Volvo which had double-parked across it. Exhausted and on the verge of hysteria as she was, this latest blow released the inhibitions of her upbringing. She leaned on the horn for nearly five minutes until the owner of the Volvo appeared and, without so much as a word of apology, got into the car and drove away, leaving Tom to placate the neighbours who had reacted angrily to Julia's indiscriminate solution.

Tom had run across the heath from Kenwood with Julia, trying to elicit from her the details of Mike's phone call. He wanted to come with her, to be as supportive as he could, but apart from gasping out the name of the hospital where Jamie had been taken, Julia did not divulge anything further. It was not clear to Tom whether this was because she did not know or because she was concentrating on running back to the car as fast as she could. Certainly, as soon as the Volvo had driven away, Julia rammed the car into first gear and drove off behind it, flashing her lights as if she was suffering from acute road rage. Tom went inside to call a cab.

There was a grisly irony in Julia's destination. The Queen Elizabeth II Hospital in Welwyn Garden City was where both her children had been born. As she drove out of London onto the A1, eyes red, heart pounding, she remembered all those ante-natal classes and the lying on the floor with Mike holding her and the regulated breathing. She also recalled the panic when the birth took place and how it didn't matter what she'd been taught because when the pain started she just wanted the epidural and any other drugs that were available.

How could she ever have imagined that one day only a few years later she would be laying that little body in a coffin? And now here she was again, caught in a similar exercise in tragedy as she drove over the endless series of roundabouts without which Welwyn Garden City would sink back into the Hertfordshire countryside out of which it had been created. Was this one of God's cruellest tricks imaginable? That she should now see Jamie die in a room only a few yards from the one in which he had been born?

What could she possibly have done to deserve such an unimaginable horror for a second time? She didn't need to ask the question. She knew exactly why she was being punished. She supposed she had always known that she would be penalised in some way from the moment she had seen Mike slumped in misery at the kitchen table. It was only a question of when and how. She just never realised it would be so impossibly cruel.

As she drove into the grounds of the hospital she saw two enormously pregnant women trying and failing to get into a small Nissan Micra. Both of them could only manage the manoeuvre once they had divested themselves of their coats. Julia wanted to stop the car and advise them to abort their babies no matter what stage their pregnancies had reached. It simply wasn't worth all the love that went into raising them. One cruel twist of fate would destroy their lives. Two cruel twists of fate were inconceivable.

On the journey she had passed cars full of people who had no troubles, people who were driving into London to spend Saturday shopping, eating in a restaurant, going to the theatre. She wanted to stop each of them, to tell them that they couldn't enjoy themselves, it was making her life even worse. Once they knew about Emily and Jamie, surely they would turn their cars round and go home.

Now that she was in the grounds of the hospital she was somehow relieved to be amongst fellow sufferers, people who instinctively knew that the only reason you were there was because of illness or accident. They averted their eyes from you in sympathy at your troubles or else because they were completely involved in their own tragedy. It was all she was fit for now — tragedy, mourning, tears.

She was directed by a nurse in reception at casualty towards a group of people sitting together, three facing her, two with their backs to her. One of the women was crying and being comforted by her husband. Another man was holding the hand of one of the women, a pale-faced, slim and well-dressed blonde woman. As Julia walked towards them she realised that the man bending forward and holding the woman's hand was Mike. Mike! A bizarre and unexpected wave of jealousy washed over her. Why was Mike holding this woman's hand? Her Mike? Then she thought about what she and Tom had been doing only a few hours before and she blushed with shame.

'Mike?' She stopped short of him. He turned round and got to his feet. He seemed much more in control of himself than he had been when he telephoned her. That seemed to her a good sign. Surely if . . . He turned back to the woman.

'Sally, this is Julia. Sally is Leonie's mum.'

Julia looked lost. She didn't remember a girl called Leonie being mentioned before but the way Mike was referring to her suggested she was part of Jamie's gang of friends.

'Jamie's girlfriend,' Mike added, seeing the bewildered look on Julia's face. 'Would you excuse us?' he said politely to the group and led Julia away, his arm comfortingly round her shoulder.

'It's OK, I've talked to the doctor, he's going to be OK, his life's not in danger but he's broken his leg and his right arm and he's quite badly concussed.'

'Oh, Mike!' Julia felt herself going weak at the knees with relief. 'Oh, thank God!' Mike put his arm round her to support her. She didn't stiffen as she had done so often lately, she positively welcomed the comforting feel of Mike's arm round her shoulder, sliding willingly into a hug of comfort and support.

'What about the others?' she asked.

He hesitated. This was what would bring back all those memories again. 'They don't think the boy who was driving is going to make it. They had to cut the car open to get him out. He was effectively dead at the scene of the crash. His parents are with the doctor now. His girlfriend seems to be OK. She's called Chloe. She was on the same side of the car as Jamie.'

'What did they crash into?'

'A tree. They were being chased by a police car.'

'And Leonie?'

'She was in the back with Jamie but on the wrong side of the car. She's unconscious. Jamie was the lucky one, the others took the full force of the impact.'

'Who are they? I mean Leonie. He's got a girlfriend? I didn't even—'

'Darling, you've been away a lot recently.'

'A few days,' she started in self-justification.

'I don't just mean in time. Since Easter we've scarcely seen you and before then you were miles away in your head.'

'Did you know about Leonie?'

Mike nodded. 'Leonie Williams. He's been lusting after her for months.'

Julia looked at Mike askance.

'He told me on the golf course. A few weeks ago.'

'Mike, I'm lost. I feel like I've just arrived from another world. What's been happening?'

He told her the story quickly. Since his triumph at Lytham St Anne's and a photograph and profile feature article in the local paper, Jamie had been officially recognised as a cool kid and as a result he had been invited to join the jet set at school. The drinking, the dope smoking, the late nights and the parties all followed. Last night they'd gone a stage further and stolen a car for a joy ride. Some joy!

'Whose idea was it?'

'We don't know. We think it was the driver, the boy who's dying.'

'Who is he?'

'His name's Rob Faulkner. Heard of him?'

Julia shook her head. 'I don't understand how he can have developed this other life. It's like he's not our Jamie any more.'

'A lot of surprising things have happened recently. Do you want a cup of tea?'

'Hadn't we better stay around?'

'The nurse said they'd find us.'

'That's what I mean.'

'They said they'd put out a message on the tannoy in the cafeteria if we wanted to have tea there.'

'Tea? What time is it?'

'Gone five.'

'Is it still Saturday?'

'I know how you feel. I've lost all track of time as well.'

'Do you know something? This is the first conversation we've had without tension for ages. It's such a relief.' Julia smiled weakly. How much tension would there be when Mike found out that Tom had just proposed to her and what the hell was she going to say to Tom?

Mike guided her towards the cafeteria where he had sat in a stupor after the birth of each of their children. It was not much changed in appearance now although the menu was a little more varied with the recent installation of a cappuccino machine and the prices had risen in line with inflation. Mike bought two of the innovative cappuccinos, a Mars Bar for himself and a plastic carton of low-fat yoghurt for Julia and took the tray over to the table where Julia was sitting with an uninterrupted view of the car park.

Julia stirred her coffee slowly, her mind flitting from Jamie and his broken bones in the bed upstairs to Tom who was presumably pacing the flat in Gospel Oak. Mike sat opposite her, knowing she needed time to deal with the complex emotions she must be feeling. Julia was glad that Mike was with her. She wouldn't have known what to have said to Tom if he'd accompanied her as she knew he had wished.

'Julia, I just wanted to tell you how sorry I am for last night.'

'Most of that was my fault. I've handled everything so badly.'

'I shouldn't have made you leave like that. I know you must have wanted to talk about things. I just couldn't face it.'

'What do you want to happen, Mike?'

'I don't want you to be unhappy. I don't want you to feel stuck in St Albans and to spend the whole time dreaming about . . . him.' Mike couldn't bring himself to mention Tom by name.

'So what do you want?'

'I want my wife back at home if that's where she wants to be. If you want to go and live with him and build a new life in California, you can. I won't stop you or turn Jamie against you. But I can't live with you acting like a bird in a cage that wants its freedom. Please make a choice. Him or me.'

'Mike, not now, please. It's all tearing me apart.'

'OK. OK. I'm sorry. Just answer me one question. And please be honest.'

'What?'

'Do you still blame me for Emily's death?'

'Blame you?'

'Our sex life disintegrated after she died.'

'It was already on the way out.'

'No, it wasn't.'

'Mike, it's not unusual for women to lose a bit of their sex drive after two babies and seventeen years of marriage.'

Mike was shaking his head violently as if in disagreement. 'It was just an accident, you know.' His eyes were beginning to water. Julia realised he was reliving all his Emily nightmares.

'I know.' She reached out and covered his hand.

'Like this . . . was an accident. Being here brings it all back.'

'I know. I feel the same way.'

'I would never have hurt Emily. Never. I loved her. I loved every minute of her life . . .'

'Shhhh! Don't.'

'Oh, I think I can cry here. If you can't cry in a hospital . . .'

'I mean don't torture yourself. How do you think I feel about Jamie?'

'Why should you—'

'Mike, I've lost him. He isn't my son. He hasn't been my son for years.'

'He's still your son, all right. He's just a teenager. Puberty is what's changed him. Remember how we used to congratulate ourselves that he was so well-behaved and never gave us the aggro that Sarah had with Rachel?'

'Of course.'

'Well, I think he was just a little slow to mature. He's now a teenager. They do stupid things like getting pissed and throwing up in the downstairs cloakroom.'

'He didn't! When?'

'It's all right. I made him clean it up.'

'Good for you. You're a good dad.'

'And you're a wonderful mother. No kid could have had better. And I'm sorry it's taken this bloody awful shock to make me realise how much . . . What?'

Julia had taken her hand away from his and lost interest in what he was saying. Instantly he felt his anger boiling up inside him again. How could she possibly—

'Hello, Tom.' Julia was looking up at a tall slim man in a blue denim shirt and smartly cut Calvin Klein jeans.

'Hi. I guess you must be Mike. Tom Johnson. I'm real sorry for barging in on you guys like this but I knew there'd been an accident. I couldn't stay in that apartment not knowing—'

The tannoy blared. 'Would Mr and Mrs Ramsey please go at once to Room 209 on the second floor of D wing immediately. Mr and Mrs Ramsey to go at once to Room 209 in D wing. Thank you.'

Julia and Mike stood up.

'I'm sorry, Tom. We've got to go. If you wait here, I'll come down after we've spoken to the doctor.'

'Julia, there's something I've got to ask you before you go.'

'No, Tom, not now. I'll see you later.'

'Julia, please,' he called after them. 'You've got to . . .'

Julia returned to the table, her eyes blazing. 'Don't be so bloody selfish, Tom. I know what you want to say and it'll just have to wait.'

'No, you don't understand,' he began but Julia turned and fled to join Mike who was waiting by the door with a black look on his face.

'Did you have to bring that bastard here?'

'I didn't. You heard him. Please, Mike, let's not fight.'

'What did he want? What was so bloody important it couldn't wait?'

'I'll tell you later. All that matters is Jamie.'

Silently, they climbed the stairs of D wing to Jamie's room, each of them nursing a grievance and regretting Tom's untimely appearance.

Jamie was sitting up in bed, his right leg in traction and his right arm in a plaster cast. His head was swathed in bandages and he sported a red bruise below his right eye which was starting to turn purple. A junior doctor was sitting talking to him as Mike and Julia came in. Though they knew he was out of danger, the sight of his damaged body was still a shock to both of them.

'Hi! I was just telling Dr Marshall that I was born here. I was, wasn't I, Mum?'

'Yes, darling. How are you feeling?'

'Sore and a bit dizzy.'

'He's been given Ibuprofen to lessen the pain and bring down the swelling but he's going to feel this way for a while.'

'I was asking about the others but Dr Marshall doesn't know. Do you?'

'No, darling. Not yet.'

'I can't remember anything. I know we got into this car because Rob Faulkner said a cousin of his had showed him how to hot-wire a car and then we were driving a bit too fast and then one of the girls screamed and the next thing I knew I was in this bed.'

'Jamie, I'm so sorry. Are you in pain?'

'I can't move 'cause my ribs hurt.'

'I'm sorry, darling.'

'I'm the one who's sorry, Mum, but it wasn't all my fault. I said to Rob we shouldn't steal the car, but Leonie wanted to see how it was done and Chloe, that's Rob's girlfriend, she was winding him up. Leonie's my girlfriend. I was going to bring her home and introduce her to you.'

'Why didn't you?'

'Dunno. Time never seemed right.'

'Why not?'

'Well, you weren't in the house together much and when you were . . .'

'We were having an argument,' Julia finished for him.

Jamie nodded.

Mike turned to the doctor. 'How's his arm?'

'It's a bad break, there's a pin in the wrist. The leg's much better. It's a clean break of tibia and fibula. Six weeks in a cast and he'll be right as rain.'

'What about his golf swing? His wrist is really important for his golf.'

'Oh yes, that was the first thing he asked me. I'm afraid he won't be playing for a while. He'll have to take it very slowly. If he feels any pain he must stop. It could take a couple of years before you'll know for sure if the damage is permanent.'

Mike and Jamie looked devastated. Julia, conversely, felt a surge of hope for all of them. She was part of their life again. The struggle ahead would be one that she could share in. She now wanted Jamie to be a great golfer as badly as Mike ever had and she knew she would be important to his recovery. It wasn't about the smoothness of his swing or the psychology of putting. It was about rebuilding the confidence of a child who had been damaged mentally as much as physically. She knew she could contribute, she knew she would be needed. The relief swept over her as surely as it had when she learned he wasn't going to die.

Mike and Jamie were talking softly together. She approached them both and waited. Unlike the old hostile exclusivity that he had so woundingly cultivated, this time Jamie looked up at her, openly and trustingly, as he had done before everything started going wrong. He held out his good hand.

'Mum, I wanted to say sorry. Soon as I left the house last night. I shouldn't have said what I did.'

'I know, darling. The last few months have been difficult for all of us.' She sat gingerly on the bed.

Jamie stiffened in case it was painful on his cracked ribs but it wasn't, so he smiled – the same smile he'd had since he was a tiny baby and his face used to crack open when she or Mike made a face or a noise that amused him. This time, though, the smile turned into a wince because of the bruise on his face.

'What about you two?'

'What about us?'

'Are you splitting up?'

'The only thing that matters now is getting you fit and healthy,' said Julia. 'We both love you, Jamie. Please don't ever do anything like this again.'

Jamie nodded. Julia leant over and lightly touched his forehead below the bandages with her lips. She stood up and Mike leaned in to do the same.

'We're going to see how the others are getting on,' he said. 'We'll be back soon.'

They walked out of the room together, not speaking, not looking at each other.

'Mike, I've got to see Tom.'

Mike wanted to scream.

'He's waiting for me in the cafeteria. Do you want to go back to casualty and ask about the others? I'll come and find you there. As soon as I've finished.'

'What did he want? What did he want to ask that was so bloody important he had to come here?'

'He asked me to marry him.'

'What?'

'Mike, please.'

'Did you tell him you were already married?'

'Mike, please, don't start. Not here.'

Mike slumped onto a National Health Service issue plastic chair, looking as devastated as he had the night Julia came home and realised that he knew about Tom. She sat down next to him and held his hand.

'Hadn't you better go and see your toyboy?'

'He can wait a few more minutes.'

'I like the touch of your hand. I haven't felt it much recently.'

Julia was silent.

'I found the letters,' Mike said.

'What letters?'

'I was tidying the loft last night—'

'Those letters were private, Mike.'

'Oh, come on, Julia.'

'I'm sorry. But I never meant to hurt you. I never even sent them.'

'I know. But I understand a lot more about everything now.'

'I just had to get my feelings down on paper. I knew you didn't want to hear about Tom.'

'Still don't to be honest.'

'But if you read them you can see that he was just a useful fantasy figure. There was no affair then. And after Emily died I just felt so cut out of your life.'

'How? How did I do that?'

'The golf thing. I wanted to join in but you and Jamie had your own little world. I was just an intruder.'

'I get so much pleasure out of seeing Jamie maturing as a golfer.'

'But Mike, how do you think I feel about it?'

'You've been opposed to it. I could always sense your hostility.'

'That wasn't hostility. That was you being obsessive.'

'I never meant to exclude you, Julia.'

'But that's what you did. You and Jamie. Boys together, talking a language I couldn't understand.'

'I'm sorry, Julia. I suppose I wanted to be his friend not his father.'

'You couldn't see it, Mike, you couldn't step outside your obsession.'

'I thought I could make him something special.'

'He is special. He's our son and we both love him but it should have been you and me together deciding his future.'

'I'm sorry, Julia. It's just that golf was the only place I could be where I felt good about myself. I knew you were unhappy. I just didn't know what to do about it.'

'We were both unhappy, Mike. I suppose I used Tom like you used golf.'

'I love you, Julia. Don't go.'

'Mike, please don't pressure me. Not now. I have to think.'

'I've got something to ask you. Remember where we met?'

'In Casualty at the John Radcliffe Hospital.'

'I fell in love with you the moment I saw you.'

'You were high on antihistamines.'

'I knew I wanted to marry you.'

'And you did.'

'I still do. If I propose to you again that makes it 2–1 to me. He can't propose twice on the same day. It doesn't count.'

'Whose rule is that?'

'Mine. I'm serious, Julia. Let's start again.'

'I have to go.'

'Please . . .'

'Trust me, Mike. Just trust me.'

Julia desperately needed time to herself before she faced Tom. She hurried down the corridor towards the Ladies'.

She looked at herself in the mirror. After the past years of domestic routine and mundane marital relations it was remarkable that the extraordinary events which had enveloped her in the last few months had not made a greater impact on her features. She still looked like the woman who commuted from St Albans to an office in central London five days a week, the woman who shopped and cooked and cleaned and cajoled. How could such a woman receive a proposal of marriage from that handsome exotic Californian, the man she had been dreaming about for so many years? What on earth was she to do about it?

'Want a piece of advice?' she heard Sarah's voice in her head. 'Flip a coin.'

It was absurd.

'It always works,' she heard Sarah saying.

Julia took her purse out of her bag and found a 10p coin. What could be the harm? Might as well see who the coin chooses. She allocated heads to Tom and tails to Mike. She flipped the coin and let it fall on the ground. It landed, inevitably, on its edge and rolled into an empty cubicle. Julia followed it eagerly, praying nobody would come in and witness this bizarre ritual. She watched the coin come to a halt. She bent down to pick it up. It was heads. Damn, she thought. Let's make it two out of three.

She rose to her feet and clutched at the washbasin. Two out of three? What was she thinking of? She wanted it to come down tails. She wanted it to be Mike. She didn't need the coin at all. She had known it all along. Known it when Tom had criticised the Italian family in the restaurant in Healdsburg, known it when he'd been so embarrassed by her presence at the winery he'd avoided introducing her to Mancini, known it for sure when he threw the little boy's ball away on Hampstead Heath that morning. Was that to be her future? Married to a man who disliked the grubby reality of kids and was embarrassed by her lack of knowledge of wine?

More to the point, she'd known it since she saw Mike making his tea with two tea bags. Mike was part of her life, and when Jamie grew up and left home, he'd still be part of her life, no matter what Tom insinuated. Tom was her dream man but that was where he belonged – in her dreams. She'd been using Tom to escape from reality. How had she been so blind all these years?

Tom was sitting at the table she and Mike had vacated, three cups of cappuccino lined up in front of him, like a drunk's empty whisky glasses. He stood up as she approached. Old World courtliness or New World guilt? she wondered. He read her mood and made no attempt to touch her. She sat down on the plastic chair. He sat down opposite.

'How is he?'

'Alive.'

'Thank God. Look, Julia, about before—'

'No, Tom, let me go first. I know I should probably have said this earlier but I'm not sure I could have articulated it all before.'

'Is it no?'

'Tom, you're a wonderful man—'

'It's no. You don't have to explain.'

'I do. For me as much as for you. You're the man of my dreams, Tom.'

'Well, thanks. Is this a criticism?'

'Only of me. I've been carrying an image of you around in my head for eighteen years but it's just an image. The reality is that much as I love you and always will, I could never live with you.'

'But I thought you just said—'

'Tom, you're handsome, witty, charming—'

'Still doesn't sound like I've done much wrong here.'

'But you're also selfish.'

'How?'

'You've never had kids. You don't know, you don't understand the sacrifices you make for them.'

'But we can try together.'

'It wouldn't work. You want a baby with me but where would we go when the buyers fly out to uncork the new vintage with you?'

'You could stay in the back of the house, or you could go away for the week . . . oh, I see.'

'You're always so handsome, Tom, so well-dressed, I wonder what you'd look like with baby puke on the shoulder of your Ralph Lauren shirt.'

'We'd still have each other.'

'But we wouldn't, Tom. That's my point. I'd be breast-feeding at four-hourly intervals. I wouldn't want to be hanging from the chandeliers.'

Tom looked at her for a while, then stretched his hand across the table. 'I guess you've really thought this one through.'

'I guess I have.'

'I think I can settle for being the man of your dreams, Julia.'

'It's a pretty good place to be. Nothing ever goes wrong up there. It's just not reality. The Tom I know doesn't belong in the Queen Elizabeth Hospital in Welwyn Garden City. Mike does.'

Tom stood up and came round the table to her, pulling her up to stand against his lean body. He kissed her gently on the lips. 'Let's not make it eighteen years before we see each other again this time. I'll be nearly sixty! Christ!'

She kissed him back in a similar spirit of friendship.

'Oh shit!' said Tom. 'You've got some explaining to do.'

At the entrance to the cafeteria Mike was standing watching them. Julia thought he was going to explode like the frog in the Aesop fable.

'Go for it, sweetheart. I'm catching a flight back home this afternoon. Call me anytime.'

Julia flew out of the cafeteria and grabbed Mike by the arm. He shrugged her away, angrily.

'Mike, please, that was goodbye.'

'Didn't look much like a goodbye from where I was standing.'

'Mike, listen to me. I came downstairs to tell him no, to tell him I love you, to tell him you and Jamie were the only people in the world who mattered to me.'

'And I came to tell you that Rob Faulkner is dead. His parents are sobbing their hearts out in a corridor upstairs. I thought you might want to be there. I'm going back to them.' He turned to leave. Julia clutched at his sleeve.

'Mike, please. This is really, really important. Help me, please, if you want us to stay together. Because I want us to!'

Mike looked at her, searching her face for signs of deceit but he knew in his heart that she was telling the truth about Tom. 'When the police came to the house to tell me about the accident, all I could think of was you. How much I loved you. How much I wanted you. How much I wanted to shield you from the news. It was like when he won that tournament, I was so proud of him and I knew you would have been too. And then I thought of where you were . . .'

'We can work it through together. Tom's going back to California. It's over. All that stuff I've been carrying around in my head for so many years is over. It's gone. I just want to look after my son and my husband.'

'How can you be sure?'

'I tossed a coin.'

'What?'

'And I won. So I got to choose you.'

'Thank you. Thank you for choosing me.'

She threw herself into his arms, not caring if he held on to her or not, just to show she wanted to demonstrate her love for him. Mike caught her and slowly moved his arms round her back to close the embrace. She lifted up her face and kissed him, inhaling that familiar unshaven smell. Now she found it almost like an aphrodisiac. They kissed for the longest time, not a friends' kiss and not a lovers' kiss but a kiss of two drowning people who were hanging on to each other for dear life. Julia broke away, her mind racing with new certainty.

'I want to talk to them.'

'Who?'

'Rob Faulkner's parents.'

'Are you in the right state for this?'

'There couldn't be a righter state.'

The grieving parents were in the corridor outside the room where their son's body lay. Her eyes were red with weeping. He had been crying but was concentrating on holding on to his wife.

'Hello, I'm Jamie's mother.' Julia sat down next to the father. 'I can't tell you how sorry I am.'

'We should be the sorry ones. It was Rob who stole the car, it was Rob who crashed it. He nearly killed Jamie.'

'Please, please, Mr Faulkner, don't apologise and don't blame anyone – not Rob, not the other kids and not yourselves. It's been nearly a year since our daughter, Emily, died, and it's almost destroyed us so many times.'

Mrs Faulkner burst into renewed sobs.

'The accident might have killed Emily but it was us who let it nearly destroy the rest of the family. Don't look for someone to blame, don't try and punish anyone. Especially each other. You don't need blame now, you just need love. Unconditional love. Mike and I'll be here for you whenever you need us. I really mean that.'

Mr Faulkner looked at her, his eyes filled with tears, and nodded. 'Thank you,' he said in a trembling voice.

★   ★   ★

'Will we?' asked Mike as they set off for Julia's car, having arranged to go home and have a bath before coming back to the hospital to sit with Jamie and the other parents.

'Will we what?'

'Be there for them? Together.'

'We will if you want us to be.'

'I want it to be just the two of us. There's been this ghost in the corner of our marriage ever since it started.'

'Gone. Exorcised. Ghosts don't exist.'

'All right, not a ghost. Tom Johnson's a reality. How do I know he's not going to walk back in and split us up again?'

'Because he throws little boys' balls away. Because he doesn't think kids should go to restaurants. Because he's embarrassed at my ignorance of wine. Because you make a cup of tea with two tea bags.'

'I'm not sure I understand much of that. But I get the drift.'

They went out through casualty which had filled up again with a whole new group of tragedies, physical, emotional and familial. The same drained, traumatised faces, the same trepidation and fear as they waited for the medical verdict. Maybe two hours ago they had been perfectly happy, entirely oblivious of the sock filled with wet sand which Fate was swinging above her head. How tenuous was family life at the best of times, thought Julia and shivered, grasping Mike's arm.

They emerged into the late summer evening which now had a slight chill in it, the first hint that autumn was on its way. In a few weeks, and with the help of nature and the NHS, Jamie would be back at school, in the sixth form, a child no longer. She could take his school uniform to the charity shop. Perhaps at half term they would fly off somewhere warm. They had talked about Sicily but had never taken the plunge. Sicily was still warm at the end of October. They could lie in the sun and let these cares drain out of them. Yes, Emily was gone but thank God Jamie wasn't and thank God Mike wasn't. She didn't want to build a strange new life for herself in northern California. She wanted her old one back in St Albans, unlikely as that would have seemed a few weeks ago.

'Where in God's name are you taking me?' Mike asked her as they headed inexorably for the sewerage maintenance plant at the back of the car park.

Julia stopped and looked around her in bewilderment. 'Where are we?'

'I thought we were going towards your car but only you know where you parked it.'

'God! I can't for the life of me remember.'

'Do we really have to wait till midnight when everyone's gone home like we did at Alton Towers?' Mike was smiling and Julia couldn't help laughing at herself. She genuinely had no idea where she had left the car.

'It's a good job I love you.'

'Even though I can't remember where I left the car?'

'Especially because you can't remember where you left the car. That's my old Julia.'

'Hey, not so much of the old, thank you. I'm only thirty-eight.'

'Doesn't matter if you're young at heart.'

Julia's eyes narrowed. She didn't know whether this was the opening shot of a new skirmish. It was the title of one of her favourite songs and the game had been taught to her by Tom. Which was why Mike had made no effort to play it with her previously.

'Who says I'm young at heart?'

'Frank Sinatra in the film of the same name.'

Julia's heart skipped a beat.

'Mike! You know the song!'

'Who doesn't? Words by Carolyn Leigh, music by Johnny Richards.'

'When did you learn all this?'

'Could I have lived with you for eighteen years and not known it?'

'You're a very romantic man, you know that?'

'I have my moments,' said Mike modestly.

He bent to kiss her and they stood together for the longest time, just revelling in the tender touch of their lips. ('The Tender Trap'? they each wondered without mentioning the other Frank Sinatra song by name.) They held each other and Mike could feel the softness of her body as she surrendered the tension that had built the invisible wall between them.

'I think I can see your car over there parked diagonally across two spaces.'

He took her pliant hand and guided her to the car. As they drove away from the hospital she recalled the same journey they had made with each of their babies. For both of them it felt like they were at the beginning again. It was odd to be nearly forty and starting family life all over again. The last time they had been with Jamie in that hospital he had been a newborn infant. Now he lay in a bed only a few floors away from where he had been born, his arm and his leg broken, his ribs and his face smashed in. Yet for all its uncertainties, Julia believed that the future was bright because they seemed to be facing it as a family again, just as they had as young parents all those years ago. Julia flipped on the radio.

'Fly me to the moon,' Tony Bennett was crooning, 'and let me play among the stars . . .'